Praise for Loving Modigliani

What a story Linda Lappin has to tell in the short life and long legend of Amedeo Modigliani, compulsive seducer, dedicated decadent and artist whose vision, like El Greco's, seemed to warp the very air. But it's the verve and authority with which Lappin centers her story on the parallel life (and afterlife) of Jeanne Hébuterne, artist and Modigliani's model and lover, that amplifies the achievement of this scintillating tale, which is also a love story, a ghost story and a treasure hunt through the decades for a lost masterpiece. Through Jeanne's female gaze, the great tapestry of Paris and its fervid art scene is rendered with twice the depth of field and emotional color. The result is a novel of high originality, page-turning pace and a poetic precision so impeccably deployed that the book unfolds like a living, breathing, 3-D spectacle in the reader's mind.

— Don Wallace, author of *The French House*

What is there of Jeanne Hébuterne that truly survives? Does her legacy exist in print, in rumor, in idle or self-interested speculation, in a handful of inherited objects, in artworks of dubious provenance, or in occasional incomplete exhibitions? *Loving Modigliani* continues the work Linda Lappin began in her novel about Katherine Mansfield, *Katherine's Wish*, extending the inquiry into the life of another marginalized woman artist of the Modernist era. This time the scenery is Paris, Montparnasse, and various places in Venice, Rome, and the Côte d'Azur, and the subject is Jeanne, the common-law wife and muse of Modigliani, whose own talent has been ignored and reputation betrayed and mishandled for over the past hundred years. Thoughtfully and with acute observation and imagination, Lappin employs a variety of genres, styles, and subject matters—ghost story, mystery, historical detail, private journal, academic inquiry, and curatorial malfeasance—to recover what there is of Jeanne that we can possibly know. These depictions, along with ambulatory evocations of our favorite city, give us an opportunity to speculate on who in fact she might have been.

—Thomas Wilhelmus

Ambitious...courageous...compelling...unique. The atmosphere in *Loving Modigliani* is so vivid and imaginative, the characters incredibly rich.

— Miriam Polli, author of *In a Vertigo of Silence*

Linda Lappin's *Loving Modigliani* is itself a declaration of love, for Jeanne Hébuterne, Modigliani's model and common-law wife, as well as a notable painter in her own right, whose suicide at twenty-one is the point of departure for a thrilling trans-twentieth-century fantasy. Ghost story, art-historical mystery, purgatorial character study, and living map of Montparnasse, *Loving Modigliani* imbues fact and counterfact with the forms, colors, and textures of classical poetry as Modigliani imbues painting with the qualities of sculpture—towards a higher vision, a higher compassion, a refined appreciation for this world and for the others it obscures. A tour de force and wild ride.

— James Wallenstein, author of *The Arriviste*

Inspired by true events and the early death of artist Amedeo Modigliani's common-law wife Jeanne Hébuterne, Lappin's atmospheric novel takes a unique approach to exploring what might have become of the woman who was a talented artist in her own right but who was largely forgotten by history. From the first page to the last, I was swept away by the imaginative adventure that spans more than a century.

Part ghost story, part murder mystery, and part treasure hunt, Linda Lappin's *Loving Modigliani* is a haunting, genre-bending novel that kept me turning the pages long into the night.

— Gigi Pandian, author of *The Alchemist's Illusion*

Praise for Linda Lappin's Previous Books

Signatures in Stone: A Bomarzo Mystery

"Readers looking for an intelligent summer mystery will find much to savor here." — *Library Journal*

"Scary and satisfying … Lappin's people are as dangerously compelling as her Italy." — Nina Auerbach, author of *Our Vampires, Ourselves*

The Etruscan

Lappin elegantly brings the characters, Italian countryside, and surroundings to life in vivid, engrossing prose. A solid, well-written tale wrought in entrancing detail." — *Kirkus*

"I was enthralled by Lappin's Italy … and by that god/demon/ boar that flits through its landscape". — Nina Auerbach, author of *Our Vampires, Ourselves*

"Captures the thin line between illusion and reality," — *Book View Ireland*

Katherine's Wish

"A dazzling piece of literary sorcery" — David Lynn

"Lappin's intensely imagined novel will satisfy readers unfamiliar with Mansfield as well as those already intrigued by her." — Desmond O'Grady, *South China Morning Post*

"Linda Lappin has immersed herself in Mansfield's life, and emerged from it with a story to narrate on her own terms, a fiction charged with the enthusiasm of a good researcher, and carried through with a novelist's verve." — Vincent O'Sullivan, editor *The Letters of Katherine Mansfield, Vol V*

The Soul of Place, A Creative Writing Workbook: Ideas and Exercises for Conjuring the Soul of Place

"Inspirational...lovely...explorative" – *Book Riot*

"Insightful exercises for writers of all levels"— *National Geographic Traveler*

"A little miracle of inspiration" — Kaia Van Zandt

"A conscious way to explore the power of place" — *Wanderlit*

"Invaluable advice for the writer and traveler" — Lavinia Spalding

"A great new resource for writers" — *Wandering Educators*

LOVING MODIGLIANI

The Afterlife of Jeanne Hébuterne

A novel by
Linda Lappin

SERVING
HOUSE
BOOKS

Loving Modigliani:
The Afterlife of Jeanne Hébuterne

Copyright © Linda Lappin

All Rights Reserved

Published by Serving House Books

Copenhagen, Denmark and South Orange, NJ

www.servinghousebooks.com

ISBN: 978-1-947175-30-3

Library of Congress Control Number: 2020943993

Member of The Independent Book Publishers Association

First Serving House Books Edition 2020

Cover Design: Lauren Grosskopf

Cover Photograph: Linda Lappin

Serving House Books Logo: Barry Lereng Wilmont

For Ginny & Gerry

Table of Contents

Part 1

Afterlife:
A Gothic Fairy Tale
Out the Window
January 26, 1920

THE RINGING IN MY EARS ceased with the dull thud of a heavy weight hurled out from a high window, crashing into the courtyard. I blacked out as a wave of pain surged through my body, traveling to the tips of my fingers and the roots of my hair. I'd barely had time to glimpse my brother André's face gawking through the open window frame, to hear the neighbor's cat yowling on the balcony below us or the precipitation of feet on the stairs. Then there I was, conscious again, rather bewildered but intact, suspended in the air a few inches above that bloody heap on the cobblestones. A taut, transparent string protruding from my belly seemed to be attaching me to it.

While André knelt weeping beside the broken thing lying amid the shards of the potted sage plants kept by the *concierge* for her digestive tisanes, my parents' faces appeared in my bedroom window, ghostly through the organdy curtains.

I wanted to reassure them that I wasn't hurt, so I dashed towards the door, but the string at my middle pulled me right back to the courtyard. I wanted to tell them it was all a mistake, and to please go back to bed. Despite the terrible row I had just had with André about what I should do now that Modi was dead, I wasn't angry at them anymore. There was no need for them to be so upset, and I was truly sorry for waking everyone up, but the words on my lips produced no sound or effect. Soon enough, my parents withdrew from the window, and my brother went back inside after an agitated consultation with the *concierge*, who had come shuffling out in her bathrobe. A few moments later, up on the fourth floor, all the windows banged shut.

The *concierge* threw a sheet over my corpse in the courtyard, crossed herself, and began to sweep up the mess I had made, muttering prayers or perhaps blasphemies, for I couldn't really hear properly. An eerie hollowness in my ears drowned out all external sound.

I waited for them to come get me as the broom licked about the edges of the sheet and the *concierge's* feet in red felt slippers padded up and down. Surely they wouldn't leave me here for long, stretched out on the gravel and dead leaves blown in from the street? Then I thought: who could carry me up those stairs at that ungodly hour? It would take at least two men in the condition that I was in, my waters ready to break. My father's back couldn't have withstood the strain. All our neighbors were quite elderly, and André couldn't have handled such a task alone. So I guessed they had decided to wait until morning before trying to move me.

The rest of the night passed without event. Unfamiliar constellations gleamed in the gutters before sinking over the edge of the roof. The neighbor's tabby, on a nocturnal prowl, scuttled up to sniff me, but ran off in a frenzy when I reached out to stroke it. Frost bloomed on the cobblestones around the bundle in the courtyard from which I averted my gaze. Finally, at dawn, Monsieur LeRoux, the dustman, making his daily rounds, collected me in his rusty wheelbarrow after a long conversation with the *concierge*. I say "me" when perhaps I should say "it" or perhaps "us"—there seemed to be two of me now—me and that thing—but I wasn't yet completely convinced as to what or who I was now.

Once in the wheelbarrow, I thought we'd go upstairs to my family and, though I sincerely wished to apologize to all three of them, I dreaded seeing them again. Our relationship had been strained long before this, ever since I had moved in with Modi and we ran off to Nice in spring 1918 to wait out the end of the war. My father had exploded when he found out I was expecting Giovanna, and my mother all but disowned me when she realized we weren't ever getting married, even after our second child was on the way. True, Papa had fulfilled his duty by coming with me to the hospital to see Modi for the last time. Still, I knew he could never forgive me for what I had just done. My father was a fervent believer, and I had committed sin after sin. As for my brother, I understood he felt betrayed, but what could I do about that now?

I steeled myself for a rough confrontation at the top of the stairs, but instead, Monsieur LeRoux twirled the wheelbarrow around, and, with its contents still modestly covered with the *concierge's* sheet, rolled out of the courtyard and into the street. Tethered, I was tugged along behind, bobbing like a balloon fastened to a baby-carriage while Paris stirred from its winter sleep.

We followed the route I usually took to Montparnasse on my way to lessons at the academy in 14 Rue de la Grande Chaumière, or to the studio where I lived with Modi at number 8. I used to love walking to school in early morning, delighting in the smells—steam and soap from the laundries, fresh horse manure in the street; the blue smoke from the chestnut vendors mingling with buttery gusts from the bakeries and coffee percolating in dim cafés where sleepy waiters would be tying on their aprons and polishing tabletops with rags. But now, although I could see perfectly well, my sense of smell had evaporated—these odors I loved were more like a half-remembered scent caught in the back of my throat and I could only hear as from a great distance underwater. It was like when you have a very bad cold and you are up in the Alps and your ears just won't pop and you feel as though your head is wrapped in cotton wool.

We rolled along the Boul' Mich, jostling street sweepers, tobacco vendors, boys shouldering bundles of newspapers, and a red-cheeked old lady draped in a shawl, just in from the country, selling tangerines from the Midi. And when I saw the luminous citrus glowing at the bottom of her willow basket on the curb, I thought: *I must buy a tangerine for Modi; they are so good for a fever*—and I reached into my pocket for some change, but to my surprise, there was nothing in my pocket at all, no money, not even a handkerchief. It wasn't even *my* pocket, but the pocket of André's scratchy wool bathrobe, which, inexplicably, I was wearing out in the streets of Paris, and I couldn't remember why. Yet no one seemed to notice, even though the robe didn't close in front because of how big I was. Also, my feet were bare, and yet my toes didn't feel the least bit cold. I plunged my hand into the basket to pick up a tangerine, but my fingers couldn't seize it.

As I observed my fingers scrabbling about in the bottom of the basket, trying to grab an elusive tangerine, my new situation began to sink in, and I panicked. But no one heard my horrified shriek, no one paid me the slightest attention, not even the fruit-vendor who frowned and recounted the tangerines in her basket. Meanwhile, the wheelbarrow was rattling on without me. Terrified that I might be left behind, I raced to catch up and was catapulted through the air and snapped back into place by the elastic string at my navel. Tentatively I touched it, but its texture repelled me: clear and stretchy as a jellyfish tentacle, and a bit sticky, like old egg whites. It shimmered like mother of pearl.

A storm of questions whirled in my mind, but I was too scared to dwell on any of them, and besides it took all my strength to keep up with the wheelbarrow.

Cutting across Rue Joseph-Bara, where Modi's friend and dealer, Leopold Zborowski—Zbo— lives with his wife, Hanka, we bounced over a pothole and my left foot poked out from under the sheet just as an elegant lady wearing a wide-brimmed black hat and veil crossed our path. The poor woman nearly fainted from shock. Monsieur LeRoux paused to help her, then carefully tucked me in again so that nothing showed, not even a strand of my hair, and we proceeded to the place I called home, Modigliani's studio in Rue de la Grande Chaumière. A sickening anxiety filled me as we approached the tall door painted Prussian blue, still closed at that hour, because I understood Modi would not be there and I had no idea where he was or what was going to happen to us now.

Monsieur LeRoux lifted the brass knocker and hammered on the door with insistent blows, which I imagined more than heard.

The *concierge*, Madame Moreau, opened, and another animated discussion ensued as the dustman must have explained to her what was in the wheelbarrow, how it got there, and what he intended to do with it, while Madame shook her head vigorously and thrashed her arms as if to say that under no circumstances could I be left there on her premises. The blue door slammed shut in our noses, so we trundled on as the sun rose and the streets bustled with an army of clerks, shopkeepers, housewives, and dandies going about their business after the little people, the true Parisians Modi loved: the sweepers, waiters, rag pickers and delivery boys, had made the city ready for them, allowing another Paris morning to take place.

The dustman was growing weary as he pushed me along the sidewalk—sweat beaded on his brow despite the winter air, and he wiped it with a dirty rag, all the while murmuring *Pauvre petite* under his breath. That's how I realized that my hearing was improving as the numb echo in my head drained away. Now the morning traffic, like a symphony by Satie—creaking wheels, chortling engines, clopping hooves—trickled into my ears as we crossed Boulevards Montparnasse and Raspail and skirted the walls of the Montparnasse Cemetery. For a moment I thought we might be headed there and I anxiously peered through the gates at the headstones, but we passed on. Modi used to walk there in early morning to visit Baudelaire. Sometimes he would snitch roses from funeral wreathes to give to girls in cafés. But he was not there now.

We stopped again outside the town hall at the Place de Montrouge, where the dustman spoke to a guard. With some trepidation, the guard peeked at me under the sheet and ordered us to park the wheelbarrow away from public view. So I was bumped up the steps to the inner courtyard and left in a corner where I waited for over an hour, perusing a noticeboard displaying marriage bans and public auctions, while Monsieur LeRoux went inside. People scurried in and out carrying papers without so much as a glance in my direction until a little girl accompanying her mother on some business there ran over to the wheelbarrow and tugged at the edge of the sheet. A furious *gendarme* barked a warning and jerked her away, whispering harshly to her mother. I distinctly heard him say the word "suicide" and I cringed when I realized he meant me. I hadn't quite thought of my situation like that.

Finally, Monsieur LeRoux reappeared, accompanied by a *gendarme*. I feared I might be whisked away and deposited in a dank, wormy cell where dead criminals are kept. But no, the dustman seized the handles of the wheelbarrow again, and together with the solemn, fiercely-mustachioed officer, we went back to Rue de la Grande Chaumière.

At that hour, art students with portfolios tucked under their arms thronged the entrances to the academies at numbers 14 and 20, and I spotted my friend, Thérèse, surrounded by chattering classmates. She was on her way to the life-drawing lesson at the Académie Colarossi, where I realized with some regret, I would never set foot again. For a moment, it seemed she observed, perplexed, the *gendarme* and dustman walking past with a wheelbarrow, and I waved to her, although of course she could not see me floating there above the street. I wanted to tell her I was sorry for neglecting her in recent months. But ever since Modi and I had returned to Paris from Nice with Giovanna, our newborn baby, and I had somehow managed to get pregnant a second time, things hadn't gone well for me. I had planned to invite her over to the studio to see Giovanna and have a cup of tea and gossip a little, as we used to do when I was a silly student who didn't know what was what. But then I had taken Giovanna to stay with the nuns because I just couldn't keep up with everything, and with this second pregnancy I was nauseous most of the time. Now I watched the students filing into the academy. Did they even know that Amedeo Modigliani, Prince of Montparnasse, was dead? *Thérèse*, I called out, but she stepped inside, and the door closed behind her.

At number 8, the great blue door to the court was open and Madame was hanging some laundry out to dry. As we rolled in, she began shouting again, but the *gendarme* silenced her, informing her that I was to be put there, in my lawful residence. After Madame had retrieved her spectacles and duly examined the paper stamped with the seals of the prefect and the mayor, she consented. I have to admit, despite my uneasiness about entering the studio again, I was relieved, as my energies were waning and I needed to take stock of myself.

The *gendarme* and dustman shunted me up four flights of stairs to the rooms where my husband, Amedeo Modigliani, the celebrated Italian painter, lay dying of meningitis just two days before. As we passed the landing on the third floor, where Modi's friend, Ortiz de Zarate, lived with his wife, two daughters, and three dachshunds, the dogs began to howl.

When the door opened, I could have screamed! We'd been robbed: all of Modi's paintings had been stripped from the big front room. The flat was an L-shape with walls painted orange and yellow. The long front room was our studio, the shorter one in the back our bedroom. The studio always overflowed with canvases on easels or stacked on chairs, sketches pinned up all over the place, sculptures preening in every corner, and piles of carnets on the worktable. Now, all that had vanished. The paintings Modi had been working on before he got sick: the great nude sprawled on a green couch with her head thrown back, the unfinished portrait of Mario Varvogli on the easel, Modi's self-portrait as a pale-faced as Pierrot—were gone. But my own paintings and sketches still gazed down from the walls, alongside the prints of Italian Madonnas from the Quattrocento that Modi never tired of studying.

The studio had hardly any furnishings: our worktable where I couldn't properly be laid out, a battered armchair where our models would sit, a stove, and a big blue cupboard that touched the ceiling.

There was no place for Monsieur LeRoux to put me, so they wheeled me into the bedroom, where the thieves had not ventured. It was just as I had left it two days ago, when Modi was taken to the hospital: the rumpled sheets stained with blood from his hemorrhaging lungs, the paint-spotted trousers he had shed on the floor, and a dozen empty sardine tins scattered all around, as that was all we had to eat in the studio. In those final few days, I had gotten too big to make it down the stairs to bring up water—there was no running water in the flat—or do the shopping, and Ortiz, who had been helping us with those chores, was away when Modi fell ill. The floor was still strewn with crumbs of charcoal—we had burned it all in a brazier trying to keep the bedroom warm when Modi's chills had set in—and bits of broken glass—Modi was always throwing bottles when he was angry, and he had kept it up until his strength ran out. Seeing the room through Monsieur LeRoux's eyes, I felt a bit ashamed that I hadn't been able to keep the place a little tidier.

The dustman and *gendarme* surveyed the disarray without comment. Monsieur LeRoux tugged the sheets from the bed and covered the mattress with a paisley bedspread he had found wadded in a chair. They lay me in the bed, and the dustman joined my hands to my breast, crossed himself, and gently arranged the *concierge's* sheet to cover me. Not knowing what else to do, I hovered there over the bed as the men went out with the wheelbarrow. Monsieur LeRoux took away the bloody sheets, saying they would have to be incinerated because Modi was tubercular.

How many times had we made love on that bed? Numbers have little meaning now. Two hundred? Three? How many times had Modi covered my bare shoulders afterward with that old paisley coverlet so I wouldn't catch cold? How many times had I turned to his body in the night, so warm with thick tufts of hair on his shoulders and the base of his spine, and wedged my hand lightly in the cleft of his buttocks—a gesture which always helped him fall asleep—that is, if it didn't get him going again. That's how I wanted to remember him, the sleeping god Amor, not the peevish invalid with shrunken limbs, coughing and writhing in bed. I squeezed my eyes shut, but could still see him there.

Restless, I wandered around the room, and the string attached to my body let me move wherever I liked. At first, I worried it might get entangled in table and chair legs, but objects cut quite through it, as through a shaft of sunlight. I moved more easily now, such welcome freedom, considering I had been almost too heavy to walk in the last few weeks. The string tugged a bit as I zoomed back and forth between the studio and the bedroom. The rapidity and the rush were like skating on ice.

Everything was a mess, but I was disinclined to do anything about it, and anyway, I couldn't have moved a hair, even if I had wanted. My hands just didn't work anymore. I took note of all my possessions still in their usual places: my sketchbooks and paint-box on the worktable. My cloche hat like a squashed purple mushroom on a hook by the window. The brass candlestick I had brought from home beside the row of well-thumbed books from the stalls along the Seine where Modi loved to browse: Lautréamont, Dante, Baudelaire, Rimbaud. He used to rip out his favorite poems from books on the stalls and stuff them into his pocket, so that he could read them to me later in bed. But now not a single book could I take from the shelf! My fingers, like sunbeams, slipped across surfaces, but could not hold or clutch. Back in the bedroom, I lingered by the bedside table, where in the top drawer, I kept my purse, diaries, and other trinkets, like the blue-green bangle of Venetian glass Modi had bought me in Nice, but I could not manage to open the drawer.

There was something unsettling, uncanny in the room: the mirror over the dresser placed at the junction of the studio and the bedroom. As I glided in and out, I could see shapes on its glinting surface from the corner of my eye. I was afraid to confront it directly, but I was also intensely curious as to what I looked like now. I wove around it cautiously at first, the way you sneak around a stray dog asleep on the sidewalk. Finally, I made myself stop in front of it and open my eyes wide—but all it gave back was the beveled reflection of an empty room in which I was not. I stood before the mirror and pinched my cheeks so hard that I could feel the blood sting in my face. I yanked at my hair so violently that strands came away in my hands. I screamed and struck the glass with my fist—but the smug, blank slate did not even crack. I seethed with rage: how could I feel such strong physical sensations and yet have no more substance than an amputee's missing limb?

And then I saw his brown velvet jacket with frayed cuffs reflected behind me, hanging on a nail in the wall. Twice had I patched its worn elbows and sewn its leather buttons back on after they had been torn off in café brawls. I went to it now, caressing the length of the sleeves, remembering the arms they once held, that once held me, and although I could not lift it from the nail, I could almost feel the smooth velvet ribs against my fingertips and cheek. Sticking my nose into the folds, I sighed deeply, and a miracle happened! I could smell again, and his scent, a ripe potpourri of tobacco, wine, turpentine, sweat, hashish, and soap, poured into my senses, and I thought I might collapse. My chest heaved with sobs, but my eyes produced no tears.

Then as my fingers crept into a pocket—an electrifying jolt! I had touched a familiar piece of crisp cotton: yes, his bandana! By an extreme effort of the will, I somehow succeeded in coaxing it just a half inch out of the pocket, and on it I noted a small brown spot of blood, perhaps, or wine, on the edge. I plucked at it desperately, but had no power to dislodge it any further. I bent down and tried to tug it out with my teeth. It would not budge, yet my lips and tongue brushed the small brown stain. From the briny taste, I knew it was a drop of my husband's blood, and a frisson shot through my entire being. I was somehow in contact with a living trace of him.

The door burst open and someone came into the other room. *Modi?* I cried out. Had he come to get me? But the warped floorboards creaked under the weight of heeled pumps and sabots clattering into the studio.

A woman's voice said, "She must be in the other room," and the footsteps advanced to where I was.

Glancing in the mirror, I saw two women and a girl: Zbo's wife, Hanka, and her friend Gosia, one of Modi's recent models for his nudes. The girl was Annie, who looked after Ortiz's children downstairs and occasionally modeled for him. Hanka carried a mop, and Gosia a broom, while in each hand, Annie held a bucket of water. It looked as though they had come to clean the flat and must have been warned by the *concierge* that they would find me there.

The three stood staring at the bed in a suspended state of shock until Annie plunked down her buckets, wailing, "Poor Jeanne." Water sloshed from one of the buckets onto the floor.

Gosia dropped the broom and put her arm around the girl. "Poor Jeanne. Poor Amedeo," she sniffled.

"A tragedy for us all," said Hanka, quickly mopping up the spill.

Gosia drew a handkerchief out of her sleeve to blot her tears, but I knew she wasn't weeping for me. She was weeping for my husband. What was I to her if not an obstacle? I knew she had been carrying on with him for months. What a fool she was to believe that Modi had cared about her. Didn't she know that he seduced all the women he painted? As an Italian, it was for him a matter of pride, which I had come—however grudgingly—to accept. Some even believed he would marry them – others claimed he had fathered their children. He just laughed at that, but he adored Giovanna, *our* baby.

He had probably rattled on to Gosia while he was painting her, daydreaming aloud about going back to Leghorn. Gosia, like all the others, did not understand that when he talked of returning to Italy, it wasn't really him talking. It was his mother speaking through him, her words he was repeating, some bedtime story she had told him once about how they would all go live in a pink house by the sea with a dining room suite and take tea like the English at five o'clock. Like a nursery rhyme, the story had stuck in his brain, and he would mumble bits of it to himself whenever he was fed up with living in cold, dirty rooms where the wind whistled under the door. But he would never ever have left Montparnasse to go back to live in Italy. He would never have abandoned me, not even in death. That was his dying promise, and I knew he would keep his word. I was the only one he loved: I, Jeanne Hébuterne, was his wife and muse. We were more married than married, he always said, under the watchful eye of his lucky black star.

Gosia stared morosely at the bare yellow walls. "This place looks so different without his pictures, without him. All the life has gone out of it."

Hanka began picking clothes up off the floor, folding them, and piling them on a chair. "Zbo took everything away early this morning. People will be coming in and out, and new lodgers are arriving after the funeral. We couldn't risk anything being taken. Soon every piece of his work will be worth thousands. Zbo will get back every centime he invested, multiplied ten thousand times. It has taken much longer with Modi, for some reason, than it did with Utrillo or Kisling, but now Modigliani's moment is finally dawning."

"*Dawning with his death! And yet what difference a few good words would have made to him—to us—just a week or two ago.*"

"Didn't Zbo want that self-portrait of Amedeo's?" Gosia pointed out a sketch near the window. It was one I had done of Modi, his fedora aslant on his forehead, his sultry lips sucking on a pipe. We were always drawing each other. Even at the very end, I drew him, and I was concerned they might now find those drawings in my sketchbook if they started poking about. Those were very private drawings, which I never meant anyone else to see. One day I had planned to show them to him: *This is you that time in January 1920, when you were so ill. Remember how scared we were? And you bound our wrists with a gold ribbon and said we were wed for eternity?*

"Oh, that's just a sketch Jeanne did." Hanka flapped a throw rug out the window, raising a cloud of dust.

"Still, it is a very good likeness." Gosia approached the sketch to study it. "It captures so well that reckless flair of his. Are you sure Jeanne did this? It is so similar to his style."

I prickled with pride. I had learned to copy his line as confidently as if it were my own by memorizing the movement of his arm as he drew and practicing it over and over.

"Quite sure. If you look carefully, you'll see that's the work of a student, not a professional artist."

"Yes, I think I can see what you mean," Gosia agreed, squinting closer at the picture, then turning away to observe the room. "Poor Amedeo, despite his great gifts, he lived and died like a pauper. He deserved better than this."

"No," I protested, "*We were richer than kings. We loved this studio. This was our home. We didn't need money to be happy!*"

"If it hadn't been for Zbo, he would have starved to death—they both would have," said Hanka, thrusting her chin at the bed. "It was a miracle he lasted as long as he did. We hoped that being from a good family, she might have some housekeeping skills: helping him mind his money, fixing him a meal now and then, keeping the studio decent in case a buyer wanted to drop by. You know how they all love to see the artist at work. Instead, all she thought about was sex. And look where it got her."

She shot a steely glance at Annie, who was still gawking at my sheeted body on the bed. "And let that be a lesson for you, too."

Annie blushed, but didn't reply.

Hanka bent down to retrieve some sardine tins from the floor and tossed them into an old pot collecting the drip from a leak in the roof.

"There's sardine oil all over the floor. Open the windows. We have to get rid of this smell."

While Gosia wrestled with the windows, I sat down on the bed next to myself and tried to explain it all to them.

"*But you don't understand. I tried really hard. I cleaned and cooked, but I had my own work to think of! You don't realize how difficult it was sometimes with him, when he wanted you, you couldn't resist. Gosia, you must know how that went! And when he was in a black mood, it was all you could do to keep from being sucked down into his whirlpool. After I got pregnant with Giovanna, I just couldn't keep up. There was too much to do. And my parents weren't any help. All they wanted was for me to give the baby up for adoption and move back in with them. But Modi would never have stood for that.*"

"We need to have her ready when the undertaker comes. Annie, you go sweep and mop the studio and gather up all the trash. Leave us one of those buckets."

Annie clumped back to the studio, with mop, broom, and bucket.

When Hanka approached the bed to pull back the sheet, both women gave a little gasp, as my green-blue eyes were wide open. Hanka lay her palm lightly on my swollen blue eyelids, but they wouldn't close. Once lowered, they popped open again.

"How odd," said Gosia, shrinking back from the bed.

"The undertaker will fix it with a dab of glue," said Hanka. "Now we have to wash her. Bring me that basin on the dresser."

How is it that an old worn thing, like Modi's cracked washbasin, can hold an entire world?

Modi always used to wash himself from head to toe after a painting session. Sometimes he was very neat while working, as precise as a clockmaker. Other times he flung his colors about with wild energy, splattering blobs of red and yellow all over himself in the most unlikely places. When he was done, he would clean his hands and nails with oil, and then setting his washbasin on the window ledge, he would scrub his whole body with cold water and a sponge, singing arias in a lusty, tenor voice that rang out across the courtyard: "La donna è mobile, Qual piuma a vento" while deliberately squeezing a few drops from his sponge down to the courtyard below, upon the laundry or head of Madame Moreau. Feeling the sprinkle on her hair, she would look up at the windows and roar, "Who is dripping that water?" Seeing him there, with his thick black curly hair, his beautiful bare torso framed in the window, laughing at her with that sparkle in his eye, she would mumble, all contrite, "Monsieur Modigliani, please be more careful," and that would be the end of it. No matter how ancient or acidic a woman might be, none could resist him.

It was this enamel basin with the cracked green glaze, over which he squatted to wash himself after we made love, that Hanka now filled with water from the bucket, and brought to the bedside. After peeling off my soiled robe and nightgown, they proceeded to wash my body with clean rags they had found in the studio, wiping away the caked blood from my forehead, limbs, and feet.

"Find me something for her to wear," said Hanka.

Gosia opened the trunk where I kept a few clothes, unleashing a smell of varnish, camphor and lavender into the air. I had brought that lavender from Nice, and now I longed to be back in the south again, lying in bed in the little hotel in Rue de France, drinking the coffee that Modi served me every morning, as I was too tired to get up and make it for him, because I had just had a baby.

"Everything looks too small," Gosia remarked, rummaging through the trunk. "In her condition, I don't think anything will fit."

"*The turquoise dress*," I suggested to the air—the only comfortable thing I had to wear when I was expecting Giovanna. It had a wrap-around skirt draped empire style from under my enormous bosom and big yellow daisies along the hem. Modi adored that dress—he loved to unwrap it and bury his face in my breasts. He said I was beautiful when I was pregnant, and he painted me in it twice. But of course, they could not hear me, and Gosia chose a dress I despised, an ugly tent-like bag of white crepe with red stripes, tight sleeves, brass buttons down the front, and a floppy red bow half-unstitched at the collar. Someone had given me this monstrosity which I had intended to cut up and use to make a Pierrot costume for Giovanna at carnival time.

27

"This looks big enough."

I cringed as they pulled the hideous thing over my head and forced my rigid arms through the sleeves like broomsticks.

"Amedeo always said 'Life is a gift,'" sighed Gosia. "What a terrible waste. She was so young."

Hanka smoothed the dress down over my mountainous belly where it hardly fit and reached under my stiff legs to yank it down behind my calves.

"She would have been twenty-two next April. I am sad and sorry for her too. But I am also very upset. After all we did for her and Modi! I dread to think what might have happened if she had leaped out the window here, and not at her parents' place. With the lease in Zbo's name, we might have had trouble with the police! I don't understand why she didn't come to us before deciding to end it all. We would have gone on supporting her and the children, if only she had turned to us first. We would have done anything to help her."

"Maybe she didn't plan it. Maybe it just happened in a moment of despair."

"We'll never know, will we?"

"Poor Jeanne."

"You have to admit, she was a selfish girl and a bad mother! Abandoning poor Giovanna like this—it's criminal. She might have been arrested if she had survived, or put in an insane asylum. She was always a bit off. You never knew what she was thinking. She hardly ever said a word in public."

Such cruelty bewildered me but then a thought pierced me to the quick: since all this had started, I hadn't really pondered Giovanna's new predicament. Our daughter didn't live with us in the studio, but with some nuns in a convent outside Paris, because Modi said that a studio full of toxic oil paints was no place for a baby whose crying would have ruined his concentration. Eventually, though, we had planned to have a real home. Now, when she'd be old enough to understand, the nuns would have to tell her she was an orphan. I *was* a monster, as Modi sometimes claimed whenever he was mad at me, which was often. When I tipped myself backwards through the window, I hadn't given a thought to Giovanna. In fact, I wasn't really thinking at all. I hadn't slept in a week and I was so numb; I just wanted everything to stop for a moment. I opened the window and the night air felt so fresh on my face and the room was so hot. With the help of a footstool, while André snoozed, I hoisted myself onto the ledge and leaned back for just an instant, the way you relax into your lover's arms to take a short nap on a train. I didn't consider the consequences.

Now I placed my hand on my belly. Modi had wanted a boy. I had killed our son. I wanted to howl. Hanka was right—I was a terrible mother.

But I also realized something else: the two women were not speaking French to each other but Polish, and despite the fact I knew not one word of that language, I could understand them perfectly.

Gosia did up the brass buttons on the yoke, pinching my dead skin with her pearly nails. "Poor Giovanna. I do worry what will become of her."

Hanka adjusted the sleeve on my wrist and fiddled with the right cuff. "Zbo and I have decided to keep her."

"No, you cannot have my child!"

"Unless, of course, his family makes a fuss, then I suppose we will have to send her to Italy. Oh dear, there's a stain on the sleeve and a button is missing, but I suppose it doesn't matter. No one will notice."

Gosia leaned over to button the left cuff and I smelled her floral perfume mixed with the faint sweaty smell of wool from her underarms. Sweet jasmine, like the scent samples my father used to bring home from the store where he worked as an accountant. My favorite was *l'Heure du Rêve*.

"Don't Jeanne's parents want to keep the girl? She is a Hébuterne after all."

"I don't think so.

"It seems so unfair to reject an innocent child for her parents' faults."

Hanka tied the bow once, frowned at the result, undid it and tied it again. "Perhaps Jeanne's father wasn't keen on having half-Jewish grandchildren."

"How sad. How can that make such a difference to them?"

Hanka shrugged. "They are very devout."

They retreated to the foot of the bed. Gosia crossed herself, and the two women studied the overall effect of their work.

"There now, how does she look?" said Hanka.

"Don't you think we should do something about her hair?" asked Gosia.

Annie came in and gave a start, seeing me there: a candy-striped mountain with a floppy red bow and my eyes wide open. "I have finished in the studio, Madame."

"See if you can find a comb or a brush, maybe in the drawer of that bedside table."

I peered over Annie's shoulder as she slid out the drawer. Inside were all my favorite little things: my diaries—a bundle of small notebooks tied together with a gold ribbon, my green purse with some cash, my blue-green Venetian glass bangle, and a wooden comb. I ached to touch them but could not.

The girl's fingers prodded the purse, as if feeling for coins, then caressed the glass bangle. It was the only ornament Modi had ever given me. "It changes green to gold to turquoise like your eyes," he used to say. He once painted me wearing it.

"*Please put it on my wrist,*" I whispered to her, "*I would so like to be buried with it.*" I had come to understand that would be happening soon.

"There is a comb, Madame."

"Well, give it to me then."

With shocking dexterity, the little thief slipped my bangle into the pocket of her coarse brown skirt and passed my wooden comb to Hanka.

"*Put that back! You can't have that!*" I tried to grab it from her pocket.

"There is also a purse, Madame," Annie reported, oblivious to my futile attempts to retrieve my bangle from her person.

"Let's have it."

"*Not my purse!*"

Hanka and Gosia exchanged a sharp glance as Annie handed over the purse. Opening the clasp, Hanka shook out some change. "Nothing but a few sous."

"*But there ought to be at least ten francs!*" Someone had taken my money, but who would have stolen it?

"Nothing else?"

"No, Madame."

But she was a liar as well as a thief—my precious notebooks were still in the drawer.

Gosia took the comb and tugged it through my tangled hair, while Hanka picked out the tiny flecks of dried leaves and dirt.

"She had such magnificent hair," mused Hanka. "Like a Botticelli. I think that's why Modigliani fell in love with her." I saw now that she was crying. So perhaps she did care a bit about me after all.

Lavender light mixed with smoke was gathering over the rooftops. Twilight would soon fall. I always loved that hour in winter and would sit by the window, gazing out through the dusk, waiting for Modi to come home from the cafés when he was out on business with Zbo. I would take out my violin, which I had brought from my parents' flat in Rue Amyot and practice a little Schubert, "Death and the Maiden." But I could never get the opening bars of the first movement to sound quite right. *Maître* Schlict, my old violin teacher before the war, always said that I was too hesitant in the attack. I needed to learn to be more assertive. I could almost hear that music now, and I looked about the room for my violin but didn't see it. Perhaps it was in the blue cupboard in the studio, which I couldn't open. Now they puffed up the pillows and propped up my head, which tilted askew because my neck was broken. Hanka crossed my arms on my breast and arranged the long hanks of hair around me like a coppery cloud, while Annie swept the floor.

"It's getting late. I hope the undertaker isn't going to wait until tomorrow," said Hanka, glancing to the window.

"Are we done here? I wanted to catch vespers and light a candle for Modi and Jeanne at Notre-Dame-des-Champs," said Gosia.

"Remember: the funeral leaves from the hospital at ten tomorrow. His brother sent Zbo a huge sum of money. We could have all lived a year in high style on what is being spent just for the flowers."

"I hope she will get a proper burial. Being a suicide."

"Her brother has seen to all the arrangements. At least we didn't have to deal with that."

"Won't she be buried together with Amedeo?"

"Zbo suggested that, but her parents objected on religious grounds. He'll be going into the Jewish section."

"And they'd deny me this one last privilege to lie beside my husband?"

All three stared at me in silence, then Hanka took Gosia's hand.

"How different it would all have been if Modi had met you first. If only he had gone away with you this autumn, I am sure you could have saved him from his devastating illness."

Gosia sniffled and smiled through her tears. "He needed someone who could take proper care of him, make him hot soups and tisanes, but Jeanne was too young and flighty."

All lies! He never loved you! And he hated hot soups!" I grasped a candlestick to throw at her, but the cold brass dribbled through my fingers like icy water. In my clumsiness, my elbow knocked against the edge of the dresser. Annie jumped, for God knows how, I had managed to produce an audible sound.

"What was that noise?" asked Hanka, alarmed, turning to Annie.

"Don't frighten her!" said Gosia.

"Annie?"

Annie gaped at my body on the bed, but shook her head. "I didn't hear anything. Did you?"

"I thought I heard…" Hanka glared at Annie, then at me. "It was probably only a mouse in the dresser."

Hanka pulled the sheet back over my body and my unblinking eyes.

"Annie, mop the room after we leave and get rid of Jeanne's dirty nightgown and robe. The *concierge* will lock up later."

"Shouldn't one of us stay with her?" asked Gosia.

"You aren't afraid to be here alone, are you, Annie?"

"No, Madame. I was very fond of Mademoiselle Jeanne."

"So why did you steal my bangle?"

"Good girl. Gosia, shall we go?"

"Shouldn't we…" She nodded towards the mirror on the dresser. "Cover it?"

"Are you so superstitious?"

"It's traditional."

"Go ahead, then."

Was she afraid I might leap off the bed and suck their blood? If there were any vampires here, it wasn't me, but them.

Gosia opened the trunk again, removed my red Indian print shawl, and spread it over the mirror. Then she noticed Modi's jacket hanging on the nail by the bed. "Oh look! That old jacket of his."

I seethed as she fingered the limp velvet sleeve.

"You don't suppose anyone would mind…."

"Take it. Zbo will be coming later to remove the rest of his things before the new lodgers arrive."

"Who'll be renting the flat?"

"Nina Hamnett and her new boyfriend."

"Not them! Sleeping in our bed!" Nina was another one who was always after my husband.

"Oh! Here's his bandana in the pocket." Gosia pressed it to her face. "It smells just like him."

I could have scratched her eyes out.

"What about Jeanne's things?" Gosia asked, wiping her tears with Modi's bandana and tucking it into her sleeve.

"Her brother is coming to clear them out."

"I'd also like to have that drawing of Amedeo with his pipe. As a memento. Do you think he'd mind?"

"Who will notice if it's gone? It's worthless."

Gosia took down the drawing.

"Annie, don't forget to close the windows or the bats will get in, and you'd better light some candles. It is almost too dark to see."

They went out, and I was left with Annie, who lit a candle in a wine bottle and set about inspecting every inch of the studio. Perhaps she had heard how I used to hide money from Modi in books and pots, but she found none, and fortunately didn't think of looking behind the cupboard, where I had my secret place, a niche in the wall. From the drawer of the bedside table, she took my notebooks, untied the ribbon, leafed through the top one. I had been keeping a diary since I was fifteen. My whole life was in those pages—shopping lists of groceries and art supplies, baby names, household accounts, my periods ticked on a calendar, doodles, sketches, dreams. She stuffed the bundle of notebooks into her apron pocket.

Leaning over the bed, she folded back the sheet and lifted the candle to my shrunken, yellow face. The flame gleamed in my lusterless eyes as melted red wax dribbled on my chin. When her dry lips brushed my forehead, I had no strength to push her away. She slid something into my breast pocket. I could feel it hard and cold against my nipple.

"Goodbye, petite Jeanne. Now don't you move. Stay right here."
Reluctantly, I obeyed.

❋

André had locked me in a closet, and I was running out of air.
Someone was knocking outside with a syncopated rhythm: *dum de
dum dum dum*. Frantic, I pounded back, screaming *let me out, let me
out*, then my eyes fluttered open. With relief I felt the sun on my face,
breaking through a chink in the wall. For a few moments, I lay very
still in the soft bed until the dream subsided.

Fully awake now, I reached for Modi at my side—but he had
already gotten up and was probably in the studio making us some
coffee on the stove in his little Italian pot, singing snatches of *Carmen*.
"La fleur que tu m'avais jetée," but changing the lyrics to something
silly or obscene.

Anticipating the taste of that hot sweet liquid, I struggled to prop
myself up against the pillows. This time I was rarely nauseous upon
waking, that came later in the day, but was always so lazy and sluggish
that I spent hours and hours in bed. Any day now, any hour, I would
be delivered—a thought that brought me both relief and dread.

I must have fallen asleep on my arm, for my right hand tingled,
half numb. Trying to knead life back into my fingers and forearm, I
noted the striped cuff of an unfamiliar dress buttoned snugly at the
wrist, instead of my white flannel nightgown. How on earth did I
come to be wearing that?

"*Bonjour*, Jeanne. *Tu as bien dormi?*"

There, on the ledge of the open window, a little boy sat swinging
his legs, knocking the heels of his dirty bare feet against the wall. *Dum
de dum dum dum*—I recognized it now. That was the rhythm I had
heard in my dream. He looked no older than ten, with a shock of
stiff red hair, a waxy face, and freckles butterflied over his cheeks and
nose. His legs were pencil-thin, and his red shirt and blue trousers so
faded and worn that they must have been washed a thousand times.
I thought he had probably come to model for Modi, who sometimes
brought urchins home off the street to pose for him. He loved their
sunken cheeks and gap-toothed grins, and the way their eyes shone

when he rewarded them with half an apple or a slice of hard cheese when his work was done.

I smiled, "*Bonjour, mon petit.* What's your name?"

"Don't you remember me?"

"Should I?" I studied his face. He did look familiar, though I couldn't say where I had seen him before.

"It's me. Pierre, the baker's son. Pierre Giraud."

I frowned. That was the name of a child who drowned in the sea at Cagnes–sur-Mer, near Nice, months ago, where I was staying with Modi. A fisherman had found the body entangled in his nets several days after the boy had gone missing. This was an unpleasant joke I didn't like at all. How could he possibly know about Pierre Giraud?

"Pierre Giraud is dead, so that can't be who you are—Modi," I called, "What is this boy doing here? Come get your model, so I can get up and get dressed."

Pierre shook his head gravely. "Modi isn't here."

His sober manner unnerved me. "Where is he then?"

He blinked at me. "You really don't know?"

His head jerked aside; his eyes swiveled showing the whites, commanding my own eyes to follow. I gasped at the sight of a plain pine coffin placed crosswise at the foot of my bed. Huge, cumbersome, bare, with no flowers, the coffin filled the whole room, blocking the view of the doorway.

That coffin hadn't been there when I first opened my eyes. Who had brought it here and where had it come from? Out the window, the bells of Notre-Dame-des-Champs clanged furiously, drowning out any possible reply. Then I remembered, like a stiletto through the heart, the funeral was today. I rammed the heels of my hands against my eyes, blotting out the images that rushed towards me from the black mouth of a tunnel. I had to push them back, to take things one at a time. Hanka had said that the cortege would be starting at ten from the Charity Hospital in Rue Jacob. So why had they brought Modi's coffin here?

I had to get ready. Surely someone would be coming for us—Zbo and Hanka, or our dear friend, Chaim Soutine, who had been like a brother to Modi, and the undertaker, of course. They couldn't expect me to walk in the condition I was in; they would have to send a car for me. I hated to be wearing this clownish outfit, but there wasn't time to change. I heaved myself out of bed and searched the floor for my shoes, but couldn't find them.

"My shoes!" I shouted, "What have you done with my shoes?" Then something tugged at my middle—shimmered like a spider's skein shifting in a draft. A glinting thread looped in the air, connecting me to the coffin. And I remembered with a resounding shock: Yesterday my body was in the bed, but now it was in that box. It was *me* there in that coffin, not Modi.

"Jeanne, never mind about your shoes. You can't go anywhere."

"But my husband is being buried today!"

"You can't, you see, as long as that's still there," Pierre said gently touching the thread. "But when it dissolves, you'll be as free as I am. I can go anywhere I like."

To prove his point, he shot out the window and then back to the ledge so swiftly, I hardly had time to take it in. "But for now, you mustn't go further than it can stretch—it mustn't break, otherwise...."

I plucked the thread, thinner now and more fragile than the day before. "Otherwise what?"

"I don't know, but it's bad if you do."

"I am sorry, but I can't talk to you now. I mustn't be late."

I somehow clambered over the coffin and ran barefoot through the studio. The door was wide open, and a chill wind blew up from the bottom of the stairs. As I tottered down the first ramp, past the door to Ortiz's flat, the thread twanged at my navel with a low thrum, and Ortiz's dogs began to howl. Pierre came out on the landing above me, shouting at me to come back, but I just kept going. Two flights down I halted—the thread would yield no further. One step more and I felt it would snap and anything might happen. I stared at the wooden steps spiraling down and my mind whirled with them.

Small fingers cold as seaweed fumbled for my hand. Pierre stood beside me on the stairs, peering up at my face. "Come back upstairs, Jeanne."

With leaden legs I climbed back up, clutching the boy's hand, past Ortiz's door and the howling dogs and into our studio, where I plopped down on a chair that for once did not wobble under my weight. Outside, the bells had ceased tolling, but the walls still tingled with their solemn vibration.

"I want so much to see him again," I sobbed.

"You will, but not now,"

I buried my face in my hands.

Cool lips touched my cheek, a hand brushed a strand of my hair from my eyes.

"Why don't we go up to the roof?" he asked. "You might be able to watch the funeral pass by from up there."

I had not been on the roof in over two years—it was dangerous to go up during the bombing—but before the Germans had begun shelling the city, Modi and I sometimes went up to enjoy the view or look at the moon. To get up there, you had to step out onto the ledge along the big studio windows, then scramble up an iron ladder fastened to the wall, used by workmen when they had to replace a broken roof tile or sweep the chimney. Modi and I would sometimes picnic up there at sunset, drinking beer or marc and nibbling pâté I had snitched from my mother's pantry. Sometimes he would toss bits of stale bread down towards the courtyard, and the fat gulls straying from the Seine would snatch them away in midair.

"Come on!"

Pierre leaped out onto the ledge and tugged me out beside him. My head spun when I looked down at the courtyard, where Madame Moreau was mopping the flagstones with bleach. The odor made me queasy. I craned my neck to look up at the roof and tweaked the string at my navel. "You are sure this won't break if we go up there?"

"Nah, it isn't that far."

I reached for the rung, which I could not grasp, but instantly, almost effortlessly, there I was poised on the crest of the roof still holding Pierre's hand.

From the Eiffel tower and the Madeleine to the Luxembourg Gardens and the Louvre, Paris lay before us. To the north, the grand boulevards were crammed with people, carriages, and motorcars like scuttling little beetles. The elms and plane trees in the Luxembourg Gardens had shaken off their leaves: spindly skeletons in tidy rows on the wintery lawns. Everything appeared in such sharp detail – the icy sparkle of water in the fountain, the frozen statues with pigeons on their heads. Inside the East entrance, the dark hatted heads of the ladies strolling there looked like rows and rows of pillboxes.

For the first time in ages, I felt free and elated. I stood on the top of a chimney pot and spread my arms wide, as the biting wind blew my hair every which way. Despite my bare feet, I didn't feel cold at all. "It's just like flying," I cried.

Pierre jumped up beside me and spread his arms, too, as the wind ripped through us, whistling between the buildings. My red-striped dress flapped and crackled like flames. I laughed when the satin bow round my neck blew away and was snapped up by the beak of a crow.

"Well, you might not actually be able to fly once the string is gone, but you'll have all sorts of fun," said Pierre, hopping down from the chimney pot and perching himself on the edge of the roof to dangle his legs over the courtyard. "You can go wherever you want, climb to the tops of mountains, even to the tip of the Eiffel tower. You will be able to walk straight into the Palais Royal and pull the guard's nose. Nobody and nothing can stop you then. And you'll know the answer to everything you don't know or didn't know before but always wanted to."

I climbed down and sat beside him. Madame Moreau had gone back inside to cook herself a pot au feu. The smell of onions and beef wafted up to the roof, and I realized I hadn't eaten in a very long time, but I wasn't the least bit hungry.

"How do you mean the answer to everything?"

"Things you never understood before will suddenly start making sense. Well, for instance, arithmetic problems from school like why zero from zero is zero, or why robins' eggs are blue, or where your lost puppy or mitten ended up—but also big questions too, ones that grown-ups think about. Do you have a big question?"

I pondered a minute and shook my head. "There is nothing I really wanted to know, that I can think of. Except perhaps how to speak Russian. I always wanted to learn to speak Russian and read Tolstoy and Pushkin."

He nodded. "Then you'll be able to."

"How can that be?"

"I don't know. It just is."

Clouds scudded over our heads as we sat in silence a while. What was my big question? The only things that had ever really mattered to me were loving Modigliani and making art, and before that my parents and my brother. I had a baby daughter but I was not a good mother. My eyes stung as I thought of Giovanna. What was my child doing now? Was she out in the cloister, perhaps for her daily breath of air? I hoped one of the younger nuns had taken her to heart, and that she wasn't being mistreated. I rubbed my arms, thinking how chilly it must be in the convent.

"I guess I would like to know about my daughter."

"Is she dead?"

I was shocked by his question. "No, she is with the nuns."

"Did you give her up to the nuns because you didn't love her?"

"Of course not! She is only a baby, barely one year old. I was just too tired most of the time to take proper care of her. And her father was very ill. We didn't want her to get sick."

"My mother and father beat me, so I ran away and stole a rowboat. Then a wave washed me overboard. It took a week to find me. They were very sorry then. They beat me for stealing five francs from the cash drawer at the bakery. But it wasn't me that stole it. It was my brother. He'd always been the favorite one, anyway. I suppose he is happier without me."

I ruffled his hair, still stiff with salt. "I am sure they miss you very much."

"I had a sister too. She died of scarlet fever. I hope I find her soon."

"Find her where?" I asked, but he ignored my question.

"So why did you want another one if you were too tired to look after the first?" He pointed at my belly.

"It just happens, when you are in love, you can find yourself expecting."

"I know about the birds and the bees. That isn't what I meant." He yawned. "It was a boy, in case you are wondering."

I stared at him incredulously. "How do you know that?"

He shrugged. "I just know. But he will probably be sent back. You won't have to worry about him anymore."

"What do you mean, sent back?"

"Sent back into life. I bet he'll be born in Paris very soon. Tiny babies never have to wait long."

I looked out over the city, and the grey rooftops blurred, but no tears came. Was it possible my poor child would be born to another life? If so, I prayed he might have another chance, with a better mother than myself.

"And will we be sent back too, Modi and I?" I wanted to ask, but church bells rang out across the city—a choir of jangling vibrations. It was ten o'clock. We stood up again to look towards Rue Jacob.

"There they are! They are coming!" he shouted.

It should have been much too far away for me to see anything, and yet, despite the great distance, I could make out the high-stepping black horses pulling a hearse heaped with lilies and roses and draped with banners of purple and gold. A brass band trod behind, playing a dirge, whose melancholy notes I could hear faintly, leading the crowd of mourners. A thousand people or more had turned out to say goodbye to the Prince of Montparnasse. The cortege crept along Boulevard Saint-Germain in the direction of Rue de la Roquette and the cemetery of Père-Lachaise, interspersed with the shiny black motorcars, in which Zbo and Hanka were surely sitting beside ladies in furs and monocled gentlemen in top hats, the sorts of people who buy pictures. I watched it crawl by slowly, and when the endless stream had petered out, it seemed as though hours and hours had elapsed. I shivered as gray clouds darted over the sun. A flock of crows rose from the naked trees in the Luxembourg Gardens, scattering across the sky.

We climbed back down to the studio, where the pine box was still waiting for me. My parents did not want to spend very much on my burial, it seemed, but I didn't care. Pierre ran his hand along the rim of the rough plank coffin, and a strange chill prickled up from somewhere deep inside me.

He knocked twice on the lid and winked at me. "Don't you want to see how you look in there?"

The thought repulsed me. "I don't think so."

"The scary part starts now, but everybody has to go through it."

"You are a wise little philosopher," I said, annoyed.

"Once they take that away, everything will be different." He rapped on the coffin again.

The coffin didn't frighten me as much anymore. It was just another piece of furniture in the room, like a table or a piano or a dresser.

Maybe I was getting used to it. I certainly didn't want to see what was inside, but I did feel anxious about what would happen when they came to take it away.

Suddenly, I felt unaccountably sleepy. I stretched out on top of the coffin and found it wasn't uncomfortable at all. I gazed up at the ceiling, which swirled round so that I had to close my eyes. And then I must have dozed off or at least there were no thoughts in my head until a noise in the studio jarred me from my torpor. I sat bolt upright. I had heard a key turning in the lock.

I panicked again. Had they come for me so soon? Did I really have to go? And where indeed would I be going? Now it was nearly night. They wouldn't take the coffin away so late in the day, would they? Perhaps it was Gosia and Hanka, returning for more of my things, or the little thief from downstairs. Heavy boots clomped across the studio towards the bedroom, and my brother André walked in, his face distorted with anger and tears. He carried a large cardboard suitcase. I flew to him, but he looked straight through me.

He put down the suitcase, strode right over to the coffin, and after a moment's hesitation, flung open the lid with an anguished cry. I flinched in disbelief when I saw myself there. I couldn't recognize that yellow witch's mask I had on, with its sunken eyes, pointy nose, and fleshless jawline.

"How could you do this to us, Nenette? How could you betray us and destroy our lives? I don't think our father will survive this."

I wanted to throw my arms around him and lean my head on his shoulder, like I used to do whenever we made up after a quarrel, but the air around his body was like solid ice. I couldn't cut through it. "*I am so sorry. I tried to catch hold of a balcony railing as I fell, but it slipped through my fingers. I know, I know I have done a terrible thing. You must forgive me.*"

"I don't know how you could live like this." He rubbed tears away with his fists. "In this bare, filthy place, just to share your bed with that… corrupter! If only you had come back to us."

"*Listen to me, André,*" I shouted, and for a moment his eyes drifted towards me, as if following a moth in the air. "*I loved him; I loved our life. I loved our child. That doesn't mean that I loved you or our parents any less. He was my husband and a great artist. Not a corrupter! Anyway,*"

I wasn't as innocent as you all believed. Before Modi, there was Foujita, yes, your friend. Things are different now, for men and women. It isn't like it was when our parents were young."

Now his tears flowed. "It's all my fault. I will never forgive myself and I will never forgive you either, and I curse the day I signed you up for drawing lessons at the Académie Colarossi."

I bent down to kiss his hand, but the ice barrier bounced me back. *"On the contrary, I will love and bless you forever, because on that day you helped me become who I really am. It is nobody's fault, except my own. My dying, I mean. I can't change it now. But nothing could ever have kept me from loving Modi; or him, me. We were born for each other, under his lucky black star."*

"Why couldn't you have been happy staying home, painting daisies on dishes and helping Céline with the cooking, or even designing costumes for the Opera? Why did you have to end up in this stinking hole?"

"Don't be ridiculous! I could not have had or wanted a different life! When we were children, we always promised each other that we would both grow up to be artists! That was our secret pact! And I kept it. I expect you to do the same and to respect my decisions."

His face stern and now void of tears, he pulled a pen knife out of his breast pocket, leaned down to cut off a lock of my hair, wrapped it in his handkerchief, and put it in his pocket. Lowering the lid gently but resolutely, he went around the room, removing my drawings and paintings from the walls and packing them into the suitcase between layers of newspaper. From the trunk in the bedroom, he took a few clothes and a scarf I had knitted, which he knotted around his neck. Proceeding to the studio, he collected my sketchbooks and carnets from the drawing table. There were drawings in them I didn't want him to see—the ones of Modigliani dying, the ones we had drawn of each other naked in bed, the anatomical ones I had drawn of myself, which Maman had once discovered hidden under my mattress in Rue Amyot.

"Jeanne!" she had cried, scandalized, "These drawings are unchaste!" I had explained that they were an experiment in life-drawing I had done at home, after my bath, with the help of mirrors so I could see "down there." She had nearly fainted at the thought. "You mean this is you?"

André now opens that very carnet, with those intimate sketches, and finds the one of me in the nude, with leg raised, foot poised on a chair, revealing the female orchid. He clenches his jaw, his hand jerks to rip the sketch from the book, then desists, and he throws the carnet into the suitcase. I want to howl, to scream, to pummel his chest with my fists.

"The human body is beautiful in all of its parts. There is nothing shameful in the human body or in the act of love. The shame lies only in the eyes of the viewer. You, a painter, should know this. But you paint landscapes. You are afraid of the landscape of your own body."

The suitcase was now so full, it couldn't hold much more, and my brother went out, carrying away all my art work, the photographs and letters I kept in the dresser, the necklaces I had made from shells picked up off the beach in Brittany, where André and I used to go walking, and, in his breast pocket, a lock of my hair. From the landing, I watched him descending the stairs, cursing and sobbing all the way down.

It seemed I was alone now. Pierre wasn't in the bedroom or the studio. I collapsed in the old armchair facing our easels, the one where our models used to sit. Modi had painted me in that chair at least a dozen times or more, always wearing a different outfit—a yellow sweater, a red hat, a pearl necklace borrowed from Hanka, with my hair coiled in a high bun or flowing over my bare shoulders.

If I closed my eyes and concentrated hard enough, I could just see him there across the room, grinning behind the easel, then coming over and bending down to cup my chin for a kiss, his warm lips and tongue always tasting of wine and smoke. The first time I posed for him, I was nineteen years old. I skipped drawing class and went to his run-down hotel, because he had invited me to sit for a portrait, but it had taken me weeks to get my courage up and present myself at his door. Four sittings later, we made love the first time, and nothing was ever the same after that.

I opened my eyes. I was sitting in our armchair in the studio, but once again a noise had disturbed me. My eyes focused on the door: another visitor was about to come in. The hinges creaked; stealthy footsteps padded in. Two black-clad figures moved in the moonlight. The taller one lit a candle, striking a match on the sole of his boot. I could just make out their faces. The one with the candle was Armand Metz, who ran a gallery in Rue de Maine and bought up pictures by the Monparnos. We would often see him at the Rotonde, wearing a bowler hat, sitting at Picasso's table with a buyer or two, negotiating some deal. He always ignored Modigliani's work and treated Zbo with a certain superiority. So what was he doing here in our studio? The other one, a stranger, looked like a roughneck—with the burly physique of a boxer or a porter at Les Halles.

"Looks like they beat us to it. Don't see no pictures here," said the boxer.

"Still, there must be something. Maybe in the other room," said Metz.

On their way into the bedroom, they banged smack into the coffin. In the flickering candlelight, its shadow danced huge on the wall.

"*Merde!* I thought you said he was in the ground."

"He is. That must be the girl who lived with him, his model. They're burying her tomorrow," said Metz.

Tomorrow? Please, God, no, not so soon.

"Was she sick too?"

"No, she jumped out the window."

"Killed herself!"

"Yes, it was tragic. She was very young and pregnant, too. Didn't want to live without him."

"*Ouais.* Quite a few women crying for him right now, I hear. Too bad, if she was expecting a child."

"*Thank you for your sympathy. I can do without it.*"

"But who knows if the baby was his?" continued the roughneck. "You know what these model girls get up to."

"*How dare you say such things! Salaud!*"

"She had already had another child by him," said Metz, lifting his candle to survey the room.

"So madcap Modi was a family man. Who would've thought?"

"Hmmm," said Metz, inspecting the pockmarked walls, "With all these holes presumably from nails and thumbtacks, there must have been dozens of pieces on display."

"Look, I don't like poking about in the company of stiffs. Let's grab whatever it is we have come for, then get the hell out of this place..."

"Relax. It is just a body in a box. She won't bite you. I am sure you have seen plenty in your line of business."

"I can't bite, oh, but if I could, you'd feel it all right!"

"What is that supposed to mean, my line of business?"

"Just look around, will you? See if you can find something."

They rummaged awhile in the dresser and trunk, but finding nothing, returned to the studio, where the short, squat one rifled through the bottom shelves of the cupboard.

"There ain't no paintings or drawings in here either, but there's a fiddle. Shall we take that? And some music too. Might get some cash for it at the flea market."

He pulled my violin case out and slapped it down with a twang on the worktable.

I winced. *Be careful with that!* My father had paid a fortune for that instrument, made in Verona.

"I am not a thief, but an art curator and dealer," said Metz coldly. "We are here only to rescue the artwork. Nothing else must be touched."

Metz studied the dark room, lips pursed, scrutinizing every object. "The girl hid things, you see, and I am sure there must be something eluding our attention."

"The only place we ain't looked is behind this cupboard here."

Panic fluttered in my chest. Behind that cupboard was my secret hiding place and I could do nothing to stop them from violating it.

Setting the candle on the floor, Metz seized the side of the cupboard, leaned his weight on it, and tried to move it away from the wall. "Don't just stand there. Give me a hand. This thing weighs a ton."

"Salauds!" Pierre shouted, and there he was astride the top of the cupboard, wildly kicking his legs in the air.

As they lurched the cupboard away from the wall, everything on the top shelf fell off, raining down on their heads: an old tomato tin full of pencil stubs, brushes and pebbles; three books of poetry; my Russian dictionary; a candlestick; two china teacups I had stolen from home and a bottle of turpentine. It all crashed to the floor with an explosion, the fragile items breaking to bits and the turpentine spilling across the floor.

But this didn't deter the thieves. "Damn it, be careful," sputtered Metz, "You'll wake everyone in the building, and the *concierge* will be up here with the police in no time."

"Not Madame Moreau. She's in with us. How did you think I got the key?"

"Madame Moreau conniving with thieves! And I considered her a decent person!"

Metz picked up the candle and shoved it into the crevice between the cupboard and the wall. "Is she now? Well, we'll see about that. Oho, here's something. I was right. There's a niche, a hole in the wall."

His arm reached in deep—I could hear his hand rustling about like a rat, then he drew out a rolled canvas bundled in newspaper. It was a painting I had put there.

"Well, well, well. What do we have here?" His teeth flashed in the candlelight. He was grinning ear to ear.

They unrolled the bundle on the worktable. There it lay: the portrait I had tried so hard to protect but hadn't had time to finish after we came back from Nice. Metz set the candle beside it and they leaned over to examine it.

"Why it's Modi– and that must be her with their baby!"

"Yes" said Metz, rubbing his chin, "I do believe this incomplete figure is indeed a self-portrait of the artist himself, together with wife and child, like the Holy Family. *Une famille sacrée.*"

"I wonder why he hid it. Or did she?"

I had hidden it to keep it safe and to keep it secret from Modi. I had asked Ortiz months ago to help me move the cupboard so I could put it there—I intended to finish it when I had more time, which sadly never happened.

"Who knows?"

"So how much is it worth, being unfinished and all?"

Metz laughed. "One day it will be worth millions."

"Well, that was a lucky find."

Pierre took my hand, and we approached the table to study the painting, pushing in front of the intruders.

"It is beautiful," Pierre said, his raggedy head bowed over the canvas.

Yes, it *was* beautiful. Modi had started it as a portrait of me with Giovanna, while we were living in Nice, but then he had abandoned it, and wanted to paint over the canvas, since he never had enough supplies. But I took it up in his place, adding his own figure next to mine, working on it in secret. I had been planning to give it to him for his next birthday, but had set it aside shortly after returning to Paris. I had only sketched out his figure and face. Giovanna's face was still a blank little moon. He had left my own face half done with only one eye and pale lavender lips. In this portrait, as in others, our styles perfectly matched. I was sure that not even an expert like Metz could tell Modi's brushstrokes from mine.

"We'll commission Kisling or someone else to do a whole series of drawings, which I'll catalogue as preliminary studies for this portrait, and then have him finish it, giving the baby a face and completing the figures of the artist and wife. An unusual subject for Modigliani— family threesome as self-portrait. I can already think of a buyer."

"Well, I will be wanting my share as soon as it's sold, and for those other things you said, too, the studies."

"Don't worry." Metz patted his mate on the shoulder, but I could almost read his thoughts. He'd never give the fellow a cent. Not that I cared.

"I wonder if there is anything else," said Metz going over to the cupboard, which was still pulled away from the wall. He reached into the niche again, but found nothing, then tapped the floorboards with the heel of his boot. "Sounds hollow," he said. "Give me something to pry up the boards with."

The other fellow handed him his pocketknife and held the candle while Metz lifted up the edge of a board. Curious I peered over his shoulder, having no idea what might be in there.

"Definitely a cavity of sorts," he said, poking around with his hand. "Quite big. Must have been a chimney running up through the floor and into the wall here where that niche is now, or perhaps a coal chute. Nothing here now."

They pushed the cupboard back against the wall, and kicked the broken cups, scattered pencils and brushes into a corner. Metz rolled up the canvas and wrapped it in its newspaper.

I stood in the doorway, my arms crossed.

"You mustn't take this away. I forbid it. It belongs to my daughter now!"

"They can't hear you, Jeanne," said Pierre.

I understood how useless it was. Nothing belonged to me anymore.

Metz tucked the portrait under his arm as if it were a baguette he was about to take home and slice up for dinner, then walked straight through me and down the stairs, and the squat one followed. I screamed at them from the top of the landing. *"I curse you and anyone else who robs me of that picture."*

The door slammed at the bottom of the stairs.

Modi had begun that painting while we were living at the hotel in Rue de France. It was just the three of us by then: Modi, Giovanna, and myself. My mother, who had been there with me in Nice for several months before Giovanna was born, gave up trying to put me on the righteous path and had gone back to Paris.

And for a moment I remembered posing with Giovanna wrapped in my Indian shawl. I had to keep shifting in my seat, for my breasts so full of milk were very heavy and my back ached intolerably if I kept the same position for too long. Giovanna was an angel, never crying or squirming, just gazing at him with her eyes wide open from in between her velvety lashes. Sometimes her pudgy fingers would reach out for the glass bangle on my wrist.

Through the open window, the breeze stirs the yellow curtains and lifts the hair on the nape of my neck like his kisses used to do. Outside I hear the voices of people passing in the street, the clanging of the omnibus, the cries of the umbrella mender and the knife grinder. The air smells fresh with a hint of brine and orange blossoms. He does not drink much while working here at the hotel and seems more patient than usual. Has the birth of our daughter worked a miracle? Sitting here in the sunny room, listening to him humming under his breath as his brush licks and stabs the canvas, I never want to leave. Paris seems so far away. I could not imagine a more perfect life.

"Quick, Jeanne, it's time. Put these on! You'll need them."

Roused from my thoughts, I stared at the sabots Pierre was holding out to me and shook my head. Those sabots weren't mine. They probably belonged to Annie who must have traded them for the leather pumps I used to keep under the dresser. What did he expect me to do with those? They looked about three sizes too big.

"Jeanne, it is time to go!" I was aware of a disturbance, the sound of voices in the other room, a bustling noise, and a scraping of furniture being moved about. Then three men burst out of my bedroom, balancing my coffin on their shoulders. I recognized one of them. He worked at the market on Wednesdays, unloading crates of fish and sides of beef.

I hardly had time to put on the sabots before being yanked along by the string still threading my navel. I knew I might never be coming back here, so I said goodbye to the place where I had been so happy and unhappy. Goodbye to the stained paisley coverlet; the pillow still bearing the impress of his head; the wise, comforting faces of the Madonnas in blue tacked up on the walls.

"Take something with you, just one thing. It's allowed. But hurry!" urged Pierre as the coffin barged through the door towards the stairs, but there was nothing left, not a hat, bandana, painting, or my glass bangle, not even a photograph. Nothing I cared about—except my violin—which the gallery thieves had abandoned on my worktable. I reached for the handle of the violin case and most amazingly, lifted it up before being swept through the door. Or perhaps it was the soul of the instrument I held in my hand—for the violin case still lay on the table even as I carried it away. But I had no time to puzzle this over.

Pierre grabbed my free hand, and we lurched down the steps behind the men, the coffin knocking against the wall at every curve of the stairs, and the string yo-yo-ing at my navel. Down in the street in the drizzling rain, a hearse with black horses awaited, but none of my family was there. There was no one but the undertaker in a worn stovepipe hat and the *concierge* remonstrating with the pallbearers for scraping the banisters on their way down. The horses looked sickly thin, the limp black plumes adorning their heads wilted in the rain. The bearers shoved the coffin up into the hearse and I was pulled up after it. The undertaker slapped a coronet of rain-drenched lilies on the lid, then climbed up in front with the driver, while the others got into the back. Pierre scrambled on after them and plunked down cross-legged on top of the coffin.

Caressing the worn leather case on my knees, I thought of the many times I had taken the horse-drawn omnibus to go to my music lesson with old *Maître* Schlict on cold rainy days like this, and how I would stop for a cup of hot coffee or chocolate to warm my hands up before my lesson.

"How is it I can keep my violin? When I tried to remove a handkerchief from Modi's pocket, my fingers couldn't even take hold of it."

Pierre shrugged. "I don't know. That is just how it is. You are allowed to take something with you right before you go. Your clothes of course, otherwise you'd have to go around naked afterwards. And something that you loved, but nothing that's alive. You can't take anyone living with you, even if they want to come. I know that because I wanted to take my dog, but it wasn't allowed."

"Take them with you where?" I asked.

"Where we're going."

The hearse bolted forward, and we set off down the street.

"This is what I took." Pierre slipped a large gold locket from his pocket and showed me a photograph of a tiny girl inside and the snippet of a blond curl. "That's my sister on her sixth birthday."

"She is very pretty," I said.

"I have been looking for her all over the place," he sighed, "I really hope I find her."

He sounded so wistful, I leaned over and kissed his forehead. "Find her? Where do you think you might find her?" And if he could find his sister, could I find Modi?

"In the other Paris."

I frowned. "What other Paris?"

"The city that's alongside this one. There is no way I can explain it. But you'll soon see."

I gripped the edge of the coffin to keep myself steady as we bounced along the paving stones. Soon the hearse reached the end of the empty street, where I assumed we would turn left and then head up Boulevard Saint-Michel towards Rue de la Roquette and the cemetery of Père-Lachaise where Modi had just been buried. Was that yesterday or the day before? I was beginning to lose track of the time. I was nervous but excited because I thought I might see Modi there in the cemetery. But instead the hearse turned onto Avenue D'Orléans, heading south.

I looked at the men half dozing in the back of the hearse with their elbows propped on my coffin. Didn't they realize that the driver had just made a wrong turn?

"This isn't the right direction for Père-Lachaise," I objected.

Pierre shrugged. "Maybe that's not where we're going."

I clutched my violin case closer and watched the Paris streets receding.

It was still quite dark. Few people had ventured out in the morning: a bent old lady shuffling to church with her umbrella; two matrons swinging their string bags along; a workman in a soiled cap braving the rain on a rusted bicycle. They all crossed themselves as we rattled by, and a *gendarme* smoking under the awning of a café tossed his cigarette into the gutter and stood to attention as we passed.

There was a market in a square crowded with shoppers despite the rain, gathered round baskets of turnips and carrots, crates of oysters and mussels, and white slabs of cod, all smelling of the sea. I thought how odd it was not to have to eat or be hungry anymore.

After a half hour drive down that ancient road where pilgrims had once set out for Spain, we came to a tidy suburb where the sign above the train station read *Bagneux*. The station was a pretty yellow building with a clock tower over the entrance and lace curtains in the lighted upper windows, where bright pink geraniums flourished on a window ledge. Under the tin roof of a kiosk by the station, a chestnut vendor had set up his stove, puffing blue smoke into the damp air. I remembered once eating chestnuts with Modi and the taste of the sweet, hot, flaky meat inside. The charred skins singed our fingers and smudged them with charcoal as we peeled them, and he drew the Hebrew letter Aleph on my cheek with his blackened finger. Now I touched my cheek. I could almost feel the warmth of his hand.

When the hearse drove in through the cemetery gates, the big black station clock was striking eight. And I thought, back over at the Académie Colarossi, the drawing lesson was about to begin. Thérèse and my other friends would be there. I supposed they must have heard what had happened to Modi and to me. Some probably had gone to Modi's funeral, but I doubted they would be coming to mine, so far out from the city. Perhaps they were thinking of me now in class, as they placed their pads on the easels. *Merde!* It didn't seem possible that I would never see any of those people or places again.

The cemetery was like a park, with tall bare lindens and drenched lawns. The hearse trundled down a tree-lined lane where squirrels hopped and hungry crows as plump as hens pecked the ground. It was still drizzling. The cold air smelled of moss and dead leaves and the tang of smoke and wet cedars. It was a very early hour for a funeral, and except for our hearse, the cemetery looked deserted. At last we stopped near a newly-dug grave where three mourners with umbrellas and a priest stood around a slot in the earth, and suddenly I felt very anxious. The pallbearers came round to slide the coffin out the back of the hearse, and Pierre jumped out. The string at my navel jerked me down to the ground and tugged me along behind, like a reluctant poodle on a leash, as they carried the coffin on their shoulders. What was going to happen to me now?

"This is awfully far to take her. There must be plenty of room at Père-Lachaise," said one of the men.

"They wanted it private, like. Didn't want nobody here except family," his mate replied. This made me angry. Why did they want to hide me away?

It was a shock to see them again: my mother, my father, and my brother, and so cruel not to be able to speak to them or comfort them. My mother weeping in her stiff black lace; my father stoic with a mourning armband; my brother sterner than a judge—all clustered together in a tight little knot, of which I was no longer a part.

I surveyed the cemetery, wondering if Modi might have found his way here, but aside from our little funeral party, there was no one about except the undertaker, the pallbearers, and the gravediggers in their blue overalls and caps, standing under an awning at a respectful distance, waiting for when their services would be needed. The pallbearers set the box down by the grave.

"This is the hardest thing," said Pierre, giving me a little push towards the hole. "You have to watch."

I took a few steps forward and was yanked all the way to the edge. Petrified, I peered down into the grave. I did not want to go under the ground. I tried to steady my feet in my sabots on the slick mud so that

I wouldn't tumble in head first. I was shaking so hard, my violin case knocked against my knees.

"It'll be all right! But stand firm," Pierre whispered behind me. I glanced back to see him grin and wave at me encouragingly.

The priest intoned only a few solemn words, and the men lowered my coffin into the earth. It took all my strength to keep from being tugged down along with it. Flowers were tossed down upon it, bunches of violets and a sprig of mimosa from the south. The elastic string, stretched almost to breaking point, pulled at my navel. When the first handful of dirt hit the coffin, the string snapped free with a prick of pleasure and pain like an orgasm, and I cried out, but nobody heard. Dissolving into a rainbow, it glinted on my father's spectacles, flashed in the puddles beside the grave, then disappeared.

As the rainbow vanished in the gray air, elation and deep sadness invaded me with equal measure. Whatever I had been before—now I was a spirit.

The service ended. I watched my mother, father, brother, and the priest file out silently, under their umbrellas, through the gate and down the street towards the station where they would take the train back to Paris and return to our flat in Rue Amyot. And there in the dining room where Céline, our maid, would have lit a fire, they would sit beneath the chandelier and eat the lunch Céline had cooked to comfort them, something hot with leeks and potatoes, perfect for a cold, wet day like this. And life would go on without me. Maman would retire to her prayers, kneeling alone in her room on the *prie-Dieu* by her bed. My father would have the little brass lamp with the green shade brought to the dining room, where he would sit perusing Pascal's *Pensées*. My brother would go to his room and pick up a drawing pad and a piece of charcoal and—I couldn't bear to think about it.

I gazed up at the sky. The rain had finally stopped. But where was Pierre? I looked about—he was gone. On the other side of the cemetery, another funeral party had just arrived, but I didn't spot him among the black-suited mourners. The gravediggers had finished their work with me and had walked off with their spades to tend the next-in-line.

I had no idea what I should do now, or where I should go, or how I was going to find Modi. I wanted to weep, but still I could not. I hadn't been able to shed a tear since all this had started. I thought perhaps my violin might weep for me. Removing my instrument from its case and setting it to my chin, I played the only thing that came to mind as dead leaves swirled down over the graves. My fingers were deft and supple, despite the cold. The crows in the tall branches cocked their heads at me, and seemed to be listening as I played.

I put the violin away. It was very quiet in the cemetery now, except for the cries of the crows and the rain dripping from the branches. I supposed I should be heading back to Montparnasse, but I didn't want to leave without Pierre, so I thought I should wait until he came back, wherever he had gone. I hoped he wouldn't be too long. I suspected things would be very different from now on, and I would be needing his help.

Something silken caressed my leg, and a faint tinkling sound at my feet made me glance down. A little gray cat with a silver bell around its neck was circling about my ankles. Canny amber eyes peered up at me with peculiar intensity: a consoling sight in this dreary place.

"You're a pretty little thing." I leaned down to pet the cat, and to my surprise, it purred and rubbed itself against my ankles again. I could see, touch, and feel it, just as I could see and touch Pierre. So, I thought, it must be a ghost-cat.

"Thank you," it said, "And you play very charmingly."

I gaped, astonished, at the animal. "A talking cat?"

"I suppose a number of things have happened that you find quite odd. So why not a talking cat?"

He stretched himself on a neglected tomb among pots of dead chrysanthemums and, catching a bit of ribbon from a withered wreathe, toyed with it madly between his paws.

A little boy from the other funeral party on its way out must have noticed the cat, for now he ran towards us among the tombstones, calling "Kitty, kitty, kitty!"

The cat jumped out of reach onto the roof of a vault, spooking a crow that hopped to the ground with a squawk.

"So that little boy can see you, too!" I said, "Aren't you dead?"

"By no means, my dear."

The mother in a black lace veil caught up with the boy.

"Come away, Jean! Leave the kitty alone," she scolded, steering the boy back towards the gate. Together they exited the cemetery.

"But you can see me if no one else can?" I asked.

"All animals can see the dead. And talk too, if you know how to listen. They always have. Nothing new there."

The crow hopped a little closer to us, as if he were listening. His black eye sparkled with amusement, and I noted that there was a bit of gold ribbon tied to one of his claws. When the cat sprang down to the ground beside me, the crow flapped up to a branch.

"If you aren't dead, how is it that I can touch you—a living creature?" I said, stroking his sleek gray fur again.

"Because I am special. I am the fisher cat, *le chat qui pêche*. I help people like you when they have just passed over."

"Is that how I should call you? *Le chat qui pêche?*"

"Oh, I have many names. But you may call me Theo."

"There was a boy helping me before." My eyes searched for Pierre again among the mossy paths running in between the graves.

"Yes, yes. Pierre."

"Do you know him? I have been looking for him. He was here just a while ago."

"Pierre is gone now. You will have to make do with me."

"Where did he go?"

"I believe I heard him say he was going to look for his sister. That's how people spend most of their time here, looking for the lost."

I was sad he was gone. "He didn't even say goodbye."

"You might run into him again. One does here, you know."

"Then I want to find my husband, the painter Amedeo Modigliani. I half expected he'd be here waiting. He died two days before me."

Theo sighed. "Truth is, decades elapse between one day and the next for the dead, and it takes a very long time to find someone once you have passed. It also takes a certain amount of luck and a great deal of patience, and of course, you can only find someone if you really desire it more than anything else in the world."

"There's no question that I want to find my husband, believe me," I said sharply.

"Otherwise, it is better simply to be resigned. It is easy to forget if one wants. Probably much easier, and not as painful." He rolled on his back, waved his legs and purred.

"Never!"

Jumping up again he arched his back and whipped his teasing tail against my leg. "You must realize there is one condition. The other person must desire equally ardently to be found by you. And also the circumstances must be right."

I stared into those amber eyes. "He promised we would never be separated, not even in death."

Modi wrapped a gold ribbon round my wrist. It was from a pastry packet someone had brought us to the studio weeks ago. Binding our hands together he said, "We are united now forever, assured of eternal happiness." His burning head was sunk deep into the stained, damp pillow. He had hardly any breath left. His voice was like a thistle about to blow away. Later I sketched our hands bound together like that with the ribbon. That was our wedding day.

"Well, then in that case, we should get going."

"Going where?"

"We have a train to catch."

Afterlife:
In the Other Paris

As we exited the cemetery gates, a freezing wind rushed at us, and purple clouds hung low, threatening heavy rain again. From the high tops of skeletal trees, fat black crows followed our movements. My feet scuffled along, chafed by the heavy sabots always about to slip off, because they were too big for me, but I was grateful to have them as the ground had turned to thick, smelly mud. The world looked strange now, wrapped in gritty, gray mist and pervaded by a faint odor of sewers, smoke, and decay. It was all quite changed from the tidy neighborhood where I had arrived a little over an hour ago. Theo padded along beside me, his tail a plume in the air.

The streets, previously deserted, teemed with people as on a market day, but without the bustle or gaiety. They shuffled along, eyes downcast. I did not like this dreary banlieue. I wanted to get back to Montparnasse as soon as possible and keep looking for Modi.

"Everyone looks so dismal."

"This is the realm of the dead. What did you expect?"

"I don't know. I suppose I didn't expect to be dead," I said.

"No, I suppose one doesn't."

I stared at the station building as we approached, marveling at its transformation. The walls were now gray, not yellow, the geraniums had disappeared from the upper window ledge, and the clock over the entrance had no hands. A shriveled little man selling false teeth and pictures of saints had replaced the chestnut vendor at the station kiosk.

We walked up the stairs and into the building, where a few people were milling around. Some studied blank charts of arrivals and departures; others huddled on benches along the dirty wall. A faded poster for Pernod, one of Modi's favorite drinks, hung above the benches. One or two men sitting there beneath it eyed me with interest.

"Those are the new arrivals," said Theo, nodding towards the benches. "Anybody you know?"

I scanned the faces slowly, hoping Modi's might be among them, but he wasn't there. I shook my head.

"Go and get your ticket. Destination: Gare Montparnasse."

"But I haven't any money."

"Then, I am afraid it will be a very long walk." He waved his tail in disapproval.

I remembered Annie had put something into my breast pocket. Reaching in, I found a coin. It looked like a 25 centime piece with a hole in the middle, but the inscription on it had completely worn away.

I showed it to Theo. "Do you think that will be enough?"

"Why don't you ask?"

The ticket clerk, a middle-aged man in a tawdry blue uniform, dozed on his feet behind the ticket window. He looked as stiff as a frozen cadaver, slack-jawed with shrunken gums exposed, but when I rapped on the glass, he stirred.

"Gare Montparnasse." I slid the coin to him across the ledge, and he slid back a ticket.

"Platform one," he said. "It's due in soon." He closed his eyes again.

Travelers of all ages thronged the platform. From their clothes, one could see that they had lived in different eras, so that it looked as though we were all in costume on our way to a carnival ball, except there was no atmosphere of fun or expectation. There were lace-clad ladies with plunging décolletages, ancient generals with powdered wigs, mantled priests, office clerks from Napoleonic days, and farm girls in white caps. Thin, ruddy-cheeked, tubercular girls and ragged paupers stood next to pockmarked plague victims and scores of soldiers from various wars with bandaged heads and missing limbs. Yet there was not a soul I knew. All waited glumly on the platform, staring into the mouth of the tunnel. They reminded me of prisoners about to be transported to some dreadful destination. No one spoke. Then, from out of nothing, two reddish eyes gleamed in the depths of the tunnel, accompanied by a low rumbling which soon grew to an overwhelming roar as the platform shook and heaved like in an earthquake. "It's coming," someone shouted. The station bell clanged furiously.

The station master, dressed in a black great coat with dull gold buttons and a purple cap, swung out from his booth along the platform. "Stand back," he shouted as an enormous black train burst out of the tunnel, its huge wheels still churning, billowing steam and spurting smoke as it braked. In the locomotive, you could see the engineers stripped to their waists, brandishing shovels, their torsos red with heat and black with soot.

The train juddered to a halt with another eruption of steam, and a tall woman in black beside me on the platform covered her mouth with a handkerchief. Turning to me, she complained, "And to think someone who has died of consumption still has to put up with this filthy air!"

As the gray mist dispersed, I could see an interminable line of purple coaches, stretching far into the tunnel. The coaches were marked first, second, and third class, and the first class ones were trimmed in dull gold. From the high windows, waxen-faced passengers scowled-ed out at us, but no one got off.

"*Station de Bagneux*," announced the station master.

Simultaneously, all the doors creaked open, and the crowd on the platform assaulted the train. It was obvious not everyone would fit. As passengers scrambled up, others behind them pushed them out of the way. People screamed, shouted, cursed. Clothes were torn; blows exchanged. An elderly woman tumbled to the platform and vanished beneath the mob.

"I'll be trampled!" yowled Theo, leaping up to my shoulder, digging his claws so deep that I winced. It was some solace that I could still feel pain.

I hid behind a pillar, watching the fray. I am a small person, short and petite, and was enormously pregnant. I was no match for this crowd.

"You have got to get on," Theo rasped into my ear. "We mustn't miss this train if you want to find Modi. It might be ages before the next one."

"*Tout le monde à bord*," called the station master.

"Hurry," hissed Theo, "This may be your only chance."

I summoned my courage, and wielding my violin case like a weapon, lanced through crowd, shoving people aside, with Theo perched on my shoulder. Heading for a second-class carriage, I seized hold of the railing and heaved myself up. A soldier tried to knock me off again, but Theo clawed his face so that he let me go, not without tearing the sleeve of my dress.

Once we were on board, the doors banged shut, the train lunged forward, and Theo sprang to the floor. A few desperate people clinging to the sides of the train were shaken to the platform as we gained momentum and plunged into the tunnel. With my free hand, I gripped a pole to keep my balance. My feet had been rubbed raw by my sabots. I had to find a place to sit down, so guiding myself along by grabbing the backs of the seats, I waddled down the rocking train. Theo scuttled ahead.

This coach was packed and so was the next. Every seat was taken, and the aisles blocked with people crouching as if asleep. Only a very few passengers had luggage with them – a hat box, an empty bird cage, a tuba. Some slept with handkerchiefs or newspapers spread over their faces. Some read feuilletons and others fingered their rosaries. A few played rummy or dice with a neighbor. Some sat idly picking their teeth, staring out at the indistinct landscape.

After I had made my way through several coaches, I reached a part of the train that was not as crowded or unpleasant smelling. Here I found a quiet coach with individual compartments, where all the blinds were lowered, except for one nearly empty compartment, where peeking in, I saw an older woman in black sitting alone by the window.

As I slid the door open, she looked up at me and smiled. She must have been about my mother's age. Over her black crepe dress, which might have been in style sixty years ago, she wore a black lace shawl studded with tiny roses of purple silk; at her throat a choker of lusterless pearls. Her hands, in iris-colored gloves, held a prayer book.

"*Bonjour*, Madame. Is this seat free?"

"But of course! Do sit down."

She watched me with detached curiosity as I put my violin in the overhead rack and settled into the worn black leather seat facing her. Theo hopped onto my shoulder and immediately fell asleep, purring noisily against my cheek. My new traveling companion was so meticulously dressed and coiffed that I felt ashamed knowing how bedraggled I must look in that hideous dress with its torn sleeve. I combed my fingers through my tangled hair and tried to make myself presentable.

The conductor entered and asked for our tickets, and I gave him my little pasteboard stub. His moustache twitched as he glared at it and handed it back to me. "I am afraid this is a first class coach, and you have only a third class ticket. So you must pay the difference and the fine, or move back to third class."

"It was so crowded and there were no seats." I protested. "And I haven't any more money."

"Madame, regretfully, you must return to third class immediately."

My companion spoke up. "Excuse me, Monsieur, but haven't you seen the condition she is in?" She stared pointedly at my belly and raised an eyebrow. "She must be allowed to stay."

"Madame, I am afraid that is against the rules. Without a first class ticket, she may not ride in first class."

"Nonsense, I know what I am talking about. My late husband was station master in Rouen. If there are no seats, women in her condition, the elderly, or wounded veterans may occupy free seats in first class. If necessary, I shall speak to the train captain myself. Please bring him here at once, and we will settle the question."

"I cannot do that, Madame, until I have finished checking the tickets of the newly boarded passengers."

"All right, then. Until you return with the train captain, you must let her stay." With a curt nod, she signaled the end of the discussion.

Grudgingly he agreed, punched our tickets and stepped grumbling out into the corridor.

"Well, that's all right," she said brightly. "We will most likely be arriving long before he returns, so you may relax and enjoy your journey."

I thanked her for her intervention and nestled back against the cushions, savoring the soothing vibration of the speeding train, the delicious warmth of the cat against my cheek. It felt good to be off my feet and not to have to think of anything.

Perhaps I dozed off, for when I opened my eyes, the woman was studying me, her prayer book abandoned on the seat beside her.

She smiled. "Buried today, were you?"

"How did you know?"

"It shows. But don't worry. You'll do fine." Reaching across, she patted my hand. Theo stirred and opened one eye. "Pretty kitty," she said, scratching his head, then considered my bulging belly. "Was it a complication of pregnancy?"

"No...an accident. I fell through a window."

She leaned back in her seat and shook her head. "I am so sorry. So tragic at your age. Where are you headed now?"

"Montparnasse. That's where I lived. I don't know where else to go."

She nodded thoughtfully.

"Have you been ... here a while?" I asked.

"Long enough to have lost count." She drew her shawl tighter around her shoulders. "I am on my way back to Paris to look for my son. He went missing in the last war, you see. But they never found his body. So I don't really know if he is down here or not. Sooner or later, of course, he is bound to turn up. Eventually everyone does. But it is all so crowded here, trying to find someone is like looking for a needle in a haystack. I haven't run into my husband yet, not that I really want to. He remarried after I died. Periodically I go traveling about, hoping to find my son, Louis. My ticket never expires, you see, as my husband worked for the railway."

"How convenient, about your ticket, I mean. I want to find my husband. He must have preceded me here. Although I don't really know where to start."

"Well, if you are certain of his date of death, it's quite easy. You just have to go to the bureau and make an application and they will help you locate him."

"The bureau?"

The *Mairie des Morts*, in your neighborhood. For Montparnasse, that will be Place de Montrouge." She glanced out the window and gathered up her prayer book. "We are nearly there now. Gare Montparnasse."

The great beast slowed its momentum. Chugging into the station, we lurched to a halt with a hissing of steam.

Theo jumped off as I stood up and got down my violin case.

"Are you getting off, Madame?"

"No, I am going on to the Gare du Lyon. Good luck with your journey. I hope you find your husband."

"And you, your son."

"Thank you. Even if I don't this time, it gives me something to do."

The Montparnasse train station wasn't located where I remembered it being. When we exited the main door, we found ourselves right in Place de Montrouge, standing in front of the *Mairie* of Montparnasse, or rather the *Mairie des Morts* XIV. It was the same handsome four-story building where Monsieur LeRoux had transported me in the wheelbarrow, but the white marble walls and tall windows were now all coated with gummy, gray dust. On the clock tower, the numbers had rusted away. A sign on the door read: *Bureau of the Dead* and beneath that, a hand-lettered notice was posted: "No pets. No animals of any kind."

"I'll wait for you outside," said Theo as I examined the notice. "But let me give you a piece of advice. Whatever they ask you, tell the truth. They are bound to find out if you don't."

I went up the steps and into the court. The noticeboard just inside, previously displaying official announcements and reports from the mayor, was covered with photographs, visiting cards, desperate messages scrawled on yellowed scraps of paper. "*Looking for Elsie Legrand, date of death April 13, 1919. If anyone has seen her, tell her I will wait for her forever at Place Saint-Michel.*"

In the vast entry hall, a man in a black uniform sat at a polished ebony desk. Behind him hung portraits of the Great Men of France, going back two hundred years or more. A purple chandelier suspended from the ceiling gleamed with a leaden light.

I approached the desk. "I am here to search for a dead person."

The attendant didn't even look up as he answered. "Second floor. Room 15."

My sabots echoed on the marble steps.

Room 15 was at the end of a very long corridor, where the threadbare carpet had been worn away by countless feet. Inside an elderly clerk with thick bifocals occupied a desk piled high with papers. Behind him rose a wall of shelves and pigeonholes tightly packed with ledgers and files. Loose papers were stacked everywhere: on the floor, chairs, and window ledges. The clerk beckoned me to enter, and I sat down across from him. Tucking my violin case between my feet and smoothing my rumpled dress over my knees, I repeated my request.

"Is the person you are looking for a family member?" he enquired.

"Yes. My husband."

"So we will want *formulaire* 129999—*notice individuelle de recherche dans l'intérêt des familles.*" He pulled out a form from a drawer, squinted at it and dipped his pen in a pot of purple ink.

"Name of person?"

"Amedeo Modigliani."

"Ah. A foreigner, not French?"

His chair creaked as he leaned back to consider me. "We only deal with French deaths here."

"He was born in Italy, but he lived in Montparnasse for many years. Paris was his home."

"All right then," he grumbled, "if he was a long-time resident, perhaps we can do something for you." He hunched over his desk again. "Spell the name please."

"M o d i g l i a n i".

"Date of death?"

"January 24, 1920."

He put down his pen and adjusted his spectacles. Behind his bifocals, his red eyelids were lined with eczema. "So recent? I doubt whether his papers have been processed. I advise you to come back later."

"But I can't wait. I need to find him. It is urgent."

He shrugged and picked up his pen. "Urgent! That word has been struck from the dictionary here. But all right. We will have a look. What is your name, please? Date and place of marriage with the deceased?"

"Jeanne Hébuterne with an H. Actually, we weren't married, yet. I was his common-law wife. But he signed a promise in the presence of a notary that he would marry me."

Indeed, he had written "I promise to marry Janette Hébuterne," misspelling, perhaps on purpose, or perhaps not, my first name.

"Ah!" He nibbled the end of his pen. "I am afraid this makes it more complicated. Any previous marriages?"

"No. Does it matter?" I was becoming annoyed.

"Well, it might, since the two of you were not yet married. The right of reunion is the prerogative of the legal spouse if there was one."

I blinked at him, confused. How was it possible that these bourgeois rules should apply even to the dead?

"Excuse me, sir, he is the father of my children. Doesn't that count for something?"

"Very well," he sighed. "Next of kin? Dead, not living."

"His father. I don't know of any others. His mother, brother, and sister are still living in Italy. And then there is our child who died with me, when I fell from a window."

There was a long pause. Stern eyes probed my face, and I felt my cheeks grow hot. Another clerk came in with a pile of papers and proceeded to stick them randomly on shelves. Youngish and more fashionably dressed, he looked familiar to me.

My inquisitor resumed his questioning. "Religion. Catholic?"

I faltered. "He didn't practice any religion, but he was brought up in a Jewish family."

"An atheist Jew, then? Mademoiselle," he said peevishly, pushing his chair back from the desk. "You should have told me you were Jewish immediately. I would have sent you to another office."

"But *I* am Catholic."

"You didn't convert?"

I shook my head. "Besides, in France don't we now have the separation of church and state?"

He frowned at me. "We aren't under the same laws here, exactly. Death place? Last known place of residence?"

"He died at the Charity Hospital in Rue Jacob, but before that, we both resided at Rue de la Grande Chaumière, number 8."

"Profession?"

"*Peintre*"

"*Peintre en batiment?*"

I drew myself up. "No, not a house painter. An artist. A great one."

"Modigliani you say? Never heard of him. But I'm told Paris is overrun with foreign painters these days." He opened a ledger and ran his ink-stained finger down an interminable list of names. "In any case," he said, "we have no record of him—yet."

He handed me the form and the pen. "Sign here, please. I don't suppose you have brought a copy of his death certificate? It might have been useful in this case."

I shook my head, dipped the pen in the little pot, and signed the bottom of the form. All I had with me from my previous life was the ugly dress I was wearing, someone else's sabots, and my violin.

"You could try downstairs in Rabbi Saltzman's office, or look on the noticeboard outside. He might be searching for you and might have left a note. If you don't find anything, come back to this office at another time, and we will try to do what we can to locate him."

"There is someone else I would like to know about." Hesitating, I placed my hand over my belly. "The child who died with me. I have reason to believe it was a boy."

"Unborn? No, no, no. We don't deal with the unborn. You will have to talk to a priest."

Still I insisted, I had to know. "I was told he may have been sent back into life. Might that have happened?"

"We don't keep the records of those who leave, Mademoiselle. All we do is try to sort out the new arrivals, and I assure you, that is quite a task with the staff we have available."

A line of other seekers had formed out the door. I seized my violin case and stood up.

The young man filing away papers turned to smile shyly at me, and I recognized him. He used to come to drawing lessons at the Académie, then I heard he had died of influenza.

"I believe I have some information about the person Mademoiselle is looking for," he said handing a dark red ledger with gold letters to the elderly clerk, who perused a few lines, nodding and mouthing to himself as he read.

"I see—I see. So this is the man buried with such ceremony at Père-Lachaise last week." He banged the ledger shut. "I am afraid we cannot help you trace this Monsieur Modigliani. It says here that he is with the Immortals. Here, you will find only the ordinary people of Paris."

The words hit me like a blow in the chest. With the Immortals! I tasted a tear on my upper lip and wiped it away. "What does that mean, if he is with the Immortals?" Part of me knew, though, it couldn't have been otherwise.

"It means what it says. He is among those who will never die," he snapped, putting the ledger away on a shelf.

"But I must find him. What am I to do?"

He shook his head. "This office can give you no further information."

"Then who can?"

"Try asking at the main desk on your way out. Next!"

The young clerk touched my sleeve as I stepped out the door and the next-in-line hurried in. "You will have to make your own way to him, I am afraid. Or if he desires, he to you. I wish you good luck."

"Thank you," I said, grateful for this kindness. "I am sorry you never came back to lessons."

He gave me an icy smile, and I realized I had said the wrong thing.

Out in the corridor, I pushed my way against the grain through the line now snaking all the way down to the floor below—ordinary people of Paris, all looking for someone they loved. My sabots made a racket on the marble stairs. One slipped off and tumbled down a whole flight of steps, echoing in the silence like a bouncing cannon- ball. The clerk at the desk scowled at me as I descended to the hall, where I retrieved my lost sabot from the bottom of the ramp.

"Mademoiselle Jeanne Hébuterne?"

"Yes. *C'est moi.*"

"Stop where you are. Don't move."

I froze in alarm.

He lifted a tarnished bell from his desk and rang it vigorously, yelling, "Guards! Arrest this woman and take her before the judge!"

"But on what charge?" I cried, "For losing a shoe?"

Two guards sprang from the shadows, grabbing my arms on either side. I was more astonished than angry or frightened. One jerked the violin out of my hand.

"What are you doing? Give that back to me right now!"

Mute as mummies, they hustled me down a corridor and in through a door.

Afterlife:
The Harrowing

I HAD NEVER BEEN IN A COURTROOM before and had only seen engravings of famous trials in the newspapers. Black chandeliers hung from a paneled ceiling of tarnished gold. Before me, ensconced in a throne on a platform, sat the judge, stiffly preserved in his faded red robe, tall scarlet hat, and bib of moth-eaten ermine. To his left, a thin man in a black robe with an immaculate white scarf tucked into the front stood perusing some papers. His head was bent at an angle so I could not see his face; his hands hidden by voluminous sleeves: the prosecutor, I presumed. Below the judge's platform, a clerk sat at a desk. From behind the judge's throne rose the jury box, from which nine ancient men in black robes peered down their pockmarked noses at me.

My left hand chained to a guard, I was escorted to a bench in the front row. As I took my place, the clerk gawked at me and then scribbled some notes on his papers. The courtroom was crammed full. All the rows behind me were packed with spectators, as were the upper galleries on three sides of the room. Scanning the upper rows, I could not pick out anyone I knew, and in all those sour faces read only disapproval and suspicion. The air was hot, thick, and stuffy, smelling of mothballs and moldy carpets that hadn't seen the sun in years. Beneath all, a hint of rot.

The clerk rang a bell and announced, "Will the accused stand?"

I was obviously to defend myself. I rose to face the judge, who read from a scroll.

"Are you Jeanne Hébuterne, born on April 6, 1898 in Meaux, France, and died in Paris on January 26, 1920, daughter of Achille and Eudoxie Hébuterne?"

"Yes, your honor."

"Resident in Rue Amyot 8 bis and by profession a student of decorative arts?"

"No, your honor."

"What's that?" He gaped at me, puzzled, as if he hadn't heard correctly.

I spoke up loudly and clearly. "My residence was 8 Rue de la Grande Chaumière, and I am an artist by profession, a painter to be exact." *That* was the truth.

I did not lower my eyes as the judge squinted at me for a long moment and adjusted his pince-nez. "Very well. May the record be amended with the accused's correct address and profession. Will the clerk now read the charges against the accused? You are to pay strict attention, Mademoiselle."

The clerk rose from his desk and threw back his shoulders. "Mlle. Jeanne Hébuterne, you stand accused of self-murder and infanticide, performed when you intentionally fell backwards from a window of your parents' home in Rue Amyot. You are charged with willful and premeditated murder in the first degree."

Murder! I had never intended to murder anyone, much less my child. But how could I not have realized what I was doing? The room churned around me, a sea of red and black. I looked down at my feet in their clumsy sabots until all held still again.

"Do you understand the charges brought against you?" the judge was asking.

I raised my head and gulped down the bitterness in the back of my throat. "Yes, your honor."

"How do you plead?"

The judge's beady eyes bored into mine. I could feel the bodies in the courtroom, all shifting, leaning forward to catch my answer. Tell the truth, I said to myself, the truth. What truth? Whose truth? Summoning my courage, I opened my mouth. "I...."

But I was cut short when someone gripped my right hand. At my side now stood a chubby, bald gentleman, only an inch or two taller than myself, who had somehow snuck in unnoticed. His black robe, several sizes too big, gave off a strong odor of camphor and cigars, and his white scarf was dotted with coffee stains. With oversized spectacles sliding down his nose, he reminded me of a rumpled owl.

His cold fingers squeezed mine again as he addressed the judge. "If it please the court, I wish to consult with my client before she replies."

His arrival must have taken the court by surprise, for the judge thumbed through his papers, glowering. "There is no mention of a legal counsel for Mademoiselle Hébuterne here. Clerk, why was I not notified?"

"I am afraid I know nothing about it, your honor," shrugged the clerk.

"This is highly irregular, sir," said the judge.

The newcomer bowed. "Your honor, allow me to introduce myself. Jacob Rabinowitz. Counsel at the High Court of Assize. I have just been assigned to this case from on high. That is, naturally," he turned and bowed to the prosecutor. "...if there is no objection."

The prosecutor observed us both with keen interest. Now that he had looked up from his papers, I could see him plainly. He had a gaunt, swarthy, intelligent face, slightly asymmetrical with eyes deep set and a brooding forehead. Beneath his aristocratic nose bristled a dandy's finely-clipped moustache. I felt certain that I had seen him before, perhaps in the newspapers—holding court at a fashionable salon, or maybe depicted in a portrait in the Louvre?

The two men exchanged an icy nod, and I guessed that they had confronted each other before.

"No objection, your honor," said the prosecutor.

"Very well," said the judge, "Permission granted. Amend the records to add the name of Avocat Rabinowitz as the accused's legal counsel."

"I was afraid I might have to defend myself," I whispered to the owl, whom I had decided to trust.

"You wouldn't stand a chance with him, my dear."

Again, I studied the prosecutor's face. "But who is he? He looks so familiar."

"Oh," he laughed, "You'll soon recognize him, I am sure. For now, just sit still and let me do the talking."

"The court is waiting. How does your client plead?" interrupted the judge.

Avocat Rabinowitz turned his round face to the judge, pushed up his glasses from the end of his nose, and in a quiet but determined voice that rang through the hall, said "Not guilty, your honor."

A murmur rippled through the courtroom. This was not the reply the judge or the jurors had expected. But the prosecutor's sly smile suggested that *he* was not surprised.

The gavel banged. "Let the prosecution proceed."

The prosecutor rose. Imposing in his flowing robe, long-limbed and lanky, he had the deportment of a military man and an actor's ease before the public. Was he a great politician or dignitary who had been cut down in his prime? A celebrated orator of the past? Certainly, he was a man of fashion. The *eau de cologne* shone on his close-shaven cheeks and the waves of his silver and black hair were slicked with pomade, though not in a recent style. He terrified yet fascinated me, and in another situation, I would have liked to paint his portrait.

All eyes turned to him as he sternly surveyed the public in the galleries, the jury in their box, and, lastly, me. Then his arm swept the room with a gesture which was like an invitation to a waltz, and I glimpsed, protruding from his black sleeve, a bright red talon with steel claws, instead of a hand. A chill shot through me, yet a powerful attraction drew me towards him.

"You see who we are dealing with," whispered Avocat Rabinowitz. "You must not address him or the judge directly unless they speak to you. Do you understand?"

I nodded and leaned back on the bench—every nerve tensed to hear what he would say.

"Gentlemen of the court, to understand the nature of this woman's infernal act, we must understand her character. Born to a family of excellent reputation—devout, respectful of the law—she threw herself into the arms of a man notorious throughout Paris as debauched and godless. His name was Amedeo Modigliani. A drunk. A drug taker. A parasite who milked his elderly mother dry of her meager earnings as a schoolteacher so that he could frequent the prostitutes of Montparnasse, calling himself an artist."

These were shocking, hateful allegations, but I had heard them all before. Always from people who did not know Modi or who had never seen his work—otherwise they would never have said such things. And as for the prostitutes—he painted their portraits sometimes, but was only a friend, never a client. He did not need to pay anyone for love, unlike a lot of dignified men sitting in the courtroom at that very minute, many of whom had probably died of syphilis. I bit my lip although his words burned.

"Good girl," Rabinowitz surreptitiously patted my hand. "Don't let him goad you. It is a technique to bring out the worst in you. This is just the beginning."

The judge rapped his gavel. "Quiet!"

The prosecutor flashed a brilliant smile towards the galleries. "I know you are all asking: who was this Amedeo Modigliani? Because none of you will have heard of this obscure individual. He was a man who would strip off his clothes at any opportunity and dance naked in the street. Who imbibed alcohol from morning till night, causing harm to himself and others. Who could not paint, in fact, except when inebriated."

"That's a lie!" I muttered to Rabinowitz, who lifted his finger to his lips in warning.

"His paintings were so pornographic they caused riots in the streets of Paris!" The prosecutor paused, held a monocle to his left eye, and extracted a paper from his sleeve. "He once claimed, and I quote from one of his letters, *We artists are above the rules of society.*"

Removing his monocle, he considered the jury, as if memorizing their faces one by one. "Gentlemen, you well know that none of us, even here, are above the rules of society. But the impecunious artist, for whom Jeanne Hébuterne abandoned her family, was a man who shirked all responsibility and knew no moral restraint. A coward who chose not to defend France in the last war." That brought out a low murmur of discontent, as there were many uniformed veterans in attendance. But the accusation was untrue. When the war broke out, Modi had tried to enlist, but they wouldn't take him because of his lungs. And as far as I was concerned, it was just as well.

"I object," spoke up Rabinowitz. "The character of Monsieur Modigliani and the quality of his artwork are not the object of this trial. The latter, I believe, must be left to the judgment of posterity. Likewise, his history of military service is not pertinent to our case."

"Objection overruled. We require a full portrait of the accused. The prosecution may proceed."

"Are you just going to sit there and let him tear apart the memory of my husband?" I hissed at Rabinowitz, loud enough, apparently, for everyone in the courtroom to hear.

"Silence!" the judge admonished.

"Just stay calm. He will pick over your entire life, yours and his, looking for every blemish. You must leave this to me."

I squeezed my knees together and forced myself to sit still.

"Husband indeed," chuckled the prosecutor, rubbing his palms together. "We will get to that. But, ladies, as I see there are ladies in the galleries, and gentlemen of the court, what could have persuaded a young, innocent girl to choose such a mate? Examining her past, we will see that she had always been a perverse child—moody, disobedient, quarrelsome, and stubborn. We know, for example, that on those occasions when her father's dear friend, Abbot Marchegal, would join the Hébuterne family for lunch on Sundays after church, at the age of sixteen, she would argue with him over questions of faith and moral behavior, much to the dismay of her family."

"C'est vrai," piped up a dry voice from the audience. "She was a most contrary and precocious child." And there he sat, the withered old abbot himself, who had so often been a welcome guest in our home. Phlegm gurgled in his throat as he spoke. "At times I feared for her future, her education, and for her soul."

I glowered at him. He had always been friendly to me. Our debates, not really arguments, about items in the newspapers, had livened up dull Sunday afternoons, saving my brother and me from the only other available entertainment—listening to our father read aloud from Pascal's *Pensées* while we all peeled potatoes in the kitchen for the evening potage. I couldn't remember what topic we had discussed which might have made him fear for my soul, but I did recall that he had strongly criticized my parents for letting me study art.

"Thank you for that testimony, esteemed Abbot. So.... The girl you see here, even when very young, craved strong sensations and suffered from a rebellious imagination. Rather than follow the sensible wishes of her family to prepare herself to become a wife and mother, she badgered them to let her enroll in an academy of arts, to become an artist, a painter, as you heard her prideful boast. But has her work ever been sold by a gallery, displayed at an exhibition, represented by a dealer, reviewed in a newspaper? In the art world the name of Jeanne Hébuterne is totally unknown. And so it is likely to remain."

I was fuming now. What right had he to judge my artwork? I gripped the edge of the bench with my one free hand, while Rabinowitz clutched my elbow firmly to keep me down.

"In any case, considering the deterioration of morals among artists, especially since the unwise decision was made to admit women to public art schools, well, we must conclude that such aspirations were unseemly and inappropriate for a young person of good family, if indeed that is what she was. But all is not as it seems."

"I object," Rabinowitz interrupted. "The morals of painters are not on trial here. Nor are we here to decide whether it is appropriate for a woman to study art. Jeanne was hardly the first female art pupil in Paris. I would like to remind counsel that women had been attending the École des Beaux Arts for least a decade by the time Jeanne Hébuterne enrolled in art classes."

I shook my head in dismay. Had he no other arguments to defend me with?

The judge yawned and waved away a fly. "Objection sustained. The prosecution is to keep to the case at hand."

"There is a connection, your honor. For it is precisely her attraction to this libertarian environment that has caused her downfall. The proximity to naked adult bodies under the pretext of drawing them, the promiscuity of persons with whom artists associate—all this shaped an impressionable mind. Alas, the accused was fertile terrain, for she also harbored an evil seed—a sensuality which matured far too early, eclipsing all organic shame. I present to the court these pieces of evidence."

He reached down to pick up something from the floor: my portfolio of dark green marbled pasteboard, the one I used to take to class at the Académie Colarossi, then hide under the bed in Rue Amyot, where my mother might not look. He removed two large drawings and handed them to the judge. I didn't have to see them to know what they were. Probably my self-portraits in the nude, or nude sketches of Modi after we had made love. People in the galleries craned their necks to catch a glimpse of the drawings.

"For decency's sake, I suggest these not be displayed to the public in which women are present."

The judge straightened his pince-nez again and squinted at the drawings, wetting his dry lips with a gray, leathery tongue, then passed the sketches to the jurors behind him, who were all leaning down from their box, straining to have a peek.

"Gentlemen of the court, I am sure you will agree, these are pornographic. May I remind you that these intimately detailed drawings were produced by a young woman of only nineteen years of age. I speak of the person who sits before us, in the condition that you see."

The jurors' eyes crawled across my body like hungry beetles. I couldn't stand it anymore. I bolted from my seat, heaving up the guard who was chained beside me.

"Excuse me! That's not true. Pornography is meant to excite the senses. These are anatomical drawings sketched truthfully from life. That's all."

Twice banged the hammer. "Sit down," shouted the judge, "You will speak at the appointed time or be removed from the courtroom. Counsel, you are responsible for the defendant."

"Yes, your honor!" Rabinowitz seized my arm again and rasped in my ear. "Try to control yourself, or it will go badly for us both."

I glared at the prosecutor, and our eyes locked. He smiled at me sickeningly and I understood that this is what he wanted: a reaction, a spectacle for all these cruel cadavers to enjoy. Well, I would not serve!

"While in art school," he resumed, " she allowed herself to be seduced by the despicable individual to whom she refers as her "husband," although they were not legally wed. She conducted this relationship with deceit, cohabiting carnally with her paramour at a time when France was at war and conceiving out of wedlock, while still of minor age."

I wanted to scream, but I clamped my teeth down on my tongue and let my rage boil inside me. "But it wasn't like that at all," I whispered to Rabinowitz. "How dare he twist my life into such an ugly thing?"

"He is the master of half-truths. Sadly, many have been undone by them."

"After all we have said here today, it may surprise you to learn that later this man himself actually made a written promise in the presence of a notary to wed the accused." The prosecutor now paused to allow his audience a moment of reflection. "I have the document here. Let me read it to you."

He swept up a sheet of paper from the bench and adjusted his monocle. "'I, Amedeo Modigliani, promise to marry Janette Hébuterne.' Note the name: Janette, not Jeanne. He has intentionally misspelled her name, thereby invalidating this document and showing his own disrespect for the law, the parents of the accused, and for holy matrimony."

A buzzing protest surged through the galleries. Shame crept through my body and into my face. A thousand times have I asked myself why Modi spelled my name wrong, and I have never found a satisfactory answer.

"I object, your honor. The intentions of Monsieur Modigliani to marry Madame Hébuterne are irrelevant to this trial."

"Overruled."

My spine prickled, and I jerked my head up. From the galleries a young woman was staring at me with a mournful intensity. I recognized her at once. A Canadian girl by the name of Simone. She had been in love with Modi before I had met him and claimed to have had a child by him. One day she had just disappeared from Montparnasse and hadn't been heard of since. So now, she was dead, too.

"He was a cad who cared for no one except himself!" Simone's voice rang out from the gallery, where she stood clinging to the railing. "Amedeo Modigliani was the father of my child, but even when I was ill and dying, he would not give me a penny to buy milk for my baby. I begged them to help me." Her spindly arm shot out through the iron bars, and she pointed her finger at me. "She could have convinced him to help me. He would have listened to her. But she did nothing."

Rabinowitz squeezed my elbow. "Don't answer."

"But it isn't true," I said to the judge, heedless of my counsel's warning. "I did not know how desperate she was, or how ill. And how could I be sure that the child was really his? Besides, I had my own child to think of, and we had so very little money and by then Modi was ill, too."

"But Modi always had enough to spend on drink!" Simone shouted.

I shut my mouth. I could not answer that, but I didn't need to. Tension in the gallery was quite high by now—Simone's accusations set them off.

"*Salauds!*" someone bellowed, and then they were all yelling and booing against Amedeo Modigliani and against me. I cradled my head in my arms to protect myself from the objects raining down: hats, coins, shoes.

The judge banged his gavel repeatedly. "Silence! Silence! Or I shall have you all removed from the courtroom. And you, Mademoiselle, one more outburst like that and you will regret it!"

The prosecutor rose and lifted his arms to the agitated galleries, waiting for the commotion to die down. When all eyes were trained on him as upon a god, he continued.

"And so, ladies and gentlemen, you have heard the plight of another young creature who fell into the clutches of this man. You have seen how unfeeling the accused became under his influence."

He gave me a sad, patronizing smile. "This woman is deserving of our pity. Doubtless, it was her deep guilt and despair which led her to commit the crimes for which she finds herself here. But we must remember that she has always had an attraction to darkness. Let me present this one last piece of evidence to the court."

Once again he rummaged in my portfolio, and I was fearful as to what he would pull out, for at this point, I had no idea.

It was a watercolor, a self-portrait: me stretched on the bed with a knife through my heart. I had painted it hours before Modi died.

I closed my eyes. I knew how they would see it.

"Do you recognize this picture?"

I nodded, eyes still shut. "Of course, I painted it."

"And are you the person depicted therein?"

"Yes." How could I tell them? How to explain the abyss into which I sank those last few hours of our life together?

He passed the picture to the judge.

"Gentlemen of the court, I believe this clearly indicates a premeditated act. Jeanne Hébuterne willfully destroyed her life and that of her child when she propelled herself through a window. She must pay eternally for her crime. The prosecution rests." He folded his talons as in prayer, bowed his head, and sat down.

Pay eternally! What did that mean? I was never a believer in either heaven or hell!

A numbing silence vibrated in the courtroom after he had finished. No one stirred or spoke until the judge cleared his throat, breaking the spell. "The defense may proceed. Please be brief."

Rabinowitz rose and straightened his dingy white scarf, and, as he did so, his glasses slid off and fell to the floor. Crouching down to retrieve them, he bumped his head on the bench where I sat, and snorts of laughter exploded through the galleries. Unflustered, Rabinowitz polished his glasses with his sleeve, put them back on, and addressed the judge.

"If it please the court, I call Jeanne Hébuterne as sole witness for the defense."

I was astounded and still in a bit of shock. How could I possibly defend myself against all the hatred and evil that had just been reviled upon me?

"Tell us in your own words what happened in the forty-eight hours prior to your death."

I shook my head. I could not relive it again.

He placed a gentle hand on my shoulder. "Stand now and tell the court moment by moment."

Tell the truth, Theo had said. All right. I would tell them my truth.

I began. "He had been unwell for several days, ever since he had returned home, soaking wet, after a night out with his friends. One evening, he took chill, and I put him to bed and wanted to prepare something hot for him to drink, but there was no water in the studio and no coal to burn. Our neighbor, Ortiz, usually helped carry up the heavy things like buckets of coal or water, because we live —lived— on the fourth floor. But he was away at the time."

As I spoke, it all returned to memory. I saw us there, the ghosts of ourselves.

"Go on," he coaxed.

"I went down to fill a small pail at the fountain in the courtyard. As you can see, it was quite difficult and risky for me to manage so many steps. There I met Madame Moreau, the *concierge,* and I begged her to send word to our friend, Leopold Zborowski, that my husband was ill and to fetch a doctor. I also asked her to have the waiter from the Rotonde send up a bowl of hot soup and some brandy.

"Eventually the waiter brought the brandy and soup, and some coffee for me, but no doctor arrived. Madame Moreau brought some more water and some charcoal for the stove, but Modigliani's fever had worsened; he began to cough blood. I stayed up all night, bathing his forehead and his lips with cool water.

"Next morning, Ortiz returned and went to get a doctor. Modi couldn't move his head; his neck was so stiff and painful because meningitis had set in, so Ortiz carried my husband down the stairs and put him in a taxi. They took him to the Charity Hospital, and there he died."

I couldn't go on, and my tears were flowing now. I kept my eyes on Rabinowitz's face.

"Our friend, Hanka, accompanied me to the maternity hospital as my child was due, but they said it was too soon, so I went home to my mother and father in Rue Amyot. I had not slept a wink since Modi had fallen ill. Back in my room at my parents' house, I tried to rest, but I was too distraught. My brother came to my room to talk to me. We argued for hours. When he fell asleep, I opened the window for some fresh air, as I felt very hot. I wanted to escape, but I had no means, nowhere to go. I closed my eyes, leaned back, and just let go. When I realized what was happening, I tried to grab the railing of the balcony below us, but then it was all over."

The judge probed my face. "Did you understand that you were committing an act of murder and that your own life would cease?"

I shook my head and contemplated the blackness of my own motivations. "I don't really know what I understood."

"If it please the court," Rabinowitz said, "Your honor, ladies and gentlemen, Jeanne Hébuterne was a young, headstrong girl very much in love, and a very desperate person who acted carelessly—certainly wrongly—but with no conscious, evil intention to murder or harm. By falling backwards, Jeanne instinctively attempted to protect her child. Her action was performed in a moment of extreme mental distress, during which she was not in the full command of her faculties." He paused to scan the faces of the judges, whom I could not bear to look at as the tears streamed down my face. Rabinowitz concluded, "The defense rests."

I wiped my eyes. Was that all he was going to say? After my whole life and character and that of my husband had been spat upon and trampled?

"You have been a great help," I muttered as the guards took me away again.

I was removed to a small cell off the courtroom to await the jury's decision, but was soon called back.

"Will the defendant rise?"

"*Bon courage*," murmured Theo from under the bench, for he had somehow snuck in and now curled round my ankles. "No matter what happens, I will be with you."

Theo was the only friend I had in the world now, it seemed.

I stood up, faced the judge, and tried to keep my body from trembling. Was I shaking with fear or rage?

"Jeanne Hébuterne, in the name of the dead of France, this court, after due and impartial deliberation, finds you guilty of criminally negligent homicide, without aforethought or criminal intent. You are sentenced to the dome of undoing for as long as it shall take."

I stared at the judge with anguished incomprehension. What could he possibly mean?

The gavel struck the bench, and the guards whisked me back to the cell where I had just been. Theo scuttled off again, among all those mummified feet in dusty shoes. I sat shackled in an iron chair. My whole body ached as if I had been run over by an omnibus. And the idea of the dome of undoing—whatever that was—was frankly terrifying. I would have prayed if I could remember how, but I seemed to have forgotten, if I ever knew.

The door opened. Rabinowitz entered and sat down in the chair across from me, but I would not meet his gaze.

He cleared his throat. "I am here to answer any questions you might have."

I sat with lips sealed. I had dozens of questions, but no faith in him.

"Come, Jeanne, the court has been clement, more than you know. I can't stay long, so we must make the most of this meeting."

I had to focus on what was most urgent, despite how poorly he had defended me. "What does that mean: criminally negligent homicide, without aforethought or criminal intent?"

"It means you have committed the crime of murder but not with intention. In other words: manslaughter."

"And the dome of undoing?" I faltered.

He sighed. "That's the best we could do, I am afraid. Believe me, it's much better than eternal punishment, which was what I feared you'd get. You are a strong woman. You'll be all right."

I didn't know whether I should be relieved or not. "What happens now?"

"Well, they will take you to the place of punishment, and there you will stay until your sentence has been served in full, or reduced. In any case, there is no appeal."

"But how long will I have to stay there—'as long as it shall take.' What does that mean?"

"You will be duly informed when your sentence is terminated. Any other questions? I have another trial soon and must speak to my client beforehand. A most unfortunate case."

"I do. My child. The one who died. I was told he might be sent back to life."

He seemed surprised by this news. "I hope so, for your sake and for his."

"How can I find out if that has happened yet?"

"It hasn't happened yet—you can be sure of that. It all depends on you, you see. They'll explain the procedure to you. It's a hard choice, and a courageous one, but absolutely the right one in your circumstances." He got up to leave.

"But wait, my husband! I must find Modigliani. They told me he is with the Immortals, but I have no idea where that is or where they are."

"You may make an application to join them, and if there is sufficient documentation of your eligibility, your reunion will be arranged by the high authorities. But it is unlikely that will happen before your term is up. And to make the application, you must go in person back to the *Mairie*. I can try to initiate the procedure for you, but there is no possibility of that until your release. Ah, here are the guards."

The cell door banged open, and a guard stepped in, unfastened me from the table, and chained me to his wrist.

"They took my violin," I cried as the guard pulled me away. "I want it back."

"I will see that it is returned to you, though it may take awhile. Goodbye, Jeanne. You must be brave and patient. If there is any further news, you will hear from me. Believe me, I have taken your case to heart."

✦

A horse-drawn police cart was waiting for us in the square outside the *Mairie*. The guard pushed me towards it, and I stumbled forward, dispersing a flock of pigeons. As they fluttered to safety, I spotted a crow in their midst, and, looking round, I saw a watchful Theo hidden behind a rubbish bin, slyly observing the birds.

The guard bodily hoisted me into the back of the cart with my hands still bound, then climbed into the front. Theo hopped on just in time before we sped off back towards the heart of Montparnasse. When we stopped outside a tall gate on Boulevard Edgar Quinet, the guard came round and ordered me to climb down, which was impossible in my condition with my hands tied. I would have toppled off head first, if he hadn't helped me down, sticking his hands all over the place.

"The keeper will take charge of you now," he said, freeing my wrists at last. Unlocking the gate with a rusty key, he shoved me inside. "You too," he muttered, giving Theo a little kick with his boot.

The iron grill clanged shut, and the key rattled in the lock behind us. The cart drove away. Before us stretched a wide avenue lined with skeletal trees, leading to a mount where a small black-domed building stood. The dome of undoing, I presumed. There was not a soul in sight. I walked towards the dome, looking for the keeper, while Theo stuck close to my heels.

I guessed we were in the old Montparnasse Cemetery, but the well-kept graves of poets and generals with their elegant headstones had vanished beneath overgrowths of black ivy and weeds. Sharp blasts of cold air breathed on us, rustling withered flowers on the graves. Eddies of wind swirled at our feet, blowing litter into the yew hedges, which flanked the wall separating us from the street.

"What sort of a place is this?" I asked, looking down at scattered scraps of envelopes and newspapers, frayed hair ribbons, and torn pieces of sheet music. "It looks like a rubbish heap." Theo trotted over to the hedge to sniff a small pile of refuse, from which a few fish bones poked out along with a pair of women's evening gloves.

"This is the cemetery of the unborn," he said. "Things that have been left undone—unspoken loves, unwritten books and symphonies, unexpressed regrets, unrealized wishes, unsolved mysteries, unsatisfied hunger—speaking of which, I say, I am starving. I am not like you. I will need to eat sooner or later. Things unfinished all end up here in this graveyard, where they remain until they either disintegrate or return to life, drifting about in the wind in hopes someone will catch them."

Is that what I was here to do, leave behind my regrets and unfulfilled aspirations? I picked my way among the tombs. I had few regrets, but how heavily they weighed. My daughter abandoned, my son unborn; my brother and parents broken by grief. My artistic career ended almost before it had begun. I had followed my husband to the afterlife, but still had no idea where to find him—or if I would ever see him again. To still have consciousness, power of movement, but to be deprived of his presence—this would be insufferable. Then it occurred to me that I might find him in the dome.

A postcard settled at my feet and I retrieved it. It showed a young man in uniform, and I thought of my brother. I let it fall, then spotted a page torn from a book – a poem, *Un Voyage à Cythère* by Baudelaire, one of Modi's favorites. "*Ah! Seigneur! donnez-moi la force et le courage De contempler mon coeur et mon corps sans dégoût!*"

As we proceeded towards the dome, I heard voices beneath the gusts of wind, heart-wrenching sobs and groans. Sometimes it seemed they were saying my name. Was that Modi's voice? I couldn't tell. The sound was oppressive; it made me want to weep. The mournful chorus grew louder as we headed up the hill. Then a low droning like the gnawing of insects filled my ears, lifting the fine hairs along my arms and on the nape of my neck, increasing in pitch to a full-blown wail. Terror seized me; my legs wobbled. I could hardly bear to hear that sound, nor could Theo. It was disintegration made manifest— I felt it could shatter walls, suck oceans dry, dissolve my very soul.

I crouched against a dead yew tree, trying to shield myself from its power, and Theo leapt into my arms. I clasped him close and buried my face in his fur, but there was no way to escape the sound that came in waves, dying down and starting up again until it reached a frenzied pitch.

"What is that noise?" I whispered when at last there was a lull.

"The sound of death—and there she is."

A hooded figure guarded the door to the dome. As it turned to greet us, I saw beneath the hood a polished white skull dotted with daisies across the cheekbones and red lips painted where the mouth should have been. Long gray hair hung down to its hips. It held something in its right hand—a long thigh bone. As the figure lifted the bone to its lips, the robe fell open to reveal an old woman's shriveled body. The bone she clutched was a trumpet, and when she played that gnawing note again, it chilled me through.

An emaciated arm with sagging skin extended towards me. "Welcome, Jeanne."

I could hardly speak, my tongue a frozen slab. "Who are you?" I finally stuttered.

"I am the mother of the unborn. Come, Jeanne, you must give up of yourself for your child to be reborn." Firmly gripping my elbow, she steered me towards the dome, and Theo scrambled from my arms, dashing down the hill in panic.

It was almost pitch-black inside, except for a dim light coming from an opening in the cupola, beyond which pale stars gleamed. I could barely make out human shapes huddled on the ground—their heads and bodies bundled in blankets, rocking back and forth, moaning in pain, as though hastening a birth. Arms thrust up to pull me down. Soon I was squatting on the floor. A piece of sackcloth was tossed over my head, and I wrapped it around my body.

The trumpet sounded once more. Hugging my shoulders, I rocked back and forth, groaning and wailing with the others until our voices and the trumpet were one. All the sorrows of the world seemed to be stirring within us. Then something moved in my womb—familiar contractions began. Suddenly, there I was on my back at the center of all, spread-eagled with hips raised, my arms pinned down, while someone held my head firm. With excruciating pain, I delivered my unborn son, and then the rest of my life emptied out—my daughter, my art, my family, my home slipped from me. They flitted about me like wraiths, and I knew they were leaving me forever now. I could not snatch them back from the air. The wail of the bone trumpet became the birth cry of a child—and for one moment suspended in space I looked down upon the sweating, radiant face of an unknown girl giving birth to a boy in a white hospital bed. Then I sank into blackness.

I was swimming through a black ocean, where a full moon bobbed on the waves. The moon became a skull with gleaming eye sockets. One held an eye like a jewel; the other was blank. The skull moon opened its jaws. "You are free, Jeanne. Your punishment has ended."

Raucous crows woke me. Opening an eye and staring up at the sky, I saw their blurred shapes flapping in the treetops and shook myself awake. I was slumped outside the gates of the Montparnasse Cemetery with my back against the cold iron bars. The hideous red-striped dress was gone. In its place I wore a penitent's robe of dirty white hemp cloth. Feeling a drop of rain, I touched a fuzzy scalp, for my head had been shaved like a nun's or a lice-infested prisoner's. Theo scuttled out through the bars and leaped purring into my arms. I ached to hold a living thing.

I don't know how long I sat there, exhausted, empty and unsure what to do. I pressed my face against Theo's warm, throbbing body. It seemed I had only one choice: to keep looking for Modi. I got up from the ground on unsteady legs, looked left towards Rue de la Grande Chaumière, and right towards the *Mairie des Morts*, and then set out in that direction, clattering down the street in my sabots, with Theo right behind.

"Where are we going now?"

"I have one last piece of business to take care of."

When we reached the *Mairie*, I told Theo to wait outside and hide by the rubbish bin. I went inside and straight up to the clerk in the entrance hall, who thankfully did not recognize me now with shaved head and penitent's robe.

"Mademoiselle?"

"I wish to join the Immortals."

He examined me from head to toe with a smirk, but did not send me away. "Third floor, room 72."

A thousand people or more were lined up along the corridor, stretching halfway down the stairs. Some were famous people I recognized: generals, actresses, statesmen. Some carried musical instruments, guns, manuscripts. I got in line behind a man holding a clothes hanger high in the air, on which were draped a magnificent evening dress of flame-colored silk and a gown of pink tulle like a cloud, the only spots of color in this somber hall. I used to love to sew and make my own clothes—oriental style. I could see the handiwork on these was masterly.

"What beautiful dresses!" I complimented him.

"Yes, these are my creations. I dressed the duchess of Guermantes for twenty years." He made a stiff, awkward bow, still holding the dresses aloft so that they did not touch the floor. "Henri La Forge, *couturier célèbre*, at your service."

"I am Jeanne Hébuterne, painter."

He studied me a moment, clicked his tongue, and gave me a wan smile. "Poor child, why are you wearing that dreadful robe? Were you the inmate of an asylum, or perhaps a victim of religious persecution? Are you sure you are in the right place?"

I nodded. "Isn't this the line for the Immortals? My husband, the painter, Amedeo Modigliani, is with them. I intend to join him."

He reflected a moment and shook his head. "I am afraid I don't know the name. I don't think I ever met him at the Duchess's salons. And believe me. Everyone who was anyone was there. You realize, of course, that you must furnish evidence to support your claim? Writers bring their books, military men their battle plans and decorations. Beautiful women bring portraits painted by renowned artists. I have brought these creations. A clerk will give you a receipt for your evidence and then a commission will examine it and inform you of the outcome. Pardon me, but you seem to be rather empty-handed. Have you brought your evidence?"

I blinked in dismay. I had brought nothing, I had nothing, except my experience.

"Lacking that, you'd need two witnesses to attest to the legitimacy of your claim: someone who could testify that you should be remembered."

I shook my head. "I don't think there is anyone who could do that for me."

"Dare I ask: is your claim to Immortality based solely on your association with your painter husband?"

"I suppose," I said uneasily.

"I don't want to discourage you, but you have very little chance of success—as do I, and most of the people here. They only approve a few people a century. But sometimes, there is an element of luck." He yawned. "I have been standing here for ages—my arm gets very tired holding this up, but the floors are so filthy, I would hate for these delicate fabrics to get soiled."

A bell rang, and then from up ahead, a murmur of protest buzzed down the line. Standing on tiptoe, I tried to make out what the consternation was about, but couldn't see above their heads.

"They have probably closed the office again. Too many people! We'll all have to come back later—what a bother! It happens frequently."

The line had broken up; people streamed in our direction. Others lingered uncertainly. "Come back when?" I asked as we followed the crowd down the stairs.

"When they open again. You have to be very persistent. I suppose they expect people to get tired of waiting and just stop coming."

The army behind us began to surge forward. "But how long will that take?"

"Don't be impatient. That will do you no good here. Besides, one must find some way to occupy oneself."

"But I must find my husband as soon as possible."

"I have heard there is an alternative way to reach the Immortals. But it isn't for everyone."

Gripping the banister in his free hand, he stopped midway down the stairs and leaned close to my ear while people elbowed past us.

"There's an underground route, right below the streets of Paris."

"You mean the catacombs?"

He nodded. "But I couldn't possibly go down there—these would get utterly ruined. But you could try. It's dangerous, though. If they catch you, you will be punished severely. And if you do get caught, don't give them my name."

"By way of the entrance at the old Place D'Enfer?"

"No, I have heard that's been closed off. You'd have to get there from...."

"*Allez! Allez!* everybody out now! Closing time." Two ushers had appeared behind us, driving the hordes down the steps with the help of long paddles, so that Monsieur La Forge and I were soon separated. I looked back to see him mincing down the stairs, holding his dresses high to protect them from being trampled while I was pressed forward and carried by the momentum all the way down to the hall. Once outside, I lost Monsieur La Forge in the mob spilling out of the building.

Before me the square bustled with people as on any workday— among the blank faces, not one I knew, but from in between the busy legs, Theo emerged, prancing across the flagstones, the bell on his collar tinkling.

"Well, what did you accomplish?"

"I will never reach Modigliani if I follow their rules."

"I could have told you that, if you had asked."

"But there is a way, through underground Paris."

"I could have told you that, too."

❊

Beneath Paris, it is well known, lies a labyrinth of sewers, mineshafts, and grottoes linked by long tunnels. Some connect to the crypts of churches; others to wine cellars or dungeons dug in medieval times, passing under the Seine. Some find their exits in wells gone dry or gutted limestone quarries. Still others lead to the catacombs where the bones of six million Parisians were interred when the old cemetery of the Innocents was disbanded.

My father had visited the ossuaries once, when they were first opened to the public, and had described to us the walls lined with skulls and the artistically arranged stacks of bones. I had never gone down there, but I had seen the eerie photographs taken by Nadar, which were published in the newspapers. Sometimes, when I wandered with Modi about Montparnasse, I used to think of all those dismantled skeletons piled up in caverns hollowed right under our feet. Entrances were said to be all over the city—even from the cellars of the art academies in Montparnasse—where students sometimes went down to hold secret drinking parties, but the official entrance was located at the Barrière D'Enfer. The Gate of Hell was one of the old gates to the city, which wasn't far at all from Place de Montrouge.

We headed up Avenue D'Orléans towards the Barrière and were soon in sight of the twin toll houses flanking either side of the Rue D'Enfer, where taxes were once levied on goods coming in and out of Paris. In the middle of the square, the Lion of Belfort dozed on his marble pedestal with a crow perched on his back. To my surprise, the entrance to the catacombs, which should have been across the square, simply wasn't there. Before us rose a wall of smooth gray stone, with no gateways, windows or doors, from behind which peeped the swaying tips of dead cypress trees. Across the square, a Ferris wheel creaked round, stuffed with mummies, skeletons, and cadavers.

"But I know there used to be an entrance here. I must have walked past it a hundred times when I was still alive." I stopped for a moment, appalled at myself. That was the first time I had used that phrase: "When I was still alive."

Theo was staring at me gravely, and I sensed he understood I had just passed a milestone.

I walked along the perimeter of the wall, around the corner and to the end of the street and back, inspecting every inch. There was no opening of any kind, and no way for me to climb up. Remembering Pierre's promise that I could go wherever I wanted, I tried to leap up to the top, but it was far too high.

"You must be thinking of the other Paris. The two worlds aren't exactly identical, you know," said Theo.

"I thought this *was* the other Paris."

"You know what I mean. Live Paris."

I sighed. "Can you manage to have a look inside?"

"Hold me up." I lifted him in my arms, and, with one graceful bound, he landed on top of the wall. With another leap, he was gone.

After I had been waiting a while, a *gendarme* came marching around the corner. Seeing me, he hastened his step and held his rifle ready. I thought it best if I played the tourist, even though with my shaved head and ugly robe, I did not look like one.

"*S'il vous plaît*, Monsieur, I am looking for the entrance to the catacombs."

He scowled at me. "There are no catacombs here, Mademoiselle. You best move on. No loitering or begging, please. This area is out of bounds."

I had no choice but to leave, so I crossed the street and sat down on the Lion's pedestal, while hearses rumbled past, pulled by exhausted horses, and the Ferris wheel rattled its skeletons round and round. The *gendarme* stood to attention along the wall, guarding the entrance that was not there, and staring at me fixedly.

At last I spotted Theo on top of the wall. Jumping down to the sidewalk, he weaved in between the carriage wheels over to the where I sat. "Nothing in there but dead trees," he reported and proceeded to lick his fur.

"There must be a portal somewhere," I mused. "A manhole to the sewers or a door in a cellar." I surveyed the street, looking for an opening but saw none. "It looks as though it's all sealed off. Why do you suppose that is?"

Wings flapped behind me; a crow squawked.

I examined the bird on the Lion's head. A shred of gold ribbon bound its claw. I was certain that this must be the same crow I had seen in the Bagneux Cemetery. It cocked its head to one side, studying me as I observed him, staring into his glittering black eye.

"I suppose they keep it closed because too many people might get in, or get out again. The two worlds might get mixed up," Theo explained, "and that would be a terrible mess. Only a few are allowed to go back and forth, such as myself."

"So how will we get into the catacombs?"

The bird croaked again impertinently and flew away towards the Seine.

"That crow has been following us since I was buried," I reflected. Again, I shuddered.

"A chatty devil, isn't he? As to the catacombs, I know a way, but we'll have to cross again to Paris of the living."

"You mean there is a way to get back?" It seemed an impossible hope.

"Of course, there is always a way back. But we'd better wait until twilight."

"But how do you know when that will be? It almost always seems like twilight," I said, gazing up at the sky where a grainy mist veiled the air. I hadn't seen the sun even once since we had arrived here, and I longed to feel it on my skin.

"There will come a moment when the setting sun will appear," said Theo. "But only briefly, and at that time, the door of return will crack open." He sprang onto the Lion's back. Lifting his head, he thrashed his tail, and his body stiffened. I could see him scent the air.

"It will be soon," he announced. "We must make our way towards the river."

The shape of the buildings and the lay of the streets were much as I remembered. I could have found my way to the Seine blindfolded, and yet the character of every street we took had changed.

There was not a butcher, baker or fruit vendor. No pastry shops or creameries or fishmongers, much to Theo's disapproval, for he must have been quite hungry. Cafés and restaurants had all disappeared, replaced by blank storefronts and shuttered windows. The few shops still in existence were selling old clothes and shoes, musty books, mildewed rugs, tarnished spoons, cracked eyeglasses, and mutilated dolls. There were windows full of medical supplies and cosmetics: used crutches, wooden legs, eye-patches, wigs. Not a newly-minted object or a spot of red or yellow, and the newspapers at the kiosk were from fifty years ago.

An organ grinder with a chanteuse in tow stood on a corner, grinding out a melancholy stream of tuneless notes. It reminded me of something I had heard back during the war, but I couldn't quite remember. It occurred to me if I stayed here too long, I might forget everything I once knew.

"Are you sure we can get back and find our way to the catacombs? I have to find Modi soon." I was too scared to express my real fear: that I might forget my husband, his voice, his touch, his eyes.

"Success isn't guaranteed you know. I told you it would be uncertain and also dangerous."

"But I am *dead*," I said. A shiver rippled through me as I pronounced that word. I still wasn't completely resigned to it. "How could I be endangered now?"

"There are other forms of disintegration which are even worse than physical death.

We passed the Pantheon and the Sorbonne, both deserted. In the Cluny garden, a brown-clad monk swept up fallen leaves. Before we reached the Seine, we came upon a narrow alley I had never seen before—a crevice between two gray, windowless walls and there at the end, the river's dull glimmer. I glanced up at the sign: Rue du Chat-qui-Pêche.

"Why that's you!"

"I lived here once, but a long time ago it was, with a friendly old priest. But that's a story for another time. We mustn't dawdle."

The buildings along the alley pressed so close I almost grazed them with both shoulders as I threaded my way through and exited right at the river. But it wasn't the Seine I knew: placid and powerful, cluttered with barges and houseboats, where lovers gazed down from the Pont Notre-Dame. Here muddy water frothed around barren islands, which had once been the Île de la Cité and Île Saint-Louis, where tree stumps poked up, covered in rags. Every imaginable kind of debris was swept along that mighty course: bicycles, cadavers, dead horses, carriage wheels, furniture. All the bridges had collapsed; down on the banks, all the trees had died. Straight across lay a charred hulk, which I realized with dismay must have once been Notre-Dame, its steeple truncated, its arches draped in cobwebs, its brilliant rose windows gouged out.

"What happened to the cathedral?" I whispered.

"You don't want to know."

I stared at it, distraught, and decided it was better not to enquire further. The adjacent buildings and monuments had all been demolished, perhaps by fire or explosion: the Hôtel-Dieu, the Prefecture, Saint-Chapelle. Further across on the other side, in the distance, a sole, familiar, solemn presence brooded over the surrounding ruins: the Tour Saint-Jacques.

"How will we cross if there is no bridge?"

"Just wait and keep your eyes on the horizon—there in that spot above the Tour Saint-Jacques."

I observed the sky where a smudge of palest pink and yellow was pushing through a cloud bank. Below us, a sound swelled above the roaring river—a cheeping and chittering accompanied by a scratching noise. Birds, I thought, stirring at twilight. Gazing down at the bank, I saw the ground itself was moving—crawling. Then I saw that it wasn't the ground at all. It was rats: thousands and thousands of them pullulating at the waters' edge.

"Theo! Look!" I cried in disgust.

"Yes, there is one for every Parisian who ever lived, and they are very anxious to return."

"How can they, if everything is sealed off?" I studied them in horrid fascination.

"Rats have a special status—they stitch the two worlds together."

From the grate at my feet, out popped a rat and then another, and soon hundreds of squealing rodents poured into the alley, scrambling across my ankles, up my legs and breast and onto my head. I screamed and tried to tear them off as their claws dug into my scalp and their teeth needled my arms. Lunging at them with a frenzied yowl, Theo managed to scare them away, though more kept erupting out of the grate.

"They sense the door is opening soon, but don't let yourself be distracted," Theo cried, "Keep your eye on the sun."

Just as I looked upwards, the sun burst through in an orange blaze and was instantly blotted out by a cloud. Dazzled—I could not see. Luminous squiggles danced in front of my eyes.

"Quick!" Theo shouted. "Behind you!"

Through my spotty vision, I could just make out a blue door in the wall, where no door had been before, open just a crack. Theo's tail was disappearing through that crack, and I groped my way behind him, trailed in turn by hundreds of rats. When the door slammed at my back, I was left in darkness; nothing was visible but a thousand glinting eyes.

"Keep going towards the light," called Theo from somewhere up ahead. I could faintly hear his bell tinkling. "I have something to attend to. I will meet you back here at six o'clock and we will set off for the catacombs."

"Where exactly shall we meet?"

"The blue door on Rue du Chat-qui-Pêche. You'll have a few hours to wander about on your own, but whatever happens, don't be late!"

In the distance, a flickering point like a firefly soon widened into a tunnel. A whooshing sound filled my ears, and I stumbled back into life.

Afterlife: Underworld

STRAY DROPS OF COOL WATER splashed my face. Looming before me rose the great fountain of Saint Michel and the devil that I had always loved ever since childhood, when we would walk here from the Luxembourg Gardens on Sundays to visit a pastry shop my mother particularly liked. The angelic warrior trampled the subjugated, but not dead, beast in triumph, attended by griffins, upon whose shiny bronze heads fat black crows had perched. All around the fountain, crowds buzzed, whirled, and jostled. I was home in Paris, almost alive again. I felt woozy and a bit dizzy, as if I had just stepped off the Ferris wheel at Place D'Enfer. Tilting my face to the sky, I fed my grateful being on sunlight.

In the other Paris, steeped in perpetual twilight, colors had disappeared. Sooty mist enveloped all, muting most colors but gray, purple, and black and draining the luster from things, but here spring rioted in blues, reds, yellows, and greens. I thought of Giovanna, and of my parents and brother. I wished ardently to see them all again. Perhaps I could find them now before going to meet Theo at the blue door.

I spun around to survey the busy square humming with voices and music from the cafés along the boulevard, where the tall plane trees were just budding out. I saw immediately something was very wrong. Was I even in Paris? Where else could I be? Around me moved small groups of soldiers and women wearing very short skirts and jaunty men's hats aslant on bobbed hair. The soldiers steering them about by the arm were definitely not French. Huge signs in German fronted the buildings along Boulevard Saint-Michel, and a brasserie on the corner where my brother André often used to go with friends was covered with placards in German. From the tall windows of the building next to it hung a long red drape with some sort of oriental cross in black, swaying in the breeze.

A group of matrons burdened with shopping bags came towards me as I crossed the boulevard. On their jackets were stitched crude yellow stars emblazoned with the word "Jude." When a small contingent of soldiers appeared from around the corner, the women scattered across the square. Some dropped their bags and did not even stop to retrieve the onions that rolled away into the gutter. The soldiers laughed at the women's timidity, kicked the onions out of their way, and marched into the brasserie. Curious, I followed.

A scabby boxwood hedge shielded the diners on the terrace from the street, where officers in brown uniforms sat, all speaking German, the strange cross-symbol strapped to their arms. Through the open kitchen door, I saw a man ladling out plates of stewed meat and smelly cabbage, which an elderly Arab waiter delivered to the terrace.

Glancing down at a newspaper left on an empty table, I felt sick as I read the headline: *Germany Victorious*. When I read the date *1941*, my legs nearly buckled under me. Over twenty years had elapsed since Modi and I had passed, and now France was at war again. I had little hope of finding my parents and was even more anxious to locate André and Giovanna. Were they even alive? Were they in danger? André's studio had been in Rue de Seine, so I hurried there.

At 12 Rue de Seine, André's name was still listed on the door. But through the dusty windows, I could see he had not been there for some time. His easels and worktables were covered in newspapers and old sheets. Unopened letters had been pushed under the door. Propped high on a shelf above a table was a yellowing photograph of my mother and pinned to a wall were postcards of camels and desert scenes. Perhaps he had fulfilled his dream of traveling in North Africa. In a corner sat a large cardboard suitcase, which I had seen before: it was the one in which André had carried off my sketchbooks and paintings from the studio I had shared with my husband.

I turned away and headed to Rue Joseph-Bara, where Hanka and Zbo had lived, but their names did not appear on the engraved bronze plaque in the entranceway. In the intervening years, the building had become more chic, with brass and mahogany fittings in the hall. Next, I gravitated towards Rosalie's, but Modi's favorite eatery, though still looking very much as I remembered it, with rough plank tables and a sawdust-strewn floor, seemed to have changed hands. A middle-aged couple was running it, Madame tending a battered pot on the stove and Monsieur pouring glasses at the counter. Like the brasserie, this place, too, was full of loud, chattering Germans. I stared at the little table by the stove, where, on cold days at lunchtime, I would sit across from Modi while he dined on Rosalie's Italian beef stew with garlic, the window to the street behind him all steamed up. He'd wash his lunch down with a carafe of red, then unhook an old guitar from the wall and pluck out a popular tune, changing round all the words until everyone howled with laughter. That Modi! What a clown, what a goof! They had no idea of the haunted man within.

A poster pasted in the window attracted my attention: a crudely drawn cartoon of one of Modi's caryatids, his Polynesian-inspired sculptures that once had populated our studio, like exotic visitors or children. Above it in bold block letters was written in French and German: *Degenerate Art.* The poster advertised a series of lectures being held at two o'clock at 14 Rue de la Grande Chaumière—which had been the address of the Académie Colarossi. I flew there.

The quiet street hadn't changed much—I lingered a moment outside number 8—the door was still painted Prussian blue with a fastidiously polished knocker, but Madame Moreau was probably long gone, dead or retired to the countryside, where her husband's relatives used to have an apricot orchard. I would see her sometimes in summer, sitting in the courtyard, halving apricots with a sharp knife and tossing away the pits. Once she even brought us a little pot of apricot jam. But I passed onto number 14, resolving to revisit our former studio after the lecture was over.

The old sign on the entrance to the academy had been removed: in its place a burnished engraved plaque read: *Kunstakademie.* The doors were open, and a few people, officers mostly, along with some French civilians, were hurrying up the stairs. I followed these stragglers into the auditorium, which was the great hall where I had once attended life-drawing classes. Easels had been moved out of the way, stacked like bones against the wall, to make room for a sea of folding chairs. Hanging on the walls all around the room were huge drawings of heroic nude figures—tall, male, with sinewy forearms and buttocks: Teutonic models in triumphant poses. The lights were low, and the windows shuttered, but a spotlight illuminated the podium, where an officer with a dozen medals pinned to his chest faced the audience. Beside him, two young soldiers held up what looked to be a large framed picture concealed by a white cloth. This, too, with a spotlight trained upon it. Above them fluttered the red drape with the odd black cross I had seen on the building at Place Saint-Michel, the same symbol embroidered on all their armbands.

The lecture was already in progress, and the speaker had just instructed his two assistants to remove the cloth—revealing beneath a painting I knew well, which Modi much admired. It was a still life of a decomposing beef carcass painted by our dear friend, Chaim Soutine. Modi and I had often visited his studio while Chaim was working on his series of rotting still lifes. Friends would bring him buckets of fresh blood from the butchers at Les Halles every day, with which he would douse the carcass so that he could work with the right tonality of red. He eventually had to stop—his neighbors objected to the stench.

A murmur of infuriated disgust swept through the audience instantly upon sight of this witty, provocative work of art, inspired by Rembrandt paintings at the Louvre—and I remembered similar reactions from the public when the painting had first been shown. It was, as Modi claimed, a punch in the bourgeois eye and stomach. But it was also, he believed, a religious painting, recalling the martyred torso of a wounded Christ.

"This grotesque still life is obviously the work of a madman," explained the speaker in heavily accented French. "An individual of an infirm mind, and a sick sensibility. Think of the conditions in which it was created, with the painter, I will not say, artist, standing a few feet away from the fly-blown, decomposing flesh, for weeks at a time. Filth, it is pure filth. The artist is, of course, a Jew, for degenerate art is often the product of Jews, Communists, perverts, and the mentally insane."

At his signal, the young soldiers set down the painting and now held another one up for view and unveiled it. I gasped. It was one of Modi's portraits of Soutine.

"And here we have a portrait of the painter, done by one of his degenerate Jewish companions." With a long pointer, the lecturer touched the canvas to indicate facial features. "Note the Hebrew characteristics —the thick lips, hirsuteness, low forehead. Indications of a dull intellect and perhaps hereditary insanity." A large photograph now appeared on a wall behind the podium, projected by a column of dusty light. In the picture, I recognized Soutine, although he had aged greatly. His hair was white, and he wore the yellow, six-pointed star sewn to his jacket. Would Zbo have had to wear one too? And Modi? He would have tossed it into the gutter.

"You see here the same features captured by objective photography. I wish to call your attention to the stubby fingers, protruding ears, and the large, ill-proportioned nose, typical of the Hebrew type."

I moved closer as another picture was lifted for display: a Picasso! This time the audience laughed and jeered. It looked like a study for one of the *Demoiselles of Avignon*—a seated nude, with legs parted, and an African mask for a face.

"This is the work of a noted Bolshevist sympathizer and atheist. Notice the perverse sexual detail—here and here. He has chosen to give the figure a primitive mask, for he wasn't skilled enough even to paint a human face. And next, in the projected photograph, you may view what decadent critics have judged to be his masterpiece."

Dismantled body parts scattered by an explosion flashed on the screen. Screaming mouths, arms thrown up in terror, a severed bull's head, a squealing horse, all in tones of black and gray. I was stunned by its force and violence, by the death and suffering it conveyed.

"This hodgepodge of dismembered anatomy could have been drawn by a four-year-old, or even by a monkey." Although the audience snickered in agreement, it was a work of genius.

But the greatest shock came next when another very large canvas was lifted for display and the cloth slid off. It was a female nude by Modigliani, one I had never seen: Gosia with golden skin, lying on Zbo's worn couch, her eyes hooking into the viewer. He must have painted it at Zbo's flat, where he went to work while I was still away in the Midi with our baby. No one spoke or whispered. I believe they stood in awe of its power as I did. I ached to see it! I had always suspected that the two of them must have made love every time she modeled for him. Now, seeing this painting, I knew it was so. I nearly choked on my jealousy, and yet I was proud of his achievement. This nude was a triumph.

"Do not let yourself be deceived by the sexual allure of this image, by the woman who invites you lovingly into her bed. Her gaze corrupts, and her embrace weakens the man who yields. It is the work of a debauched Jewish painter, who destroyed himself with alcohol, drugs, and unclean women. This very picture demeans those who look upon it."

"Rubbish. You are the one who is speaking filth and lies," I cried. But of course, they could not hear.

More paintings were shown and ridiculed: works by Kisling, Chagall, some I did not know, but several I recognized. In fact, many had once belonged to Leopold Zborowski; I had seen them stacked about his dining room. How had they come into these Germans' hands? And what had happened to Zbo?

In the back row, near the door, I noticed a woman with a hat slanted low across her forehead, scribbling notes throughout the lecture. Hers was a face I thought I had seen before, someone from my past, but I couldn't quite place her. I went to stand over her chair to see what she was writing, which turned out to be a list of the names of the pictures exhibited and of the artists who had done them. My eyes were drawn to a blue and green flicker around her wrist, half hidden by her jacket sleeve as her pen flew across the page. I was not mistaken. My own green and blue glass bangle—the one Modi had given me, the bracelet Annie had stolen from the drawer of my bedside table! I studied her face. This woman, neither young nor old, not yet forty years of age, was Annie herself.

"You little thief, I have found you at last." I tried to wrench the bangle off, but could not grasp it. She shivered and looked about her, and I knew she had sensed my airy touch.

The lecture was ending now, and I directed my attention towards the speaker to catch his concluding words. "You will be pleased to know that these and other monstrosities are being collected at the Jeu de Paume. All degenerate works such as these belonging to Jewish or foreign artists, patrons, or galleries—will be confiscated, evaluated, and, if necessary, destroyed." The audience clapped and cheered.

I was sickened with rage. Destroy the works of these artists? Of Amedeo Modigliani? Of Chaim Soutine, Pablo Picasso? Of Moïse Kisling or Marc Chagall? Insanity!

Annie gave a gasp, which she disguised with a cough, and a soldier sitting next to her glowered at her.

"No, no, they cannot! They must not," she whispered to no one, or perhaps to me. Closing her notebook, she rose and made for the door.

At that moment, the soldiers in the audience sprang from their seats and raised their arms in a rigid salute, which sent a chill through my being. Annie looked back with a horrified grimace and darted down the stairs. I followed.

I didn't need to go far, for Annie walked briskly a few feet to number 8 and was greeted by a burly matron, who might have been Madame Moreau's incarnation, sitting in the *concierge*'s cubicle beside a cup of tisane. She was dressed as her predecessor invariably had been, in a blue serge dress, checked apron, and red felt slippers.

Annie crossed the courtyard, where a small stone basin had been added to the spigot, which was once our source of water, and entered the annex where the studios used to be. Numb as a sleepwalker, I climbed behind her to the third floor, to Ortiz's studio. As she unlocked the door, I glanced up the dark coil of stairs to where our studio had once been—who was there now? Was there anything left there, of our old life? Some old piece of our furniture still knocking around? I wanted to know, but then I didn't.

Ortiz's old flat was no longer an artist's studio—at least there was no sign of any work being done there. The paintings had been stripped from the walls, which showed the dirty impress where frames had once hung. Striped orange curtains had been added to the tall windows. At present they were pulled open and tied back with ribbons. The far end of the room was partitioned off by a boldly painted folding screen that nearly touched the ceiling. Boxes of papers, books and supplies encumbered a trestle table by the window. Other boxes and parcels, tied up with string, were strewn about the room, ready for mailing. I glanced at the address—*Manuel Ortiz de Zarate—Berne, Suisse*. So I learned he had left Paris.

A tiny closet of a kitchen had been set up in the other corner, where Ortiz's charcoal stove used to be, furnished with a cook stove and a scarred porcelain sink where a few dirty dishes and eggshells were piled. Annie lit a small gas ring with a match and set a red enamel pot on it, heating up some coffee she must have brewed earlier. The scent seemed heavenly to me, and I wished I could taste it.

Through the window, she surveyed the courtyard below and the windows directly across, then drew the curtains, pinning them tightly shut with a clothespin. She moved some boxes from the table, lay out two cups, a packet of madeleines, and her steaming coffee pot, then went to the other end of the room, where she folded the screen aside, revealing a wardrobe built into the wall. I remembered having seen that wardrobe years before. Ortiz had built it himself and used it to keep his painting supplies along with a stock of wine and brandy. It was positioned more or less below where our cupboard had been placed in the flat above. When Annie opened the wardrobe, I was surprised to see it was empty, with all the shelves removed. Reaching for a broomstick tucked inside, she knocked twice gently on the ceiling. A reply of three soft knocks sounded from above, to which Annie answered with one sharp tap. Then with the clatter of a bundle tumbling down a chute, a pair of feet in socks and two long trousered legs dangled down inside the wardrobe, and moments later, a man's body slid down into a groaning heap.

"I am getting too old for this, I am afraid," said the visitor, slowly rising on creaky knees. I first recognized the voice and then the man: Armand Metz, the gallerist, the thief who had stolen my painting from behind the cupboard, while claiming to rescue it. He looked about sixty now and clasped a roll of canvas to his chest. "Isn't it rather risky so early in the day?"

"Come have some coffee, I have some things to tell you. What's that you have got there?"

"Something I want you to take care of."

He put the canvas on the trestle table, and sat down, drawing his chair back so that the protruding edge of a sideboard partly shielded his face and figure from the doorway. He sniffed, then savored a first sip of coffee she poured out into a yellow cup. "Real coffee, my girl, and madeleines! I won't ask where or how you got these."

"It's easy enough if you have the right contacts."

"You are so kind to take such good care of an old man like me." He coughed, and his chest rumbled. "Did you remember the cigarettes?"

She drew a blue packet from her pocket, and they both lit up.

"I have just been to the so-called *Kunstakademie* for the lecture on degenerate art. They have their hands on the whole collection," she said, blowing two plumes of smoke from her nostrils, just like a man. I loved the smell of cigarette smoke. It reminded me of Modi. "The Picassos, the Modiglianis, and the Soutines."

Metz pressed his hand to his forehead. "They came to the gallery, took a blowtorch to the vault, cleaned the place out. I was lucky to get out through the cellar without being shot."

"*Who? Those German soldiers? But why would they do this?*"

"I know. But it's worse than we thought," she said seizing his forearm across the table. "The ones by Jewish painters risk being destroyed. Modigliani, Soutine, Kisling, Chagall…."

"I don't believe it. They're not stupid. Surely they would want to sell them, or to keep them as investments. Propaganda—that's what it is. They would not dare. They know how much they are worth. Why do you think they have not arrested Picasso? Everything he produces is worth a fortune. They will confiscate them for the private collections of the Führer and his lot."

"Would you care to see the list of what they showed today?" She handed him her notebook.

His eyes skimmed the list, and he threw the notebook down. "I am glad Leopold did not live to see this day. He must be turning over in his grave."

Zbo! He was dead. And Hanka?

"Well, I am sure he turned when Hanka sold his collection to you."

"Ach." He clutched his heart.

"What's the matter? Are you ill?"

"No, I am disgusted with humanity."

There came an abrupt knock at the door—they eyed each other in fear. "It's probably the *concierge* again, that damn woman. Quickly!"

Annie snatched Metz's cup from his hand and dashed the coffee out into the sink. She plucked the cigarette from his lips, and, pinching it once between her own so that it was imprinted with her lipstick, squashed it in an ashtray.

"Madame Rosier!" shrilled a voice from behind the door.

"*Oui, Madame Avril. J'arrive. Un petit instant.*"

Metz scrambled back into the wardrobe. Annie locked the doors but neglected to unfold the screen back across the room. Kicking off her shoes and peeling off her skirt, she threw on a faded pink kimono grabbed from the back of a chair. Hastily knotting the sash while the knocking continued, she ran to the door in her stocking feet.

The door flew open, revealing the red-faced *concierge*, who peered over Annie's shoulder towards the kitchen where the canvas had been left on the table.

"Madame Avril! I was just about to draw a bath. What can I do for you?"

"Your curtains are all closed. I was checking to find out if everything was all right." The table was in full view, with only one cup, the little red pot, the packet of madeleines, and one cigarette burning in the ashtray. "Is there someone with you? I thought I heard voices."

"No, no one. As I said, I was just undressing to have a bath, so I closed the curtains. Those soldier boys across the way are always playing peeping tom. Besides, I have a bit of a headache and the light bothers me." She ran her fingers across her forehead.

Madame Avril's eyes were still fixed on the table, where she had noticed the packet of madeleines.

"Are you hungry, Madame? I have some madeleines. Please take some. I must be careful of my figure. There's more than I can possibly eat."

"Don't mind if I do," she said, taking two steps forward, swiveling her head left and right. Annie wrapped some cakes up for her. "And some cigarettes too?"

"*Oui, merci.*"

Annie saved four cigarettes from the pack and pressed it into the *concierge*'s hands, along with the cakes.

"Here you are. I hope you enjoy them."

"Thank you." When Madame Avril turned to examine the wardrobe, Annie stiffened. I could see her swallowing her fear.

"You're sure everything is all right?" asked the *concierge*.

"Of course, Madame. Please forgive me, but I must have my bath and a rest before going out again."

"If you have any problems, remember to come to me first."

"Yes, thank you." She smiled and hugged the robe close to her body.

The *concierge* withdrew, and Annie shut the door. She stood motionless for five long minutes before bending down to peek through the keyhole, but I could have told her that Madame Avril was still there too, on the other side, with her ear to the door. They remained poised like that five minutes more, listening for the other to make a move. I could almost feel Annie's heart jumping in her throat as if it were my own. After the *concierge* had clomped back down the stairs, Annie liberated Metz from the wardrobe.

Collapsing into an armchair, he held his head in his hands.

"I can't stay here any longer. One word from that woman, and we'll both be on the next train for the camps. Inhuman things are happening in those places. And in any case, it is time you got out. Did you do what I told you?"

"*What camps?*"

"Yes, I did as you instructed." From a purse, she drew out a passport.

I peered over Metz's shoulder as he examined it with a magnifying glass he had slipped out of his trouser pocket. The passport had Annie's photograph but someone else's name. "Excellent job they did," he commented, handing it back to her. "There is a train tonight, for Zurich."

"Not there. I will be going to Rome." She slid the passport back into her bag.

"To Rome? But it is not safe with that mad Mussolini."

"I will be safe. I know someone there who will help me. But what about you?"

"I am making arrangements. It is best if I not tell you."

She nodded. "Yes, it's best."

"Very well. Then you must take that with you and make sure it is kept in a safe place." He pointed to the canvas he had left on the table before Madame Avril had arrived.

"You still haven't told me what it is," she said.

"Have a look and tell me what you think."

Annie cleared off some space on the table and unrolled the canvas, but I had already guessed what it was: our painting, of Giovanna, myself, and Modi, which Metz had stolen from our studio after Modi died. Amazement blurred my tears when I saw that it had been completed since I had last seen it, and quite beautifully. All three figures had been finished, and a gypsy cart added to the background. Giovanna had been given a sweet little face, and Modi, now with elongated legs, wore a red harlequin suit. His left hand held a palette, the other rested on my shoulder, which was wrapped in a gypsy shawl. I stared at the layered blood red texture and the supple, wavy lines of Modi's legs—characteristic traits of Soutine's style! As for Giovanna's infant face, the wide-spaced eyes with long lashes, the impish smile, and cool blues reminded me of Kisling's portraits. Modi's closest friends, who had been like a family to us, had finished the painting for us.

"*La famille sacrée*," whispered Annie. "*C'est magnifique.*"

"You are looking at Modigliani's very last painting. A self-portrait including his wife and child, unique among his works, which has been out of circulation for two decades. His wife, Jeanne, is portrayed as a Tzigane, symbolizing his anti-bourgeois, free-spirited attitude, his childlike playfulness, and at the same time, it pays homage to the harlequins of Picasso, the circus figures of Chagall, and the gypsies of Soutine's rural Russia. Garbing himself as a harlequin suggests his close ties to Italy, to Venice, and to a philosophy of life that claims that all the world's a stage. Yet the deep blue of Jeanne's dress with its star pattern on the hem evokes the Tuscan and Umbrian Madonnas of the Quattrocento, bespeaking his classical training."

This lofty lecture made me laugh, but I was enchanted by the painting's effect, and truly the figures portrayed did suggest all the things he said: gaiety, freedom, playfulness, and love. Things I had forgotten had ever existed. Things I would never have experienced, had it not been for Amedeo Modigliani. What mattered most now was keeping the painting safe. These two people, whom I had believed were thieves, were turning out to be my allies and defenders.

"I think I have seen this before. In a very early stage—the star pattern on her skirt looks familiar. But back then it was only a portrait of Jeanne and her baby, a Madonna, when I saw it in their studio after Jeanne came back to Paris with Giovanna." She touched his sleeve. "Is it authentic?"

"Of course, it is authentic," he burbled—although I knew better. "But it wasn't in Zborowski's catalogue. I obtained it directly from the artist's studio right after he died. It's true, I had to have a few details filled in. Kisling and Soutine helped with that. I meant to sell it years ago, but became too attached to it. Now, after a lifetime's career as one of the great dealers in Paris, friend and patron to the most celebrated names in art, this is all that I have left. It is a remarkable testimony to those times. To a life that will never come again." His voice cracked. "And I now entrust it to you."

Annie lit another cigarette as she studied the painting. "You know Modigliani's daughter is in Paris? You don't want to give it to her for safekeeping?"

Giovanna! What joy to learn that she was still alive!

"My dear girl, as Modigliani's daughter, she is no safer than I am. But she is not in Paris at the moment, I have heard. She is a very brave girl. You know she is with the Resistance." He pronounced this last word as if it were a prayer.

Annie nodded gravely.

What is the Resistance? Against whom or what does it resist? Tell me where she is, at least!

"And that is why I certainly cannot give her this painting," Metz continued. "If it should fall into the wrong hands...."

"It will be safe in Rome. And when this is all over, it will be returned to you." Annie rolled it up quickly.

"When this is all over, I will probably be dead. I dread to think what will happen if Germany wins this wretched war." Metz began to cry softly. "Forgive an old man his foolishness." He wiped his eyes with a gray handkerchief. "Now, please give me something to eat."

"I gave nearly all the cakes to that witch. Let me fix you some eggs."

As Annie set about poaching some eggs, I inspected the wardrobe on the other side of the room. Peeping inside, I saw a large hole had been cut in the top of the wardrobe. The hole bored straight through the ceiling, creating a direct passage to the studio above, right where our old blue cupboard had once stood. So that was what the loose floorboards around the cupboard had concealed! If Modi had known about this secret connection between the two studios, he had never mentioned it.

I found it easy to hoist myself up, and there I was in our studio. Our blue cupboard had been painted brown and moved to the opposite wall. A small red carpet lay rolled up near the hole. There were, thank goodness, no signs of our previous life. The bright orange walls had been painted white, now streaked with old soot from a charcoal stove. In the bedroom, two rusted bed frames with horsehair mattresses had replaced our large lumpy bed, and the shelves, mirrors, and pictures had all been taken away. I couldn't bear to stay more than a few moments in that room, remembering everything that had happened there, so I went back out to the main studio, now flooded with sunshine, and there on a battered table by the window, illumined by a ray of yellow light, was my violin case. Overjoyed to find it again, I opened the case, removed the instrument, put it to my chin, and played all that I remembered of my favorite Schubert pieces. I hadn't forgotten a single note.

In the other Paris, time never passed, but here the minutes were ticking by. I did not realize that the afternoon had begun to wane until violet shadows deepened across the courtyard, just as they used to do when I practiced my violin in the dusk, waiting for Modi to come home from some appointment with Zbo. How long had I been here? I had just drawn my bow, the final note quivering in the empty room, when I saw two figures reflected in the darkening window: a young girl and a young man embracing. Then the door burst open behind me, and two people stormed in, making such a ruckus I almost fell out of my chair. But it wasn't the young couple I now saw mirrored in the window, but the *concierge* and a German officer.

"Where is the music coming from?" growled the officer. "Are you hiding anyone here?"

"I heard nothing," Madame Avril replied, but her worried eyes hooked into mine, reflected in the window.

She knows! She has seen me! I shut the case with bang, and she jumped.

"If you heard music, it must have come from there." She pointed out the opening in the floor across the room. "Those vermin must have a wireless."

The heels of his boots resounded on the floorboards as he strode over to inspect the hole.

"*Jah!*" He sprang into the hole, and, reluctantly leaving my violin behind on the table, I slid down after him, although I had no idea what power I might wield to aid my new friends.

But I needn't have worried. When we rolled out of the wardrobe, the apartment below was empty: both Metz and Annie had decamped, and the painting was gone. Smoke spiraled up from their cigarettes in the ashtray.

As the bells of Notre-Dame jangled for vespers, I followed the Seine towards Rue du Chat-qui-Pêche. Carloads of helmeted soldiers rattling along the Quai de la Tournelle passed me as I ran. The second-hand booksellers—where Modi and I used to browse for cheap editions of Huysmans, Rimbaud, Baudelaire, Poe—were closing up their stalls. Brightly colored books leaped out at me as I passed: *La Vraie Histoire de Modigliani Peintre Maudit.* The lurid cover showed a wild-eyed Modi tippling from a bottle and in the background, a caricature of one of his great nudes lying on a couch. There were other books written by names I recognized: *Montparnasse* by Francis Carco, the critic who had once praised my husband, and *Memoirs* by our friend André Salmon. I wished I could read what they had said about Modigliani, and perhaps, about me, but there was no time, and besides, I could not even turn the pages, had I lingered to examine those books.

Across from the Quai de Montebello, plum trees exploded in pink and mauve blossoms, enfolding the cathedral. My eyes drank in the frothy colors, which I could almost taste like the pastel water ices Modi used to buy for me from the Sicilian *gelataio* in Nice. I shivered, recalling the vision of Notre-Dame as a charred ruin, which I had glimpsed in the other Paris, hoping that would not happen for centuries to come. Down on the banks where the plane trees had leafed out, I saw scores of teeming rats heading like me, I supposed, to the door of return. When I finally found the spot, Theo was waiting for me, pacing up and down and swishing his tail in annoyance.

"But doesn't this lead back to the other Paris?" I asked, gazing at the blue door, where I was puzzled to note Hebrew letters painted in a circle. Modigliani sometimes used to paint Hebrew letters on his canvases—but would never explain to me what they meant.

"This door leads anywhere you wish, including the catacombs. It is one of the safest entries left. The others are heavily guarded. Luckily, this one isn't marked on any map."

"You should have told me that the world was at war."

"What difference would it have made? You can't choose the era in which you return. It chooses you."

At that moment, there came a groaning of reluctant hinges, and the door popped open of its own accord.

Once inside, we found ourselves on a staircase descending into darkness, widdershins. A strong smell of earth, mold, and damp wafted up from the depths.

From the street above drifted eerie echoes I thought I recognized as the wheels of cars, the omnibus, voices, and footsteps. But as the light dimmed, these sounds gradually grew fainter, too, until there was nothing left but the trickling of distant water. Still, there was no need for torches or candles. Theo's eyes cut beams through the gloom, lighting our way. Rats on the ledges, catching Theo's scent, scattered squealing as we passed. I felt we were descending the whorls of a giant conch shell towards an invisible ocean. When the stairs ended, we stood at the mouth of a narrow corridor, which branched off into different chambers.

"How do you know which way to go?" I asked Theo as he scampered forward, the silver bell at his throat tinkling in the dark. Lifting his head, he indicated the arrows I had not noticed painted on the ceiling. Each chamber led to a dozen more. On and on we went through the tunnels, following the red arrows, discovering signs of habitation: bed frames with moldy covers, charcoal stoves, old wine flasks, barrels, rusty lanterns, and candle stubs.

"So people sleep down here, or are they hiding?" I thought of Metz locked in Annie's cupboard and hoped they were both safe.

"This, my dear, is a veritable parallel universe."

We came across crude pictures, graffiti scratched on the walls, and rough stone sculptures made perhaps by the quarrymen who had worked here decades ago. We splashed through stinking canals covered with green scum where rats paddled and clambered across rickety scaffoldings of rotten wood. Occasionally street signs were posted, indicating exactly where we rambled beneath the streets of Paris—though here, twenty, thirty, fifty feet below, you could have no sense of what was going on above. We passed a jewel-like pool of turquoise water, illuminated by sunlight breaking in from who knows where. Further on, stalactites hung from the ceiling and fossils of ferns and shells were impressed on crumbling walls.

Then there came a feeling of something uncanny, both a physical sensation and a smell: moldy, sweetish, and musky, a little bit sickening; thick and suffocating as chalk dust. Theo sniffed the air and whipped his tail about. A sign, I had noted, of agitation.

"What's that odor?" I said, covering my mouth with the sleeve of my robe as it grew overpowering.

"Bones, my dear. Disintegrating bones."

Turning the corner, we found rising before us a mound of greenish skulls embossed with mold and a wall of bones six feet high, stacked in herringbone patterns. We had reached the ossuaries where the dismantled skeletons of millions of Parisians had been interred. On the stone lintel, a warning had been chiseled: *Arrête, c'est ici l'empire de la mort!* As I now belonged to the realm beyond, I knew I should not be afraid, yet I was stiff with fear, and my teeth were chattering.

Theo dislodged a skull which rolled along the ground, colliding with a row of empty wine bottles, knocking them over.

"Who's there?" barked a guttural voice as a soldier burst from the shadows, a headlamp fending the darkness before him. Red sparks flew from the binoculars strapped to his face. As the dancing red spots dazzled my eyes, I was caught in the beam of his headlamp. The soldier stumbled towards me, rifle ready. His face paled; his mouth dropped open. God knows how, but through those binoculars he *saw* me.

"*Mein Gott!*"

I gaped back, unable to move. He cannot endanger me, I thought, but then he threw down his gun and grabbed a camera strung round his neck, pointed it towards me, and held it steady with both hands.

"Watch out!" cried Theo. "This way!" The tip of his tail vanished into a hole at my feet just as lightning crackled in a gash of blue light. I dived in after him, but could barely squeeze through.

"Come back! Halt!"

The hole led to a narrow passageway, where I propelled myself along on my elbows and stomach, the blue light flashing at my heels. Then something gave way: the bottom fell out from under me. I plunged twenty feet, landing belly down in a pile of sand. Grit filled my eyes, and, when I finally blinked it away, I was aware of waves breaking nearby, not the lulling of the ocean—but a low, unquiet thunder. I sat up. We had escaped. The soldier had not followed us here.

I spied the cat further down the beach, grooming himself. "Theo! Are you hurt?" I called.

I got to my feet and gathered up my sabots, which had been flung yards away.

We stood on a vast beach before a black, gelatinous sea, where the broken masts of sunken ships bobbed, leviathans rolled in dirty foam, and desperate hands shot up to beg for rescue. I knew that ocean. Modi had often described it to me, and I had seen it in my dreams: Lautréamont's sea of Maldoror. A dock of rotting planks extended far out over the viscous waters. Stinking algae lined the sand, where decaying limbs had washed up among sponges and mussel garlands.

Theo prowled along the tideline, sniffing about, in search of something edible. He tasted a mussel, but spat it out.

A black star gleamed low in the purple twilight, and far across, dim red, green, and gold lights glittered along tall walls, domes, and towers. I knew that across that water, where no rope could reach, Amedeo Modigliani must be waiting for me. His lucky black star had led me to the other shore.

"Is that the realm of the Immortals?" I asked.

"I don't know what else it might be," said Theo.

I surveyed the beach in all directions: its desolation stretched as far as I could see.

"So what now?" I asked.

"Heavens, if I know. But it does seem you have three choices: wait for a boat, swim, or return from whence you came."

"I won't go back until I find him."

"Well then, the choices are not three but two."

I knew from reading *Maldoror* I had few chances of crossing those annihilating waters. The beach was strewn with the remains of those who had tried, whose beings had been chewed up, sucked dry, spit out. Was that what Theo had meant when he spoke of a disintegration worse than physical death?

We stood awhile watching the inky, congealed waves until we noted a long, twinkling shape on the horizon, strangely elastic, like a caterpillar. Gradually, it grew larger as it approached, until, incredulous, we made out the hulk of a white ocean liner, decked out with colored lights, its portholes all aglow. A foghorn sounded a thrilling bass note, and we ran to the rickety dock as the ship cast anchor. Two sailors clambered down ladders thrown over the side and hurried to secure the ropes. Out shot a gangplank, and a white-clad officer stepped onto the dock. He seemed to be waiting for us, standing to attention with a black notebook tucked under his arm, while we scrambled towards him. Theo pranced from plank to plank, as the dock swayed and shifted beneath us on the slimy black waves.

"Where is this ship bound, Monsieur? I must join the Immortals," I asked, pointing to the lights across the way.

"Your name, Madame?"

"Jeanne Hébuterne, with an H."

He consulted the black leather notebook. "I cannot find your name in the passenger list. Which class should you be traveling in?"

"Third or second?" I faltered.

He checked the list. "No one here by that name in any class. Do you have your ticket?"

The foghorn blew a second time—a warning, vibrating in my being.

"I am afraid I don't have one. Perhaps there is a reservation in my husband's name. Amedeo Modigliani. He might be in first class," I added.

He read through the list again and shook his head. "Without a proper ticket and reservation, you may not board." He snapped the black book shut.

"Please, Monsieur. I'll do anything—scullery work, cleaning, mopping, mending, minding children, manicuring ladies, if only you will take me, take us with you," and I scooped up Theo to show the officer how adorable he was.

"I am sorry. Captain's orders."

Salt poured from my eyes now, as I clasped the squirming cat to my chest. "You must take me with you! I have been through so much." I thought of pushing the man into the sea and running aboard—but I knew I'd probably be imprisoned and thrown into the sea myself.

The tittering of annoyed voices drifted down from the upper decks, where a group of women in evening gowns leaned over the railing, observing us. "Good gracious, ensign. What's going on? Why have we stopped in this desolate place? There is a most offensive smell."

Only then did I realize how frightful I must look to them, like an escaped inmate from an asylum, as Monsieur La Forge had described me.

The officer retreated over the gangplank, which was hastily drawn back in. The ship blew its horn a third time, weighed anchor with a rattling of chains, and departed. The waves generated while the ship maneuvered were so violent that they lifted the planks of the dock:

we barely managed to keep our balance without being tossed into the sea. Away it sailed, impervious to the evil that festered in those waters. Violins and clarinets tweedled out melodies from operettas as the passengers waltzed on deck under a brooding sky.

After the ship had gone, we sat on the edge of the dock, looking down at the luminous jellyfish swirling there. Theo crouched alert in a hunting position. Something silver flickered in the water, his paw shot out, and then I saw clutched in his claws a small fish, which he carried off in his teeth and devoured on his own.

Feeling exhausted, I lay down on the splintery planks, and stared at the black star gleaming in the twilight. I closed my eyes and surrendered my body to the soothing movement of the dock in the water. For a brief moment, I remembered abandoning myself to the weight of Modigliani's body on mine and to the waves of pleasure.

A sound roused me—another boat horn. Thinking perhaps I was dreaming, I shook myself and blinked. Sitting up, I saw approaching a *bateau mouche* piled high with cargo. The barge tooted its raspy horn twice as it puttered up to the dock. A bewhiskered man in a blue knit cap waved at me. Beside him stood someone I knew: Pierre.

"Jeanne! Jeanne! Look, I have found my uncle and my sister too!" A little blond girl knelt on deck, playing with a doll. It tumbled away as the girl stretched out her arms to us. "Pretty kitty! *Viens ici!*" Theo had reappeared and was staring as if hypnotized at the children.

"Come, Jeanne, come with us back to Paris. You can stay with us there forever. The cat can come too," coaxed Pierre.

"I can't. I have to find Modi. But perhaps, Monsieur," I asked, addressing the man in the watch cap, "you would be kind enough to take me there." I pointed across the water.

Squinting at the distant lights, he shook his head. "I am afraid not, Madame, it isn't allowed. I just go to Paris and back. You are welcome to travel with us that far, if you wish. But night is coming, and we must be on our way. The sea out here can get mighty rough."

"No, thank you." I mumbled and looked away, so they would not see my tears.

"But you will be here all alone, Jeanne. Come with us, please," said Pierre.

I shook my head.

"This is where we part company, I am afraid," said Theo, piercing me with his candid yellow eyes. "I don't know how to swim, and I confess I despise walking on this sticky, wet sand. I mustn't waste this chance to get back home. I hope you understand."

He leaped aboard and was swept up into the little girl's arms. I heard him purring effusively.

"*Au revoir!*" They all waved as the barge headed out. I clung to it with my eyes until it had disappeared entirely.

"*Non c'è due senza tre,*" Modi always used to say. Things happen in threes. Two boats have passed—surely there will be a third. I would just have to wait.

Nothing happened. Not a gull moved in the sky, or a crab on the sand. There was no movement but the waves and the swirling jellyfish. Further out circled the ravenous sharks of Maldoror. I walked up and down the beach, searching for materials to make a raft—branches and planks, reeds, bits of rope and wire. The planks were wormy and the bits of rope all rotten. I amused myself by populating the beach with mermaid sand sculptures and stringing black cockle shells on rusted wires to make wind chimes, which I hung in the withered branches stuck in the shoreline, except there was no wind. Finally, I sat and gazed out at the waves—my hair had grown back into a tangled mop like seaweed, all the way down to my feet. I buried my face in my knees and wrapped my hair around me. I had been marooned here for ages unknown. Even if I had wanted to return from where I had come, I did not remember where that was. There was a blue door somewhere in Paris, with Hebrew letters painted in a circle. That I knew, but I had no idea how to find it again. All my memories were drying up. I could not conjure up a single scene of my past life to comfort or distract me.

Then plop! Something fell at my feet from the sky—a shriveled red rose bud. The only spot of color in view. But where had it come from? A crow cawed. I looked up to see the creature spinning overhead, laughing at me as crows do. It brought me joy to see it again, and I waved. The bird looped and dipped. I could see it wanted to communicate something, but I could not make it out. It squawked three times and now seemed annoyed. Puzzled, I watched it fly out to sea, then return to croak at me and fly away again, as if urging me to follow.

I slipped off my sabots, shed my rough hemp robe, and walked to the water's edge. The scummy tide stained my toes with algae. Offering up a prayer, I stepped naked into the waves and a putrid blackness swallowed me whole.

Part 2
Ghosts of Montparnasse:
The Missing Madonna
1981

FROM THE BUSTLING STREET, I pass through the dark blue portal away from the clatter of traffic and cafés into a cobbled courtyard. The concierge isn't in, but I know where to go: straight through a door at the back and into an inner court, where the art studios of Gauguin, Modigliani, and Ortiz de Zarate used to be. Finding the annex door wide open, I slip inside and start up the winding staircase as a staccato of hammers and the whining of saws tumble down from above. The door on the third floor also stands open, revealing fervent renovation in the works. Stepping into swirling clouds of sawdust, I sneeze conspicuously, and a carpenter intent on fitting a shelf into the wall looks up at me and frowns.

"Bonjour. Je cherche Monsieur Gérard...."

"Bonjour, Mademoiselle."

An elderly man in a gray track suit picks his way toward me through a labyrinth of electric cords running the whole length of the flat. I have been given this appointment as a favor to my art history professor back in the States. I have come to Paris for a year to write a thesis on the Chilean artist, Manuel Ortiz de Zarate, whose studio was once located on these premises in the glorious years of Montparnasse. Through my professor's connections, I have been granted an opportunity to have a peek at the place. Monsieur Gérard, the flat's current owner, who has cordially consented to give me a tour, is well-versed in the history of his property.

"Ortiz lived in this apartment only for a very short time," he explains, guiding me with a touch of my sleeve through the empty, high-ceilinged room, where all around workmen are busy stripping moldy wall paper, ripping out rusted wiring, and prying away cracked tiles. "He and his family soon moved to the main building across the courtyard, a slightly more comfortable setting, but he kept this space as his atelier. He came from a very well-to-do family and preferred a greater standard of comfort than his upstairs neighbor, the Italian painter, Modigliani. His grandfather had been President of Chile— but you must know all that." He gives me a sidewise glance to gauge how much I do know.

"Yes," I said.

The doors have all been removed from their hinges, giving me stark glimpses of a tiny kitchen, a squalid water closet, a miniscule bathroom with

125

a grubby, lion-footed tub and sink, all just off the entrance and emitting the characteristic Paris stench of over-chlorinated water and bad drains.

"Running water wasn't put in until just before the war. Electricity instead a bit earlier." We stand in a large bare room fronted with huge windows. "This is where he worked. You see that protuberance where the wall curves outward? That was once a small fireplace, now walled up, the only heat they had. Here a platform for the models probably stood." He pauses as if giving me time to picture it as it was.

The room is unfurnished, except for a scarred trestle table and a straw-bottomed chair, illumined by a forty-watt bulb dangling from a wire overhead. I try to imagine the walls hung with Ortiz's paintings, models sprawled on threadbare couches, and the trestle table loaded with opulent displays of orchids and bananas, which Ortiz loved to paint. Maybe some messy palettes and crumpled tubes of paint strewn about. It feels like a room you could work in. I can see myself sitting at the table before the large windows, drinking coffee and typing away on my Olivetti Lettera 22, perhaps even writing a novel.

"Fifteen years or so before Ortiz occupied this space, Gauguin worked here briefly on his last visits to the capital before disappearing forever in Tahiti. Twenty years later, upstairs, as I said, lived the Italian painter, Modigliani, with his companion, Jeanne Hébuterne. You know the story?"

I nod. Who hasn't heard the Montparnasse myth of these star-crossed lovers? After Modigliani died of TB, Jeanne, pregnant with her second child, jumped to her death, unable to face life without him. She was twenty-one at the time, five years younger than I am now.

"Let me tell you something. The books have got it wrong. They say she jumped from her parents' flat over near the Pantheon. But that it isn't true. She fell from the studio upstairs." He hesitates, perhaps for effect, then continues earnestly. "When I was a child, there was a woman living in the building here who remembered that sad event and described to me how Jeanne looked, lying there in the courtyard, like a plump swan with a broken neck."

It sounds to me as if he has rehearsed this line before. Proud of this tragic legend and his resident ghosts, he points to the wide front window overlooking the courtyard, and I take a step closer. The image of a mangled, pregnant girl with long Pocahontas braids impresses itself vividly on my eyes, and I blink it away. He indicates a row of scraggly boxwood bushes in planters arranged around a shallow stone basin, from which emerges a dribbling spigot.

"That was where they got their water."

I see the girl again, bending to the spigot in a full blue skirt as water gushes into a tin pail, then carrying it heavily up all those steps.

"You aren't the first you know. People come all the time, asking to see the place. First, they go upstairs to see if someone's there, then, disappointed, they come here but I have nothing to tell them. That flat up there has been empty for at least ten years now. There have even been break-ins! They think that maybe Modigliani or Jeanne hid something there. One of his paintings, you know, behind a wardrobe, or a sketch rolled up and stuck in a crevice, or a portfolio under the floorboards. But there is nothing to be found there, nor here!" He looks at me sharply. "Modigliani's dealer, Zborowski, picked the place clean. And a dozen treasure-hunters have been over it since then."

When the tour is over, I thank him for his kindness. He gives some instructions to the men about closing the flat and steps out with me to the landing. "That was Modigliani's studio," he points up the stairs. I can see nothing but a helix of worn wooden steps rising in the gloom.

We go out to the courtyard and make our way to the exit. A light is on in the concierge's cubicle, where he stops to exchange a few words with a grim woman in a plaid housecoat and felt slippers, who gives me a long, hard stare. Perhaps she disapproves of my fedora, my jeans, my youth? Of young Americans in Paris?

As we say goodbye, I seize courage. "Would it be possible for me to come again, perhaps on a day when the workers are off? I would be so grateful. I feel it could help me in my research."

He gives me a canny look with his glacial blue eyes, "There is nothing here to be found, Mademoiselle."

"I am not looking for things," I bumble, "but rather atmospheres. Being in the place where Ortiz de Zarate lived and worked might help me identify with him, connect with him, in a way." I am astonished at myself for how bold I am being in French, but I press on, "I will touch nothing. I will just sit, read, think, and write for an hour or two."

He cocks his head at me in a Gallic way and gives me an ironic smile. "From six to seven on Sunday. You may ask the concierge for the key. Goodbye, Mademoiselle. Good luck with your research."

Pressing my hand with cold, dry fingers, he turns away and disappears down the street.

I can hardly believe my luck.

Sunday evening at six o'clock, the concierge hands me the key. As I climb the laborious steps, jazz from a radio somewhere worms out onto the stairs. I feel excited, apprehensive. The stairway seems dimmer, steeper, and much more slippery than I recall, and the light on the landing goes out before I reach the top. I stumble up the last few steps and grope for a switch. Overhead a feeble lightbulb flickers on with a crackling sound to illuminate the doorway. The key with blunted teeth fits deep into the lock. I prod until something clicks, and the heavy door swings open into the dark entryway.

Stepping inside, I hear a faint sound, like the scrape of a chair on a wooden floor, and I feel a prickling of panic. Suppose someone is hiding in here? No light comes when I flick the switch just inside the door. With blood beating in my ears, I hold my breath and listen keenly to faraway sounds, then decide the noise I heard must have come from a neighboring flat. There is still enough light straying from the windows to guide me inside, so I pull the door shut behind me.

The workers have cleared a path through the studio amid stacks of shelving and tangled cords. The wide windows present me with an arresting view of gray slate roofs and chimney pots against a lavender sky. Across the courtyard glitter bright yellow window squares with sheer curtains, behind which figures move. Looking down, I see once again the sad picture of the dead girl on the cobblestones. I close my eyes until it fades.

The February dusk is deepening over the Paris rooftops, and I didn't think to bring a flashlight or even a cigarette lighter or matches as I don't smoke. If the workmen have turned off the electricity, I have no idea where to look for the fuse box. I locate a light switch on the wall, and to my relief, the bare bulb overhead flashes on.

I sit down to the battered table mapped with deeply engrained blobs of crimson, cobalt, and dirty yellow. I fantasize that Ortiz worked here on this very table. From my backpack, I pull out a handful of reproductions and postcards, spread them out, and take out a notebook and pen. I read through my notes on Ortiz's Cubist period, which corresponded to when he had first occupied this studio, jot down impressions, but my eyes are drawn to the window, where the sky has darkened to a coppery cobalt, edged in the west with a luminous line of green.

Instead of Ortiz, I find myself still thinking about the girl who jumped and musing on the circumstances that led her to such an end. I have to remind myself why I am here: to soak up the atmosphere as inspiration for my work. I succeed in drafting a paragraph on Ortiz's still lifes and am soon absorbed. Then I become aware of a disturbance from upstairs.

Someone is walking, pacing rather, in the room right above me, in heavy shoes, in clogs or sabots. Three paces—stop. Two paces—stop; four, five, six—about face, and the footsteps turn in the opposite direction. I register this first only as an irritation— two things I hate when trying to concentrate are people walking overhead or loud music, but then a realization comes. The upstairs flat is supposedly empty and uninhabited, so who could be making that noise? The concierge, perhaps cleaning? Maybe what I hear is the knocking of brooms? As the footsteps persist, it occurs to me that if someone has broken in or entered without permission, I might be suspected, being a stranger in the building, if later something should turn out to have gone missing or been damaged. I close my notebook, stare at the ceiling, and attune my ears. The pacing has stopped, but now I hear distant voices: a man's angry tenor and a woman's plaintive wheedling. Unlike the footsteps, the voices are more diffused in space, I cannot tell if they come from upstairs, downstairs, or next door. Then a glass or bottle falls and shatters, shards skittering across the floor right above my head, as a man's hysterical, high-pitched voice screams, "Monstre! Merde!"

I jump in my chair, look up, and catch a ghostly face in the window before me.

"Excusez-moi, Mademoiselle," intones the concierge, who has come into the flat and crept up behind me in her silent slippers. "My orders are to close the apartment at seven."

Rattled by this apparition, I gather up my papers, give her the key, and leave the apartment. Hands on hips, she watches me from the top of the stairs as I make my way down the twists and turns, the heels of my boots resounding on the old worn wood.

Once outside again, my heart is pounding as if I have been going up and not down, and I feel relieved of some obscure oppression. The concierge's unexpected intrusion gave me quite a start, and I am puzzled by the ruckus I heard upstairs, which I surmise she must have heard as well.

Clearly it wasn't her slippered feet I had heard clunking around on the top floor. Before going out the door to the street, I glance up at the windows, where not a gleam of light appears.

❄

In my little black moleskin, Jules Renard headed my list of Paris contacts. He was a professor emeritus of the Sorbonne and had been mentoring my project on behalf of his former colleague, my thesis director back in the States. An expert on Montparnasse in the 1920s, he had furnished me with books, articles, bibliographies, letters of presentation for galleries and archives, all invaluable resources for the work I had come to do, and also a list of phone numbers and addresses of people to contact: scholars, dealers, experts. A few of these had been helpful, but many had led nowhere. One professor was away on sabbatical; another had died; a curator at a small museum would be unavailable while the place underwent renovation. Since my arrival in Paris two months ago in December, I had contacted nearly everyone he had recommended, except for Madame Annie Rosier, who had once modeled for Ortiz, and for a time also worked as babysitter for his two daughters. I had often tried phoning her, but no one ever answered. But that evening, after my first visit to Ortiz's flat, I called her number from a phone in a café on Boulevard Raspail. On the tenth ring, a withered voice replied.

"*Bonjour.* Madame Rosier?"

"*Oui?*"

"Professor Renard gave me your number."

"Who?"

"Professor Jules Renard, an art history professor from the Sorbonne."

"Never heard of him."

Oh dear, perhaps she was senile.

Still I pressed on. "I am an American art history student working on a doctorate on Manuel Ortiz de Zarate. Prof. Renard said you had known the artist personally and suggested you might be available for an interview."

"*Peut-être. Vous êtes américaine? Quel age avez-vous? Vous êtes étudiante, vous êtes artiste?*"

She asked several questions, including the spelling of my name and that of my professor, then after a deliberation so long I feared she had already hung up, said, "I do not remember meeting your professor and have no idea as to how he obtained my phone number. But you may telephone me next week, and I will give you my answer."

Every two weeks or so, Professor Renard and I would meet over coffee to discuss my project when he returned to Paris from his weekend place in Bordeaux. I didn't know many people in the city, and even fewer Parisians, and I spent my days poring over tomes in libraries and visiting museums alone, so I particularly enjoyed our encounters, always at a swank café in a different neighborhood. In his late fifties, suave, affable but reserved, he treated me as a younger colleague rather than a student and always picked up the tab, even when I insisted on paying. He was greatly knowledgeable about the period I was researching, and every café visit turned into an absorbing lecture.

At our next meeting at the Au Chien Qui Fume near Les Halles, he was curious about my visit to Ortiz's flat. "Did you discover anything of interest?" he asked as we sipped our coffee.

"That lots of people come looking for the traces of artists they love and admire."

"Did anyone come while you were there?"

"No, but I did hear someone upstairs where Modigliani used to work, which is supposedly uninhabited. Monsieur Gérard told me the studio has been broken into several times over the years."

"The Modigliani atelier has been more picked over than an Etruscan tomb, probably. After Modigliani died, it was occupied by Nina Hamnett and her Polish lover, who claimed they had found drawings and sketches tucked all over the flat, but it was later discovered they had fabricated them all. For a while they had a cottage industry going there, selling Modigliani sketches and even palettes! After them, an army of scavengers descended, looking for souvenirs, mostly. Some perhaps looking for the famous lost portrait by Amedeo Modigliani."

"A lost portrait?"

"Legends die hard in Montparnasse. A portrait of Jeanne Hébuterne and their child, which was said to have disappeared from the studio after the tragedy."

"A missing Madonna?"

"Perhaps! Other sources say that it was a portrait of the three of them, including Modigliani. But it may have been destroyed—by Modi himself, who often took a knife to his own canvases if he felt they were unsuccessful, or simply painted over them, as he sometimes did when running low on supplies."

"And it is believed it might be hidden in the flat?"

"Oh, that is one of many suppositions. Or in Nice where Jeanne gave birth and where they lived for a very brief time as a family. Or that the Germans confiscated it during the Occupation, or that it is concealed in a cave in Italy, and so on and so on…." He shook his head and threw up his hands. "If it existed at all."

I drained my café crème, musing on the legend.

"Better be careful," he warned, with a playful shake of his finger, "Or you, too, will be caught in the net of the *Cas Hébuterne* and deflected from your proper course. I am responsible for reporting on your progress to your university, after all."

"It is an intriguing story," I said, slightly annoyed by his patronizing attitude. "I also finally managed to contact Madame Rosier," I informed him. "She hasn't consented to an interview yet. She'll let me know next week if and when. By the way, she said she didn't know who you were."

He grimaced, and, tapping his forehead, leaned forward with a leery smile. "Old age is the devil. True, I have only met her once or twice, though we corresponded some years ago over a matter of mutual interest. Keep in mind she has a reputation for making things up. You can't be sure of everything she says. But she is a goldmine of anecdotes, gossip, and odd little facts few people know or remember, so it is worth taking the time to talk to her. But I hear she is mercenary. Prepare a fat little envelope." He summoned the waiter with an elegant flick of his hand.

"I am only a poor student on a grant!" I protested as he paid for our drinks with a handful of change.

"I'd suggest one thousand francs for an interview," the professor continued, as we wove our way between the tightly-packed tables out into the street where he hailed a cab. "Remember what I said, about Jeanne Hébuterne," he said, climbing in. "She is like the siren and leads only to a dead end. And if Madame Rosier tries to sell you an original sketch or watercolor, don't bite!"

❋

On Sunday around six p.m., I find myself just a block away from Rue de la Grande Chaumière, puzzling over a linguistic conundrum as I savor a glass of Sancerre. Monsieur Gérard said he would leave the key on Sunday from 6-7. He did not say "dimanche prochaine," but just "dimanche." This could be interpreted from a single Sunday to a stream of them. I reflect that the concierge must keep the key to give to the workmen or delivery men who don't work on Sundays, so it was probably still in her possession at this moment and available. If so, there would be no harm in going to ask for it. She could always say no and send me unceremoniously on my way.

From behind the floral curtains of her cubicle, pinned tightly shut, I hear the tinny sound of a television, the familiar theme song of Bonanza. I rap loudly on the glass. The curtain swishes aside, and Madame glares out. "What do you want?"

"May I please have the key to the studio?"

I expect a protest or flat-out refusal, but instead, she plucks the key from a rack, opens her door a crack, and drops it into my outstretched hand. The metal key is cold as ice, as if fresh out of the freezer.

"Remember. Only until seven o'clock."

Cooking smells, the rich odors of beef and onions braised in wine for a pot au feu, invade the staircase as I climb up, feeling furtive, like someone on the way to meet a secret lover.

The lock yields instantly, and the door swings open. It must have been oiled in the meantime. Inside I see the painters have been in. The floors are covered with plastic tarps, cans of paint are set about the room, and sample swatches of pink, lavender, and lime streak the walls. Two walls of the big studio room are freshly painted in a pale orangey yellow much in fashion this year. A mattress wrapped in plastic stands propped against the far wall, next to a box of kitchen things. Someone is moving in, and I am intruding.

I sit down at the table, take out my notebook and pen, and browse through my notes. I have written nothing about Ortiz since my previous visit. Soon enough, my concentration is interrupted by fleeting footsteps overhead. Then a long, low, tremulous note from a violin penetrates the dusk, riveting me to my chair with its unexpected intensity.

133

I soon recognize the melody: the opening bars of "Death and the Maiden," clumsily played by a student not quite in control of his instrument. The music stops abruptly and resumes as the same few measures are played over and over, at last unraveling into scales in a minor key.

Upstairs there is no thief or scavenger, I realize, but a musician who, perhaps, has arranged to use the apartment as a practice room, so as not to disturb the neighbors on the lower floors. Inexplicably, I am seized with curiosity to find out who is up there, and maybe have a peek inside the apartment. Given Ortiz's long friendship with Modigliani, my sudden interest seems justified in the name of my research. I step out of the flat and head up the stairway as the scales continue.

The stairs grow narrower and steeper near the top, and I am quite out of breath as I reach the landing. Outside the door, a threadbare green mat bears a dusty impress of small, round-toed shoes— those of a child or maybe a young woman with dainty feet. To the right, a brass doorbell with nameless plaque. I touch the bell, then press hard. It makes no sound as the music inside persists. I knock resolutely, and the music stops. A chair scrapes. I hear footsteps, a door closing. The timer clicks, and the light on the stairs goes off, leaving me in total darkness. I knock again, put my ear to the door, but can hear nothing more.

I find the light switch and descend to the next floor. When I unlock the door to Ortiz's studio, the door on the landing above me opens, and a chill breeze sweeps down the stairs, teasing the hairs on the nape of my neck. Someone stands there at the top, listening to me, as I listen back. Then the door upstairs creaks shut, and the breeze dies away.

An uneasy voice calls from below. "Qui est là?" The concierge appears round the curving stairway, feet clad in soundless slippers. "Ah, c'est vous. It's almost time." She peers anxiously up the steps towards the top floor. "You should go."

I retrieve my things and return the key, which she pockets without pausing, climbing past me on her way further up. I hear a loud knock from the top landing as I reach the bottom step.

"Assez! Assez!" Her voice booms down the stairs. "We have had enough of you and your violin!"

❋

I knew her at once, sitting in the cavernous shadows of the café, swallowed up by the cushions of a red plush sofa: a frail, shrunken woman in a mauve silk dress, with silvery hair glued in stiff waves to her skull, and a pasty mask of thick rouge and lipstick on her face. Before her a flute of champagne, its bubbles winking in the half light of a smoked glass chandelier dangling overhead.

"Oh, but you are very young," Madame Rosier said as I introduced myself. Then, "Why do young women wear these dockworkers' trousers? They are so unfeminine. Aren't they uncomfortable, hot and rough to tender skin?"

She gave me no time to apologize for my outfit, as her next comment was, "I am terribly hungry. Do you mind if I order a little snack while we chat?"

The waiter arrived and sized us up with a blink. Were we an odd couple? This figure lifted from a Toulouse-Lautrec, and me with my blue jeans, long brown hair beneath a fedora and a single silver earring of Navajo turquoise? The waiter gave no sign of having any opinion at all.

Madame ordered oysters and more champagne. I asked for a Perrier with lemon and nervously checked the prices on the menu, calculating sums in my head. I would have to use my credit card to pay for her snack. It was only to be used in the direst emergencies.

"But I do like your hat," she said.

"I bought it in Florence at a market." I was working hard to make my choppy French seem nonchalant and worldly.

"Ah, l'Italie. Yes, such a beautiful country," she sighed.

A platter of oysters on the half shell nestled in crushed ice was set down ceremoniously before her. She smiled in obvious pleasure, lifted a first oyster, speared it out of the shell and into her mouth, then tipped the shell to her lips. "It tastes of the sea. You sure you won't have one?" She proffered a shell in my direction. "They are very delicious." On her bony wrist, she wore a pretty bangle of Venetian glass, blue, green, and gold.

I declined politely.

"You Americans. You like everything sanitized. What is it you would like to talk about?"

"I am doing research on Manuel Ortiz de Zarate."

"You know I modeled for one of his great nudes: *Deux Nus*. I was the figure on the right. You have seen it?"

"Yes."

"Of course, you must have. Ortiz had two children and a very high-strung wife: Edwige Piechowska. I was hired to look after the brats; clean their bottoms and noses and braid their hair. When I first went to work for them, I was sixteen and fresh in from the country-side, but I was physically very mature. At that age, one was, then. And I caught his eye. Ortiz used to go into ecstasy over the rosy color of my skin." She patted her mouth with a napkin and took a sip of champagne.

"When painting of course, nothing improper ever happened between the two of us. He was a very respectable person and a devot-ed husband. Not like his upstairs neighbor, who made a point of seducing every model who walked in the door as a matter of pride. Like a true Italian."

"Amedeo Modigliani?"

"Ah, yes!" she smiled. "You have done your research! Poor *maudit* Modi. One heard things going on up there! *Mon dieu!* Bottles crashing to the floor! Him cursing like a demon in French and Italian. Jeanne did her best to keep him in line, poor dear. But she was just a young thing herself. And too soon carrying a child."

She caressed the bangle, and her eyes drifted away, then darted, puzzled, back to me. "What was I saying?"

"You were telling me about Modigliani and Jeanne."

"I was there when it happened, you know. When she jumped, or rather, purposefully fell out." She attacked another oyster.

"In Modigliani's studio?" I frowned.

"I know there are different reports in the books, but they are wrong. I witnessed the event. I was in Ortiz's studio, mopping the floor because one of the girls' little dachshunds had made a mess and I had to clean it up. I heard the thud in the courtyard and ran to the window. There she lay, face up, like a plump swan with a broken neck. It was heartbreaking."

She shook her head. "But that was so very long ago."

She sipped her champagne and smacked her lips.

I noted that those were the very words Monsieur Gérard had

used to describe Jeanne after her fall.

"I have visited Ortiz's studio," I said. "The owner let me have a look around. It's being renovated."

"Everything in Paris is being renovated. I suppose there is someone living upstairs, too?"

"I was told that it has been empty for years, but I believe I heard voices up there: a man and a woman arguing, and the sound of glass breaking. And the following week, I heard music."

She stopped swallowing oysters and stared at me fixedly. I could not read the emotion that flickered in those piercing eyes, which, after the briefest pause, now crinkled into silent laughter. Leaning forward with a smile of conspiracy, she slapped my hand lightly and whispered, "A violin. Schubert. "Death and the Maiden.""

"How did you know?" I was flabbergasted.

"She struggled so with the opening, with the attack. Couldn't get it just right. Practiced those few notes over and over. Dum de dum dum. I can almost hear it now. It used to bother Ortiz. He said it made his eardrums vibrate, but he never said a word to her about it. He was too much a gentleman."

"Who do you mean? Who struggled?"

"Jeanne, of course. Who do you think?"

I stared at her a moment—was she senile, or having me on? "Are you suggesting that I heard Jeanne Hébuterne playing her violin? Or her ghost?"

"Oh, what does that word mean—ghost? No, not exactly. But there are traces, traces that remain in the walls."

She punctuated those words with a penetrating stare, then drained her glass.

The café had filled up. At the adjacent table sat a pensive teenage girl, fingers wrapped around a cup of tea. A young man with long, prematurely gray hair, very Oscar Wilde, with a grubby silk shirt and floppy bow tie, puffed a Celtique and scribbled intermittently in a notebook, shooting glances at the girl drinking tea. Nordic tourists in unsuitable footwear dawdled over café crèmes and argued over a map of the metro.

I studied the old woman across the table, who seemed lost in her thoughts again. It was very odd that she knew exactly what music I had heard being played. It was also odd that she had repeated Monsieur Gérard's very words, but she may well have been the originator of that story. In any case, I was confident that a rational explanation for both these coincidences could be found if you poked around enough. Professor Renard had said that she was not 100% reliable, if at all, which made me wonder: why had he suggested I fork over 1000 francs to her for an interview if he believed her testimony was worthless? Obviously, he did not really think so.

Her eyes sharpened again, and she glared at me, piqued. "Ah, yes, Mademoiselle, you would like to interview me about my relationship with Ortiz. It was so very many years ago, and I have previously spoken to journalists and researchers about this all, and I am sure if you look hard enough you can find those interviews published somewhere. I don't think I have anything new to add."

I was grateful that the conversation had shifted from ghosts, but now had a more awkward topic to pursue. I might never have another chance to speak with someone who had actually known the person I was writing my thesis about. This woman, mad or not, was a piece of living history. I fumbled in my bag, drew out an envelope, and handed it to her.

"To express my thanks and my hope of being able to interview you in the future."

She peeked into the envelope and sighed.

"You are a young, idealistic woman. A scholar? An artist, a writer? It is kind of you to be interested in an old person like myself. Though truly, I lived through some remarkable times, the likes of which you young people today cannot possibly imagine."

She put my offering into her bag, a pink Chanel clutch, and snapped it shut. It occurred to me that I had just made a dreadful mistake.

"Why don't you visit me at home where I can show you a few photographs, paintings, and other relics of the past? Do call me in a week. I believe you have my number."

She rose shakily, picked up a silver-headed cane discretely tucked out of sight, and limped towards the door. Greeting the waiter familiarly, she went out to the street and disappeared into a taxi.

❀

The staircase tilted up towards the wall, so it was like climbing the whorls of a seashell, and the effort gave me a slight sense of vertigo. How did Madame Rosier manage all these stairs at her age and with that cane? I rang the bell. When the door flew open, there stood Madame in a sober blue dress with a pea-green scarf wound around her neck and crimson lips. A bluish rinse had been applied to her silvery waves since I had last seen her, and her nails painted blood red. From somewhere nearby came the shrill burst of a tea kettle. She led me to a cluttered salon, where not a free inch of wall space remained; crammed with mirrors, pictures, and faded photographs in chunky gilt frames, all in need of dusting. In the center of the room was a sagging couch draped with a sheet of worn green velvet, piled high with red plush pillows scattered with a few tufts of white dog or cat hair. On an end table by the couch were several photographs of Madame Rosier in the company of a young, dark-haired woman and a white Maltese dog.

I presented the bouquet I had bought, which she took in shaking hands, vanishing into a tiny kitchen to fill a vase with water and make some tea. As I sat down on the couch, a small cloud of dust wafted up from the cushions. Well-thumbed movie magazines and several shoe boxes brimming with photos, letters, and memorabilia were assembled on the coffee table. I took my tape deck out of my bag and set it on the table, as she wheeled in a squeaky cart where a teapot, cups, and a plate of pink macarons were deployed.

"Do you mind if I record our conversation?"

Sitting down beside me, she lifted the teapot, hovering over a cup as if to consider my request, then shrugged, pouring out a stream of yellowish liquid. "Why not preserve my voice for posterity?"

The fine china cup she handed me was cracked with age, chipped on the rim, as was the plate with two macarons. I took a nibble. The cookie tasted stale and sickly sweet, so I put it down. Madame touched neither tea nor cookie. I turned on the recorder.

Pushing horn-rimmed glasses over her powered nose, she set a box on her lap and plucked out a photo. "Now here I am at fifteen, before I went to live with Ortiz and his family...."

Nothing of this plump, buxom young girl remained, except the shrewd, challenging eyes, now lost in leathery folds.

Of the many photos she removed from the box in the hour that ensued, very few showed Ortiz or his work. There was a very faded one of Ortiz with Chaim Soutine taken in a studio in 1922. There was a recent one of herself in a sombrero, standing next to an Ortiz nude in a gallery in La Paz, pinned to a faded newspaper clipping in Spanish about the model's visit to a show of works by Ortiz. There wasn't much of interest for my research. I glanced at the other boxes on the coffee table, wondering if they held more of the same and how long it would take to go through them all.

"Do you have any photos of him in his studio while working? Or together with other artists, at exhibitions?" I asked, hoping to speed things up.

"There must be something of that sort. Now, here," she said, unfolding a piece of yellow paper, "we have a poster for the artists' carnival in 1919! That was an event to remember! Nothing nowadays can compare. The war had ended. People were celebrating, after all those senseless deaths."

Here was some information that might be worth recording. I opened my notebook, sat with pen poised. "You mean the Carnival of the Institute of Beaux Arts? Did Ortiz attend?"

The paper trembled in her hands. "Well, you can't expect me to remember that! He probably did. Everyone who was still alive wanted to be there. The 1919 Carnival was special because it could be publicly advertised with a poster. During the war, they had supposedly stopped all that—there was a curfew. Cafés closed at eight. But still, on occasion, especially during carnival week, smaller private parties were held even at the art academies in Montparnasse, midway through the war. That is how Jeanne and Modigliani met, in 1916. There were many celebrations around the quarter, in private studios and houses, in cafés and clubs; in the very streets. You'd see people in costumes parading about. One year the theme was Ancient Rome; another it was Egypt. I was supposed to stay in, at Ortiz's flat, looking after my charges. But now and then I managed to sneak out for a bit of fun of my own. As a popular model, I always could arrange an invitation wherever I desired." She adjusted the scarf around her neck, and her eyes glazed, perhaps remembering that time and how popular she was.

She shuffled through the box again and drew out another photo, held it to her nose for a long examination, and sighed. "You have no idea how rare this photograph is. A man from Israel came and offered me a good deal of money just for the privilege of making a copy, but I refused. I have no idea how he knew I had it." She handed it to me.

An intense young woman, dressed in a long, dark dress, stood beside an easel with a brush still in her hand, frowning as she studied her model: a man in a floppy-brimmed hat sitting across from her, one leg thrown over the other in a casual, dynamic pose. It was taken from a side angle, so that the woman was in profile, and the model's face was turned three quarters towards the camera. I peered closer at the man, thinking it must be Ortiz, but was surprised to recognize the fiery face of his upstairs neighbor: Amedeo Modigliani. One of Modigliani's great nudes hung on the wall in the background, next to another large painting, of which only the lower part was visible. It gave me a bit of a jolt to see that famous nude, quite recognizable in the photo, although blurry and faded, in the context of the studio where it was painted, instead of in a book or a museum. Studying the two figures, the girl at the easel and Modigliani in the chair, I assumed that the artist and his model had exchanged places when they posed before the camera, as a sort of game.

"It is the only photo in existence of the two of them working in the studio together. Ortiz took it. When Oritz emigrated to America by way of Switzerland, he left behind a bundle of papers which he entrusted to me and I found this among them."

"So this must be Jeanne Hébuterne."

"She was an artist, you see. Not many people knew that. A very talented artist. He was not only her lover, her husband, and the father of her children, but also her *maître*. He was teaching her, guiding her artistic career. He was a god in her eyes. Her passion for Modigliani was equaled only by her passion for her art. As a mother, well, she was too young to have taken on that responsibility, and he was certainly not much help."

I considered the woman holding the brush. "I didn't realize she was a painter. I thought she was just a model."

"Of course, you didn't know that! Hardly anyone does! It's been a secret all this time. Only her closest friends knew how talented she was."

"Kept secret by whom? Why?"

141

"By her family, of course. By her brother, André, first of all. He loathed Modigliani. He was furious with him for stealing his sister's affections while he was away at war. And then, maybe he was jealous that her talent might outshine his."

"Her brother was an artist?"

"An illustrator—a painter of landscapes and later exotic desert scenes."

"I confess I have never heard of him."

"I must have a photograph of him." She poked about in the box and drew out a postcard, showing a stern young man in a soldier's uniform. "Yes, this is André. He did all right in the end; made a name for himself. But her work had sparkle! It had true élan. After she died, he took it all away and locked it up in his studio, where it still is today, probably, if it hasn't rotted from mildew. Luckily, a few pieces escaped."

"It seems so unfair. To hide her work away from the world."

"Artists can be very competitive. Look at Picasso, for example. Now Ortiz, he was a generous man."

"And no one asked to know what happened to her work? No one ever wanted to see it? It just vanished, like that?"

"Jeanne was very reserved, rarely spoke in company, so that many people in Montparnasse thought she was not very intelligent, and believed her work could not interest anyone. But they were wrong. It was very difficult for a woman to be a painter back then. It took courage, determination. Today a woman may be whatever she desires, except perhaps… a woman. Not then. At the Atelier Julien, women students had to pay more than the men for their lessons!"

"It seems so sad that your own brother would censor your work and stifle your aspirations, and him being an artist, too!"

"That's not how it was exactly. André had been teaching his sister to paint. So it was doubly painful for him to lose both a beloved sister and a devoted pupil. And you can't blame him for disapproving of Modigliani, who was no ideal husband or companion. This is what her brother could not understand: Jeanne's acceptance of Modigliani's worst faults, the drinking, the other women, the drugs. André could not forgive her for choosing death with her lover and not life with her brother. Nor could he forgive himself for being unable to save her. He loved her dearly."

I scrutinized the photo of Jeanne and Modigliani, trying to guess the emotions of the two figures—what tensions, attractions or repulsions were threaded on their gaze. I felt as though I were peeking through a keyhole at some intimate exchange, at a moment torn from time and saved from ruin.

"So what this photo shows is her painting him rather than him painting her."

Madame nodded.

"Fascinating."

"More fascinating for what it doesn't show than for what it does."

"You mean the canvas on her easel we cannot see?"

"You are a sharp one. Yes, there's that, and then there's this."

As the withered finger with lacquered nail pointed to a detail in the background, the sleeve of her dress slipped up to reveal her wrist, encircled by the bangle of green and blue Venetian glass I had first noted at the café.

She was pointing to a canvas hanging on the wall, of which only the lower part was visible in the photo.

"You can look in every Modigliani catalogue ever published, and you won't find anything that matches this painting."

You couldn't tell much from the black and white photo—the hem of a dark skirt printed with a star-like pattern, and a pair of dainty women's feet.

"Another portrait of Jeanne?"

"A very special portrait."

I thought a moment. "Of Jeanne and her baby?"

"You are very clever!" she beamed at me.

"And what has become of it?"

She shrugged theatrically, with all the air of knowing the answer to that question.

A clock somewhere softly chimed six, and Madame yawned. We had been talking for nearly an hour and had hardly said a word about Ortiz. I tried to steer the conversation in that direction, but she was too tired. I punched the off button on the recorder.

"You will have to go now," she said. "Mimi will be waking soon, and we must have our constitutional."

143

I hadn't realized there was someone else in the apartment with us and I certainly did not want to overstay my welcome.

"Take these," she said, handing me a bundle of old magazines. "All I have had to say about Montparnasse and Ortiz can be found here. But return them next week, please. You may telephone me when you want to come."

I thanked her and put the magazines into my bag, along with my tape recorder and notebook. "I couldn't help noticing your bracelet," I said. "It's very pretty."

"Ah! The bangle. I never take it off. It was hers. He gave it to her when they were in the south of France, when Paris was being bombed by the Germans. It's Venetian, of course. He loved Venice. All painters love Venice. It is the ancestral home of all art."

"Did she give it to you?"

"Poor dear. No, Zbo's wife did. Leopold Zborowski was his dealer and patron of sorts. His wife, Hanka, gave it to me as a memento, because on that horrible day, I helped wash and dress poor Jeanne, and then after the funeral, the apartment had to be cleaned and made ready for its new tenants. It was a terrible mess, empty tins and bottles, and bloody rags all over the place. Jeanne wasn't much of a housekeeper, and in the last weeks of her pregnancy, she had let everything go, and then Modigliani fell ill. Hanka and Zbo gave me a few things of Jeanne's—nothing of any value, of course—as keepsakes to thank me for my help."

She accompanied me to the door. "I admired her you see. I, too, wished to paint. But I didn't have the courage. Or the money to take lessons. Not then. She was only three years older than I."

"Did you ever? Become a painter?" I gazed round at the scores of paintings, mostly mediocre, cluttering her walls.

She shook her head. "It is my one regret."

We said our goodbyes. I stepped out to the landing and began a careful descent down the whorls.

"Don't forget," she called, as I rounded the helix into invisibility. "Don't forget to go back and see Jeanne. She gets lonely up there all by herself."

❅

I spent the next few days reading the interviews in *Elle, Vogue,* and *Art News*, which were of mild interest. The articles were more about Annie Rosier herself than anything to do with Manuel Ortiz de Zarate, but I suppose I couldn't have expected more. Still, I managed to glean a few useful biographical details about life in Paris at that time. As Sunday approached, I grew apprehensive. I was intrigued by the ghostly violinist but intimidated by the bad-tempered *concierge,* and concerned that perhaps the new tenants had already moved in. I made my decision rather too late, for it was already ten past six when I turned the corner onto Rue de la Grande Chaumière: a narrow street of gray and cream-yellow stone buildings with dark blue fixtures and black iron grilles. Cool and reserved on a late Sunday afternoon, it probably looked very different now from what it must have been when the Académie Colarossi was operating just a few doors away from Ortiz's studio. The streets would have been flooded with scruffy artists from all over the world, lodging in flop houses around the corner and dining *chez* Rosalie nearby in Rue Campagne-Première.

That afternoon, the sophisticated bookshops, boutiques, and the print shop were all closed. Only a café with its vintage façade reading "*Vins et Liqueurs*" was open, the waiters setting tables for the evening shift.

I saw immediately that something was wrong as I quickened my pace. The dark blue portal was shut, and there was no bell to ring. I stood outside the door in acute disappointment, then wandered back home to the flat I was subletting on the Île Saint-Louis.

The next day, when I phoned Madame Rosier to arrange a time to return her magazines, a different woman answered. I heard the staccato yapping of a dog in the background.

"*Qui êtes-vous? Que voulez-vous avec ma tante? Tais-toi petite bête!*"

My awkward explanation about the magazines was continuously interrupted by the dog's furious protests.

"*Bon.* Bring them back by four o'clock. After that I am going out."

At a quarter to four, I rang the bell and the door to Madame Rosier's apartment opened. A busty, youngish woman in tight jeans and enormous sunglasses appeared, obviously just on her way out, a cigarette hanging from pouty, painted lips. From one wrist dangled a string shopping bag; in the other hand, she clutched a red leather leash attached to the rhinestone collar of a long-haired, well–combed little white Maltese. Its nails skittered across the floorboards as it jumped up and down in excitement, barking like mad.

"I have brought back Madame's magazines, and a gift." I held out a little package of pink and green macarons from Fauchon and put my offering and the magazines on a table in the entryway.

The woman took a puff of her cigarette as she considered the package and exhaled a plume of smoke in my direction. For some reason, she seemed faintly amused.

"My aunt can't eat those, I am afraid. She's diabetic. And at the moment she is on a liquid diet at the Salpêtrière hospital."

"I am so sorry! Is she very ill?"

"Not ill, just old and worn out. And lucky to have lived as long as she has."

"When was she hospitalized?"

"Last night. Cardiac crisis. I doubt that she'll ever come home again."

Looking past her shoulder, I noted changes had already been made to the flat. An Indian bedspread now covered the sagging couch, and many pictures had been removed, leaving bald rectangles on the walls.

"Is she able to receive visitors?"

She scrutinized every inch of me and inhaled lengthily in deliberation. "Why not? Might cheer up the old bird." She stubbed out her cigarette in an ashtray on the table, as the dog tugged the leash.

"How do I find her? That hospital must be huge."

Still restraining the prancing dog, she reached for a pen on the table, tore off a scrap from the cover of one of the magazines I had brought, and scribbled something across it.

"That's the building number and ward. On the second floor. Just ask at the front desk right at the entrance."

I went straight to the hospital from Madame's flat.

Salpêtrière isn't just a hospital but a city within the city. Originally built in the sixteenth century to house the vagrants and homeless of Paris, it soon became one of the world's most celebrated insane asylums. Now a functional general hospital in the heart of the city, with countless buildings, annexes, and lanes running in between, it is a veritable labyrinth.

I ascended a staircase, followed a white corridor of anonymous, closed doors of steel and glass, and at last found the room with two white beds in hushed semi-darkness. To the far left, an inert body lay facing the wall. To the right, by the window, Madame Rosier dozed, wrapped in a pale blue robe, for once relieved of her make-up mask. A lowered blind filtered out the afternoon light. I looked about for a place to put the red and purple anemones I had purchased at a stall near the entrance to the hospital. There was a bedside table with a flask of water and a cup, an eyeglass case, and a magazine, but no vase for flowers or any space for them.

I sat for a while on the folding chair next to the bed, clutching the bouquet in my lap and watching her breathing. She stirred, coughed, and turned her head on the pillow. Her eyes fluttered open, and she frowned.

"Hello, Madame Rosier. Do you recognize me?"

"*Oui, oui. Je vous reconnais!* For a moment I thought you were someone else. How did you know I was here?"

"Your niece told me when I returned the magazines."

"Never mind the magazines." Groaning, she shifted in the bed. "Give me my glasses. There on the bedside table."

I removed them from the case and handed them to her. "How are you feeling? I hope you recover soon."

"Recover! Isn't it obvious I am going to die here!" She put her glasses on. "Far away from my darling Mimi."

"Your niece?"

"*Mon dieu*, that bitch. No, Mimi is my adorable little Maltese! She'll get it all now, what she has always wanted. The apartment. The dog. The paintings. But this is nonsense. I don't know what I am doing here. I swallowed some air and started to hiccup. The next thing I knew she had called an ambulance. *S'il vous plaît, un peu d'eau.*"

Placing my bouquet on the foot of her bed, I poured her a cup of water from the flask on the bedside table.

"She poisoned me, the ingrate. Has been doing it for years. Hence I am in this state."

With both hands she lifted the cup to her trembling lips, quaffing the water down like a survivor from the desert.

"It is good of you to come. Did you go back to see Jeanne?"

"You mean back to Ortiz's studio? No. Well, I went there, but found the main door closed and I couldn't get in."

"You were lucky to have heard the music even once." She took a deep, wheezing breath. "Have you progressed with your work? You are writing a book, was it? About Modigliani and Jeanne?"

"No, I am writing a thesis on Ortiz. I interviewed you about that."

"Ortiz, a worthy subject. But Jeanne and Modigliani, so much more to say." She noticed the bouquet on the bed. "Anemones! Is it spring yet?"

"It's February, so not quite."

"*Oui*. In the spring, we will go to Nice. To see the almond and cherry trees in bloom." Her breath snagged again, and she closed her eyes. Her head sunk deep into the pillow.

I got up to leave so that she could rest and moved the flowers to the window ledge.

"Open the blind a bit. I want to see the light," she said.

I complied. Outside I could see orderlies wheeling shrunken old people bundled in blankets in the cold bitter light.

"Open this drawer, please," she ordered sharply, with a complete change of tone. Her index finger jabbed towards the bedside table. I slid open the drawer to find a rosary and a wad of tissue inside. I thought she wanted the rosary.

"Is this what you want?" She stared at me uncomprehending and shook her head.

"*Pas ça*. That's not mine. The nuns bring those to everyone. There must be something else."

I picked up the tissue wrapped around an object: her blue-green glass bangle.

"Your bracelet?"

"*Prends–le*." Her eyes were closed again, and she had switched to the informal address. *Tu*. Did she even know who I was?

"Take it."

I thought she meant that I should hand it to her. "*Le voilà*," I held it out to her.

"No, it is for you. *Un cadeau*."

She obviously didn't know who I was or what she was saying. "I can't accept this. It means so much to you. Are you sure you want to give it away?"

"That is exactly why." Her eyelids popped open like a doll's, and she glowered at me. "It means so much. It mustn't get lost! Don't be stupid. Here one of the nurses will steal it. Or she'll get it! *Et puis*, it has no value. Put it on"

I slipped the glass circlet on my wrist. It caught a ray of light from the window and gleamed eerily.

"It fits you perfectly and looks very pretty. I am sure Jeanne won't mind you having it."

"Thank you. I shall treasure it," I said uneasily and caressed the cool glass.

"And well you should! And there is another thing." She glanced furtively to the far side of the room, where the woman in the other bed lay motionless. "Is she asleep or dead, that neighbor of mine? No matter. Come closer. The walls have ears."

I bent down so that she could whisper in my ear. "There is something you must do for me."

"If I can," I said, hoping it wouldn't be too problematic.

"At the end of my street is a shop selling secondhand books. Tell him I sent you there and ask him to give you the envelope."

"Tell him? Tell who?"

"Monsieur Ravi. The bookseller. Show him the bangle." She sat up to clasp her fingers around the bracelet she had given me, then fell back on the bed. "He'll know what it means."

"*Bonjour!*" A nurse breezed into the room and swiftly closed the blinds again.

"*Enfin, Madame a de la visite.* Are you a relative?"

"Just a friend!"

"Madame must have her medicine now. We can't have her tired out. You may come again tomorrow."

"I left those flowers on the ledge, as I didn't know what to do with them."

"I will take care of them—just leave them there." The nurse busied herself with reading through the patient's chart, then stuck a thermometer into Madame Rosier's armpit.

Madame Rosier sought my hand and squeezed it hard. Tears glinted behind her glasses.

"I will come back tomorrow, if you'd like me to," I said.

"Tomorrow is too late. Come closer. I have left something there with Ravi. Whatever you do, don't let her have it or know anything about it. You mustn't tell a soul."

"Madame Rosier, you mustn't get excited. Your friend will come back tomorrow." The nurse prepared a cup of pills. "She is very tired. Sometimes she speaks nonsense. Come back when she has rested." She removed the thermometer, checked the temperature, and seemed satisfied.

"I trust you'll know what to do with it," hissed Madame Rosier.

"I'll do my best," I said uncertainly. It seemed such a strange request.

"You must," she said urgently.

"That's enough, Madame. Your medicine." The nurse held out the cup of pills and a glass of water. She gave me a sharp look and rolled her eyes, suggesting that the patient wasn't quite in her right mind, and in any case, I should leave.

Madame Rosier swallowed her pills, then lay back rigidly, eyes wide open drifting in the dim room.

Coming out of the hospital, I got out my map to figure out what bus route to take home, but I couldn't make heads or tails of it. A light blue Citroyen Dyane was parked across from the entrance, and a man was sitting inside, probably waiting for someone.

I walked over and rapped on the window, which, after a moment, slid open.

"*Excusez-moi.*" I leaned into the car. "I am bit a lost and I need to go to Île Saint-Louis." I pushed my wrinkled map towards him. "Where can I get a bus?"

The man seemed quite startled by my question and rather amazed to see me. I thought I had woken him up from a doze, or perhaps had interrupted some other activity. Or maybe he just couldn't understand my French. He had an odd, angular face with pale gray eyes and a nasty scar on his cheek. I suppose he didn't really look like the sort of person you should ask for directions. But after a brief hesitation, quite cordially, he took the map in hand and pointed out where to get the bus for the Gare d'Austerlitz, which would continue on towards the Île. Then sliding the window shut, he drove away.

✽

150

The next day was lost. Part of my grant obligations included giving a series of five lectures to art history students on a study abroad program. The day after my visit to Madame Rosier, I was informed by the program leader that my first lecture had been rescheduled, in order to cover for one of the other professors who had taken ill. I had only two days to prepare a talk on women artists and the female nude. I spent the next twenty-four hours holed up in the apartment I was subletting on the Île Saint-Louis, going over my notes and accompanying slides. Needless to say, I had no time to check out the bookshop in Madame Rosier's street, or even to go back to the hospital, which I felt very guilty about. I planned to go see her the afternoon right after my lecture.

Only seven students showed up to my lecture that Monday—all women, except one male student, older than the others, my age or perhaps a year or two younger. With typical Gallic ruddy coloring and long sandy hair swept over a broad forehead, he had a fleshy mouth and blue eyes set in a perpetually amused look, which in American men would have seemed smug, but in him seemed attractive. He had a good build, disguised by sloppy, paint-smudged combat pants, and wore a thick cotton mustard-colored sweater, and red sneakers. He sat alone in the front row and followed with rapt attention, and as I expected, or perhaps, hoped, came up to speak to me after it was over. He introduced himself as Paul Marteau, a performance artist, who was auditing the course to improve his English. He asked several vague questions I couldn't answer properly, partly because I was in a hurry to get away. In the meantime, two girls had come forward to speak to me as well, probably drawn by Paul's presence, and he suggested we all go to a café to carry on the conversation. I declined, for though I found him intriguing, I wanted to go over to the hospital to see Madame Rosier before it got too late.

"I'm sorry, I will have to take a rain check," I said, putting my slides into my backpack.

He looked at me blankly, and I laughed, realizing that he didn't understand this idiomatic expression. "You say that when you can't accept an invitation, but you'd like to do it another time."

"Oh, I see!"

"I'd love to talk to you, but I have to see a friend at the hospital.

She's at Salpêtrière. I can't be late, or they might not let me in."

"I am sorry for your friend. Do you want me to take you there with my scooter? You'll get there faster."

"Yes," I said, although I had never ridden on one.

And there I was flying through the thirteenth arrondissement, holding onto my hat with one hand, my other arm entwined around Paul's waist, and one cheek pressed to his dirty sweater reeking of turpentine, tobacco, and sweat. Bumping over cobblestones and weaving in and out of traffic, we tipped dizzyingly on curves and were finally delivered to the entrance of the building where Madame Rosier's ward was located.

"Be careful getting off. Don't touch the exhaust pipe," he warned. Awkwardly I dismounted, grateful for my sturdy boots as I smelled singed leather when my ankle grazed the pipe.

"Well, thanks so much. I suppose I'll be seeing you at school."

"A friend of mine is having an opening in the Marais. Tonight. Any time after nine."

I felt tempted but tired, and hesitated to reply.

He pursed his lips in a pout. "Please come to 34 Rue des Archives. I will wait for you."

With that, he sped off.

Faint cracks of light were visible through the slats of the blinds, tightly drawn. Drooping in a glass of water on the ledge were the anemones I had brought days ago, half their petals shed. Madame Rosier's bed was empty.

I glanced at the other bed, where Madame's neighbor, now awake, lay watching me, propped up on her pillows.

"*Elle est morte ce matin*," she said drily, then yawned. "Poor thing."

I was aghast and saddened by the news and cursed myself for not having visited her again. I looked about for a nurse to ask further information, but there didn't seem to be anyone around.

In tears, I ran back out of the building and found my way to the bus stop and then to the metro. I went straight to Madame Rosier's street, planning to search for the bookshop. It wasn't a very long street, and I walked up and down it several times, but couldn't find any booksellers. By now it was after seven, and places were closing up or already shut. There was a butcher, a wine shop, a cheese shop, a shoe shop, a shop selling wigs, a dry cleaner's, a button shop, a newspaper kiosk, two cafés, a pharmacy, and a small church—but no bookshop. One or two storefronts were boarded up. Peering in, I saw abandoned mannequins and dusty, dismantled shelving; they had gone out of business a long time ago.

I asked the shopkeepers if there had ever been a bookshop on the street. Only the wig-seller vaguely remembered a place from ten years earlier or more. Occasionally, as the man at the newspaper kiosk informed me, street peddlers came by with old books.

An elderly man stood browsing newspapers at the kiosk as I questioned the proprietor.

"*Mais oui. Vous le connaissez.* Monsieur Ravi. The Indian gentleman. He had a shop where the shoe shop is now. He dealt in old art books."

"I wouldn't know. I took over this kiosk only five years ago," grumbled the proprietor. "The shoe shop was already here then."

"Yes, you still see him bumbling around the neighborhood. On Fridays sometimes when the market sets up in the square. Every other Friday."

"Wednesday. The market is every third Wednesday," the newsagent corrected him.

"Wednesday, you say? Perhaps you're right. That would be the way to find him, Mademoiselle. When he brings old books to the market."

"That would be next week on Wednesday," said the proprietor. "You should try then. Now are you going to buy something or not before I close up?"

I bought a copy of *Paris Match* and then found my way to the Marais, thinking that a little company would do me good after the shock of Madame Rosier's death.

❃

"Here's your drink," said Paul, holding out a glass of cherry-colored fizz with a sharp vodka bite, David Bowie's "Ashes to Ashes" booming in the background. The bar from which he had served my drink had been fashioned from a supermarket cart which he was wheeling around to the guests while on roller skates. The large drafty space where the party was going on must have previously been a storehouse and now was the swank private studio of one of Paul's friends. The rooms were packed with bizarre sculptures made of medical skeletons, stringed instruments, and supermarket carts assembled in surreal sequences. Somehow it fit in with my most recent visit to Salpêtrière.

"How's your friend at the hospital?" he asked as we sipped our drinks in a quieter corner.

"Actually, I just found out she died. I went to the hospital, and she was gone."

"What a terrible shock."

"It was. But she was quite elderly, and apparently had a heart condition. Perhaps it wasn't that unexpected."

"I am sorry. Were you quite close?"

"I didn't know her that well. Her name had been given to me as a possible resource for my thesis project. I interviewed her a couple of times. But I liked her, even though she was a bit eccentric."

"How so?"

"I think she believed in ghosts."

Paul laughed. "Paris is full of those."

I wasn't in the mood for dancing, so Paul took me to his own atelier in the studio and showed me a project he was working on—a layered collage of hand-drawn, annotated Paris maps with bits of rubbish glued to them. He explained that he asked friends and strangers to draw him a map of their favorite corner of Paris and send it back to him with something they found in the street. There were cigarette butts, paper scraps, lost buttons, matchboxes, and a rhinestone earring. I found both the project and Paul clever and engaging, so when he suggested we might meet occasionally for language exchange, I was thrilled. I didn't know many people in Paris. The other teachers at the study abroad program were older, settled expats, with their own circle of friends and activities. They were nice enough, but I hadn't really hit it off with anyone there. I spent a lot of lonely evenings and weekends on my own.

"My English is so bad," he grumbled with self-deprecation, "And I will help you with your French, which is much better than my English."

I smiled at his compliment, which of course wasn't true. "I don't agree, though. It seems to me your English is excellent."

"You're too kind," he said. When he squeezed my elbow, sparks traveled up my arm.

We arranged to meet again on Sunday after lunch, at the Tuileries Gardens, to visit the Maillol sculptures.

"Tell me about your project," said Paul as we rambled on barren lawns beneath a black lattice of naked branches. I told him about Ortiz, Professor Renard, and Madame Rosier, and as I rattled away, he gently corrected my French verb tenses.

"We have friends in common," he said, plucking my sleeve as we sat on the cold iron chairs in the gardens, contemplating one of Maillol's busty bronze ladies.

"Who?"

"Jules Renard. He is the one who suggested I attend your class at your school to improve my English a bit. He was one of my profs at the Sorbonne."

"Oh really! I am surprised he didn't mention it to me, so that I could look out for you."

"He probably was afraid I might embarrass him, knowing what a poor student I am," he grinned.

"He must be very brilliant. He seems to know a lot about Modigliani and Ortiz."

"I believe he is working on a new book about Montparnasse."

"Madame Rosier was a walking history book on that topic. I could have listened to her for hours. She must have known them all personally. I will miss talking to her. Even though...."

Crows swooped down from the wintry trees and pecked the ground near our feet. One came so close, I could have caught it in my hand.

"Even though?"

"Professor Renard said she often embroidered the truth, which may be why her stories were so intriguing."

"In what way?"

"Well, for one thing, Jeanne Hébuterne's death. Most sources have it that Jeanne fell from her parents' flat, but Madame Rosier says Jeanne fell from a window in Modigliani's studio and that she herself was there when it happened, downstairs in Ortiz's flat. She used to babysit his children. That's why she was there."

"Why would she say that if it weren't true?"

"To impress people or acquire authority in some way. It makes for a good story when talking to journalists, especially if they are paying for an interview. Or maybe she was a bit senile. I don't know."

"Never trust an eyewitness!" he laughed.

"And then she was almost obsessed about a portrait of Jeanne Hébuterne and Modigliani's daughter, which she claimed has gone missing."

"I have heard stories about missing Modiglianis—probably just rumors put in circulation by the forgers."

"Could be. But Professor Renard mentioned it too. And when I visited the atelier, the owner told me people had been breaking in for years to scavenge the flat."

"You have visited the Modigliani atelier?" His interest had quickened.

"I visited Ortiz's atelier, on the floor below. My professor back in the States happens to know the owner and put me in contact with him, so I was allowed to have a peek. It's odd though. When I was there, I heard footsteps, voices, music, and a violin upstairs in the old Modigliani atelier, even though the flat was supposedly empty. Madame Rosier suggested I had heard their ghosts. She seemed quite convinced of that."

I suddenly felt uncomfortable as I said this and thought perhaps I shouldn't be talking about these things. Not that I believed them. Or did I?

He laughed again. "Perhaps she was pulling your leg?"

I shrugged.

"Then what do you think about it?"

"Those old buildings with wooden beams and floors transmit sounds in odd ways. The noise could have come from downstairs or next door."

I looked at my watch. It was five o'clock. The gardens would probably be closing soon. "Would you like to see the apartment? The owner leaves the key for me so I can go up and work for a bit. I like being inspired by the life that went on there." I instantly regretted my words. Monsieur Gérard might not like me going there with other people, especially with a man. He might get the wrong idea of why I wanted the key to the flat.

"How far is it?"

"It's only a half hour walk from here, straight down Boulevard Raspail."

"And do you think we will meet the ghosts?" he teased.

"I don't know."

"*Allons-y.*" He pulled me up from my chair.

✳

Bonanza is on again—the concierge drops the key into my open palm through the crack of her open door. Paul stands discreetly to one side near the staircase, and she doesn't notice him at all. Climbing up, we hear music and laughter from the other apartments on the landings. I precede him up the steps.

I fuss with the lock while Paul leans close, lightly pressing his hand to the small of my back. I feel flustered and excited. I am not sure myself why I have brought him here, but from the warm pressure of his hand, radiating through layers of denim and wool, I understand he has his own idea of what is going to happen here.

When the door swings open, I see the renovation has progressed. Two lime-green armchairs have been delivered, and several packing cases have arrived. Someone is definitely moving in soon. I hope they won't choose this evening to make a visit to the flat and discover the two of us here. I switch on the light.

"Sympa! Give me a tour."

Tugging him by the hand, I take him through the rooms, then we return to the studio to stand before the big front windows overlooking the courtyard, watching the dusk fall over the rooftops. When he starts kissing me, I have to keep coming up for air, until he hoists me onto the table by the window and pins me down with his knees. My feet in my boots stick out beyond the table edge in a very uncomfortable position, yet my body yearns for his. Even so, I am not ready for this.

"Wait," I say, twisting away from him, trying to prop myself up on one elbow.

"Why? Why else did you bring me here?" he smirks.

"I don't really know," I say, "I like you, but you are going too fast."

The bare bulb overhead shines straight into my eyes—an incandescent gash flicks over my retina. It occurs to me that anyone across the way might see us through the wide, uncurtained windows.

"At least turn off the light," I say.

"Why?"

"Please," I said, "Turn it off. Someone might be looking."

"An American prude," he mutters. I can't tell if his tone is joking or annoyed, but he complies with my request and reaches under my shirt to unhook my bra.

Just then a bottle breaks straight overhead—splinters skid on the floor.

I untangle myself from him and sit up, staring wide-eyed at the ceiling. "There! Did you hear that?"

He frowns at me incredulously. "Quoi? I heard nothing."

※

The next Monday, Paul didn't show up for my afternoon lecture. I waited ten minutes before starting, in hopes that he would arrive and afterwards went home in a gloomy state. By Tuesday night, still no news. There was no way to contact him unless he came to the school. He hadn't asked to exchange numbers, and anyway there wasn't a phone in my flat. I was very disappointed by his disappearance and cursed myself for taking him to see the atelier. Given the astonishment on his face when I remarked on the noise from upstairs, he probably thought I was nuts. And what if word had got back to Monsieur Gérard that I had been there with a man? All things considered, that had probably been my last visit to the Ortiz atelier.

When Wednesday morning rolled round, I headed over to Madame Rosier's neighborhood to see if I could locate Ravi, the bookseller. The mystery attached to this task at least helped keep my mind off Paul a little. As promised, amid the junk stalls set up in the square beneath a barren plane tree, were several carts of old books. A gaunt young man with pea-green eyeglasses and a red-checked shirt stood near the cart—I couldn't tell whether he was a customer or the vendor. I browsed through the crates stacked high with cheap paperbacks in various languages: nothing much of interest and certainly nothing artistic.

"Monsieur Ravi?" I asked doubtfully.

The man in the pea-green eyeglasses glanced up at me from his paperback.

"I am looking for Monsieur Ravi. I am told he sells books here."

"You'll find him over at that café." He pointed across the street where a plump older man with a goatee and an astrakhan hat sat perusing a newspaper.

Crossing the street, I approached his table.

"Monsieur Ravi?" He looked up at me through bifocals as thick as an aquarium wall, where dark eyes darted. I could smell the pungent fennel in his glass of steaming tea.

"Madame Rosier," I began, and his brow furled at this name, as though hearing it caused him pain or displeasure, "who lived here on this street at number 32…."

"I know her very well," he said impatiently. "What do you want?"

"I am sorry to tell you she is dead," I blurted out. "She died a few days ago."

He seemed startled by this news, and his manner grew gentler. "I am terribly sorry. Please sit down. What can I do for you?"

Announcing Madame Rosier's death to this stranger had almost brought me to tears. The strength had dwindled in my legs, and it was a relief to sit down. He motioned for more tea to be brought. The sweet herbal brew was so hot it burned my tongue, but after I had taken a sip, I could continue.

"She said she had left something for you to give to me. I have no idea what it is. It's in an envelope."

He stared at me intently.

"She said I was to show you this." I thrust out my arm to reveal the blue glass bangle beneath my jeans jacket sleeve.

"Ça suffit," he said, and his warm brown hand with hairy knuckles clamped over mine to hide the bracelet from view. From across the street, the gaunt man in green glasses was following our conversation with interest.

"We don't want to attract attention. Yes, she left a packet. Please come with me to my storeroom when we have finished our tea."

We sipped in silence and then he asked, "What happened to Annie?"

"I didn't know her well and I don't exactly how she died. She was hospitalized for a cardiac crisis. When I went to see her, she seemed all right. That's when she asked me to find you and show you the bangle. But when I returned to visit her after the weekend, they told me she was dead. That was a week ago Monday."

"A very, very great pity. Come with me now." Rising, he tossed some coins on the table.

Across the street, the man with green eyeglasses was talking to someone—a tall man with stooped shoulders and a pork pie hat. There was something familiar about the tall man, about the way he held his shoulders, although I couldn't see much of his face. Or maybe he just resembled someone from the school. Now seeing that I had noticed him, he turned his back to me and picked up a book.

"Something wrong?" asked Monsieur Ravi.

"Nothing," I said, after the slightest hesitation, and shook my head.

I followed Monsieur Ravi into an unlit entryway, and down a treacherous spiral of steps where everything stank of drains. We passed a room with overflowing garbage cans, then wound further down to an old iron door. Switching on a dim light, he produced a key, and we entered a cave of books, bric-a-brac, and broken furniture. There were books crammed on shelves, piled on every surface, spilling out of crates. The strong smell of moldy pages and damp earth made me sneeze.

He vanished among the stacks, where I heard him rummaging about, moving piles of books and boxes until he must have found what he was looking for. He returned with a brown envelope and plunked it down on the cluttered surface of an old rolltop desk near the door.

"I assume that is what you have come for."

"I have no idea. She said it was important."

He looked at me hard as he handed it over. "Good luck."

"Thank you."

"And again, my condolences for your friend."

❋

I headed back up the stairs to the noisy, sunlit street, leaving Monsieur Ravi in his musky cavern. Not knowing what treasure I held in my arms, but bursting with curiosity, I peeked inside the envelope as I waited at the bus stop. I discovered a bundle of the same movie magazines I had seen that Madame Rosier collected. Perhaps she was senile after all.

Once I got home to my flat, I dumped the contents out on the couch. The smiling faces of Alain Delon and Audrey Hepburn spilled from the envelope, along with candy wrappers, cancelled bus tickets, receipts. In the midst of this litter, a tightly folded newspaper from June 1960 was wrapped around a small parcel that felt like a book. Unpeeling the pages, I found three old notebooks bound together by a frayed gold ribbon with a handwritten note pinned to the front.

To whom it may concern:

On the afternoon of January 26, 1920, I was asked by the art dealer Leopold Zborowski to accompany his wife Hanka to Amedeo Modigliani's studio at 8 Rue de la Grande Chaumière, where I was to assist her while she tended the poor pregnant body of Jeanne Hébuterne, Modigliani's wife, who had committed suicide by falling out the window after Modigliani died at the Charity Hospital on January 24. The studio was in a terrible disarray—remains of meals, bottles, paint tubes, trash, blood-stained linens, and rags were everywhere. All that had to be got rid of, and the place wiped down with bleach, as Modigliani was consumptive. The apartment was going to be leased to a new tenant, and I was asked to help clean the rooms and make them ready. In exchange for my service, Hanka gave me a small memento—Jeanne's glass bangle that she always wore, which Modigliani had given her during their time in Nice. After Hanka and her friend, Gosia Lisiewicz, prepared Jeanne for the undertaker, I remained alone in the studio to finish cleaning up, and while doing so, I found a small notebook , which I knew to be Jeanne's, for I had once seen her writing and sketching in it at the Café du Dôme. I knew Jeanne well, as I lived with Ortiz's family in the studio below, and I selfishly wanted to keep this memory of her.

I didn't tell Hanka or Zborowski or anyone about what I had found, nor have I revealed it to a living soul. It is my wish that once these pages have been studied and evaluated by a person of competence, they are to be consigned to my notary Monsieur Henri Legrand, or his heir, who will then, at his discretion, decide what to do with them—whether or not to render them public at this time and to deal with claims of ownership surely to come forth from any remaining members of the Hébuterne or

Modigliani families.
    In faith, Josephine Annie Rosier.

I opened the first notebook and leafed through it to find sketches, watercolors, and fine line drawings; pages of a diary blotched with yellow and brown stains, written in ink so faded it had become transparent; postcards, visiting cards, and photographs. The pictures included a baby in a christening dress with a spit-curl in the middle of her forehead and a young, dour-looking man with thickly brushed hair above a broad forehead, whom I recognized as André Hébuterne. There were shopping lists, accounts for groceries and paint supplies, snippets of poems, and a tarot card, "the Lovers." Some entries were carefully dated with the day, month, and year; others only had the name of the month scribbled at the top. In some places, you could see that several pages had been ripped out. Pinned to the back cover was a postcard picturing the Promenade des Anglaises in Nice with the message MONSTRE scrawled on the back, addressed to Jeanne Hébuterne, at a hotel in Rue de France in Nice, postmarked Paris, 1919.

I reached for a plaid blanket, sank back on the cushions, and was lost in the story of Jeanne.

Part 3
The Notebooks of
Jeanne Hébuterne

Notebook 1

Saint-Michel-en-Grève, July 19, 1914

I like to sit here on this rock and look out over the ocean as I scribble in my notebook. I could spend hours gazing at those inky clouds, drinking in the colors with my eyes and my skin. I love the ocean in all weathers, even like today when the wind is raw and the salt stings in my throat and the mud from the field clings in globs to my shoes and dirties the hem of my cape.

I've always been attracted to storms. When I was still very small and we were on holiday in Finistère, I'd slip outside and ramble towards the headland whenever I heard the wind rising. As soon as Maman saw I was missing, she would send André out to find me. He always knew where to look: perched as close to the edge as I could get. Shouting my name into the wind, he'd run to me through the scrabbly heather.

"Come away from there, Nenette, you'll fall!" Gently, he'd draw me away from the precipice. But I knew how to keep myself steady: I'd just look down at my shoes on the salt-frosted furze and feel my feet in the earth. Hand in hand, we'd squint out at the waves of steely water. I kept hoping we'd see something burst up from the foam. A whale or a seal. A sunken ship up from the deep, dripping seaweed and barnacles from its sides, a skeleton at the helm!

I can't explain why I keep watching the horizon, but I feel that my real life is waiting for me out there somewhere across the water. Who am I? Who will I become? Maman says I am going to be beautiful—but that my hips are too round, my face too full, and when I am older I will have a double chin, like hers. But my eyes are the color of southern seas in summer, changing from green to gold to turquoise. I have seen those waters in the pictures of Gauguin, who is my favorite painter.

I am J.H. and I am sixteen. Everyone has an idea for who I am and what I shall be. For Papa, I will marry an engineer, or perhaps a doctor, like Rodolphe, the young country doctor who treated his grippe last winter. I will become a proper wife and mother, accomplished in music, bookkeeping, and domestic skills, like turning tough chunks of old beef into edible stews.

Maman would rather I marry Charles, who is the son of the neighborhood apothecary, Thibideau, in Rue Mouffetard. He is a friend of André's, and when he comes to visit, he always brings Maman licorice or lavender pastilles, but he is not beautiful like André and doesn't know anything about art or poetry. He spends hours in the laboratory, helping his father make pills and suppositories, and his clothes and hair smell of ether, valerian, and cod liver oil. Maman opens all the windows after he leaves. I cannot imagine living with such a presence, much less being touched by those fingers.

Sometimes after dinner, when André has gone out with his friends, Maman and Papa discuss the merits of both, debating which one would suit me better as a husband. I sit there smiling as I listen, sketching or sewing a hem.

"A doctor is a fine addition to any family," says Papa.

"But an apothecary will do just as well and if he owns his own shop, why, he'll be richer than a doctor."

They are both so absurd—they never ask me what I think. How can they imagine I'd ever be caught dead with someone like Rodolphe or Charles? The man I marry will be someone special. An artist or a poet. And he must be as beautiful as a god.

Papa thinks women should not work outside the home, unless economic circumstances require it. Maman says that teaching is a respectable profession for a young woman, if she wants to do something useful in society. She thinks I could be a teacher—of English perhaps, so she is always making me study English grammar. But I find it hard to concentrate on English verbs. I'd much rather learn Russian. But what I love to do most is paint. It is a passion I share with my brother.

André is studying at the Académie Ranson in Rue Joseph-Bara in Montparnasse, where the *Maître*, Serusier, says he is very gifted. Over the bed in my room back in Paris, I have hung a painting he made of a poplar tree, which he copied from a postcard when he was only sixteen. There is life in that tree—you can feel the leaves flutter as the summer wind shatters the heat and makes shivers run up your arms. When a painting makes you feel, hear, smell, and taste, the artist has talent, or so Serusier says.

On every excursion to country fairs or old churches here in Brittany, I buy more postcards for André to copy so he can develop his talent. André plans to become a professional artist—though it's a secret between us! Papa and Maman don't know yet that what they believe is merely a hobby will be his career.

André thinks I have talent, too. After every lesson at the Académie, he teaches me something new, and this week it's been about landscapes, but I'd rather paint people than cornfields. In any case, the human body is a sort of landscape. I like to study how our bodies are made—the waves of muscles and hair and the textures and colors of skin. The dimples in elbows and knees fascinate me, like the labyrinths in ear whorls and fingernails. I also like the way clothes fit on bodies, and the crisp turnings of caps and collars like the Breton women wear and soft draperies in long clean lines and a bit of fur on a jacket cuff.

André says I should become a clothes and costume designer because I have a way with fabrics. And I love making clothes for myself, though Papa and Maman think my turbans and ponchos are too fanciful. This dress I am wearing I designed and sewed myself, inspired by a Pre-Raphaelite painting. Sometimes I wear my hair in two long braids all the way down to my hips, with a beaded bandeau around my forehead, just like an Indian princess. Other times, when I want to look older, I let it flow loose, under a black velvet cap. I made a promise never to cut it, and when I am old enough to have a lover, I will wrap him in my hair and keep him safe.

July 22, 1914
Here in Saint-Michel, every day André and I go out painting, morning and afternoon. But if it is raining, he stays home and reads or sketches, but I get restless and have to go walking for an hour or so along the beach and up to a spot on a cliff where an old *paysan* keeps his goats. I watch the goats for awhile, then traipse home through the sand and mud, clean my boots, hang my cape in the doorway, and shake the rain from my hair. Soon Papa will go back to Paris, and we will follow a few days later. Although I love it here, I admit, I am starting to miss Paris too!

I go straight to the kitchen, where fresh sole are sizzling in melted butter and thyme on the stove. Maman is grating celery root into a big blue enamel bowl, and Céline, the girl who helps in the kitchen, is whipping up *crème fraiche* and mustard in an old stone crock. The leather-bound volume of Pascal lies closed on the sideboard. Papa has stopped reading aloud for the edification of the ladies and is now absorbed in his newspaper, but I can see the news is upsetting: his pink mouth scowls above his gray goatee. André sits on the edge of a chair, long legs crossed, puffing his new pipe by the open window, reading a book of poems.

"War is coming," Papa says, rustling his newspaper. "André will have to go."

"I am not afraid," André says. His voice, so determined and grown-up, makes me feel proud and scared.

"But I am," says Maman. "I don't want my son to go to war. Against the Germans."

She grates the root vigorously. Flakes fall like snow into the bowl.

"I won't wait to be conscripted. I will sign up and defend my country."

Papa stares at him, proud and apprehensive, then folds the newspaper and sets it aside.

"And you, Achille?" my mother asks.

"All able-bodied men will be mobilized," Papa replies.

Mama puts down the celery root. I can feel she is sick with fear. We always have similar reactions. Our minds work the same. I go over to her and take her hand. Her fingers are cold and damp from the celery root, her wrists are threaded with fine lavender veins. I cannot believe that both my father and brother will be sent to war, though I know, all over France, men will be leaving their families. I squeeze her hand to give us both courage.

We eat our lunch in silent dread. The food tastes like ashes in our mouths.

July 23, 1914

Why am I a person of such extremes? When I am here in Brittany walking in the wind, I am happy for an hour or two, but then I feel gloomy and begin to miss the little alleys around Rue Mouffetard: the noise and turbulence, the bookstalls, street vendors, and cafés. But once I am back there again, soon enough I feel I can't breathe, even the Luxembourg Gardens seem like a prison to me, and I long to escape to the seaside. It's always back and forth with me—I never can decide which place makes me happier. But now that we know that André and Papa will have to go war, I don't want to go back to Paris at all. Why does André have to enlist in the army? I asked him this afternoon while we stood on the rocks above Ploumanach, where we had come to spend the day painting the pink cliffs.

"A man has his duties, Jeanne. Otherwise, he wouldn't be a man. Making a choice and sticking with it is what gives a shape to our life." He was painting a brooding seascape in bold lines of cobalt, with a fine thread of yellow foam scribbled across the sand.

I added the last strokes to my watercolor. "I know I change my mind too often."

"That is because you are only sixteen-years-old, Jeanne, and you don't know yet what you want out of life."

"And you, aged philosopher? Do you know what you want out of life?"

"Yes, I want to paint! Doesn't matter where. Here in Brittany, in Paris. Or maybe when the war is over, I will go to Morocco or Egypt...."

"To paint blazing deserts, camels, and exotic women in yellow silk veils?"

He laughed. "You would look charming in a yellow silk veil. But show me what you have done today."

I step back from my easel to let him have a look at my work, holding my breath as I watch his face. I can guess his reaction by the way his mouth tightens at the corner and his eyes squint. He is never very generous with praise. But today he says—

"Not bad, for a girl of your age. You have captured the lay of the shore in that sweeping line quite admirably. Your brushwork in the clouds here is a bit clumsy, but the colors are subtle. This violet, tangerine, and gray truly give the sense of an impending storm." He holds up the picture to study it closer, then nods. "There is feeling and emotion in it."

The ocean wind scrambles a loose strand of my hair, blowing it into my mouth and eyes. "Passion," I suggest, brushing the hair from my face. "Violet and tangerine are the colors of passion."

André rolls his eyes. "*Peut-être*. But why not red, scarlet, orange, fuchsia? Besides what would you know about passion?"

I shake my head and do not answer, kicking at a stone with the scuffed toe of my shoe.

Finally, I say, "Who will teach me to paint if you go off to war?" But what I mean is, "How can we possibly live without you?"

"I know you are sad that I have to go. All of you." He blinks and turns away, so I won't see his face. "They say a war can't last long. I will probably be home again in a matter of weeks."

We are silent for awhile, looking out at the ocean. Far below the pinkish cliffs, we can hear the waves pounding the shore. Along the yellow beach, a little boy in a red jacket runs along the sand with a prancing dog. It must be the lighthouse keeper's son, and I wonder if the keeper will have to go to war, like André and Papa, and if the lighthouse will be left deserted.

I swirl my brush in black and purple and daub some more paint in my clouds. "Perhaps I could enroll in a school to study painting while you are gone." I say this partly to change the subject, but also because it is something I have been thinking about for a while.

André looks at me, surprised. Clearly, it never crossed his mind that I might want to go to art school. Now he ponders the idea and says at last, "Why not? Many girls enroll in the School of Decorative Arts, these days. There are courses for decorators at the academy of Montparnasse in Rue de la Grande Chaumière. You might learn a skill you could practice at home."

"But I want to paint portraits and nudes." He raises his eyebrow at that. "I want to make art! Not decorate teapots with rosebuds. I want to be a painter! A real painter."

"Being a painter is a very hard life, even for a man."

"But Marie Laurencin and Susan Valadon—they are successful women painters."

"Yes, but for a woman to be a painter, she must be rich and have an independent income! Or she must be the lover of a very important painter herself, and being a painter's mistress or lawful wife is almost worse for a woman than being a painter. I don't say this to discourage you from painting. But it cannot become your profession. Maman and Papa would never want you to lead such a life."

"But *you* will lead an artist's life."

"Girls don't become painters for the same reason they don't become soldiers, or chefs or the President of the Republic."

"And why is that?"

André sucks in his cheeks and doesn't answer straightaway. The granite cliffs seem to take on animal shapes as the violet dusk deepens around us. Overhead, screeching gulls reel back to their high nests. My brother puts away his paints and folds up his easel. It is almost time to go home.

"If you don't know the answer to that question, it means you haven't grown up enough."

Why must he always treat me like a child? I turn on my heels and stalk off towards the old lighthouse, leaving my easel and paint box behind, forgetting, just like the child he accused me of being, that this might be our last lesson for a long time to come. I glance back to see him packing up my things, then gazing out at the ocean. He looks so miserable and lonely that I run back up to him and throw my arms around him.

"Let's never argue, my little Nenette! You will be what you wish! The gods will decide." He kisses the top of my head.

July 24, 1914

When Céline is out shopping and Papa and André are not at home, Maman calls me to the kitchen to wash my hair. She says I can't go back to Paris with my hair full of brine. It is almost the only time when the two of us are completely alone, a ritual since I was very small. My hair is so long and thick now—it hangs down to my hips—I could never wash it without her help.

I sit with my back to the marble-topped table, my arms bare in my thin chemise, and a towel draped round my shoulders. The white kitchen doors are open, and I can see our reflection in the tall mirror in the hall: Maman, in her blue apron, stands over me with a tin pitcher of hot water; a copper kettle heats on the red-tiled stove behind her; on the table, the blue enamel basin and a pile of grated castile soap. A perfect domestic scene: *La Toilette de la Jeune Fille.*

171

As I dip my head back over the basin, the blood rushes to my brain and black spots swim before my eyes, but my mind clears instantly when warm water from the pitcher hits my scalp. Maman scrubs the grated soap into my hair so vigorously, it makes my teeth chatter. Relief comes when she rinses all the lather away with smooth, caressing strokes and rubs almond oil into the roots. Twisting my hair into a long squeaky snake, she wrings out the last drops of water. Now the torture begins, as she tugs a comb through the tangles, humming under her breath. At last I find the courage to tell her what I have been thinking about.

"Maman, I have decided to enroll at the Académie Colarossi." I have chosen the Colarossi as it is cheaper than the Julien, and the Ranson where André studies doesn't take women students. I watch her reaction in the hall mirror, spotted with steam.

"Have you, my dear?" She goes on humming her old Breton tune. It is as if I have said, "I have decided to swim to England."

"I am going to take drawing lessons and learn to paint. I want to be an artist like André. He says I have talent."

The teeth of the comb dig into my scalp and rip a knot out by the roots. "An artist! Goodness child! What ideas has your brother put into your head?"

"I could become an illustrator of books. André says it is a respectable profession for women that can be done at home."

"And what about your music lessons? Your father would be disappointed if you stopped studying the violin."

"There is no reason why I can't do both."

"I don't know. You must ask your father." She studies me in the hall mirror, her eyes puzzled as she wraps the towel round my head.

"Go sit in the sun and dry your hair now."

She wipes her hands on a towel. "There is going to be a war. Our life may change. I can't promise you anything. In any case, it is your father who must decide."

❋

July 26, 1914

Abbot Marchegal came to lunch, as he sometimes does on Sundays. Midway through, he peered at me across the table, and said,

"You haven't been to confession for awhile, Jeanne."

His fork trembled in his frail hand. As he speared a large piece of roasted eggplant, it shot across the plate and into his lap. I pinched my lips to keep from laughing and primly patted my mouth with my napkin. "No, I suppose I have nothing to confess."

"Jeanne!" Maman's eyes flashed.

I turned to her scowling face. "It's true. I haven't murdered anyone, told any lies, stolen anything, hurt anyone, or performed lustful acts. However, I am lazy and indecisive at times. I suppose that counts." I took a sip of watered red wine.

"And the sin of pride is no stranger to you," said Papa.

"And she is as stubborn as a mule!" said André.

I clamped my mouth shut and stared at my plate.

"Our daughter is rather a free thinker," Maman apologized.

"I promise I will soon," I said, looking down demurely as I chewed some bread, hoping that the conversation would move on, and it did, until almost the very end of lunch, when the coffee was served.

Shifting his thin body in the wobbly cane chair, the abbot set down his cup and addressed my father.

"Have you thought about a career for your son, for when the war is over? Will he pursue accounting like you have, Achille?"

"I am afraid I don't have father's head for numbers," said André, not waiting for Papa's reply. He nudged my foot under the table. I nudged back.

"Well then, young man, what are you thinking of? A military career?"

"Heavens no!" cried my mother.

"Civil service. He would make an excellent clerk," said Papa.

"Actually, I am fond of painting," said André.

I stared at my brother wide-eyed, and he winked back. This was the first time he had announced his plans to our parents.

"Painting—well, that's a fine hobby, but not a profession, surely," said the abbot.

"This is the first I have heard of it," sputtered Papa.

"If I can have a go at it, well, I'd like to try. If I fail, I can always do something else. I will be taking a studio, together with some other students from the academy."

Maman stared at him. "And where would that be?"

"One of my classmates has a place in Rue de Seine he's willing to share. When I am back again, and things return to normal, in a couple of months, I expect, I will move in with him."

"André is very talented," I said. "His teacher, Serusier, thinks he could make a living as a landscape painter. And I want to study painting too!"

"We were thinking of enrolling Jeanne at the Academy of Decorative Arts. Girls nowadays want to be active, and not just sit at home and brood," said Maman. "And it's just around the corner in Rue D'Ulm,"

"It will help her pass the time while André is away," my father added.

"I understand. I thought you were studying music. The violin, wasn't it, Jeanne?"

"I love music and languages, but I love painting more."

"You should be learning the feminine arts, to prepare for becoming a wife and mother," the abbot sternly suggested.

"There's more to a woman's life than just cooking and cleaning and taking care of babies," I answered.

"You sound ambitious. Perhaps too much so," said the abbot.

"Is that a sin?" I gazed straight into his eyes.

Paris, July 30, 1914

I show André my portrait of Maman at the piano. It is my first attempt with oils, inspired by Gauguin. Yesterday I was so proud of it, but today, the more I look at it, the more I hate it. The face is too rough and naïve, and the hands are ugly bird claws. It doesn't even look like Maman, so I am amazed when he praises me: "Yes, but the arms and wrists are graceful, and even if the eye is crudely drawn, it shows inner concentration. You have caught the mood and intensity of the model, if nothing else."

He is silent when I show him my new self-portrait with my hair in two long braids and an orange bandeau around my forehead. He studies it abstractly, as if he did not want to recognize that it was me in the picture.

"Is that really how you see yourself?"

"How do you mean?"

"Stern, angry, determined, perhaps. Impatient, too. An irritated angel, like the one in Durer's *Melancholy*. Not at all like the sweet young girl you are."

"I don't know that picture."

From the bookshelf in his bedroom, he takes a huge volume of prints he bought from a stall along the river. We study it together, sitting side by side on the bed, the heavy tome in our laps. André puts his arm around my shoulder. I nestle close as we leaf through the pictures.

"You see, she has the same brooding expression in her eyes as you. Ready to punish the world."

We look at Durer's *Knight, Death, and the Devil* and prints by the Pre-Raphaelites and Gustave Doré. A faint smell of mold wafts up as he turns the pages.

"You could have modeled for Dante Rossetti, with that thick hair of yours!" He wraps a strand around his finger and tugs it twice.

"Ouch! That hurts!"

He wags a finger at me. "That is a warning. You must never cut your hair the way some girls are doing now."

"Don't be silly. I'd never cut it." My hair is my most distinctive feature. It makes me who I am. Why should I want to cut it?

"While I am gone, you must be good. Help our parents and behave yourself."

I sigh. I am in for another lecture. "I am always well-behaved."

"Hmmph. Don't argue with Maman too much. And be sure to write me frequently. I intend to keep on painting, or at least sketching, if I can, so you'll need to send me supplies!"

"Anything you like!"

✺

André lets me take the book back to my room where I can look at it before going to bed.

I love how the clean, black lines look on a white background, so stark and defined. I'd like to make woodcuts or etchings to illustrate a story. You possess part of the story when you put it in pictures of

175

your own, as Doré has done with Dante's *Inferno* or Beardsley with the story of King Arthur.

I am fascinated by the figure of death, and the hourglass that the knight ignores in Durer's print, but that night I dreamed death dressed as a priest peeked into my bedroom while I was asleep and I woke up terrified.

August 1, 1914

War has been declared. Recruiting posters went up all over the neighborhood—men must report to their local headquarters to be drafted into the army. Papa says he will probably be assigned to an administrative office: perhaps in Paris, or nearby. André, after training, will be sent to the front. There are crowds of men at the Gare de l'Est, waiting to be mobilized.

August 5, 1914

The first soldiers left today. All of Paris turned out to see them off. The officers looked so handsome in their red trousers, dark blue jackets, and mauve helmets. Each man had a flower stuck at the end of his rifle as they marched down the boulevard.

I tried to get close to the curb, but there was such a mob I could only get a glimpse. In that legion of faces, how could I hope to pick out André? They poured through the streets like a river about to burst its banks. Crowds cheered, threw flowers, and waved flags.

When the band marched by with its gleaming brass, we all sang "la Marseillaise." A freckled young woman in rumpled white linen grabbed my arm halfway through, and pointed out a helmet bobbing by.

"That's my fiancé. Marcel! Marcel!" She waved her flag in rapture, but of course he couldn't hear. "Isn't he handsome?"

"Aren't you afraid for him?"

"By no means! Those Germans are no match for our men. They'll march up to Berlin, settle things, and be back by Christmas time."

I slip through the crowd and head home through the deserted streets. The cafés are empty, except for a few old men warily peering out—foreigners, probably. Everyone else is along the boulevards to watch the men march away.

Maman had a bad headache, so she and Papa did not go to watch the soldiers. They stayed home with all the shutters closed against the heat. He sits by the dark window, with Pascal's *Pensées* in his lap; Maman is slowly raveling a skein of yarn—already knitting a scarf for André for when winter comes. She reaches out to pull me to her side, and I put my arm around her. Papa lays his hand on her knee, and we stay like that, unmoving, while people pass through the street below, still singing "la Marseillaise."

August 30, 1914
André's first letter has come; tucked in the envelope was a picture of himself in uniform. He has already grown a moustache and goatee—apparently it's regulation. He looks stern and determined as a soldier should. Maman puts the photograph in a silver frame and sets it on the mantel in the dining room. His absence is now canonized. She took me to Notre-Dame today to light two candles to the Maid of Orléans. As we were crossing the great square, we heard a man say that the Germans were only fifty kilometers from Notre-Dame!

August 31, 1914
A bomb has fallen over Paris, launched by a German plane. We tremble in our beds at night.

September 18, 1914
Céline has gone back to Brittany. Her father is ill and needs care, and there were free trains for people to leave the city. Even the government has moved to Bordeaux, and Papa has followed them there to work in an office, counting sacks of flour and pillow cases for the army. Perhaps Maman and I will leave later this autumn. Papa says that food may run out in the city come winter, and we might need to relocate to the countryside.

It is just the two of us now at home, and Maman hardly eats at all, saving what she can of our rations. I spend the day helping around the house, practicing the violin, drawing, and painting in my room. For the moment, my violin lessons have stopped. *Maître* Schlict has gone back to Germany. There is no hope of studying painting now, either. Maman says I must wait till the end of the war, or until things have settled down.

Reims Cathedral has partly collapsed, destroyed by German bombs. Yet the news from the Marne is hopeful.

The Germans have been pushed back, although many men have died. I pray every night that André and Papa will be safe.

Here ends the first of the three notebooks

Notebook 2

April 6, 1916

Today was my eighteenth birthday, we are back in Paris again, and André is home on leave! Maman brought me coffee and toasted bread with a pad of real butter—there is not a croissant left in Paris—in bed, and then I got up and got dressed, taking all the time in the world to pin up my long braids like a wreathe around my head.

My brother was in the kitchen, sipping his coffee with Papa, poring over the newspapers when I came in to say *bonjour* and receive my birthday kisses. When he saw me in my new green silk dress that fits so snugly in the bodice and flares out at the hips, André's eyes popped. I suppose he was startled to see that I have grown up since he has been away. Papa blinked at me in astonishment, and Maman, too, studied me sidewise, as I turned on tiptoes before them to show off my outfit. I think she knows I have retouched the dress, taking in tucks here and there to fit it more nicely to my form. I am a better seamstress than she thought, for I have learned to take invisible stitches. But, for once, she didn't criticize, just gazed at me with that mournful look of an old mother hen, pecked me on the cheek, and told us not to be late for lunch.

I love to go walking in the city with André. Some people say we look alike, but I think we are as different as night and day. I am petite, dark, and brooding while he is as handsome as Apollo. School girls swoon when they see him in his uniform, and fine women in fabulous hats smile at him in cafés. They all imagine he must be my fiancé, but he is not even engaged.

The Luxembourg Gardens have always been my favorite place to go for a walk with my brother. We'll sit for awhile on the cold iron chairs, staring up at the lacework of black branches in winter or the first green flickers of spring. We talk about everything under the sun: books and holidays and our plans for the future. But mostly we talk about art. He worships Cézanne and Turner, but I prefer Gauguin. Before the war, on Sunday afternoons, he used to take me to exhibitions in Montparnasse or Montmartre and explain the pictures to me. Every year we'd go together to the Salon D'Automne and discuss each new work for hours—sometimes even days, as we did with Matisse's *Blue Window*. I love looking at paintings with André. He is so knowledgeable about all the technical aspects you must notice. A painting is a window into another world that dwells in your head. Sometimes I think I would like to paint a picture and disappear inside it.

Today, though, he is sterner and more silent than usual. I try to ask him about his life at the front, but he won't talk about it. "One day when you're older I will tell you about it. Let's make the most of our day. You can't imagine how much I looked forward to spending this time with you." He squeezes my arm as we walk along, and my eyes fill with tears. I have missed him so much.

We rush home for lunch from the Luxembourg Gardens without even stopping for an aperitif. Maman and Céline, who is now back living with us again, have made all my favorite dishes, after saving rations of butter, sugar, and flour for weeks. While we eat, Maman can't take her eyes off André, bobbing her head as he takes a second and third helping of everything on the table. "Eat, eat," she insists, passing him a plate of goat cheese, which Céline brought us from the countryside. "You are much too thin."

After lunch I open my presents. From Maman, two shimmering swathes of turquoise silk to make a dress for myself—already I have in mind something daring, a mermaid's sheath of transparent waves. From Papa, as always, Muguet perfume, a proper scent for young ladies, which he buys at a discount from the Bon Marché, where he worked before the war. He also gave me some Debussy scores for the violin— hoping, I suppose, to inspire me to practice more—though I know I won't. There is so much to do in one day: study Russian and English, paint and sketch, help Maman with chores, read about the war in the newspapers, and practice the violin. I love Schubert's "Death and the Maiden," but I will never master the opening bars, no matter how hard I practice. I have a new violin teacher, since *Maître* Schlict returned to Germany. *Maître* Dupré is very elderly and frail. He agrees with *Maître* Schlict: I am not decisive enough at the very first note. Some people might say that it is unpatriotic to play Schubert, but *Maître* Dupré says that art transcends war.

But the best present of all was André's gift: a big bundle of drawing pads, pencils, tubes of gouache, and charcoals! I know why he chose that—he's tired of me stealing his home art supplies for my classwork at the school of decorative arts. I have been going to lessons there for six months now.

After lunch we went out again— but we didn't tell Maman where we were going. Back up to Montparnasse to see a gallery there and browse about the studios of a couple of artists André knows in Rue de Maine.

Coming back, we stop to buy a bouquet for Maman from a girl with a wheelbarrow full of violets. I decide to confess my plan, and perhaps engage his help.

"I am going to enroll in the Académie Colarossi this week."

"Aren't you happy with your classes at the School of Decorative Arts?"

"I enjoy them. But they are too tame! I want to do figure drawing and sculpture and oil painting."

"You are determined then!"

"Yes. I want to be a real artist. Like you."

He studies me for a long moment, then slaps his hand on his thigh, as if to say his mind is made up. "All right. We will go tomorrow and enroll you, and I will tell Papa it's time you moved on."

But his smile is sad, and I think I understand why. While he is away, I will be painting and learning for him too.

April 10, 1916

I sit under the red-fringed canopy of the Rotonde with André, writing in my diary while he studies a battle map in yesterday's newspaper.

It is not yet noon, and we have just returned from the Académie around the corner in Rue de la Grande Chaumière, where I have signed up for the life drawing and painting classes. The waiter brings hot chocolate for me and a Pernod for André. Both our drinks are watered down. I have only been here to this café twice before, always with André. Along with the Dôme, which is across the street, this is the café where all the Montparnos drink. Inside there are pictures tacked up all over the walls. There's a Picasso over the cash register, a

Braque collage over the beer taps; sketches by André's friends, Kisling and Dorignac, pinned up next to the menu chalkboard.

It is almost lunchtime—an in-between hour and with so many men at the front now, the cafés are not as full as they once were, and everything costs twice as much. Yet life still goes on. The poor foreign artists, who have slept here under the tables and washed up in the lavatory at dawn, must have wandered elsewhere for the morning, to a studio or a park bench. It is too early for the students who come here after lessons at the École and the Académie. Soon I will be joining them!

I am wearing my lilac dress with a green turban and tall felt-topped boots. I can feel the men at the other tables, studying me with interest, and I look up from my writing to glance back from the corner of my eye, making sure André doesn't notice.

A handsome, well-dressed older man with a beard, a Russian or a Pole, perhaps, sits waiting for a colleague or mistress while he reads the *Figaro*. A woman in a magnificent hat with a lavender plume drinks champagne alone, smiling at André. Two soldiers on leave at the next table are discussing the progress of the war as they sip their aperitifs and ogle the lady in the hat, who doesn't seem to mind in the least. The three girls at the table nearest the street must be factory workers. They wear dull blue serge dresses and black cloche hats—Père Libion, the owner, will turn away any woman not wearing a hat—and their hair is bobbed at shoulder length. They are laughing and talking loudly. One of them is smoking a cigarette and blowing her blue smoke in our direction, much to André's annoyance. He thinks women with bobbed hair are bad enough—but *smoking!* But I like the pungent smell of tobacco.

A Japanese man crosses the street, steps up from the curb, and heads right for our table. He is dressed so strangely that for a moment I am afraid he is mad and might harm us or ask us for money. He wears a lampshade on his head, gold hoops in his ears, sleek black bangs combed low over his forehead, and thick black-rimmed eyeglasses like motorist's goggles. A bold-patterned shirt with kimono sleeves is wrapped over his sweater. To my great surprise, André jumps up to embrace the stranger, introducing him to me as Foujita, a painter from Japan. The Japanese painter bows deeply with such dignity that I cannot laugh, even when the lampshade starts to slide off his head.

"This goddess is your sister? I would be honored if you would pose for me, Mademoiselle."

"If you will pose for me! I love the pattern of your shirt."

He bows again at the compliment, clasping his lampshade to his head with one hand. "I see the Hébuternes are a family of artists."

"We have just signed her up for lessons at the Colarossi." From the tone of his voice, André sounds so proud of me—something I did not expect.

"I start the day after tomorrow! Until now André has been teaching me," I say.

"Excellent! Then you will be one of ours in Montparnasse. My studio is just here in Rue Delambre. You must come and visit soon, both of you, for tea. I am usually in after five o'clock." To André, he says, "You know where to find me."

"Jeanne will come, but I am afraid my leave is up. I return to the front tomorrow."

A dark crease appears between Foujita's eyebrows, thick as caterpillars behind the warping lens of his goggles.

"I see," he bows again.

André invites him to sit down with us, but Foujita declines, "I have to return to my cats."

"You have cats?" I ask.

"An army and always hungry. What a concert they give if I am late with their food. And these days finding enough food for them has been quite a chore. It has been a pleasure, Mademoiselle," He kisses my hand, then bows to André. "Goodbye, dear friend. I hope we will be seeing your new work at the exhibition next spring."

"Of course. I intend to keep working, if at all possible."

As Foujita turns to leave, André adds, "Watch out for her, will you, while I am away? I don't want her to get into any trouble."

I cringe at his words. Why must he always embarrass me in front of other people?

"It will be an honor," Foujita says, and, unseen by André, winks at me from behind his goggles. I am curious to meet his cats.

Leaving the Rotonde, we decide to visit a gallery where André always goes to see the new trends.

It's not really a gallery, but more of a junk shop where some of the

Montparnasse painters sell their work for a few sous so they can buy themselves a hot dinner at one of the cheap canteens in Rue du Maine.

As we turn the corner, we see a small crowd gathered in front of the gallery window, where an angry man is shouting and gesticulating. Drunk probably. People swarm the entrance; perhaps it is the opening of a show. Curious, we approach and push our way to the window, where two large nudes are displayed right in front, along with a portrait of a man, some old broken furniture, and a tarnished tea pot. Watercolors and sketches are pegged up with clothespins on a line stretching across the whole window.

More people arrive, trying to shove me out of the way as I stand there under a spell. The nudes make me want to cry out with joy—heavy round breasts and golden skin, offered to a lover's eye; their smiles secretive and sensual. They radiate an electricity you can almost feel sizzling on your skin. I stare at a portrait by the same artist of a dark-skinned man with a mask-like face—one eye seems to weep and the other to laugh—and his smile is full of sadness, passion and scorn. I want to kiss those warm, brown lips, and I know just how they will taste—like the skin of sweet black figs from the south, warmed in the sun.

I try to make out the scrawl in the lower right-hand corner of one of the paintings. "Modi…." It's a name I am not familiar with.

A hand jerks me away from the window. "Don't look at those!" André sputters. "They are obscene!"

My mouth drops open in amazement. What is he talking about? "What's wrong? These paintings are beautiful."

"They are not for innocent eyes."

André and I have looked at nudes, male and female, by Michelangelo, Titian, Renoir, and Manet many times. He never reacted like this. When he grips my shoulder even tighter, I plant my feet on the ground, unwilling to turn away.

Meanwhile, the shouting around us grows more agitated as people pour out of the gallery. I try to get another eyeful of the paintings before André tugs me away again, and then I realize what he finds so scandalous. It is the bit of fuzz between the women's thighs and in their armpits. Not just a shadow— the painter has painted fine threads of real hair. I giggle at my discovery. André turns purple, and his Adam's apple throbs, as if he had something stuck in his throat.

"Come away from there. Besides, the police are coming. Maman would never forgive me for letting you get caught in the middle of a scandal."

A dark-faced policeman strides through the crowd and into the gallery. As André pulls me away, I look back to see two blue-sleeved arms reach up in the window and take down one of the nudes. I am outraged! The artist did not deserve such treatment.

André steers me along the street by the elbow. People stepping out of shops with parcels stare at us as we pass, squabbling.

"But why is it worse to paint hair in a woman's armpit than it is to paint a moustache under a man's nose?" I ask.

"It is obscene. Women should not be painted with hair on their bodies."

"But nature makes it grow there."

"Art is art. It is not reality. It is not nature. It is an idealized vision. Hair on a feminine body isn't part of the canon."

"Maybe I don't believe in the canon."

We don't speak for the rest of the way home, but by dinnertime, our quarrel is forgotten. Tomorrow he will take the train back to the front. Although we pretend this is a normal evening like any other, the atmosphere is strained, and Maman's hand shakes as she lifts her wine glass. André chats to them about our trip to the Académie Colarossi, but he says nothing about how we have argued or about the scandalous pictures. After dinner, Papa blissfully refrains from reading philosophy aloud to us and just sits in his chair, smoking meditatively, watching Maman darn a sock. I leave them like that and go off to bed.

Later, I lay dreaming of those pictures in the gallery window. I think André is wrong. The whole body is sacred, even the hair in a woman's underarm and every inch of her body. The man who painted those nudes must feel that too. He knows the beauty of a woman's body comes from deep inside her, and not from someone's idea of how she ought to look.

How could André not understand that?

I want to meet the man who painted those pictures.

April 11, 1916
André and Papa have gone again. The house is a tomb. Maman spent most of the day in her bathrobe and did not even get dressed.

April 13, 1916
Today was my first day in life drawing class. As soon as I stepped into the classroom, I thought I would suffocate. The room was packed, the air dense with smoke from a charcoal stove puffing in a corner, so that you could hardly breathe. And the smell! Sweat, garlic, mildewed clothes, unwashed socks, tobacco—all mingled in the baking air. They keep the room warm for the nude models, with only one window cracked open to prevent general asphyxiation.

The men are mostly foreigners, of course, as the French boys are all at war, and there are twice as many girls as men.

On a platform at the front of the room, the model—fifty-five if she's a day—sprawls beneath a glaring electric light, her skin glistening with sweat. While students sketch, Colarossi's son goes around the room collecting money for the lesson from everyone, then barks an order at the model to tell her to change pose. Obediently, she rolls over on her side and stretches out a pudgy arm.

Poses last all of five minutes, and you must work in a fever to get much of the figure down. I strain to concentrate while a running conversation in six languages buzzes in my ears, and a young Slavic man with long hair and a velvet coat tosses paper wads at a girl in the row in front of me, who looks as though she has been up dancing all night, with red-rimmed eyes and tussled hair. Twice his missiles land on my sketchpad, and once in my hair, causing them both to giggle, and the silly lout does not even apologize. I wonder how I will ever do serious work in this place.

I scowl at the drawing I have just done. The breasts are dumpy and the head too tiny. I want to rip it from the pad, throw it in the stove, jump on the next omnibus home, and never come back!

"Not bad," says the girl beside me, glancing at my pad. "I think you have done the elbows well."

I peek at hers, so much better than mine, with sinuous lines and delicate cross-hatching. How has she done it so fast?

"I'm Thérèse." She is thin, pale, and older than me. Blond hair cut short like a boy's, in the manner of *les Anglaises*. She has bluish half-moons under her eyes and frayed cuffs on her shabby velvet jacket. I doubt if she gets enough to eat.

"Jeanne."

We press hands. From the warmth of hers, I know we'll be friends.

Now the teacher makes the rounds, poking his long nose into each student's work, pointing out flaws with a charcoal-smudged finger, giving a word of advice, rubbing out a line to make a correction, and more rarely offering a bit of encouragement. Chatter ceases instantly throughout the room when he speaks: everyone leans forward listening to his old, brittle voice, hoping to learn something new.

When my turn comes, my face flushes and sweat prickles in my underarms. I have never shown my work to anyone except André, or Mama and Papa at home. At the academy of decorative arts, I drew mainly patterns and geometrical designs, controlled and repetitive, completely different than figure drawing, in which you must take risks.

"I have never seen you before, Mademoiselle," the *maître* says.

'No, Monsieur. Today is my first class."

He stares at me a moment, then smiles with faint recognition. "You're the sister of André Hébuterne, aren't you?"

"Yes."

"Very well, then." He glances at my work for less than a second. "Keep trying. One step at a time." Patting my shoulder, he passes on to Thérèse.

Tears of humiliation sting in my eyes as I hear him praise her fine shading and make a technical suggestion or two. He hardly even looked at my drawing. Obviously it wasn't good enough to deserve a comment. A tear falls on the paper, blurring a charcoal line. I give up for the rest of the morning and just watch Thérèse, envying her skill and keen eye.

It is such a relief when class is over. Thérèse and I walk down the stairs and out to the street together.

"I came from Nantes to study fashion, but then I switched to art. By the way, your outfit is most chic. Did you make it yourself?"

"Yes, it was inspired by a Burne-Jones."

"The necklace too?"

"Yes, I made it from pieces of glass that washed up on the shores of Brittany last summer."

"It does look like something a mermaid might wear. Clever girl! How old are you?"

"Eighteen."

"Heavens! A baby! But you look much more mature than that. I am twenty-three. Where do you live?"

"With my family in an apartment in Rue Amyot."

"Where's that?"

"Not too far from the Contrescarpe."

"Sounds lovely!"

"It is bourgeois." My cheeks scald with shame as I spit the words through my teeth.

"I am sure it is nicer than where I am staying over in Rue Campagne-Première. When I put out the gas light at night, the walls fill with bugs. And in the morning, the place stinks of rotting garbage and piss from the courtyard below. There isn't even a tiny charcoal stove in my room. I have to cook my eggs and heat my coffee directly over the gas jet. And last January the water froze in my pitcher. It was so cold!"

"But at least you are independent. Nobody tells you what to do, I bet."

"Yes, you are right about that! I live as I please. Now, where shall we go, to the Dôme or the Rotonde?"

She links her arm in mine, and men smile at us as we walk to the square.

We go to the Dôme and sit in the very front row right along the street. The waiter brings us two noisettes with a little hot milk. I greedily take a sip, but Thérèse grabs my wrist.

"Don't drink it so fast! You are a Montparno, little girl, and you have to learn to drink like one of us, whether it is wine or coffee. When you don't have much money, the trick is to sip very, very slowly, to make it last as long as you can."

With studied elegance, she lifts the cup to her lips almost in slow motion and takes a sip, then with deliberation, puts the cup back down, setting it carefully in the saucer.

"That way if it is cold outside, you can stay in where it's warm. The waiter won't chase you out if you haven't finished your drink, and you'll have so much more time to watch people around you, and maybe spot the man who will buy you your next drink—or something more!"

I follow her advice and take such tiny sips I can barely taste the coffee on my tongue. We talk about art, our classmates, and favorite painters, and by the time we finish our coffee, it is stone cold.

"What do you plan to do with the rest of the afternoon? I am going to the anatomy class to sketch a few cadavers. Would you like to come with me?" she says.

I shake my head.

"It isn't as bad as it sounds. The other day there was a lovely girl, not more than sixteen. They say she drowned in the Seine. She was so undamaged that it looked as though she were asleep."

"Poor girl. Was it suicide?" I ask.

"Probably. I know it's sad."

"She must have been terribly unhappy to want to end her life. Her family must be devastated," I say.

"If she had a family, she wouldn't be lying on a table in the anatomy class. She'd be having a proper burial with flowers, a priest, and a tearful fiancé. Or maybe she would still be alive. No one will even ever know her name or where she came from, although it is easy to guess what she did for a living."

Thérèse sighs, then smiles, patting my hand. "I forget. You are still young and impressionable! You'd be better off drawing Greek statues at the Louvre than drowned bodies from the Seine."

"I thought I'd go for a walk in the Luxembourg Gardens, or maybe visit Foujita at his studio."

"He's a crazy one, that Japanese, but his work is very respected by the Montparnos. You know him well?"

"He's a friend of my brother, André, who is also a painter, studying at the Académie Ranson."

"You don't say! Two painters in the family! What rotten luck for your parents!" she laughs. "One day you'll have to introduce me to your brother. I'd say good looks run in your family. Does he have a fiancée?"

"Not yet. He lives for his art, but he is very handsome. You can meet him when he is back on leave. He's away at the front."

"Oh, I am sorry," she sighs. "So many have gone. They say there won't be many men left in Montparnasse in a month or two, except cripples and consumptives. But don't worry about your brother. He will come back just fine."

"How do you know that?"

"I am psychic." She winks at me.

"It isn't something to joke about."

She lays her hand on my sleeve. "I am sorry. But I do have a sixth sense, and I believe your brother will be all right."

Thérèse pulls a mirror from her beaded purse, inspects her mouth; wipes it clean with a napkin. Then taking out a little pot of lip rouge, she daubs some on her lips and holds the pot and mirror out to me.

"Put some on. You're as pale as death."

I rub some rouge on my lips, grimace at the mirror, and hand it back to her. I have never colored my lips before. It tastes strange and sticky.

She inspects her hair again, holding her mirror high at an angle, then rasps, "Oh my God, there he is!"

"Who? Where?" Curious, I crane my neck to survey the boulevard behind her.

"He's just come out of the building by the apothecary, three doors down. Don't do that. Don't look! Drink your coffee as if you haven't noticed anything. He is coming our way."

"But I have already finished my coffee."

"Then pretend to be drinking it. Don't sit there gawking like a goose."

A sturdy-looking man, not very tall, swarthy with black hair, wearing a brown suit, a red scarf knotted around his neck, lopes towards us up the boulevard, a canvas under his arm, graceful as a cat.

I stare hard at that face, familiar yet new, feeling the cold bite of the empty cup against my teeth, and the cold iron seat beneath me. Squeezing my knees together, I sit up very straight and lift my chin as he comes closer, willing him to look at me just once, but he passes by, squinting into the sunlight without a glance in my direction.

I turn my head to watch him walk away, studying him from behind. I note the swing of his legs, the slight sway of his buttocks and shoulders; the cocky angle of his head, tilted to one side as if he were amused or perplexed. It is the most perfect body in motion I have ever seen, though he is small, like the Greek god Mercury at the Louvre.

When he disappears down Rue Delambre, Thérèse siezes my wrist.

"Isn't he superb? I adore him."

"Who was that?"

"I thought everyone knew Amedeo Modigliani. That's the famous Modi of Montparnasse! The one whose nudes caused such an uproar, and the police closed down his show! Reputedly the best lover in Paris and an unsung genius as well."

I smile and say nothing, trying to hold his image in my mind like a candle flame as Thérèse rattles on.

"They say his current mistress is an old English witch, a poetess, at least forty, who lives with that madman, Max Jacob. They say she's completely cuckoo and goes around with live ducklings in a shopping basket."

"Why would she do that?"

"Who knows! She's crazy."

"Maybe she takes them into the bath with her."

"I'd like to take him into the bath with me! She can keep the ducky. Quack, quack, quack!"

Her duck imitation is so convincing, the waiter pokes his nose out the door to see what is happening, and we both laugh so hard, we nearly fall out of our chairs.

Later that evening at home, I draw a sketch from memory and hide it at the bottom of a drawer. I'd say he is exactly my type.

May 5, 1916

Foujita's studio is like an oriental art museum, filled with Japanese prints and pottery along with odd broken objects retrieved from the street, like warped bicycle wheels and old flattened tins. In a corner stands a sewing machine, which he uses to make his own clothes—a passion we share. Paper dolls of himself dangle from ribbons on the wall above a well-worn red velvet couch, where his models pose. I sit on the couch while he kneels on the floor, as there are no chairs, and he serves me smoky-tasting tea in a bowl and little rice cakes wrapped in lettuce leaves, which he prepares himself. The place is crawling with plump, well-kept, mischievous cats and dozens of drawings and pictures of the same. Cats rub up against my ankles and peer down on us from the top of cupboards, waving restless tails.

I ask him about the cats.

"I paint them when I have no women to pose for me."

"Which do you prefer: women or cats?"

"Well, they are very much alike, you know. Just add whiskers and a tail to a woman, and there's no telling her apart from a cat. And in any case, cat pictures sell well, even better than women."

I finish my tea and set the bowl down on the low table before me, wondering what will happen next. Will he try to kiss me—and if so, should I let him? Will he ask me to sit for a portrait or, perhaps, to undress? I have heard he has a mistress, but it doesn't look as though a woman lives here.

"Would you like to see my bathroom? I have recently installed a tub with running water, thanks to my sales of cats. One of the first in the neighborhood. You can have a bath if you like."

"No thank you. I can bathe at home."

"I forgot you still live with your parents."

"Yes, I am bourgeois."

He laughs, then lunges forward and leaps up on the couch beside me. "You are a goddess with eyes of ocean foam." He kisses the inside of my wrist, where no one has ever kissed me before.

"I love the ocean," I whisper, not knowing what else to say.

His smooth-shaven cheek shines with sweat. His lips, when he kisses me, taste of the smoky tea and salt. I have been kissed by a man before: once quickly, in a corridor in a gallery in Rue de Maine. Somehow I am expecting more—but I feel nothing. It's like kissing a stone statue of Buddha, and when he slips his hands under my blouse, his cold fingers make me shiver.

June 5, 1916
Today I have had a letter from André.

Dear Jeanne
I am happy to hear that your drawing and painting lessons are going well and that you have made some new friends in Montparnasse. Foujita is a gentleman. I trust him to behave respectfully towards you. Thérèse

sounds like a nice girl, but she is a bit older than you, with more experience of the world. Don't get in over your head, and be careful when you go out to private parties at studios. The Swedes particularly like to lace their champagne with gin or even paint thinner, a dangerous combination!

I won't tell you what it is like here. Or the dangers we face daily, which it is best not to think about. In my free time I copy the postcards you send, but I am running out of supplies. I am enclosing with this letter a list of things I need, which you could pick up for me at Sennelier's and send them along to me here.

At night I dream of the peace of Lanmeur and the cliffs of Ploumanach.

—A.

Saint-Michel-en-Grève, February 1917

Maman, Céline, and I have left Paris and come up to Brittany for a few weeks, and I have left my lessons. Maman has been ill again with headaches and dizziness, and the doctor thinks the change of air will be good for her heart. The weather is so miserable that I have caught a bad cold and so I rarely go out to paint. Mama and I sit in the kitchen, drinking tea by the stove, and I make sketches of her, while we wait for the post to come. Papa sends a card every other day. André writes once a week.

Today I received a letter from Thérèse:

Dear Cocanut!

When are you coming back to Paris? Aren't you tired of that soppy weather? And sleeping in blankets stinking of mildew? Montmartre and Montparnasse are a desert. Most of the painters are gone, except a few foreigners, and those few who are too sick to enlist. Lessons at the Académie are still being held—with a few bums coming in off the street to keep warm—and ogle the models and the pupils. But I must say the model we had today was so old, decrepit, and flabby that I am sure next week we will find her laid out on display for the next anatomy class. And she coughed and hacked too, as we all did, because the stove smokes so much. When you pat your face with a handkerchief, it turns black.

I am working on a sculpture now—a nude, but I am furious with her because her buttocks won't hang right and her arms are out of joint! But one day she is going to stir to life and walk down the Boulevard Raspail, go into the Dôme stark naked, and stand us all a round of drinks! And then they will see that Thérèse is a real artist and no dilettante. And then we will have an atelier together and go out in our wonderful clothes, and everyone will admire us

But would you let me know how that daredevil of a brother of yours is doing?

The cafés are all but empty. People seem depressed—But here is the news! In spite of the general air of mourning—or perhaps because of it—the Académie has decided to organize a private carnival ball. A party in costume and all the pupils—current and former—can come and bring whoever they like. You must be back in Paris by then, and why not see if your brother can get leave?

—Thérèse

February 20, 1917

I love being back in Paris again, walking to the academy in the early morning when all the smells are so intense: fresh coffee and baking bread and damp cobblestones and horse droppings and steam billowing up from a grid in the street.

Carnival revelers, up all night, strut down Boulevard Raspail. Silver harlequins, woolly satyrs, bare-chested Roman slaves, all fortified by wine and hashish, brave the cold, shoulders and loins exposed to the icy air. In Rue Delambre, a blue devil pokes me with a cardboard prong and throws a fistful of confetti in my face, and a fur-clad cave woman proudly reveals to passers-by that she has nothing on underneath. Some people say that it is unpatriotic to celebrate while men are dying in the trenches, but life must go on. We need some distraction.

After drawing class, I must put the final touches on my costume for tonight. I am going as a Russian doll: a striped peasant dirndl green and gold, a white gathered smock, tall green boots and a gold bandeau for my hair. Over that, I will wear a green wool cape with orange tassels. I am sad that André won't be back to see me in my outfit and dance with me at the ball, handsome in his pirate's costume, the one he always wears for such occasions.

That night, when Thérèse and I arrive at the academy, we hardly recognize the place. The auditorium on the ground floor has been transformed into a dance hall. Panels of black canvas cover the tall windows because of the blackout. Red paper lanterns dangle from the ceiling and supply the only light. An orchestra of clarinets and guitars thrums and toots in a corner, but their melody is drowned out by the wild rhythms of frying pans and chamber pots. Dancers sway in spasms, their faces lit by red gleams, and the air is thick with the smells of sweat, wine, hashish, and turpentine. Some worktables have been lined up end to end against the wall to make a catwalk, where dancers parade up and down, showing off their costumes and tearing off beads and feathers to toss to grabbing hands.

Thérèse and I worm our way to a table where drinks are being handed round, but the wine and brandy have run out. There is nothing left but mud-colored punch, into which a harlequin is pouring a dozen different bottles. The first sip burns my lips and throat, but with the second I get used to it.

Thérèse gasps as she tastes it. "Watch out. Too much of this will knock you flat, and then I won't be able to get you out the door again. What will your parents say if two days later you are still stinking drunk?"

"I'll be careful not to drink too much," I promise.

Thérèse whirls off with a Cossack, and I am left alone. I stand to the side, sipping my tongue-numbing drink and wishing André were here. Then, out of the blue, pins and needles prickle up my spine: someone is staring at me! That happens sometimes on the omnibus. A funny tingling on my skin warns me I am being watched, and when I look round, there's some old man eating me with his eyes. As I scan the crowd, I catch the haunted gaze of a gypsy woman observing me intensely. I frown back—I believe I know those black eyes, that scornful, sultry mouth. The gypsy nods stiffly to me as she tangoes off with an Orpheus in leopard skins, and I wrack my brain trying to remember where I have seen her before.

The stove in the corner is roaring now, and beneath my costume, sweat drips down my arms and the insides of my thighs. The dancers' make-up of rouge, kohl, flour, and soot has begun to melt away, revealing underneath the blurred red mouths and swollen eyelids of people I recognize. That's the delivery boy from the grocery in Rue Delambre. And that's the girl who cleans the stairs in the building where Kisling lives, and that's the man who sometimes washes dishes at the Dôme and comes to my drawing class on Wednesdays. I do not see Thérèse or her friends anywhere. The gypsy, too, has gone. I dance for a while alone until my legs get tired in my boots.

The music pulses in my brain, faster and louder, as a chain of half-naked dancers snakes through the crowd, beating out a savage rhythm with bare feet and swinging hips. The chain moves as a single being as more dancers strip and join the frenzy. I hang back in the shadows watching, fascinated, until a man in the chain notices me standing there all alone. Breaking free, he rushes at me, ramming his hips against mine and pinning me to the wall. I shout out, but no one can hear me above the ruckus. I feel him hard through my dress.

I know him—it's an old man who models for drawing class, completely drunk. He stinks of sweat and alcohol. I try to shove him away, but he is much too strong. Looking round for help, I see only leering faces when he pushes me to the floor.

The gypsy swims into view, and I call to her for help. Seizing the man in her stout arms, she hoists him up and twirls him across the room in a teetering waltz, and they are both swallowed up by the crowd.

I get up and stumble away, colliding with other dancers. There is no place to sit down; no water to drink. Someone sticks a tin cup in my hand, I taste the fizz of champagne first, then an acrid tang like turpentine, and I feel like I am going to be sick.

I need fresh air to settle my stomach, so I press through the crowd towards the door. But the people waiting to get in thrust me back inside again, and I have to fight with my fists to force my way out, though I am on the verge of fainting.

It is a relief to be out in the cold air, where I can breathe and where my ears stop buzzing, but my face is boiling. I lean against a wall and find myself shivering—I realize I have lost my cape. It must have slipped off while I was dancing, but I can't go back inside to look for it. There are too many people thronging the door.

The streetlamps are out and the cafés are closed. In the moonlight, a dog noses through the rubbish piled on a corner. Next to a hole in the pavement, where water pipes are being repaired, someone has left the tiny flame of a red paraffin lantern burning, forgetting all about the black out.

The back of my dress is so drenched with sweat it clings to my skin like a wet bathing suit. I know I'll catch pneumonia if I stay out too long in this state. But I can't go home. I told Maman and Papa that I'll be staying tonight with Thérèse. It is past two in morning, and the *concierge* will have gone to bed, and, besides, it is too long of a walk back to Rue Amyot without a coat in this freezing air.

I take a deep breath. I must go back inside to look for my cape and try to find Thérèse.

The rasp of a cough makes me wheel round, and there stands the gypsy woman, bundled in a dirty blanket. She has followed me outside.

"*Pauvre petite!* You'll catch your death," her voice is mellow, pleasing, slightly foreign.

She folds me in her blanket. It stinks of wood smoke and old wine, but I am grateful for its warmth. Poking about the garbage piled on the corner, she picks up an orange crate. Setting it in a doorway, she dusts it off with her hand.

"Sit down, my daughter. You are tired."

I sit. She brings the paraffin lantern from the barricade and puts it on the ground before me, then crouches down on her haunches until we are eye to eye. In the dim red light, I see a sallow, finely-lined face, powdered with flecks of cocoa and charcoal to make it swarthy, thick black eyebrows, and a stubbly shadow of beard. The liquid eyes are grave.

"I will tell your fortune, but you must cross my palm with silver."

I fish a coin from my skirt pocket. It is warm from my body heat, and when I drop it into her outstretched fingers, a spark passes from her hand to mine.

The coin vanishes into her skirts, from which she draws out a grubby pack of fortune telling cards. One by one, she lays the cards on the cobblestones between us. I study the fingers dealing out my fate: finely tapered with paint-flecked nails; yellowed with tobacco; knuckles ridged with dark fuzz.

The first card is the Star: "You are a seeker, and you will stop at nothing to seek your heart's desire."

The second card is the Fool: "A wise fool will show you your way."

The third, the Lovers: "You will have your moment of bliss…"

The fourth, the Tower: "…to which unexpected circumstances will try to put an end."

The fifth, the World: "Your love and beauty will illuminate the world for a century or more. Like the light of Beatrice."

"Will I be happy then?" I ask.

The gypsy seizes my wrist and pulls me so close that her lips graze my face. I am not afraid, but excited. I can smell the brandy on her breath and the sweet cocoa powder dusting her cheeks. Her hand on my wrist is hot and firm. The foreign words she murmurs like a spell raise every single hair on my neck.

"Jeanne! Jeanne, why there you are." Thérèse, tipsy, still in the company of her Cossack, tumbles out to the street. "We've been looking all over for you."

"I must go," I tell the gypsy. The warm brown fingers release my wrist, and I rise up on stiff knees from the crate.

Thérèse holds out my cape. "You silly girl, you left your wrap inside! We found it for you, but it is all trampled and stained with wine. Come along. We are going over to Serghei's studio to make some spaghetti. I can try to remove the stains with some lemon juice."

I throw off the dirty blanket to put on my own cape. Turning to hand the blanket back to the gypsy, I see she has gone, so I leave it on the crate. One Tarot card lays face up on the ground: the Lovers. "*You will have your moment of bliss…*"

"Who was that you were talking to just now?" asks Thérèse.

"A fortune teller," I say, reaching down for the card and putting it into my pocket. I don't tell her who it really was: Amedeo Modigliani.

❀

Ash Wednesday, 1917

The next morning on my way to the Académie Colarossi, I see him outside the Rotonde, dressed in his brown corduroy suit, a red scarf knotted at his neck; his hat slouched over one ear. A smudge of charcoal remains on his cheek from the make-up he wiped away. He's picking up cigarette butts along the pavement and sticking them in his pocket. Seeing me, he gives me a dreamy smile, doffing his hat like a courtier, and recites a poem in Italian. I understand only three words: *Cuore, Spirito, Amore.*

He points to a table on the terrace, inviting me to sit down, so I do, although I know I'll be late to class. Slinging himself into the opposite seat, he leans forwards on his elbows and studies my face. Shyly I study him back. Last night I would have known him any-where, despite his gypsy disguise, simply by the heat of his nearness, or is it the heat he kindles in me? My heart is racing, and I can't think of anything to say. I clutch my portfolio like a shield before my breasts.

"*Permette?*" He eases the portfolio from my grasp and unties the ribbon with a wicked smile as though he were untying my chemise. When he pulls out the drawings and lays them out on the table, I want to die of embarrassment. Papa by the woodstove. Maman at the piano, André in uniform with his beard neatly trimmed. A tidy interior of mirrors and flowers. The little life of the bourgeoisie. This morning I thought these sketches were good enough to show Thérèse after class today, which is why I have brought them along with me, but now I wish I had torn them to bits.

He surveys them all quickly, smiles again, "*Ah, che bella famiglia!*" then scrutinizes them one by one.

"With such a patriarch's beard, this must be your grandpa."

I shake my head. "My father."

"A stern man, no doubt, but an excellent *père de famille*. And this lady at the piano must be your mother."

I nod.

"I can see a close resemblance. Very sensitive, a worry-wort; per-haps, even a bit hysterical. You will look just like her when you are old. Double chin and all."

He tickles me under my chin, and I blush and look away. His fin-gers stink of cheap tobacco.

Now he studies a sketch of André in uniform, smoking his pipe. "I see I have a rival. Don't tell me you are already engaged?"

"That is my brother, André," I blurt out. "He's away at the front."

His eyes narrow to a piercing glance. "You miss him very much?"

"We are very close. He is an artist, too. He was teaching me to paint."

"And now you have no teacher?" He leans back in his chair and folds his hands over his stomach. "That's easily remedied. Plenty of teachers in Montparnasse."

"I am studying at the Colarossi now."

"I sometimes go there to draw the models, but I have never seen you. I would remember if I had."

"I was away for nearly a month. Maman was ill, and the doctor recommended sea air."

The last drawing is a still life of our dining room table, with the mantelpiece and clock in the background, which he examines so long I begin to feel nervous. I used to think it was the best piece. Seeing it through his eyes, I am horribly ashamed.

"This is your home."

"I know it's not very good."

"On the contrary, it is very charming, and so are the others. You have a certain talent. I mean that, Mademoiselle…?"

"Jeanne, Jeanne Hébuterne with an H."

"Jeannette."

He stares at me a while without speaking, and I don't know what to say or do, so I just sit there and gaze back into those unsmiling eyes until I think I might lose myself there.

With his index finger, he caresses my cheek, eyelids, and forehead, as though he were drawing them on a blank canvas. When he traces my lips, my whole body trembles, and I have to stop myself from biting his finger or kissing his hand.

Abruptly, he pulls his hand away. Tearing a blank sheet from my carnet, he slips a pencil nub from his breast pocket and makes a quick sketch of my face with my braids hanging beneath my turban.

I fumble in my bag for some coins—I have heard that he asks five francs. Far too little, for a sketch, but he won't take it.

"Come to me next week, and I will paint your portrait." He saunters off before the waiter arrives.

I put the sketch away carefully, then order a noisette and drink it very slowly, the way Thérèse has taught me. I can still feel the hot touch of his hand on my face. The coffee tastes sweet and dark on my tongue.

March 1, 1917

Thérèse loaned me a book to read by Neel Doff, which almost won the Goncourt prize. It is about a girl who is abandoned by her parents and becomes a prostitute in order to feed her brothers and sisters: *Days of Hunger and Misery*. I have never read such a powerful story. Every other page makes you sigh or weep. I lie crying in bed as I read it, imagining myself in Neel's shoes. Rejected by all. Considered dirty and low, while trying to save her brothers and sisters from starvation. How could her parents have been so cruel? No one offered to help her—no one. But everyone blamed and accused her. How can people be such hypocrites while claiming to be Christians?

Stepping into my room with the laundry basket, Maman is startled to find me in tears. "What is it, Jeanne? Are you ill? What's wrong?" She places her cool hand on my forehead to see if I have a fever.

"I'm all right," I sniffle, gazing up at her from the bed. "It's just this book. It is such a sad story."

She looks relieved but also puzzled, and strokes my forehead, gently pushing strands of hair back behind my ears the way she used to do when I was a child sick in bed.

"With all the tragedy in the world and your brother at the front, you are weeping for a book?"

"All Paris is talking about it."

"You are too sensitive, my dear." She puts my freshly pressed chemises away in a drawer and goes out.

I know this is the book I have been looking for. I will make this story my own by sketching illustrations of the moments that mean the most to me. Other people will know the pain I feel.

March 5, 1917

When André is back home on leave, I proudly show him my carnet of drawings for *Days of Hunger and Misery*. He examines each one carefully and sighs when he comes to the last one where I have added a caption from the text: "All alone crouched on my bed, I raged and wept."

"It is a very sad story. Why do you like it so much?"

"The author is a true heroine. Abandoned by her mother and father, she willingly sacrificed herself in order to feed and protect her younger brothers and sisters. I think that is the noblest sacrifice—gladly accepting the scorn of society to express the highest love."

André snorts. "What example did she set for the children in her care by becoming a prostitute?"

"She was too poor to have a choice! Besides, prostitutes have their dignity too. Mary Magdalen was a whore."

"Watch your language! Did you learn that word from your friend Thérèse?"

I am too furious to answer. We always used to agree on everything! Or almost.

"Anyway, I think you're wrong," he continues. "She might have taken the children to an orphanage and found honest work for herself as a rag picker, or a laundress, or a dozen other jobs that poor women can do in Paris without degrading herself. She might have made other choices."

"But at an orphanage, the family would have been split up. The poor children had no one but her. Orphanages are such cruel places! To survive, they needed to be together!" My head is swimming; I am almost screaming with rage.

André stares at me, suddenly calm, his lips pale.

"In any case, your life is nothing like hers," he says in a complete change of tone. "You are surrounded by love, comfort, and even luxury, while brave men are dying so that you may maintain your style of life. You will never starve or find yourself without a roof over your head. Not if I can help it!"

"You are right," I surrender. "I am bourgeois. I am spoiled when so many fine artists have nothing to eat. But there are other forms of starvation, you know."

"What are you talking about?"

"The starvation of the soul."

"What in God's name do you mean?"

I shake my head, gather up my drawings, and go to my room. It is no use talking to André about Neel Doff. There are things about me he cannot understand. Perhaps no one can.

❋

Soaking in my bath, I look down at my pale body, at my breasts afloat above the waterline. I am lovely and old enough to have a lover now, although my only experience so far was with Foujita, and that was not a very happy one. Thérèse had her first lover when she was sixteen. She says she felt no pain, and that if you are with the right man, it won't hurt at all. Foujita was clearly the wrong person. But just sitting near Modigliani warms me from inside. Would he like my body? What would he say about the slope of my shoulders, the round line of my hips; the whiteness of my breasts?

I climb out of the tub when the water gets cold and inspect myself, naked, front and back in the mirror, as I often do. Last week Maman came in after my bath and surprised me, looking at myself from behind in the nude. I think she was worried I had something wrong—a rash or a wart—and I said that I was examining the mole I have high up on the back of my thigh.

"That's not a mole," she said, "but a birthmark. When I was expecting you, I had a craving for prawns, and your father would bring me some from the ocean. I ate so many that you were born with a sign: a little red crescent. Now I can't even stand the smell of them! But dry yourself off, child. You'll catch cold!" and she wrapped a thick white towel around me.

"It doesn't seem like so long ago that you and your brother were just toddling around my skirts. And now when I think André must return to the front, I think I will go mad."

"Then don't think of it, Maman. We must believe that he will be all right. Otherwise, how can we go on?"

"You are both so precious to me. I could not bear to lose either of you."

"You mustn't worry. You won't lose us," I say, but my voice lacks conviction.

April 6, 1917
Maman and I were alone for my birthday. With André and Papa both gone, we weren't in the mood for celebrating. Papa sent me Muguet perfume, as usual, and André sent a postcard. Maman gave me a little bottle of almond oil and a new notebook.

April 12, 1917

I knew the moment I opened my eyes that today was the day I'd go see him. I have been thinking about him for weeks, ever since that morning we met outside the Rotonde. I keep remembering the touch of his hand on my face, and my lips trembling. His finger was rough, and his knuckle was covered with fuzz. The warmth I felt when he leaned near was like when a cloud moves away from the sun.

I caught sight of him last week at the Dôme, talking to Kisling. When he glanced at me across the sea of hatted heads and round tin tables, his eyes burnt into my skin. He nodded and I nodded back and I knew just what he meant: *I am waiting for you to come to me whenever you are ready.* And then he turned back to Kisling and didn't look at me again, yet all the time I felt he was following me from the corner of his eye. There was a thin golden thread strung across the room from his body to mine, like honey dripping from a spoon.

Thérèse was there at the Dôme with me as we were meeting her Russian friends, and she noticed him too, but I don't think she saw the sparks that flew through the air when our eyes made contact. I still haven't told her how we met at the café, or that he has asked me to come sit for a portrait.

I could lie here all morning wrapped in my pink satin comforter thinking of him, but the bliss is about to end. I hear Céline clomping down the corridor from the kitchen, bringing me my bowl of coffee and milk along with a hot roll.

"Jeanne, you lazy girl! You'd better get out of bed, or you won't get to class on time!"

"Thank you, Céline, I will be up and dressed in a moment."

Putting the tray on the bedside table, she studies my face a moment.

"You look pale. Is it your time of month? Is that why you are dawdling in bed?"

"Not at all. Now leave me be while I have my breakfast."

"Well, hurry up. I have to get the beds made before I go out for the shopping." She shuts the white door behind her.

Today lessons at the academy have been cancelled because the *Maître* is down with a head cold. They put up a notice on the door late yesterday afternoon, saying no lessons until Monday, which Thérèse and I read as we walked past on our way to a café. I said nothing about it to Maman, so I am free all day to do as I wish. I will walk over to Montparnasse and wander about for awhile, then, around noon, I will see if Modigliani is hanging about the Dôme or the Rotonde. If I can't find him, I will ask Père Libion at the Rotonde where he is living now. They say he never stays in one place for long, but he has broken up with that English poetess, the one with the ducks in her purse.

I prop myself up on the pillows and reach for the coffee. The cheval mirror in the corner by the great armoire gives me back myself. My dark hair streams down over my shoulders in my chaste white shift, with its collar edged in lace made by the knotted hands of an old Breton woman. I gaze about the room as I sip, at the writing table piled high with notebooks and sketchbooks, my precious violin in its battered black case neatly tucked on a shelf, a hamper of drawing and painting supplies and on top of that my sewing basket. Stuck in the oval mirror above the washstand with its skirt of rosebuds is a photograph of André in uniform—with a dedication *to my darling Nenette*—and next to the photograph is the Tarot card of the Lovers. This is the room of a proper *jeune fille*, the person I am outgrowing or perhaps have never been. It is a room where Modi will never set foot, where his smile will never be caught in the mirror. Yet the thought of him fills every room, every space I go, and replaces the air in my lungs.

It takes me longer than usual to do my hair. Braids are too school-girlish and virginal. I sweep it all up in a simple chignon, to look older and more sophisticated. Then I carefully choose my colors. A yellow sweater—I have heard he likes yellow—a white silk blouse, and a purple skirt are clothes I'd wear to class, so Maman won't suspect I am going anywhere special. But underneath I have on my nicest chemise and underwear, and I have squirted myself all over with Muguet perfume and rubbed my body with almond oil.

She is in the salon, at her writing desk, worrying over some bills as I head out the door. The light glints on the spectacles she has started to wear as she looks up to inspect me.

"Your hair looks nice. You look—so grown up. Hmm. You smell nice too. Come back straight after class."

"Yes, around five."

"Maybe I can find us a nice treat for tea. Now kiss me and go."

I spend an hour window shopping, then dawdle at a café in a side street, scribbling in a notebook as my coffee grows cold. At noon the jangling bells of Notre-Dame-des-Champs wake me from a daydream, and I walk back to the Rotonde, heart fluttering, stomach churning. I can barely catch my breath. But he isn't on the terrace or inside; in fact there is hardly anyone at all about, so I go over to the Dôme where a few rowdy foreigners are drinking aperitifs on the terrace, and inside an old man is reading a newspaper. Anxious, I return to the Rotonde, and go straight to the bar, where Père Libion is removing blue seltzer bottles from a wooden case and arranging them on a shelf.

"And why would you want to know where Modigliani lives?" He grins at me in a way that makes me feel ashamed.

"I need to speak to him as soon as possible." My ears are burning; my face is hot.

"Well, come back later and maybe you'll find him."

"I am telling you, it's urgent."

"I can see it is, Mademoiselle, but you look a bit young to go calling on the likes of Modi."

"Please." I grip his wrist in his grubby sleeve.

He spits out an address, and I almost kiss his hand. I know the place—a crumbling hotel where the rooms are rented out to artists and prostitutes for a few sous. I run all the way there, and when I catch my reflection in a shop window, with my cheeks bright red and my chignon coming all undone, I stop and try to calm myself down by poking the pins back in.

I pass through a cobbled courtyard into a dark hall, where the front desk is deserted. A few rusty keys dangle on nails stuck in a board behind it. A fat gray cat curled on the lumpy sofa lifts its head to yawn at me. What a dreary place he lives in! Outside I hear a rattling of bottles and a banging of bins, and a stout woman in a long black dress appears from the back of a court, dragging a sack of rubbish. The cat jumps down and scuttles away as she comes in through door.

"*Vous désirez?*"

"*Bonjour,* Madame. Please, what room number for Monsieur Modigliani?"

Hands on hips, she sizes me up. "Who wants to know?"

"I am a model here for a sitting."

"*Vraiment!*" She laughs—a raw, rough sound. "So now he is after girls of your age, is it? Third floor." She nods to the stairs.

She watches me go up, her laughter swirling up around me like bats in an attic.

In the air hangs a sickening smell of boiled cabbage and cat piss. Orange peels and cigarette ends litter the unswept stairs. After a few steps, I realize I shouldn't have come. I should have waited for him at the Rotonde. And then, if he had asked me to sit for a portrait, I could simply have got up and followed him here and climbed these stairs behind him, holding that warm, brown hand with fuzz on his knuckles. What if I find him working or in a furious mood—I have heard stories about how he flies into a rage if he is disturbed at his easel, slashing his own work with a stylet. Or he might not even be in. He may be in bed with a woman. And what if he has forgotten that he asked me to come…. But I can't slink back down and face that Medusa at the bottom of the stairs, so I force myself to go on. My mouth is dry, and a bitter taste like dread clings to the back of my throat

"Monsieur Modi?" I ask a man coming down the corridor, breathless from the climb, or is it terror? He points to a door and passes on.

I knock.

"Go away," says a voice inside. It's him.

"Modi, it's me, Jeanne."

"*Petite* Jeanne? *Ma petite* Jeanne?"

I hear a scurrying about inside. The door opens just a crack, and two black eyes peer out at me. He flings the door open and pulls me into the room.

"You told me to come for a sitting. So here I am."

"So I see! *Bien! Bien!*" His shirt is open, revealing thick curly hair on his chest.

Behind a screen, a woman—a model—is putting her clothes back on. From the unmade bed with its dingy sheets all askew, I understand that they were together just before I knocked. Scowling at me, she hurries towards the door, her feet bare, breasts poking out the front of her open blouse, her shoes and stockings in her hand. Modi, his palm on the small of her back, pushes her out gently with a teasing goodbye, "Till tomorrow, same time!" and shuts the door.

I stand in the middle of the room and look around, for a moment dizzy with panic. What am I doing here? Then I see the Madonnas. Tacked all over the walls are reproductions of the Annunciation by Italian masters: Piero della Francesca, Giotto, Simone Martini. They peer at me from beneath dark blue veils studded with stars—prim, secretive, tender. They tell me to be calm, and all will be well.

Now I notice his paintings, his portraits, propped up against the walls, and stacked on the dresser. An army of heads fill the room. My curiosity blots out all fear.

A Chinese woman with a red face and puckered lips squints beneath a black fur hat. A cellist embraces his instrument with closed eyes while dreaming his music. A stern woman with a flounced collar stares out accusingly. Although some have blind eyes with no pupils, all the faces are alive with thoughts that you can almost touch, thoughts tingling in the air around them.

"Please sit down." He clears off the only chair in the room, tossing the books and clothes piled on it to the floor, and I perch on rough, prickly straw.

This is such a squalid room. An old piano shoved against the wall. A small charcoal stove, empty tins and wine bottles, rags, papers, and books all scattered on the floor. A rusted washstand with a cracked mirror, a green enamel basin, and a comb. His red bandana hangs on a nail in the wall.

"Do you play?" I point to the piano.

"It is broken, only for decoration. Do you?"

"Only the violin."

I sit with my knees together in my purple skirt, and my chin raised to make my neck look longer, falling naturally into a pose. I try to squeeze my life through my eyes in hopes he will find me worth painting.

"Then one day you will play for me."

"Of course."

He puts a canvas on the easel and stands there staring at me for a very long time, unsmiling, his eyes traveling over every inch of my body. I sit still and stare back until the roaring in my ears dies away and my heart is quiet again. An ocean lies between us that I must swim across to reach him, like a drowning person to an island. After an hour, or is it two, he comes to me, pulls the pins from my chignon and arranges my hair around my shoulders. He studies me for awhile with my hair down, then lays his hands lightly on my shoulders. I look up into his eyes and then bend my head to touch his hand with my cheek, my lips.

When he unbuttons my blouse, my heart pounds.

"You have never had a man before?"

"Not completely." I hardly have any voice at all.

"Are you afraid?"

"No," I say, but he laughs. He can see how terrified I am.

"But you are shivering. You are cold."

We lay down side by side on his bed, and he strokes me, as if I were a cat or a frightened child until I fall asleep.

Four visits later when the portrait was done, we became lovers. He ripped my underwear, and I had to sew it back up before going home.

❋

May 7, 1917

Maman is out when I return. The clock on the mantelpiece ticks loudly in the empty room, where the red-damask curtains are drawn, and the piano closed with a paisley shawl thrown over it to keep off the dust. With André gone, there's no life in this house. A fly drones above a dish of apples on the dining table. A petal falls from a drooping tulip on the sideboard, where Maman keeps André's letters on a tray, but today there are no envelopes or cards, only a folded newspaper. While walking home, I was scared I would be punished with bad news about André, but there is nothing at all.

Is it true that you can tell a girl is no longer a virgin simply by looking in her eyes? I examine my face in the mirror above the mantelpiece. Soon it begins to whirl, recomposing itself into portraits I don't recognize: I am a woman, a boy, a very old man; I am a tusked animal with yellow eyes. I wait until the whirling stops and the silver depths grow calm again, showing me the mask of my face I always wear, and, behind me, the familiar dining room with its mahogany table and sideboard where the headline on the newspaper appears printed backwards.

Then I see something impossible. A small blue door with a brass knocker stands there in the distance behind me. Black Hebrew letters are painted in a circle on the door, and, as I study them, they begin to move while everything else in the room is still. I know I am only imagining something like in a painting. If I turn and look, I will see there is no blue door leading off the dining room; there are no dancing letters. Yet from here, I see it all so distinctly in the mirror. All I need do is reach back for the knob, pull it open, walk backwards, and pass through. Into another room. Another time. Another Paris.

Modi says there is no barrier between this world and the next. That the other world sometimes appears in dreams, mirrors, and reflections in water. And sometimes even in the pictures we paint, unawares.

"Jeanne!"

I jump at the sound of my name and break the spell of my gaze.

Maman in her best hat and coat bustles in, carrying a pink packet from a patisserie like in the old days before the war. She puts the packet on the sideboard. "Have you just come in?"

"I was out with Thérèse." I have never lied so blatantly to her before. I have been silent sometimes, but I have never lied, and now I feel ashamed.

"You seem to be seeing a lot of her recently," she says, unbuttoning her coat. "You have been neglecting your music." She steps out to the hallway to hang up her coat on the rack, chatting to me as she unpins her hat and readjusts her hair.

"I have bought two small pastries. Your favorites. Heaven knows I was lucky to find some in these times. The baker must have moved heaven and earth to get the flour and sugar! Certainly he charged me as though they were baked and delivered by angels. But we won't tell your father that."

"I am not hungry."

"What did you say?" Coming in again, she gives me that pinched look of hers.

"I said I'm not hungry,"

"Are you all right? You seem…."

I glance up to meet her eyes, and she stares right through me as if I were a ghost. She knows, I thought. She knows they are losing me.

"...Flushed. Are you sure you don't have a fever? There's flu going around." She claps her hand to my forehead. "You are a bit warm."

"I am tired. Perhaps I should go lie down."

"Yes, darling, go and lie down. I will bring you some tea later."

In my bedroom, I take all my clothes off and study my body with my hand mirror—all the places where he touched me, which now have new life. The violet shadow under my breast, the fuzz in my armpits; the delicate folds of my sex like fleshy pink orchid petals. I take my drawing things and begin to sketch my body. This body is me. It belongs to me, and there is no reason why I should not draw it.

❀

May 20, 1917

I like to sit up in bed and watch him sleep in the afternoon—one limp arm dangling over the mattress to the floor, where a book has slipped from his hand. I love the smell of his skin and hair after we make love. Sometimes I draw him. His eyes closed with their fringe of black lashes and his thick black hair slicked back from his brow. One arm thrown over his head on the pillow, fingers splayed, palm open like a corpse. A meaty forearm with undulating muscle. An almost womanly foot. His buttocks tufted with soft, dark hair. Drawing him like this, finally I possess every inch of him.

Maman and Papa don't know where I spend my afternoons and evenings. But they have begun to be suspicious since I am away from home so often after class. I tell them I am with Thérèse. André will find out sooner or later, and then he will eat me alive! He has so many friends in Montparnasse, and everyone here knows that Modi and I are halfway living together, though we keep moving to room to room, wherever he finds a place to work or sleep. But I must keep up the pretense until the ax falls, and then I will make my choice. But for now, I shall go on leading a double life.

Papa is stationed now in Paris, so he is sometimes home at mealtimes, which is so much better than when it was just Maman and I hunched silently over our bowls of bean soup. The three of us sit at table, with André's place empty. His picture on the mantelpiece stares mournfully at us as Papa says grace. Our meals are more frugal now with the high taxes, restrictions, and rationing on everything: eggs, meat, sugar, milk. Every week, two meatless days, and bones get boiled over and over for broth. Even so, I am lucky to enjoy food in a comfortable home, while so many of my friends in Montparnasse are starving. Although if they have enough to drink, they sometimes don't seem to care. Like Modi. He never gets enough to eat, but is too proud to complain. Every sip of broth or mouthful of bread I eat at home with my parents I feel I should be sharing with him.

The other day I snuck him some food from home: a jar of milk, a few lumps of sugar, half a Parisienne, a hunk of cheese, and three oranges all wrapped in a piece of newspaper. Céline saw me taking food from the kitchen and accosted me at once.

"It is for Thérèse," I say, stowing my bundle into a string bag. "She is a poor art student and she is ill with flu. I must take her something to eat. Please don't tell Maman."

"And if she sees something is missing from the pantry? What will I tell her then? I don't want to be blamed. You know how hard it is to find fresh food? You must have a ticket for meat, one for sugar, and one for milk."

"Tell her that I came home ravenously hungry, and you could not refuse me a snack. Please," I pleaded. "It is for a dear friend who needs my care." This part at least was true.

"All right, I won't interfere with Christian charity. But make sure you don't catch whatever she has got." She went back to mopping the floor with bleach.

But my lover just laughed when he opened the packet and the oranges rolled out on the worktable among the crumpled tubes of paint.

"Ma petite Jeannette, like a good wife, you wish to feed me. But there is no need. I dine like a king at Rosalie's and never pay a cent. And unlike Cézanne or Matisse, I am not a painter of fruit. But I'll share this with poor Soutine, who is always hungry."

"But you need to eat fresh food too, and oranges are good for the lungs!"

"Are you worried about my lungs, my dear? Afraid you might catch something from me?"

And how could I say, but there was blood on the pillow again today?

"Of course not, would I be here if I were?"

Scowling, he sniffs an orange. "Anyway, what do the French know about oranges, a southern fruit? Now, back home in Livorno, we had orange trees in huge clay urns in the yard, and the perfume in spring when they bloom, mixed with the fresh smell of the sea," he drew in a deep breath, "was unforgettable. Besides this shriveled ball is not an orange. It is as hard as rubber."

He tosses the orange into the air, grabs the other two, and begins to juggle them before my nose, like a circus mountebank.

I snatch an orange out of the air, as he lets the others drop to the floor. Digging my nail deep into the skin, I peel it, and lift a segment to my mouth. It tastes dry and sour, but I swallow it and hold a piece out to him. With a smirk, he eats it. Segment by segment, I dismantle the oranges, handing him each piece, as I would to a child, and I think tomorrow I will bring him boiled eggs.

May 30, 1917

His pockets are full of poems—Lautréamont, Dante, Baudelaire, and Rimbaud. He reads them to me in bed. Yesterday we sat beneath the Tour Saint-Jacques and he recited Nerval. "*Je suis le Ténébreux, – le Veuf, – l'Inconsolé, / Le Prince d'Aquitaine à la Tour abolie.*"

May 31, 1917

Every day, when classes are finished, I go to the Rotonde, where everyone gathers at lunchtime—artists, models, and dealers. Sometimes, Thérèse comes with me, but lately our friendship has cooled since I have been spending so much time with Modigliani, and she more and more time with her sculptor friend, Serghei.

Modi saunters in sooner or later, usually with Soutine—and throws himself into the chair I have saved for him. He chats with anyone sitting near, whether stranger or friend, dashing off sketches or accepting drinks from anyone who'll pay as the saucers pile up in front of us. If he notices my green portfolio propped against the wall, he'll reach for it, untie the black ribbon with a sly smile, and remove my poor sketches. One by one, he subjects them to his terrible scrutiny, pointing out all the flaws, and even handing them round to the other artists present for further comment. I hated him at first for this, until I saw that it meant he takes my work seriously. The few words of critique he gives me are so much more than what I get at the academy from the drawing instructor. And I think Thérèse is jealous, because he rarely asks to look at her drawings, and if he does, gives only encouraging praise and slips them back in her portfolio.

If Soutine is there, Modi will make sure he gets something to eat as well as to drink, and help keep him in line as Soutine's table manners are atrocious. When Soutine first arrived in Paris, it was Modi who taught him how to use a fork and a toothbrush, neither of which he had ever seen before. If Picasso or Ortiz is present, then they are bound to launch into long discussions of philosophy or technique, and all the while, Modi will hold my hand under the table, pressing my fingers, so that the sparks run up my arm, and all I can think about is when we are going to be alone again and fall into each other's arms.

Then finally, after another drink or two, we hurry to the room where he is staying, pull off our clothes, and make love on a prickly horsehair mattress or anywhere else he likes. Afterwards he is always hungry, so we go to Rosalie's in Rue Campagne-Première, where he orders her Italian style stew, mostly potatoes and hardly any meat, but lots of rosemary and garlic. I only eat a morsel from his dish, because Maman expects me home for dinner. I just sit and watch him, smiling at the pleasure he feels as he chews his tough beef and drains his liter of Italian red wine, chattering in Italian with Rosalie. Sometimes he will take the guitar down from the wall and strum a tune like a harlequin.

When he has finished, we walk arm in arm towards the Contrescarpe, taking a roundabout route to my parents' apartment. He talks to me about Italy and life in the south, and about when we will go and live there. He never comes all the way home with me, for fear someone in the neighborhood might see us and report back to my parents, or worse, our *concierge*, but leaves me there at the corner near a little weed-choked garden at the end of the street or on the steps of the church of Saint-Étienne. After a chaste kiss or a pat on my cheek, he turns away in the dusk. They say he goes out drinking all night, stumbling into bed at dawn, if he manages to make it home.

The dour *concierge* glares at me as I go in the door and head up the four flights of steps. Maman and Papa are already at table, waiting to say grace. And as I slide into my place across from them and lift a spoon of fish soup to my lips, I can think of only one thing—the next time I will see him again—when our mouths and tongues will meet and our bodies join in a bliss I know I cannot live without. I'd rather die than lose him.

Thérèse doesn't approve of our affair. Of course, she must be jealous. She liked him too. But she claims she is worried about me.

"His lovers are legion," she says one day, as we were having coffee alone at the Rotonde.

I know. There was the Russian poetess, the English poetess, the prostitutes, the models, and the many little friends of friends.

"There is even a baby he wouldn't claim as his own. The mother they say is dying of consumption. Her name is Simone."

I shrug. "Yes, I have heard. None of that has anything to do with me."

"But the same thing could happen to you."

"It won't."

"How do you know?"

"Because we are careful, and I watch the calendar."

"That's all? The calendar? No sponges?"

I shake my head. I don't even know what she is talking about.

"Then you're a fool." Now she shakes *her* head. "This affair will end badly."

"Why do you say that—oh, of course, you're psychic."

"It doesn't take a fortune teller to see where you're headed. You're probably already in trouble."

I protest, but I want to know about those sponges.

"You silly goose, I have to teach you everything."

And leaning forward over our empty coffee cups, she explained about the sponges and vinegar and how to put them in to avoid getting pregnant.

June 15, 1917
Now that classes at the Académie are over, I am free to spend all day with Modi, who continues painting portraits of me in every imag-

inable outfit. Right now, he is staying in a cheap room near Rosalie's with a horsehair mattress on the floor. I dream of a place of our own. Returning home, I tell Maman I have been out with Thérèse, whom I haven't seen since classes ended, or visiting other artist friends in their Montparnasse studios—which isn't really a lie.

Yesterday Modi took me to see Hanka and Zbo, his patron and dealer, at their home in Rue Joseph-Bara. Opening the door, Zbo beamed at us with his birdlike face, deep-set eyes glinting above a patchy red beard.

"And who is this delightful creature?"

"Jeannette, *ma femme et ma muse.*" His words thrill me. I am his Wife and Muse!

Zbo's moustache prickles me when he kisses my hand. Cool-eyed Hanka leads the way to a tiny salon that doubles as a dining room.

Zbo is a good man who has helped Modi so much, buying him painting supplies, giving him money; sharing his dinner of boiled beans and bread night after night in the worst times; occasionally even selling a piece. From what Modi has told me about him, I feel I can trust him, but I don't know about Hanka. She seems so proper and superior. Modi says she is a true aristocrat.

In a book-lined room where the lamps have pink silk shades, we sit on a worn green velvet sofa. Hanka serves us tea, pastries, and dark, chewy seed cake. Modi, completely sober and neatly dressed, does not touch the tea or cakes. Zbo pours him brandy out of a silver flask as they talk about some prospective clients in the south who might buy his work, and Modi gives him a list of paints and supplies to buy. I sit there listening as I always do when Modi is talking business with someone, drinking my tea while Hanka inspects me from top to toe.

I am wearing my robin's egg blue dress, a gold damask turban, and a necklace I made from twisted copper wire. She wears a prim dark blue dress with a stiff, pointy white collar, which makes her look sallow and brings out her sharp Slavic cheekbones. She wore that dress in a portrait Modi painted, set off by a string of pearls, but she sold the pearls and gave the money to Zbo to buy paints, canvases and food for the several artists he maintains. I must not criticize her. I know I must be grateful.

Hanka asks Modi to help her with something in the kitchen. I am left alone with Zbo. We hear them in the next room, rattling dishes and cutlery around, and Hanka laughing at something Modi has said. I look down at the red Afghan carpet, where my feet are placed dead center of a dark green lozenge, illumined by a ray of sunlight. I can feel Zbo studying me with some curiosity as we sit awkwardly for a long moment, not speaking, waiting for them to come back from the kitchen.

Zbo breaks the silence. "How old are you?"

I look up and smile. I am not threatened by this question. Whenever Modi introduces me to someone, this is what they always ask first. "Nineteen."

"Hmmph! He has a difficult character."

"I know."

"Given to excesses of all kinds: women, drink, sometimes—drugs."

This must be a test, I think, so I nod. "I love him." I have nothing else to say.

"And your family? You are still underage! What do they say about your liaison with the Italian painter?"

I shrug. "I don't talk about it much with them." How can I say: They know nothing!

Zbo's eyes narrow in his red cheeks, and he peers at me with mistrust. "He is not well. His health isn't good."

"I know."

"If he is to work, he must get better. And to get better he needs care."

I nod.

"Can you give him that care, Jeanne?"

I look down at the empty cups and plates on the table, thinking that in my life with Modi, there will be no china dishes or afternoon teas, or comfortable sofas like this one. I touch the white linen napkin, neatly starched and pressed like those at home. I crumple it in my fingers.

Again, I nod.

He takes my chin in his hand, tilts my face towards his, and stares me straight in the eyes.

"Can you?"

I don't answer with words, only with my eyes, with all the inner force I have.

"Yes, I think you can." He lets go my chin and smiles at me. After a pause, he says, "Modi cannot go on living in abandoned buildings, train stations, or cheap hotels if he is to do any serious work. He needs a space where he can paint undisturbed and show his work to buyers. A painter is nothing without a studio of his own. I think I have found the right place."

July 3, 1917

Zbo has found us a place at 8 Rue de la Grande Chaumière, right next door to the Académie and just around the corner from the Rotonde and the Dôme. Our new residence is a large L-shaped flat on the top floor of an annex in the courtyard, fronted with huge windows and flooded with light. The short stroke of the L is the bedroom—the longer one is the studio, furnished with trestle tables and even a charcoal stove for cooking and heat. Zbo has promised to pay for the fuel.

Gauguin once had an atelier in this building, and Modi says it is a good omen. Our downstairs neighbor is Manuel Ortiz de Zarate, who studied with Modi in Venice when they were young. Ortiz has a wife and two girls. He is brawny with powerful arms. He will help to bring up our water and coal. Modi cannot lift heavy loads without hurting his ribs and lungs.

With Rosalie in Rue Campagne-Première and Zbo and Kisling in Rue Joseph-Bara, both just minutes away, we are at the heart of the universe. And it is only a twenty-minute walk to Rue Amyot, by way of the Luxemburg Gardens.

Zbo and Hanka have brought a few furnishings—a bed, some chairs, a dresser, a worktable, a few old dishes, pots and pans, and even an Italian coffee pot! I snuck a few things from my bedroom: books, a candlestick, a piece of blue striped cloth to spread on the bed; some fabrics to make a curtain, though Maman suspects nothing. Soon I will bring over all my things, but then I will have to tell them that I am moving in with Modi. I know they will take it badly.

July 5, 1917

In my little bedroom in Rue Amyot, I keep a portfolio under the bed where my secret things are stored: drawings of myself, of Modi, naked in bed. I have been meaning to take them to the studio where they will be safe, but I kept putting it off, and now the worst has happened. In one of her cleaning fits, Céline found the portfolio and Maman opened it to see what was inside.

Returning from Modi's in late afternoon, I find Maman in her apron, sitting on the freshly made bed, leafing through a sketchbook, with other drawings spread around her on the white lace coverlet. She glares at me as I come in, her eyes burning with anger and shame. "Jeanne, we must talk about these drawings of yours. They are indecent!"

"No, they aren't. They are just nudes, as we are taught to draw." I reach out to ease the sketchbook from her grip, but she clutches it tightly, staring at a portrait I did of myself.

"But some of the details are so explicit. A lady mustn't draw such things or even see them. If I had known that this is what you were doing at the academy, I never would have let you attend lessons there. I don't know what your father or brother would say if they should see these. The mere thought makes me feel ill."

"My brother would probably understand that these are anatomical exercises for art class." But as I say this, I know it's a lie. Remembering his reaction to Modi's nudes, he wouldn't understand at all. "Anyway, I didn't do these at the academy. I drew them here at home with the help of a mirror."

The idea horrifies her at first. "You mean that's you? You drew yourself—like that?" Disgusted, she tosses the sketchbook aside, and I sweep it up and stick it in the portfolio, clasping it firmly under my arm. One by one, I pick the sketches up off the bed and slip them into the portfolio, which tomorrow will be transferred to my new home, where I will not be required to explain what I draw and why I draw it.

"It is not that scandalous, Maman," I say caressing her arm. "The human body is beautiful in all of its parts. Besides no one else but you has ever seen these drawings—except myself, of course."

"You haven't shown them to anyone?"

"No. They are private experiments in technique."

"I see." She sounds doubtful. "What about the drawings of the man? Who is that?"

"No one in particular. Just a model from the academy. I don't even know his name."

She sighs in relief and stares at me, examining my appearance.

"Dearest, you need to wash your hair. Tomorrow. Today I am too tired."

She rises slowly from the bed and smooths the apron over her skirt.

"This knowledge you have, Jeanne. This knowledge of your body. It is not seemly for a young woman, for a lady of good reputation. Your virginity, your good name, our good name are the most precious things you have. I raised you and your brother to understand this. I know you will not disappoint me."

Stepping out to the corridor, one hand on the brass doorknob, she says, "I hope you will have the good sense to keep these out of sight. If I find them again, I will destroy them."

Later, I stand naked before the cheval mirror. My hair cascades to my knees—so dark on my pale skin, and my orange nipples showing between the glossy strands. This is the body of Eve, of a Pre-Raphaelite maiden. The body I have given to Modi. The body I refuse to let my mother control.

I pick up my steel sewing shears to make the first cut. The long tresses drop to the floor like the shed skin of a snake. I cut my hair all around, with the help of a hand mirror, leaving it just shoulder length, then shake out my mane like a lion might do. How much lighter it feels! Now my hair will be easier to take care of, and I can wash it at the studio alone, if need be. I sweep up the clippings and wrap them in tissue to make a small packet. Tomorrow I will sell them to the hairdresser in Rue Rivoli, who makes wigs for old ladies, and I will use the money to buy paints.

I smile at my new face in the mirror, and decide it's time to claim my freedom: I need to tell her the truth about "that man in the drawings," and that I am going to live with him.

Maman stares at me, aghast, as I step out of my room in my bathrobe. "What have you done to your lovely hair?"

"Women are cutting their hair now. It's modern. Haven't you seen them all over Paris?"

"Your father and brother will be heartbroken."

"It's not their hair. They have no idea what a bother it is. Getting it snagged in doorways, blowing into my face, keeping it up with pins poking my scalp. You of all people know what a burden it is. Women nowadays have better things to do than spend an entire day washing their hair."

Despite the row we have just had, a faint smile flits across my mother's lips. Her anger dissolves and so does mine. I stroke her arm.

"You don't know how many women would die to have hair like yours," she says.

I notice the white streaks at her temples. Her hair started turning when André went to war. "Anyway, it will grow back by the time André comes home, thicker and longer than before," I say.

"If he comes home," she says mournfully.

I suck in my breath. She has said the words we never say aloud, but we think and fear every single day.

"Maman! You mustn't talk like that. He is going to be all right."

"I know I must not dwell on dark thoughts. But it is so hard for me, to have him away, and to see you—growing up so quickly, so eager to lead your own life, and not confiding in me anymore."

She has always been able to read my mind. I reach for her hand and give it a guilty kiss.

For the moment I shall say nothing.

❋

July 6, 1917
"Are you afraid of death, Jeanne?"

We were lying on a tomb, watching the clouds. He had promised to show me a garden where he often goes to meet a friend and pick the roses he sometimes brings me. Red or white, edged in brown, with swollen buds drooping on the stem—hot house roses that never fully bloom, retaining only the ghost of a scent.

I was surprised when he stopped at a gate on Boulevard Edgar Quinet. The park he meant was actually the Montparnasse Cemetery. The friend he had come to meet was Baudelaire—who has two tombs, or rather a monument and a grave in two different places in the cemetery. One for himself and one for his shadow, or so Modi claims. Baudelaire was interred in a family tomb, where the list of his stepfather's accomplishments took up all the space on the headstone. For Baudelaire there was barely room to engrave his name. And yet, no one knows or remembers his stepfather anymore, but Baudelaire is immortal.

Modi takes a piece of paper from his pocket, a page torn from a book, and sitting down on the tomb begins to read to me from *Un Voyage à Cythère*.

"It's disrespectful to sit on a grave," I protest, looking round to see if there are mourners present who might object, but we're the only people in the cemetery. Modi grabs my hand and tugs me down.

"He won't mind! He likes the company."

He lies back, and I lie back too and cradle my head on his shoulder. The stone is cold and scratchy with lichen.

"I am afraid," I said, "A little. And you?"

He wraps his arm around my shoulder and softly chants a stream of words I can't follow but which make me want to weep. I cling to his side.

"It's the prayer for the dead," he says, and a chill runs through my bones.

"You're so cold," he says and rubs my arms to bring warmth back into me.

"You there! What's going on?" An attendant with a rake appears from behind a tombstone, and we jump up and run laughing hand in hand towards the gate.

July 7, 1917

Zbo bought an armchair for us at a flea market, so our models would have a comfortable place to pose. I have no idea how Ortiz managed to get it all the way up the steps to the studio. Chaim Soutine is our first model to be painted there. All morning Modi and I work side by side in the studio, while Chaim sits half sunk in the chair, smirking and smoking incessantly.

As I work, my eyes dart back and forth from my canvas to Modi's, to observe his process. He always begins with the eyes. He says it is the person's gaze that creates the atmosphere of a portrait. First, he must know and understand the eyes, then the rest will come. He leaves the sockets empty or fills them with sky.

Next, he traces the shapes with long, fluid brushstrokes in black or dark blue, never hesitant, every stroke clean and pure. This is the secret of his style—that simple, elegant line that sums up a personality.

I try to follow his guide, leaving my arm muscles lax, almost as if floating on water. Only the muscles of the hand and fingers are tensed in holding the brush, so the energy may flow straight to the tip. It is like when playing the violin or making love—too much tension cuts off the flow.

Sometimes he disappears behind his canvas, not a word or a breath breaks his concentration. Other times he fights with it, curses it, lashes at it like a fencer with a sword—as if to attack or murder a dreaded enemy or intruder.

He works simultaneously on background and figure—like a sculptor pulling a statue from stone. Then comes a moment when the background falls away, leaving a stark shape traced upon an empty space of vibrant color which is both an outer atmosphere and an inner one.

Each face and figure is splendidly proportioned, as dictated by his classical training. Often he will slyly point out to me the geometrical lines of the Golden Mean he has applied to a face or figure like an invisible skeleton. Yet it seems so natural, without any forethought. You would never suspect it was there. I think that is why his bodies and faces are so satisfying to look at.

He is so unlike me. I let myself be guided by the colors of feeling. Every color has a feeling; every person has a dominant color. I love a naïve approach, in which background and settings are part of the person, a sort of extension of personality. I find that clothes and furnishings are ways people, especially women, express their identity. Women see the world and their bodies differently than men.

But on other days, when Zbo has found him a paying client for a portrait, Modi prefers to work alone, so I retire to our little bedroom and find myself something to do. At first, I brought my violin from Rue Amyot, and practiced, but that disturbed him, so now I sew or write in my journal, or paint small gouaches of what I can see through the window: a little tree down in the courtyard. A woman reading, framed beneath a gable across the way.

I keep waiting to hear the door shut when the model leaves, so I can join Modi again and see how his work is progressing. He tries to finish in as few sittings as possible, even in a single session, and afterwards he is exhausted. Sometimes he asks for water, sometimes for wine; sometimes he needs me to massage his shoulders. Then he takes a basin of water, no matter how cold, and washes himself from head to toe. It is like a ritual ablution. Perhaps he feels he must wash away the guilt of having painted a human form, which the religion of his family forbids. Other times he is so excited he wants to make love right there, but the floor is too hard and strewn with bits of charcoal and glass, so I lead him back to our tiny bedroom, where the green gauze curtain I sewed shifts like seaweed in the breeze through the open window.

I could not imagine a more perfect happiness.

July 13, 1917

Yesterday Kisling stood a round of drinks for everyone at the Rotonde to celebrate a major sale to Jonas Netter. Foujita, Brancusi, and Matisse are all selling well, and the critics fill newspapers with praise. But Modi has so few buyers. In his pocket, he carries a clipping from a Swiss newspaper, with an article by Francis Carco, praising his work to the stars. It is so crumpled and dog-eared by now, it is disintegrating, but he clings to it like a saint's relic and can recite it by heart the way my mother recites her prayers.

Zbo wants Modi to produce some large canvases, fewer portraits, more nudes, and perhaps landscapes, which Modi despises. Zbo says these types of paintings sell better and have universal appeal. Who wants to buy a portrait of someone they don't know or care about? A pretty country scene or tasteful nude, however, are sure to find a place in the homes of the bourgeoisie.

I told Zbo that I would be happy to pose nude for a major painting. It's normal for a painter to portray his wife or mistress in the nude, and Modi has done a few sketches of me undressed. But he doesn't want me to model for one of these new pictures for Zbo. To paint your wife naked and let everyone see is not the Italian way, he says. Perhaps he's worried what André or my parents might do, if they should see such a picture hanging in the Salon D'Automne and recognize their Jeanne.

I am still going back Rue Amyot to sleep, and sometimes also for dinner when Papa is home. I just can't make the break while the war is on and André is away and in danger. I sometimes think of what he must be experiencing, the terror and the fear. I want to break free, but not to break their hearts.

224

Yet in some ways it might be easier to tell them the truth, with André gone. I expect there will be a terrible row when he finds out I am no longer the pure sister of his dreams. How can I convince them that my loving Modi doesn't mean I love them less? That living with Modi as his wife doesn't mean I have become a whore? Just because I draw my body in the nude doesn't mean that I'd let just anyone touch me.

Still, every time I step through the door at Rue Amyot and into the dining room, I flinch, as my eyes search out the mantelpiece, where Maman props up the latest card or letter from André, to make sure that we will see it. This time will it be a postcard to cheer us up—or a black-bordered telegram? Will I find her weeping in the chair by the fireplace where André loved to sit and puff his pipe? Will fate punish me for the love they will never accept?

July 20, 1917
In the mornings, when I hurry to the studio from Rue Amyot, I usually bring Modi some bread left over from breakfast and brew him coffee on the little stove. But this morning the flat is empty. From the rumpled sheets, I can't tell if he has spent the night here alone or in company, or elsewhere. I go out to comb the cafés looking for him, but he is nowhere to be found, then return to the studio to work for awhile on a piece of my own. Then I eat the bread I brought him, undress, and lie down in our bed to wait for him. The bells of Notre-Dame-des-Champs pealing at six o'clock wake me up.

I rush to the Rotonde, where I find him drinking with Zbo and Gosia, a Polish girl who sometimes models for the Montparnos. He waves me over to their table, tugs me down next to him, and pecks me on the cheek. He has been drinking heavily again. His eyes glitter, and his cheeks are red. I order a glass of beer.

"Where have you been all day? I was waiting for you!" I lower my voice and look him straight in the eyes. "In bed. But you didn't come!"

He laughs and gives my arm a squeeze, "With Zbo! I am painting over at his place now."

"Are you?" I glance at Zbo, who gives a curt nod.

"He'll be working at our flat for awhile."

"What is wrong with our studio?" I ask.

"He can concentrate better if he is not disturbed," says Zbo.

"Are you saying that I disturb his work?"

"The models complain that the place is as hot as a furnace with all that light pouring in through the windows," Zbo says.

"But it's July. It's hot everywhere in July. At your place too, I expect."

"Well, at least there is a suitable sofa in our flat where they can lie down and be comfortable," says Zbo.

Gosia giggles and hides her mouth with her hand.

The waiter brings my beer and I take a sip. "I see."

"Don't sulk," Modi says, "It is a perfect arrangement. You'll have me out of your hair. A man needs some time on his own."

I understand perfectly. Modi doesn't want me around if he is going to be painting girls in the nude. He doesn't feel free to concentrate when I am at the studio. I suspect he even makes love to them on the worn cushions of Zbo's musty old sofa.

I drink my beer in silence while Zbo makes empty chat.

"I've got to go now." I stand up. Usually Modi accompanies me home, but today he just sits there, sipping his wine, smiling at me; not making a move.

"So soon?" says Zbo.

"My mother is expecting me for dinner."

Modi lifts his glass of red wine. "To your mother."

"Aren't you coming?" I blurt out but immediately regret it. He obviously isn't. He hates for me to be direct when other people are around. He wants me to read the signs of what he wants and what he doesn't want and then expects me to comply.

"We are in the middle of a conversation. A business conversation."

I walk away quickly, so they won't see my tears, then turn round to catch his eye, but he is chattering away and pays me no attention.

I stop at the fountain on the corner of the Luxembourg Gardens to splash some water on my face before I get home, not wanting the *concierge* to speculate about my red-rimmed eyes.

Stepping in the door, I find no sign of dinner yet. Céline is bustling about with small packages from the apothecary and bundles of freshly ironed underclothes. Maman calls to me from her room where I find her bent over a suitcase on the bed, stuffing clothes into it. For a moment, I fear something might have happened to André, and she is leaving to go to him. But her face is flushed with pleasure and nervous excitement.

"Are you going somewhere?"

"Your father has rented a farmhouse in the Sarthe for a month. He'll be on leave. We are going to have a vacation!"

She adds a prayer book and an icon of the Virgin to her bag. "Our train leaves tomorrow morning at eight. Your father will be at the station to meet us when we arrive. You should pack your things. Unfortunately, André can't get leave to join us, but it will be a relief to be away from Paris for awhile."

"I can't leave Paris now!"

"Why not? Aren't lessons at the Académie over? The fresh air will do you good. You have been looking so pale, lately. And there is even a vegetable garden. Heaven for your father, who has been dreaming of homegrown salad and fresh eggs. Speaking of which, Céline has made us an omelet for dinner. Céline!"

Céline pokes her head in through the doorway. "Oui, Madame?"

"Now that Jeanne is back, we must eat. Set the table, please."

"Très bien, Madame," she says, giving me a little smirk before heading off to the kitchen. Perhaps she knows where I spend my afternoons.

"Listen to me, Maman. I have things to do. My friends. My work. I was planning to spend every day at the Jardin des Plantes, sketching trees."

"Your friends and the Jardin can wait until we return. And there will be plenty of trees to sketch in the countryside. Go start packing, and don't forget your violin. Papa will want to hear you play. Have you made progress with your Debussy? You are hardly home to practice anymore."

"I will stay in Paris here alone."

"Of course you cannot stay here unchaperoned. Your father would never allow it."

❋

August 2, 1917

I simply can't live with them anymore. Just one week *en vacances* in the Sarthe nearly drove me mad, but Maman and Papa are in their element. He spends hours in the vegetable garden, hoeing, weeding, watering; cackling like a hen over every marrow or pepper produced, which Maman stews or bakes with tomatoes and onions. They reminisce about the old days for hours.

My hands and nails are stained from pitting peaches and plums to make preserves to send to the troops, and all the while I stir the bubbling pot to keep the fruit from burning, my father sits in his undershirt by the window and reads to us from *Dionysius the Areopagite*.

I refuse to spend an entire month like that.

Modi did not write to me once the whole time I was there, although I received a letter from Thérèse, telling me that Kisling is going to be married soon, and that I should come back for the party.

So that is what I am doing now—heading back to Paris on the train. I feel very brave and reckless, with so few civilians traveling. The train is packed with soldiers, all staring at me while I write in this notebook. We keep stopping in lonely stations where no one gets on or off and there we sit for hours.

I told Maman and Papa that I couldn't bear the mosquitoes, that they have ravaged my skin. It isn't exactly a lie.

❋

It is past seven o'clock when I get back to Paris. I go straight to the studio, without passing by Rue Amyot—even though I have a key, which Maman consented to give me. But he's not there. I find him at the Rotonde where he has been drinking too much again and making a fool of himself, taking off his clothes, throwing chairs around, and generally creating havoc.

"Jeanne! I am glad you are back," Père Libion says to me. "Take him home to bed before the police come! He has had way too much."

Modi, completely naked, is slumped on the floor with his back leaning against the base of the bar. I have never seen him quite this bad. On the far side of the room, Picasso stands near the wall, with a glass of wine in hand, grinning at the pitiful spectacle. He nods curtly to me as I make my way to Modi. Some of the people at the tables are laughing at Modi, others ignore him, but all scoot their chairs to make room for me to pass.

I crouch down beside him and sweep his dark curls off his fore-head—has he fallen or hit his head? Is he injured? I pat his face with my cool hand—it seems to me he has a fever. Torn pieces of a sketch and a few coins are scattered around him, alongside the worn trousers and shirt he has shed.

"Modi."

He opens his eyes, but does not recognize me at first. I try again, gently shaking his arm. "Modi, let's go home."

"He falls apart when you are away, you know," says Libion.

Everyone is staring at us now. Although I know them all by name, they seem like strangers to me. Only Père Libion comes to my aid and squats down to help me put Modi's clothes back on.

Like a huge spineless doll, he flops about as I try to guide his feet in through his trouser legs. Libion helps me pull them up as we stand him up and prop him against the bar. His flanks are so lean, we must fasten his trousers around his waist with a piece of string to keep them from slipping down again. With his arm clasped around my waist, bearing his weight on my hip, I manage to get him out to the street, where he collapses on the pavement. I sit by him on the curb for over an hour, watching him, making sure he is still breathing.

A carriage clops past, the woman inside gapes at us from between the parted curtains, but Modi doesn't notice. He is out cold. A *flic* walks by and sneers, "What's the matter, is he dead?"

I give him my most demure smile. "It is Modigliani. He has drunk too much." The *flic* laughs and goes on. He knows all about Modi. They all know his reputation.

At last he wakes with a sputtering, cavernous cough. Painful to hear, it rips my own ribs. His head jerks up. Seeing me, he grins, "*Ma petite* Jeanne! You have come home. When did you get here?"

I pull him up. He is sober enough to stand up and walk with my support. We sway and stagger all the way home, just around the cor-ner—to number 8 Rue de la Grande Chaumière. "My head, my head," he moans.

We meet Ortiz down in the courtyard, where he is filling buckets of water to carry upstairs. I am relieved to see that Madame Moreau is out, and she won't have to see Modi in such a state. Ortiz helps him up the four flights of stairs and rolls him into the bed. I undress and lie down beside him. His body is soaked in sweat.

I wake at noon to the sound of the bells, my face in the dirty pillow; my body glazed in sweat. A scorching heat radiates through the high windows. Modi has already gone out. His pillow is mapped again today with chocolate–colored stains. He is coughing up so much blood now. It is too hot to light the stove for coffee. I wash my face with water from the basin. There is hardly any left. I must beg Ortiz to bring up a bucketful to refresh our stores. On the worktable I find a note from Modi, asking me to fetch him at Zbo's at three.

At three o'clock, Zbo's friend, Lunia, opens the door. "I am here for Modi," I say.

"He can't be disturbed. He's working."

I put my hand out to push the door back before it shuts in my face. "He told me to come for him at three. Please let me in."

"Come back in an hour or two."

"I'll just wait inside until he is done."

"I am afraid I can't let you in." We stare at each other as my fury mounts.

"Modi," I shout. "I am here."

Zbo appears in the dark entryway. "Lunia, what is all this fuss? I told you he mustn't be disturbed. Oh, Jeanne, it's you. Please come in." His smile is slick and embarrassed.

Lunia steps aside, grumbling, to let me pass.

"Just come into the kitchen and wait until he has finished. He is working in the dining room," says Zbo.

Zbo and I sit down at a tiny table in the kitchen pervaded by the stink of boiled cauliflower. The sink is full of dirty pots and dishes. From behind the closed door to the dining room, I can hear Modi shouting and cursing. A bottle crashes.

"Hanka is out at the moment. I wanted to wash up the dishes, but the rattle of plates would bother our painter," Zbo apologizes.

I shrug. It doesn't matter to me whether Zbo's dishes are dirty or clean. The dining room door bangs open, and Modi steps out. I peer through the open doorway and see Gosia still lying naked on the couch.

"What the devil was all that ruckus?" Modi says, bursting into the kitchen.

"It was me—they wouldn't let me in." I rise and go to him.

His anger abates. "Don't be ridiculous. Where I go, you go." He starts to put his arm around my shoulder, then pushes me away, "But I will smudge you with paint. I must wash."

Dutiful Lunia hands him a kettle and a small towel, and he goes off to Zbo's bedroom to wash up.

I tiptoe into the dining room, where Gosia has just vacated the green couch to put on her clothes behind a screen. From the steamy smell in the room, I can tell that they have been making love. I approach the easel. The painting—the nude—is magnificent. I feel a sharp stab of jealousy for he has never painted me like that, with such desire and such power.

August 12, 1917
Kisling has got married. The party went on for days. Modi drank incessantly. He is losing all control.

September 12, 1917
I am painting a portrait of myself painting, a palette in hand, brush raised. It is a study in triangles—those sharp-edged shapes that define all relationships. All life is connected by triangles, says Modi, by conflicts and attractions that interconnect and resolve. Once he drew the tree of life for me and showed me how it is made of triads. He says we can follow the chain back to the moment of our conception. Sun—Moon—Earth; Demon—Angel—Man; Man—Woman—Child; Love—Hate—Desire; Life—Death—Eternity. Between every opposing pair, he says, the antagonism is resolved by a third force. Pain—Joy—Art.

What is the third reconciling force between me and Modi? Modi—Me—André? Modi—Me—Gosia? Modi—Me—Art? I don't know.

September 13, 1917
Maman is busy at her desk writing letters when I come in. As always, I greet her with a quick kiss on the cheek. She does not look up from her papers, at first.

"Who is that man you were with?" she says casually and goes on writing.

I flinch. "What man?"

"The one with dark eyes and the large hat."

I just stare at her and don't answer.

"You were seen holding hands in Rue Monge." She peers up at me from behind her thick glasses, her pen poised in the air.

So, now she knows. There is no use holding back or lying.

"His name is Modigliani. He is a painter from Italy. I met him in Montparnasse."

"A foreigner?" She glances down at the letter she is writing and sets it aside. She does not look at me while I speak.

"Jewish," I say, just so they will know from the start, if they have anything against that.

"And you have been seeing him for how long?"

How could I tell her that we have been together since the beginning of time, so I say, "Not quite a year."

She gasps in disbelief. When this revelation has sunk in, she says, "He is much older than you."

"Does age matter so much?"

"Why isn't he in the army, like all able-bodied men?"

"He tried to enlist last August, but his lungs are weak."

"So, he is in ill-health, too. At least, is he a successful painter?"

"He is the best in Paris. One day the world will celebrate his name!"

She says nothing to that, only shakes her head. "When you left us in the Sarthe to come back to Paris…"

"I went to his studio, Maman. That's where I am going to be living from now on. I have been meaning to tell you for some time."

"Have you? Well, we noticed something odd in your erratic comings and goings, but you have always been moody and susceptible. But I certainly didn't expect anything like this. I won't allow you to go and live with this person. He is a grown man. You are still hardly more than a child."

"You can't stop me."

"You will kill your father. I cannot let you do that."

"I don't want to hurt anyone. I just want to lead my life in peace with the man I love."

Maman reflects on this for a long moment and finally looks at me again. "Very well. I cannot lock you in your room. But for your father's sake, you must keep up a pretense. You must come home at night at a decent hour. I will not have the *concierge* spreading rumors to everyone in the street! I have always let you do as you please. So this is as much my fault as yours! We have been too lenient with both you and your brother. But he is a hero, and you—!"

"And I?"

"You are a foolish girl."

Here ends the second of the three notebooks.

Notebook 3

January 12, 1918

Zbo gave me 300 francs today. "Don't give him any to spend on wine. I will buy that for him when needed. Save it for daily expenses. I am counting on you to take care of him."

I put the money in a drawer in the bedside table and keep careful accounts in my diary of how much we spend for food and supplies. But there is no logic in the way we live. Modi would gladly share his last centime with a hungry beggar and often gives our money away to perfect strangers at cafés. He wears his poverty like a king.

In Livorno, his family was comfortably off and well-respected. Here, to every new acquaintance, he spits out the words "I am a Jew," as if he despised himself. Even though he is not religious, his Hebrew background is deeply engrained. He often speaks of the Kabbalah, the Talmud, and mysterious Jewish traditions: of letters and numbers that come alive and tell destinies, of demons shaped in clay. That is why he is so close to Soutine. They share an understanding of those things.

With every kiss, his lips taste of tobacco and pastis; hashish and brandy. It seems to me he is drinking more now, and his cough is getting worse. Yesterday one of his teeth fell out! Empty wine bottles are lined up like sentinels all along the walls of the studio. He can't be bothered to take them away, and there are too many for me to carry down the stairs. When he is angry, he will sometimes throw one out the window, where it crashes in the courtyard near the *concierge's* cubicle. It is up to me, then, to pacify his tantrum and afterwards, hers. I go down the steps, help sweep up, toss the shards into a bin, smile sweetly, and apologize.

At the Rotonde or the Dôme, he'll play the poet sometimes—reciting Shakespeare or Dante at the top of his lungs to an enraptured audience. Other times he plays the buffoon, stripping off his clothes and dancing across the tabletops while everyone howls with laughter, except me.

These antics are only the prelude to his black moods, which sweep up from nowhere like storms over the ocean. Modi calls it the *Nigredo*, the dark power inside us, the negation of All. When those moods descend, he lashes out—vicious, sarcastic, cruel, sparing no one, not me or himself. He takes a knife to his own work; smashes glasses and bottles on the floor. He once shoved Beatrice Hastings through a window, and the shards of glass left scars in a thousand places all over her body.

Monster! He calls me when I tell him to stop drinking, come to bed, eat something, or come home. I never thought he would be violent with me, but lately that too has begun to happen. He pulls my hair by the roots or twists my arm; trips me up to make me fall. The other day, he pushed me against a railing at the Luxembourg Gardens. André Salmon, who happened to be passing by, saw what was happening and tried to intervene. I told him to leave us alone, I didn't need any help, but my ribs were badly bruised afterwards, and it still hurts when I breathe. I know it is Modi's illness that makes him behave this way.

Zbo believes those black moods are caused by his frustration from his lack of success, and that sooner or later, the wheel will turn. His work will be recognized at its true value, and we will become happy and prosperous. We must bear up until then.

His friend, Paul Guillaume, agrees with me and thinks that it is ill health that brings on these tempests. Modi has suffered from pleurisy since childhood, and he wears himself out with his painting raptures and his nightlong bouts of drinking. Guillaume gives Modi hashish pills to soothe him, but when he takes them, he lies listlessly for hours, smiling at nothing until he falls asleep. I don't like it when he takes those pills. His eyes glaze, his lips taste bitter when I kiss him; he drifts alone in a place where I can't reach him. He has no desire, no ardor. Once he made me swallow one, promising me I would taste music and hear colors, but it only made me sick to my stomach. I would rather have him angry than in a drugged stupor caused by those pills.

Once the storm is over and he is himself again, he will beg me to forgive him and beat his head on the wall, whining about how miserable he is, about what a failure he is. And then I take him in my arms until he is calm. When all seems lost, all I can do is hang on to him tightly and try to stay afloat to keep us both from drowning. Even when he shoves me away or pursues other women, I know I cannot—I *must not*—desert him. I must remain fixed with my feet firmly on the ground, as I used to do while watching the waves break below the cliffs of Finistère.

March 10, 1918

I am sitting at the Rotonde, waiting for Modi, and sipping my coffee slowly. A chanteuse and an organ-grinder are standing right along the curb—she is warbling "Madelon" completely out of tune. Zbo comes in and heads straight to my table. He is alone.

"Hello, Jeanne. May I sit down?"

Zbo orders coffee. Although he is calm and smiling, I am ill at ease. Has something happened to Modi?

"There is something I want to talk to you about. You have seen what is happening in Paris with these bombs."

I nod. Who hasn't?

"It makes for a nerve-wracking environment. It is very hard for Modigliani, for any artist, to work under such conditions."

Again, I nod, wary as to where the conversation is going.

"That's why I have arranged to take Modi, and a few of our artist friends, Soutine and Foujita, to the south, near Nice. I think a change of air and better climate would help our dear Modi get over that cough he has. And in the more tranquil atmosphere, he'll be able to work better. I have also been in contact with some buyers, who would like to see his work. I know you understand how important it is for his work to sell and his name to be known."

My heart pounds, and I clench my fist on the tabletop until the knuckles turn white.

I have barely enough breath to speak. "For how long will he be away?"

"That's just it, Jeanne, I don't know. Several months, perhaps even a year, until the war is over."

He clasps my wrist. "Jeanne, he is very ill. He is destroying himself here with alcohol and drugs. I had hoped that meeting you, he might calm down. He is a bit better, but it isn't enough."

"I don't know how to stop him," I protest, almost howling, "If I ask him not to drink, he just laughs. If I bring him healthy food, he won't eat it."

"I have to get him away from Paris for his own good."

I don't ask if Hanka's friends, Gosia and Lunia, have been invited to come. I know they both are in love with Modi, like nearly every other woman in Montparnasse.

Instead, I say, "And me?"

"That is why I needed to see you."

My heart stops. I can't breathe. He is going to take Modi away from me.

"You must come too," he continues. "He won't go without you."

Relief floods my body, and my face grows hot and then cold. My shoulders finally relax, and I can breathe again.

"Of course I will come."

"But you are underage, Jeanne. What will your parents say?"

"I will convince them to let me go."

Papa sits by the stove, reading reports of the recent bombs in a newspaper. Mama mends a chemise, holding the thread taut in her pale violet hands. My parents look old and tired. This week we have had no letters from André.

"It just gets worse! Yesterday a bomb fell in Rue de Rivoli, killing twenty-eight people and leaving a huge crater in the middle of the street. It might have hit the Louvre!" says Papa.

Maman squints at her mending. "To think I passed by there just the other day."

Papa looks alarmed. "What were you doing there?

"I was there to see the curate's niece, Madame Lisette, who is too ill to go out, with her rheumatism. I took her some fruit and a cataplasm from the apothecary."

"That is my wife, always ready to do a good deed for the more unfortunate."

"There's a butcher, on the corner, well known throughout the quarter, and I stopped there to buy the veal brains you had last night."

"I told you not to go gadding about Paris. It is so dangerous now."

"But it is also dangerous to lie in one's bed."

Papa rustles his newspaper in disapproval.

At last I find the courage to speak up. "I am going to the south with Modigliani. He is not well, and the climate will be good for his health."

Maman stares at me in sullen amazement, her needle poised in midair.

My father's face shows no reaction. It is as if I haven't spoken at all.

"Zborowski and his wife will be coming," I say.

"You can't imagine that your mother and I will let you go alone with that man and his friends," my father says.

So he knows. Maman has told him. "That man's name is Modigliani," I say.

"I know what his name is."

"And what will you do to stop me? Lock me in my room?"

"You are too young to understand what you are doing, what he is."

"What he is? A painter, an artist? A foreigner? A Jew?"

"That is not the issue. He may be a fine painter, but he is not a suitable companion for an innocent young girl. You will ruin your life if you don't give him up, and you will ruin ours, too," he says.

"I am not as innocent as you may think."

"Oh, Jeanne, please!" Maman fixes me with her mournful eyes.

"I am a woman now, don't you understand? I have the feelings and needs of a woman."

Maman draws a sharp breath as a small red stain bleeds across the white lace.

"And how long do you intend to stay in the south? Who will pay for your journey and lodgings?" my father asks, finally putting down his newspaper.

"Zborowski will pay for everything, and I suppose we will stay until the money runs out. Zborowski hopes to sell some of Modi's work to rich collectors in Nice."

"I see."

Maman and Papa exchange a long, painful look, and then Maman turns to me to announce, "It is not proper for you to live openly with that man in the same house. I will come with you."

Papa gapes at her as if she has gone insane. And perhaps she has. She glares at him defiantly.

"You just said yourself—Paris is getting dangerous. Jeanne and I will have our little vacation in the sun and get away from this madness."

She picks up her mending again. "You may tell Monsieur Modigliani and his friend that if you wish to go, that is my condition. But I shall pay my own way."

❊

Haut-de-Cagnes, May 15, 1918

The house where Maman and I are staying looks out over the sea and has a terrace with a jasmine pergola. The others are lodged in a dilapidated villa a little further up the hill, with a garden full of weeds and overgrown vines. Their villa has been cobbled together, floors and stairs haphazardly slapped on, over a century or two. Modi and Soutine have an atelier on the very top floor. Soutine has already done three paintings of the place—a wobbly *"maison ivre"* about to tip over.

Nearby lives an Italian farmer with a young wife and a brood of children. Modi was delighted to make their acquaintance and speak Italian with them. The wife has been very kind to us, bringing us baskets of lemons, eggs, and salad.

Maman and I do our shopping in the village market at the bottom of the hill, then walk up with all our groceries. Halfway up, my legs feel heavy, and my head spins. It is the heat and light, Maman says. I am not used to it. Modi comes every evening for dinner, and Maman has learned how to cook food that pleases him: stewed rabbit or roast chicken, which we get from the Italians. Sometimes she makes steamed mussels or clams, but he won't eat them. Neither will I. They are not like the ones from Finistère: I cannot digest them. We dine on the terrace under a bougainvillea arbor, and Maman says that Modi, despite his worn brown velvet jacket with patched elbows, has the manners of a prince in disguise. It almost seems that those two might get along one day—something I never dreamed could happen. They speak of art and literature, while I listen half-amused and pick at my food.

In just these few days, Modi's depression has lifted, and even his skin looks less sallow in the golden light. All day he works feverishly in his studio. Zbo has commissioned him to produce some landscapes, which he usually despises, but here he has found new inspiration—

perhaps because the light reminds him of home. I have set up my own studio where I work during the day, when I can overcome the strange listlessness I feel. I have missed two cycles and have put on weight, even though I hardly have any appetite.

Maman watches me closely whatever I do, wherever I go. I am only allowed to see Modi at mealtimes, and sometimes, for a Sunday walk after lunch when we are all together: Foujita, Zbo, Soutine, Hanka, Modi and me. I have only been to the studio twice, always accompanied by Maman. She and I live like two nuns in our cells. She would be appalled to learn that Foujita and I almost became lovers before I was with Modi.

But sometimes, Modi and I manage to meet secretly, at night in the garden of a house midway up the cliff, where no one is living now. After Maman retires for the night, I unlatch the window of my room and scramble down through the bushes, where I keep an old kerosene lantern hidden to light my away along the road.

I follow the low yellow wall up to an old pink villa with a turret on top. The gate creaks open, and I step inside the wild garden—the air drenched with the scent of jasmine, so sweet it is almost sickening. Fireflies tremble in the tall weeds, where a path worn by children and cats winds through the shadows to a niche made of ragged palm fronds, which shield a rusted bed frame.

I spread my yellow wool shawl on the bed frame, then sit down, blow out the lantern, and wait in the dark, looking up at the summer sky. The spirals of the Milky Way peep through the thick foliage.

Thirty minutes; an hour passes until I hear the gate open and his feet hissing through the tall grass.

He sits beside me and throws his arm around my thickening waist. With just one whiff, I can tell how much and what he has been drinking. Tonight is not as bad as other nights.

"Aren't they beautiful?" I ask, tilting my head back to look at the stars.

"Yes, but the most beautiful ones are invisible."

"You mean the ones that are too far away to see?"

"No, I mean the black stars that pulse at the center of the cosmos."

"If they are invisible, how do you know they exist?"

"You can feel them. When you sleep, when you dream, when you have an orgasm, you pass through the portal of the dark star, and when you die, you just remain there forever."

He slips his hand under my skirt, up between my legs; touches me in the secret place. I loosen the front of my dress and lay back. The metal mesh of the frame digs deep into my spine. My breasts ache with pleasure as he cups them to his mouth. I give myself to him, and the sky slides from view.

"*Je t'aime. Tu m'aimes?*" I prop myself up on my elbow and touch my lips to his sulky mouth, which tastes of wine and hashish.

He laughs. "Every bourgeois says that to his mistress. It means nothing. There is love, there is sex, and then there is something stronger than both—Fate."

June 7, 1918

For days I have fought back against the bile rising at the back of my throat. Nothing can wash the bitterness away, not cold water or tea or the lavender tisanes Maman makes me every evening. In the morning, my head spins when I get up from the bed. The floor turns to sponges when I walk across it. Coming back up the hill with my load of groceries in the morning, I can hardly get my breath, and my stomach churns all day long.

Before lunchtime, in the kitchen, the smell of mussels steaming in wine and olive oil is so overpowering I have to rush outside again. Then comes a wave of nausea, and I am violently sick. I run inside to rinse my face and go lie down in my room.

Mama stands at the foot of the bed, studying me slowly and gnarling her hands in her apron.

I press my head to the pillow then turn my face to the wall. I cannot bear to look at her.

"Jeanne, you aren't pregnant?"

"I don't know. I might be. It has been over two months since...."

"Why didn't you say anything?"

"I didn't know. I didn't think...."

She sits down on the edge of the bed and forces me to turn my face to hers.

"He must marry you."

I jerk my chin free. "I don't want to get married."

"In your condition, you have little choice."

"No!"

"If he will not marry you, then you must give the child up for adoption."

"I don't believe in marriage."

"There is now a child to think about. What you believe and don't believe no longer matters. Have you told him?"

I shake my head.

"I thought not! He will desert you when he finds out."

"No, he won't."

"He is not faithful to you, my daughter."

"And how do you know that?"

"That Italian woman, the farmer's wife, our neighbor. She goes to him several times a week. I have seen her walking up the road towards their villa."

"That proves nothing. She takes them vegetables and eggs, just as she does with us. And he is painting her portrait."

"I have seen him going to her. Even yesterday, she was in the yard, hanging up sheets on the clothesline. He came up behind her to embrace her and put her hands over her…. I could see them from our terrace. Do you understand me? They have no shame. In the village, they say she is pregnant again…."

"She is nothing to him."

"And you are?"

I have nothing else to say. How can I explain that we are tied by the black star, by fate?

"I curse the day I sent you to art school! Your brother will never forgive me."

Later at lunch, under the bougainvillea arbor, it is just the three of us. A white tablecloth, slices of melon on a blue plate, pink and white frangipane in a bowl, and the meal that Maman has made. I leave my food untouched, but Modi is ravenous. Despite the hot sun, I feel a chill and wrap the yellow shawl around my shoulders. A stray black cat Maman has adopted prowls at our feet.

I stare at the spoons and forks on the table, at the carafe of cold white wine beaded with moisture, at the sharp knives on the tablecloth pointing straight to the heart. I must cut from her now, forever, soon. Modi is happy today. His work is going well. He is producing, but so far there have been no sales. He is polite and genteel with Maman and compliments her on her cooking. He does not seem to notice that today she is sullen and silent and is not chatting to him about art.

When the meal is done, Maman brings coffee for the two of them and a fennel tisane for me.

She drains her cup, and places it in the saucer, settling into herself before attack.

"If you are going to continue to eat with us, then we must come to an understanding," she announces.

"Jeanne and I have a perfect understanding."

"You must marry my daughter, Monsieur, in a Catholic ceremony. The sooner, the better."

He smiles, toying with the spoon in his saucer. "I cannot do that. Firstly, I am a Jew, and secondly, I do not believe in marriage, Madame. It is a bourgeois institution, and I am not a bourgeois. I love your daughter. She loves me. That should be enough."

"You have responsibilities to live up to!"

"I am an artist. My responsibilities are to my art. Nothing else. Besides, Jeanne does not care about marriage." He reaches out for my hand.

"No, it's true. I don't." I take his hand. I grasp it firmly. My own fingers feel like ice.

"Artists don't need to live by the rules," he says.

"You have ruined my life, and you have ruined hers. She has chosen her fate. But I won't let the two you ruin the life of an innocent child!"

Modi frowns. "What are you talking about?"

She bolts upright from her chair and gathers up the empty cups on a lacquer tray.

"Tell him! What have you been waiting for?" She carries the tray back into the kitchen.

He stares at me, puzzled—not a clue as to why I have been so listless and moody these last few weeks, and why I hardly eat at all. I pluck at the dark silky hair on his wrists.

"Modi, we are going to have a baby." He gapes at me incredulously, so I repeat. "You understand—a baby!"

His uncertainty explodes to joy. He leaps to my side, sweeps me up in his arms, and sets me down again, babbling in Italian and then in French. "…And we will go live in Italy in a lovely house with a dining suite and lemon trees in the garden. This calls for a celebration."

He pours a glass from the carafe, gulps it down, pours another for himself, and half a glass for me. "For you, only a sip! You are carrying my child! A Modigliani on the way! I will write to my mother at once. If it is a girl, we will call her Eugenia and if a boy…."

"André?" I suggest.

"We will see. He must have an Italian name. He must speak Italian."

Maman returns from the kitchen to remove the last things from the table. Clearly, she did not expect such a celebration. She gazes at us, wide-eyed, as though we have lost our senses.

Modi, tipsy now, lifts a glass to her, "And a toast to you, *grand-mère*! I hope you will have the pleasure of meeting my mother. I think the two of you will get along very well. We are now officially a family!"

September 1918

Today Modi and I went to Nice by tram car, where we had tea at a grand café along the sea front. We stopped along the beach at a stall selling Spanish fans and Venetian beads and glass. He brought me a circlet of blue-green glass and slipped it on my wrist. "You see it is the color of your eyes." It was the first time in weeks I have left the house, for I am too heavy to walk much, and my breasts and back ache if I stand up for long. I don't think I will go out again until after the baby is born.

Every evening at dinner, he fights with Maman, and I go to my room, lie down, and cover my head with a pillow. I cannot wait for this all to be over.

Zbo brought some rich clients to the studio. They bought a few paintings by Foujita and Soutine—but none of Modigliani's. How can they not understand? But perhaps Modi put them off, with his hollow eyes and sarcastic laughter. Zbo is depressed—there is no reason to stay on here. Perhaps he will leave next week. More gallerists are flocking back to Paris, and he has arranged for a show in London. If not in France, Modi will be celebrated elsewhere.

November 12, 1918
They say the war is over, but I am too tired to celebrate.

Nice, December 10, 1918
The baby has come. She was born on November 29. Her name is Giovanna—the Italian for Jeanne. Sometimes I call her Jeanne, sometimes Giovanna. Her face is mottled red; her shrill cries penetrate our sleep. She has her father's broad brow, dark hair, and thick eyelashes. Maman was with me throughout the ordeal, gripping my hands as I heaved and screamed; my body wracked with spasms. I felt as if every organ inside was being squeezed out of me. In making little Jeanne, I guess that is what happened.

I haven't heard a word from my father. Maman sent him a note when Giovanna was born, but he did not reply—or at least not to me. Maman has not told André about the child—she says he is angry with her and with Papa for not taking me away from Modi.

We have moved to a little hotel in Nice in Rue de France, which costs less than the villa. Zbo and the others have gone back to Paris, and Maman left this morning. At last we are free to live as husband and wife, like any family with a new baby. Maman tried to make me give the child to the nuns, but I refused. Modi already loves little Giovanna so much. Besides, an Italian would never give up his child to strangers. It is not the Italian way.

But sometimes I am terrified of this creature we have made. I feel exhausted all day. I don't seem to have a motherly instinct. I panic at moments, not knowing what I should do to soothe her. Maman would not help me. I don't have enough milk to feed her. My nipples are painfully chapped and swollen because she sucks so hungrily and desperately. We have brought in a wet nurse, an Italian girl, who has been a great help.

Modi says he loves me even more now that I have borne his child. Nothing can ever separate us now, he says. Our destinies are bound up forever in the body of this tiny being. He claims he will paint a portrait of me with the child, a Madonna, to rival the works of Piero della Francesca.

January 1919

Our daughter is lucky to have been born at a moment of great celebration. But last week, when Modi went to register her birth at the town hall, he got swept up in the raucous festivities that are still on going, and when he reached the office, it had closed early. Tomorrow or next week he said he would go back to register her. In the end, I had to send the wet nurse, and our daughter was registered as Jeanne Hébuterne. I haven't told Maman that Modi hasn't yet given our baby his surname.

In the morning, we rise late, Modi brings me milk and coffee in a yellow bowl, then goes to work furiously at the studio he is sharing with Osterlind, a friend from Paris who has moved here with his wife. Modi doesn't want to work here at the hotel. Giovanna's crying disturbs him. I get up, feed the baby, tidy our rooms, and pile the bedding in the window so the air will freshen it. When my chores are done, I take Giovanna out in the carriage lent to us by the hotel owner's wife and do the shopping. Oranges, fish, and milk, which gives strength to the lungs. He is coughing now more than ever.

With Maman gone back to Paris, we must be very careful with money for food and cannot eat often at taverns or cafés. I keep a careful list of the household accounts, wash his socks and underwear, brush his corduroy jacket, gather up empty bottles for the rubbish man to take away. I put our painting supplies in order. I have no time for work of my own, not even a sketch.

March 1919

Today we began the new portrait, though sitting for long is so tiring. I have to keep shifting in my seat, and, with my heavy breasts so full, my back hurts if I sit straight in one position for long. The hotel owner does not want us to use our room as a painting studio—he is afraid we will soil the walls or bedspread, so we work secretively with the window wide open to let out the smell of fresh oil paint. When Modi has finished, he cleans his brushes so carefully, not a speck of color remains to smudge anything.

My hair has grown out again, I wind it in braids around my head. On my wrist sparkles the blue-green bangle, which he claims captures the changing color of my eyes. Giovanna tugs at it with her tiny fingers and tries to taste it with her tongue. I am wearing a turquoise shift with yellow daisies along the hem which Hanka gave me last summer. It is the only thing I can still wear comfortably. In the new portrait, Modi has transformed those daisies into stars, while Giovanna is swathed in an Indian shawl of red, pink, and gold, against a background of powder blue. His name for that color is *carta da zucchero*, the color of heaven and spirituality found in Italian frescoes of the Quattrocento. Modi says that this color transmits silence and calm to the soul. I think back to my first day with him at the hotel, when I came to sit for a portrait, where the Madonnas in their blue veils looked down on me and seemed to give me their blessing.

Little Jeanne is so good during these long sittings. Even when she wakes, she doesn't cry or squirm, but lies inert, her great brown eyes staring straight ahead. They say that babies can't see at such distance, and the world around them appears only as an indistinct blur of colors, but I am sure she can feel the love he radiates towards us, and even the intensity of his gaze like a soft wind on her skin.

Through the open window, the breeze ripples the yellow organdy curtains and lifts the hair on the nape of my neck like his kisses used to do. Outside I hear the voices of people passing in the street, the clanging of the omnibus, the cries of the umbrella mender and the knife grinder, and a girl selling oranges and lemons from a cart. The air smells fresh with a hint of the sea and orange blossoms. He does not drink much while working here at the hotel and seems more patient than usual. Sitting here in this sunny room, I never want to leave.

But none of his paintings have yet been sold. Zbo sent money from Paris for Modi's art supplies, telling us that our hotel is paid for only until the end of the month and that he is organizing a show later in the year, hoping to sell the new work.

Before Maman returned to Paris, she left me almost 600 francs. I divided the money into bundles. I hid some under a tile; some in an old pot. The rest I put in the worn green purse we keep in the drawer of the bedside table. This morning, when I went to get money to buy milk, 100 francs were missing.

When Modi returns, I can see he is not himself again. His eyes glint, the pupils are dilated—his fine lips, a twisted sneer. He has been taking those hashish pills, or perhaps something else. He goes straight to the bedside table, opens the drawer, and pulls out the green purse.

"You mustn't take any more money from there. We need that for our milk and bread and to pay for the room next month, if Zbo doesn't send more money in time."

"I needed it and now I need some more," he snaps.

"What did you need it for?"

"I took the money to buy a new shirt. I am going to meet some buyers and I must look decent."

"So where is it, your new shirt?"

He is wearing the same shirt I have bleached with soda and wood ash a hundred times to try to whiten it.

"I gave it to the girl to press." He opens his arms in that Italian fashion, still smirking, as if to say—see, I am right and you are wrong.

"Still, you must not take anymore."

He pulls out the rest of the bills and flaunts them in my face.

"Put the money back, Modi."

"Get some more from Zbo. How much do you need?"

"Just put it back." I snatch at the money, but he grabs my wrist and viciously twists my arm.

"I hate you when you're like this. You are not yourself. Let go! You are hurting me."

He leers at me, shoves me to the bed, and Giovanna wakes with a cry.

"*Je est un autre.*" His toneless voice terrifies me.

He pulls a flask of wine from the shelf and tips it to his lips.

Giovanna is crying inconsolably now. I pick her up and try to comfort her, bouncing her on my hip.

"You monster, you have woken your child," he says, holding the bottle out to me. "Give her some of this. It will make her sleep."

"Don't be like this!"

"Like what?"

Catching sight of the portrait on the easel, he snarls curses in Italian now. I have learned the meaning of all those unrepeatable words.

With a jerk of his hand, he splashes wine from the bottle all over the canvas, then drops it at his feet. The glass breaks; a red stain seeps across the tile floor.

Giovanna howls.

"Can't you ever make her shut up?"

Slamming the door, he goes out.

In tears, I wipe the wine from the canvas with a cloth, then mop up the puddle and broken glass.

Then I hide the painting where he will not find it.

❀

June 1919

Modi has gone back to Paris. He says he must get the studio ready for me to return with Giovanna. At present, it isn't suitable for a baby. Hanka and Gosia will help him. But the good news is that he is to have a show in London, and five or six new nudes are needed. An article has appeared in the British press, naming him a great talent of his generation. Perhaps at last the wheel is turning for us. Zbo will send money for me to return to Paris as soon as the studio is ready.

Now that he has gone, I have taken out the painting and propped it back up on the easel. Everything else has been packed up and sent to Paris, but I have kept a small supply of brushes and paints for myself and spread them on a newspaper on the table in our hotel room. I must be very careful not to get paint on the floor or walls or sheets. The hotel owner told us that if he found paint smudges, he'd throw us out. But I have no other place to go, and while Giovanna naps, I work on the portrait, nibbling on cheese and bread for lunch. I have added Modi's figure standing beside me.

In the early afternoon comes a knock at the door while I am still at work. My dress is unwashed, and my hair all untidy. I am still wearing my paint-smudged apron. If the hotel owner finds me like this, he will surely tell me to leave.

"Just a minute." I tear off my apron and throw a cloth over the worktable. In a panic, I try to think how to hide the easel.

The knock is repeated. "Jeanne? Are you there?" I know that voice. It is André's.

When I open the door and see him standing against the lemony light, I want to throw my arms around him, but we eye each other in silence. I cringe at the fury in his face.

250

"How could you deceive me like this!" He storms into the room. "You kept everything from me! And our parents never breathed a word of what has been happening here! How could you all have kept me in the dark like that, about your liaison with that man? With me away at the front all that time, risking my life, dreaming of nothing but coming home to you all—and you running around like a little whore with that—! You have no idea what I have been through—in those stinking trenches, with everyone around me being blown to bits."

I retreat to the wall. "We didn't want you to be upset. There was nothing you could do about it. Besides, it's my life, not yours!"

Giovanna wakes up screaming again in her cradle. I pick her up and rock her in my arms until she stops.

"And now we are a family," I say.

André hates arguing. Soon enough, he sinks into a chair, and studies the squalid room where I was happy for such a very short time.

"Are you happy living here like this?"

"Very happy," I lie, for how can I be happy if Modi isn't here?

"I'd like to see you in a more comfortable setting and eating hot food."

"You mean living like a bourgeois?"

"And what is wrong with that? It takes money to live, and to make art. What life will you give your baby? Is this any place to keep a child?"

"Do you care about our daughter—your niece? Have you kissed her, or asked to hold her in your arms?"

I hold the child out to him, but an expression of disgust flits across his face.

"You've always been so headstrong. I don't want a war. I want you to listen to reason. Give him up and come home to us with your child."

"No."

He gets up and begins to pace up and down the room, then stops before the easel.

"I wish to God I had never signed you up at that académie! It is all my fault. If I had been with you, this never would have happened."

I shake my head. He has no idea. "This would have happened anyway. You couldn't have stopped it."

Grimly, he examines the picture, and the red stain blotted across the faceless child at my breast.

"If you come to your senses, you can find me in my studio in Rue de Seine." He stalks out.

I put on my apron again and turn to the easel. My hand is as skilled as Modi's, but it shakes as I pick up the brush. Carefully I paint over the red stain, until it is disguised. Only I know it is there. Only I know its significance. I will finish this portrait for our daughter. I will give my child a face.

Tomorrow Giovanna and I will take the train back to Paris. Modi has been alone there with Gosia, Lunia, and his other admirers long enough.

I feel sick in the mornings now. I pray to God that I am not pregnant again.

Here ends the third of the three notebooks.

Part 4
The Missing Madonna 2

Paris, 1981

Hours passed as I lay there reading and rereading—I didn't sleep all night, and when I finished, I felt as though I had returned from a very vivid dream in which I was Jeanne Hébuterne. There was a connection between the two of us that I did not quite understand.

I had no doubt that these notebooks were genuine. The postmarks on the postcards, the faded photographs, the receipts from Sennelier's art supply shop in sepia ink, and the yellowing, brittle paper were all signs of authenticity, and the story was so touching, intimate, and real. I knew I had to protect the diary and yet also follow Madame Rosier's instructions. I still could not fathom why she had shared it with me, and not with the Modigliani or the Hébuterne heirs, or with some well-known scholar, or even some museum. But she had expressly stated she did not want to do that.

I thought of phoning Professor Renard at once and telling him of my find, but that would mean disobeying Madame Rosier's last wishes. I would need to try to locate the notary, but I wanted to hold onto the notebooks as long as I could.

When I finally came back to earth, I realized there was no food in the flat, so I went out for a snack at the café St. Regis on the corner, still reeling with the import of Madame Rosier's gift and unsure as to what I should do about it.

Returning home, I found an envelope stuck under the door to the street, addressed to "*Mademoiselle américaine au chapeau.*" Although I wasn't the only américaine in the building, I was the only one who went about in a signature hat. The others were older too, and would surely be referred to as Madame.

I thought it was some kind of joke played by one of my students, or maybe—I hoped—by Paul, who could have obtained my address from the school office easily. On the card tucked inside was scribbled a time and place: *Café Metro:18h00,* but no date. Looking at my watch, I saw that I could just make it to the Café Metro by six. It was exciting to be summoned by a stranger, but I had already convinced myself that Paul had left the note.

The yellow streetlamps had just flickered on against the bluish twilight as I emerged from the Maubert metro stop to approach the bustling café. At this hour on a Thursday evening, the tin tables along the street were packed with people sipping aperitifs, chatting, perusing newspapers, and waiting for friends or lovers, despite the cold air. I scanned the animated faces looking for Paul, and, not spotting him, checked my watch again, to see I was five minutes late. Perhaps he was inside?

As I stepped through the glass doors, a beefy, white-aproned waiter touched my elbow and steered me to the right, whispering "*On vous attend*." With a thrust of his cleft chin, he indicated a table set apart in the very back, where a figure in a black overcoat and a wide-brimmed fedora pulled low over its forehead, sat alone before an empty champagne flute. For a moment I felt disoriented. The person in the overcoat was definitely not Paul nor anyone I knew. It was a man, or so I thought at first, but then seemed to recognize the avid, colorless lips. As I made for the table, the face looked up. Two glassy blue eyes pierced mine from beneath the brim of the hat. I gasped as my suspicions were confirmed.

"Madame Rosier! They told me you were dead."

She flicked her hand in the air, as though chasing away a fly. "Nonsense!" she huffed. "Old, yes, dead no. Who told you such a thing?"

"I went to visit you at the hospital ten days ago, and you were gone. The woman in the other bed told me you had died that morning."

"That senile old wreck! As you can see, I am perfectly fine. They had probably taken me away for a bath. Sit down, dear. We don't want to call any attention to ourselves. There are spies everywhere."

I slunk into the worn leather couch across from her. As far as calling attention to ourselves: she looked ridiculous in that get-up, and we were both wearing conspicuous hats, but no one else seemed to notice us at all.

"You look rather pale. I know just what you need." She hailed the waiter with an imperious gesture. "*Garçon*, a Pineau des Charentes for Mademoiselle! She is ill. And for me, another glass." She leaned forward to scrutinize my face. "What is the matter with you? You're not…."

"I am just surprised, astonished, rather. I'm afraid I told Monsieur Ravi you had passed away."

She laughed at that and patted my hand. "Oh, no matter. At least he will stop pestering me about the money I owe him, for a while, until he finds out the truth."

"How did you get that note to me? How did you know where I live?"

"That wasn't hard. You said you lived on the Île. It's like a village there, you know. I asked if they knew an American girl with a hat. The boy from the wine shop on the corner said he had noticed you around and said you were staying where the old bakery used to be, so I asked him to stick the letter under your door."

The waiter brought our drinks. The wine she had ordered for me was very sweet and strong, while she drank more champagne.

"If you saw Ravi, then you got the envelope. Did you open it?"

"Yes."

"So you read it, then. Good. What did you think of it?"

"It is quite moving to read the story of that young woman." These words were inadequate to express my mounting obsession with Jeanne Hébuterne.

She nodded. "It's in a safe place?"

"I believe so." I had hidden it in a drawer in the kitchen, under a stack of dish towels.

"Very well indeed. You must realize how valuable it is."

"Do you want it back?"

"Oh no. It's too much responsibility. And I am too old to hang on to it. It must be preserved for future generations who will want to know about Jeanne."

"But why did you choose to give it to me?"

"The Hébuterne and Modigliani heirs would only fight over it, like the Montagues and the Capulets. Someone would doubtless end up dead, and they might stick it in a vault for another fifty years. My niece Danielle is such a gold digger. I trusted you would know what to do with it, as a scholar." She drained her glass and signaled the waiter to bring another. "But it was Jeanne who decided."

"How do you mean?"

"She let you hear her music. That is how I knew. Not everyone can hear it, you know. Only a chosen few."

"The *concierge* heard it, and she even told whoever it was playing to shut up."

"The *concierge* has lived in that building for over thirty years. I dare say she has learned to listen to what the walls have to say." She picked up a menu to fan her face. "Goodness it's hot in here."

"Then take off your coat," I suggested, though it didn't feel all that warm to me.

"I can't," she croaked, smiling mischievously, and unbuttoned her coat collar to show a glimpse of a blue hospital gown. "I hope you won't mention to anyone that we have met, not Ravi, or anyone, least of all my niece."

"Of course."

"I just left the hospital last night without signing myself out. I unplugged myself from the drips, put on my robe and slippers and shuffled out the door. It was very late, and the night nurses were God knows where. In a wardrobe near the staff room I saw someone had left this coat and hat, so I grabbed them and snuck out unnoticed, like a thief, at three o'clock in the morning."

This sounded preposterous, but there she sat in her hospital gown. "Where did you go at such a late hour?" I asked.

"Oh, there are places. Paris is full of them. But now I need your help."

Inwardly, I cringed. She was going to ask me for money.

Seizing my wrist across the table, she whispered, "I can't go home you see. Danielle is there. She would just put me back in the hospital, or worse, do me in. I need some clothes to wear. I am not even wearing any underwear—they take it away from you when they check you in. I also need some cash, and I am terribly hungry. The food in hospitals is so bad."

Here we go again, I thought, more oysters and champagne.

She let go my wrist. "I have some very important business to take care of at the bank, but I can't do it dressed like this. They'd arrest me before I got through the door. If you could just loan me five hundred francs, I could take myself off to a little place I know and get fixed up in no time. I will pay you right back—tomorrow, I promise."

I stalled for time. Five hundred francs was a lot of money to me.

"Well, let's order something to eat, if you're hungry."

"No, we have been here too long. My niece will have put a private detective on my trail. Just give me the money, and we'll leave the café separately. I'll go first, and head for the taxi stand, and go right on the boulevard. Wait at least a half hour and then when you leave, go in the other direction. I will meet you tomorrow on the banks of the Seine, below Quai de la Tournelle. But be careful. The stairs there are treacherous. And if you see anyone following you, just wait for me in the café on the corner next to the violin-maker's workshop. At ten o'clock sharp."

I reached into my bag and opened my wallet, wondering why I was doing this. "I can't give you that much. I can give you only three hundred." I handed her the cash.

"All right," she pursed her lips, took the money, and tucked it into her pocket.

She got up slowly, clutching the edge of the table to steady herself, and I realized then just how frail she was. She fumbled for her cane, which had been tucked out of sight.

"Don't turn around to watch me as I go out," she warned, and hobbled towards the exit.

I finished my drink and sat a while, brooding about Jeanne and Madame Rosier. When the waiter brought the check, it took nearly all the cash I had left to pay it, scraping out all the loose change from the bottom of my bag. It would be another week before I would get the next monthly stipend of my grant money. Slinging my bag over my shoulder, I wove in between the tightly-packed tables and out the door. Right on the edge of the crowded terrace, a man sat alone observing at me. With one glance, I noted his hunched shoulders, colorless eyes, and the crescent-shaped scar on his stubbled chin. In some ways, he resembled the man parked in the Dyane outside the hospital, whom I had asked for directions after visiting Madame Rosier. But his hair was all wrong. This fellow was blond and had a moustache, while the man in the car had been dark and clean-shaven. If this was the detective she feared had been following her, he may have been on her trail even before she went AWOL from the hospital.

Next morning, I descended the mossy steps to the embankment along the Seine below Quai de la Tournelle, carefully inspecting the area to see if that man was about—but I didn't spot anyone. A blustery wind was blowing, and gulls sailed above the swollen river. A strong smell of disinfectant hung in the air, masking a ranker scent of sewage. It wasn't the sort of place I'd choose for a morning stroll. At present it looked deserted except for an elderly man walking a poodle. A barge passed, and its occupants waved: a bearded boatman in a knitted blue cap, and two children playing on the deck with a plump gray cat.

I waved back, watching the foaming wake the barge left behind and soon spied Madame Rosier, still in her purloined overcoat and hat, making her way slowly beneath the scrawny plane trees flanking the river. A huge pair of black Dior sunglasses had been added to her disguise.

She was wearing bright red lipstick again, and her nails had been expertly manicured. A strong floral perfume wafted from her skin. On her feet, dainty patent leather heels had replaced her woolen slippers, reflecting the wintry sun. Wherever she had gone to get herself up—as she said—with the money I had loaned her, they had done it in style.

"Thank you for coming," she said, squeezing my elbow. "I knew I could trust you. Now I need your help again." From her pink Chanel shoulder bag, she removed a bundle wrapped in a handkerchief and plopped it into my hand. Cold, heavy, and metallic, it felt like a gun, but unwrapping it, I found a rusted chisel.

"My hands are too stiff from arthritis. You see that stone?" She pointed to a spot high in the wall of the embankment behind us. "I need you to pry it free."

I must have looked doubtful, for she went on to explain, "I've hidden something there that I need to get. It will be to your advantage."

It was almost out of my reach, and most definitely out of hers, but I thought I could manage it standing on tiptoe. "Did you bring a hammer, too?" I asked.

She shook her head.

"Then get me a rock."

I looked about to see if anyone was watching us, but no one up on the street seemed to take notice. After twenty minutes of tapping and prying, I succeeded in freeing the stone from the cracked cement that had once bound it to its neighbors. It slid out easily, exposing a cavity in the wall.

"It's in a plastic bag," she said.

Reluctantly I stuck my hand into the hole. My fingers prodded cold, damp earth; bugs, perhaps, grit and rubble.

"There's nothing here," I said.

She glared at me. "You wouldn't lie to me, would you?"

"Of course not!" Why would she think such a thing? "I can't really reach that far inside. I'd need a ladder and flashlight."

"Don't be ridiculous. Everyone would see us. Perhaps it's slipped further back."

With one last wrenching of my calf muscles and shoulder, I hoisted myself up and groped further back into the cavity. Bingo! I recoiled at the touch of a hard, slimy object.

"I have got it!" I shouted and pulled it out.

I was holding an ancient Celtiques pack, wrapped in several layers of squishy, dirt-streaked plastic.

"Is this it?"

Madame Rosier had removed her sunglasses to inspect the object. "Yes, yes! Now open it."

With squeamish fingers, I peeled off the layers. Inside was a dirty bundle the size of a thumb, which contained a rusted key.

With a hyperventilated "*Ouais,*" Madame Rosier snatched the key from my hands. "And now we must rush to the bank before they all go to lunch."

I understood then that it was the key to a safety deposit box and had probably been there for years.

I sat at a café across the street while Madame Rosier entered the glittering palace of the Société Générale on Boulevard Haussmann. Piled on the chair beside me were her hat, sunglasses, and coat—the disguise she had shed to reveal a pink-checked Chanel suit underneath, appropriate for tending to business in such a place.

"Keep a look out for anyone suspicious," she had warned. But who could have been more suspicious-looking than ourselves?

I sipped a café crème while I waited, my eyes on the door, my hat pulled low over my brow. A man came in, frowned at me, and went out again.

Madame returned, smiling abstractly, humming a tune, her bag swinging on her shoulder. In one hand she carried a mailing tube, the other clutched her cane.

261

"Now, I will have something to show you," she said, joining me at my table. She surveyed the premises with a furtive look, then removed the end stopper from the tube and drew out a tightly rolled sheaf of papers.

Half a dozen drawings opened. "This is a Kisling. This is a Foujita. This is a Soutine. And this little jewel was by Pablo, but alas, he failed to sign it… and this is a Modigliani."

I stared in awe at the drawings. The Modigliani nude sketch was superb, created with such an economy of line. To examine them so closely in an intimate setting, spread out on a café table, seemed so incongruous—a privilege for only the very few. I could not even imagine their value.

"That's where old Libion tacked them up on the walls of the Rotonde!" She chuckled, pointing out some holes in the upper corners of the sketches.

When I put down my cup to pick up one of the drawings, she nearly jerked it out of my hand.

"Be careful. Don't spill your coffee on it."

"And here," she said, handing me the last one, "is a self-portrait by Jeanne Hébuterne."

At the very first glance, I experienced a flash of vivid recognition. I had just read her diary, and here was a sketch of the woman herself: a melancholy face beneath a funny squashed cloche with a plume sticking out of it; short pigtails hanging below the brim. She sat musing at a café table, chin in hand, with a book and a teacup beside her, waiting, perhaps, for Modigliani. Time vanished as I stared at the sketch. She was of our time; we were of hers. In some ways, I *was* her.

"You see, she had just cut her hair, so it was 1917. Écoute, I promised to pay you back—and so I shall. This one is for you, if you should like to have it, in repayment for my debt."

Now along with Jeanne's diary, I was being offered this rare sketch. Both the drawing and the priceless original notebooks were the stuff scholars dreams of, obtained only after years of painstaking research and expense. But to me they had been handed, as it were, on a silver platter—like the key to Ortiz's flat, with hardly any effort on my part. I was thrilled and humbled.

"But it must be worth so much more than three hundred francs!"

I protested, then remembered Professor Renard's warning: If she tries to sell you an original drawing, don't bite! But he had said nothing about what to do if she wished to give me one.

"Of course it is, and it isn't. To the world she was nothing more than an art student, or what do you call them nowadays, a group-ie? For an art dealer, this has no value today. And there is no market for the papers and drawings of Jeanne Hébuterne, yet. Ah, but one day this sketch will be worth thousands. And you," she tapped her lacquered fingernail on the table, "will help with that."

"How do you mean?" I was intrigued, but also wary.

"You will write the story of Jeanne and her art and tell all America about it. It is time someone did." She plucked the drawing from my hand, rolled the papers up and tucked them back into the tube. "And there are quite a few more where these came from."

"More of those drawings?" I couldn't fathom it—they must be worth a fortune. As for writing the story of Jeanne and her artwork, I supposed it could be done, if resources could be located. My brain started ticking.

"*Ouais*, and a whole carnet of Jeanne's sketches, which no one else has seen in sixty years. As I said, this is yours, if you would like to have it, but not quite yet. There is one more little thing you must help me with."

"What's that?" I knew there had to be a catch.

"You must help me rescue Mimi."

❋

At nine o'clock, the tall green door with the iron grille opened and out stepped Danielle with Mimi straining at the end of her red leather leash. The dog tugged towards a small tree planted in a square plot along the sidewalk, sniffing excitedly. Danielle unhooked the leash to let the animal do its business unhampered while she contemplated a shop window and rolled herself a cigarette under the streetlamp. It was bitter cold. Nothing was open so the street was quite deserted.

When Madame Rosier inched forward from the doorway where we were concealed, the dog instantly sensed its mistress's presence, losing all interest in the tree. Mimi looked around wildly, nose in the air, trying to locate the source of what must have been a fond, familiar smell. Whimpering faintly with wagging tail, she peered expectantly towards our hiding spot.

"On the count of three," Madame Rosier rasped. "*Un, deux, trois....*"

I pounced out of the doorway, scooped the dog up, and plopped her into a small burlap sack Madame Rosier had provided. Veering down a side street, previously indicated by Madame, I ran with the squirming bundle clutched to my breast, while my elderly friend shrouded in her overcoat lumbered along with her cane. Danielle gave a shriek and set out in pursuit, but in her high heels, the cobblestones were an impediment.

In the small square where the side street ended, a taxi had been pre-arranged by Madame Rosier. We clambered inside, giggling like maniacs to defuse the tension.

"*Allons-y!* Pont Saint-Louis," squawked Madame, and the taxi was off like a shot.

Mimi wriggled out of the bag. The obvious joy they both felt on their reunion was infectious. Mimi bounced in her mistress' lap, licking the tears streaming down Madame Rosier's face, and yapping with pleasure.

"My little treasure!" She took my hand in the taxi and pressed it twice. "How can I thank you for what you have done?"

I only hoped no one had seen and recognized me. I wouldn't want to embarrass the school or even lose my scholarship over trouble with the law. I also wondered if she really would give me Jeanne's drawing after all.

"Can you drop me at my apartment on the Île?" It had been a long day, and I was tired.

"Aren't you hungry? Mimi is starving. There's a little place I know on the Île that serves Moroccan food. Mimi likes the way they do their steaks."

"I don't really have much money left for dinner out," I confessed.

"Don't worry about that! This time you are my guest."

I was hungry, and there wasn't much to eat in my flat, so I thought, why not, as long as she is paying? The taxi pulled up outside a restaurant just around the corner from my building.

I had noticed this Gothic-looking place with massive medieval ceiling beams several weeks ago, but had never ventured inside. From the menu posted in the window, I had seen it was quite expensive. Madame Rosier, instead, was a regular. The handsome Moroccan waiter greeted her warmly and led us to a roomy corner on a heated, glass-enclosed terrace, where there was plenty of space for Mimi. She ordered our dinner, including a filet for herself and one for Mimi, who was provided with a plate of her own.

"The poor dear is undernourished," said Madame, watching indulgently as Mimi gobbled up her filet cut up into bite-size pieces by the waiter. "Danielle probably never fed her."

My chicken tajine arrived in a large clay platter with a peaked cover like a magician's hat. Lifting the lid, I inhaled an exotic explosion of cumin, coriander, cinnamon, turmeric, pears, and apricots, and the first taste was no disappointment. Madame and I shared a carafe of Shiraz.

"I feel like a human being again. I was afraid I'd die in that place. But now to us. If you have read through the diary, you will have read about the portrait."

"The missing portrait of Jeanne with her child?"

"What other portrait is there that interests us both? She hoped to finish it herself, making it a family portrait of the three of them, but things worked out differently."

"In the diary, Jeanne says Modigliani had left the faces undefined of mother and child. Do you think that was a sign he no longer loved her?" I asked.

"There is no doubt that he loved Jeanne deeply. But he was very high-strung, hot-blooded like all Italians, and even a bit vindictive."

"You speak as if you knew him well."

"Well, I did know him and Jeanne. And I know the Italian character. My second husband, Renzo, was Italian. Modi loved being a father, and he adored his baby daughter, Giovanna. But he was also very ill by that time and infatuated with another young woman who modeled for him and who tried to steal him away from Jeanne."

"Do you mean Hanka's friend, Lunia Czechowska? I know he painted several portraits of her." Jeanne had mentioned Lunia in her diary as a rival.

She shook her head. "Not her. He was fond of Lunia of course, but not smitten. This was another Polish girl, Gosia, who modeled for two of the last great nudes. Zborowski found her in Montmartre and immediately saw she was the long-necked, buxom type, with a vast experience in men that would appeal to Modigliani. Mind you, it could have been anyone. It was the idea of being free from Jeanne and the baby, from all bourgeois routine, that made him rebel. But he would never have left his little family to run off with Gosia. She imagined they'd even take the baby. What a fool she was."

"What happened to Gosia?"

"She drifted about Montparnasse for a while and came to a bad end after she collaborated during the Occupation. She was nothing—nobody compared to Jeanne! You see, he couldn't reconcile the two parts of himself: the vagabond and the bourgeois. Oh, he railed against the bourgeoisie, artists should be able to do as they like, behave as they like; fuck whom they like. He'd take off his clothes and dance on tables whenever he got tipsy enough. But beneath it all was a man who dreamed of sitting in a cozy armchair, wearing a pair of warm slippers, while his wife fixes dinner and his children piddle about drawing pictures at his feet. But I am not sure that is what Jeanne wanted. She wanted excitement, fulfillment, beauty, and meaning. She wanted her life to be art, and art, her life."

Who doesn't? I thought—isn't that what we were all doing in Paris? Isn't that what the city promises us?

"Are you sure the portrait still exists?" I asked. "I have read that he would destroy a painting rather than drop it, or just paint over it or on the back if he needed supplies. Didn't you say it doesn't appear in any official catalogue or inventory?"

Her eyes narrowed slyly at this suggestion. "Modigliani wasn't good at keeping track of his own works, and in any case, he had abandoned it, so it wouldn't have been included in any official lists made while he was alive. And I am sure Jeanne had to hide it from him to protect it. She used to hide lots of things from him, like money. He was spiteful at times, as I said, and near the end could be terribly violent. He was always throwing things, and sometimes he hit her. I could hear them upstairs whenever they went at it. Monster, he'd shout—that was his nickname for her even when they were not quarreling because she tried to make him take better care of himself."

Monstre—that was the message scrawled on a postcard I had seen addressed to Jeanne. "Why did she put up with it?"

"She just bore up because she loved him. She knew it was his illness that made him behave like that. Tuberculosis doesn't just destroy your body. It eats away at your mind and your relationships. In that way, she was wise and long-suffering beyond her years."

I looked down at my hands on the table. "I don't know if I would have done that for anyone."

"Then you have never really loved, as Jeanne did."

"I suppose not." For a moment, I felt oddly unsettled.

She sighed and touched my sleeve. "You are trying to decide whether you are in love or not with some young man, *n'est-ce pas?*"

"No," I snapped. "Why do you think that?"

"At your age, my dear, that is all one thinks of. That is all Jeanne could think of. Hers was a love of a lifetime. Of many lifetimes. And it was both a blessing and a curse."

The waiter emptied the carafe into our glasses and took away the dishes. We both declined dessert, but a bowl of cream was ordered for Mimi and promptly brought.

"In any case, that portrait was obviously very important to Jeanne. There exist no photographs of Jeanne with her daughter, so it is a unique testimony. That is probably why she kept it hidden from Modigliani, and probably also from her brother. More than their parents, he was the one who couldn't accept Jeanne's love for Modi and the child it produced."

"If André Hébuterne removed all Jeanne's artworks from the studio after she died, isn't it logical to presume that it would be among the things he took away?" I asked.

She shook her head. "No, I know for fact that he didn't take it away—you see, I saw the portrait myself during the war. It had come into the hands of a famous collector of those days named Metz, whom I knew. Only a handful of people, Metz's closest friends, ever saw it, as he supposedly kept it in a vault. Later they said it was cursed because of what happened afterwards." She drained her wine glass.

Madame Rosier certainly knew how to keep a listener on the edge of her seat. "Jeanne's suicide you mean?" I asked.

"Partly, but not only. Metz's great collection was dispersed during the Occupation, and he died at Auschwitz. Those were terrible years. You young people cannot imagine it."

"So people think that the portrait might bring bad luck?"

"That's just ignorance," she huffed. "It may well be the only painting of Metz's collection that survived, so I'd say the contrary."

"And so, what do you think might have happened to it?"

"I think it may be in the south of France. Oh dear, what's the time?"

I checked my watch. "Almost eleven."

"The train leaves in a little over an hour from the Gare du Nord. We must hurry."

"Train?"

She pulled two tickets out of her bag and put them on the table like a Tarot reader laying the cards.

"Nice, and then on to Cagnes-sur-Mer by bus. You will enjoy it. *Garçon!*"

I stared at the tickets. "I can't go with you to Nice at the drop of a hat."

"Why not? Have you anything better to do? It is just for two or three days. You are a scholar. It's for your research. Don't you want to find that portrait by Jeanne and Modi? Think of what it would mean for your career. You'd be settled for life with one book. Maybe you could even buy a flat in Paris, or a little place on the coast. It is an opportunity not to be missed."

"But I have things to do here."

She gave me a disparaging look.

"Why does it have to be me? Isn't there anyone else who could go with you?"

"Who can I possibly trust with such a task? You cannot imagine how much that painting is worth. At my age, I cannot travel so far alone. I need an assistant. I feel you can be trusted. And your expenses will be paid. Besides," she said, leaning forward and lowering her voice, "after what has just happened with Mimi, we'd be wise to make ourselves scarce for a couple of days. Danielle will be furious and she can also be very vindictive."

The waiter returned. She paid our check with a bundle of bills and picked up Mimi, still licking the cream from her dish, off her chair.

"Midnight sharp, platform five, Gare du Nord, car number twelve. *Le train bleu.* If you run now, you can get your things together and make it in time. But you will need a taxi to get to the station. I have some business to take care of beforehand. I will see you on the train."

She pushed a wad of money into my hand. It was over 1000 francs. From impecunious, she now seemed to have a generous supply of cash, after that visit to the bank.

The flat I had sublet was just around the corner. Madame had known that when she had chosen our dining spot on the Île, where she had her own informers. I rushed back to my apartment and quickly stuffed a few clothes and toiletries into my backpack. I wasn't sure why I had agreed to go, but perhaps the dognapping incident had something to do with it. Perhaps it was wise to lie low. Or maybe I knew the adventure would surely keep my mind off of Paul, who hadn't been back in touch. And yes, after having read the diary, I was curious about the missing Madonna.

I tucked cash and passport into a neck purse I always wore under my shirt while traveling. Afraid to leave the diary in the flat while I was away, I slipped it into my backpack, although I did not relish the idea of carrying it around with me.

The buzzer rang. I ignored it. It rang again twice insistently. Peering out between the slats of the shutters, I could see Paul holding a bottle of wine. I buzzed him inside.

He grinned at me when I opened the door but gave off a strong scent of alcohol, and his eyes glinted. The attraction was strong, but I stepped back.

"How did you find me?" I asked.

"I enquired at the school, and they gave me your address. Walking past, I saw the light on and wondered if you were in. I picked this up at the shop on the corner. Are you busy? Ah, I see I am interrupting something. You are escaping!"

"I am going to Nice for the weekend with a friend. I am sorry but I am in a terrible hurry."

He cocked his head and gave me an ironic smile. "With a friend?"

"I am going with Madame Rosier." I don't know why but I felt I had to explain.

"You are going with a ghost?" he frowned.

"There was a misunderstanding. She wasn't dead after all. I just had dinner with her, as a matter of fact."

"Oh, a minor misunderstanding! So will you be hunting for the missing Modigliani?"

"Don't be silly. She is taking me to see some pieces in a private collection owned by a friend."

The lie tripped so easily off my tongue.

"I am glad that your research is going so well. Will you give me a rain check?"

"I certainly will, but I am sorry, I have really got to go. The train leaves in half an hour. Can you give me a lift to the Gare Du Nord?"

"I don't have my scooter with me. I came by foot. But we can get a taxi just near the bridge. *Viens!* Allow me!"

He hoisted my backpack on his shoulders, and we headed out the door. I turned the key twice and buzzed us out to the street.

A waiter greeted him as we passed the Café Saint-Louis.

"This is one of my favorite neighborhoods in Paris," he said. "I know some nice places for a meal. That café has great music on Saturdays, and that one is famous for its ice cream. We'll go there when you come back."

"I'd like that," I said, but I was getting nervous that I might miss the train.

"There, a taxi is coming!" He strode to the curb and lifted his arm—so athletic, I thought. *Pas mal.*

The taxi stopped. Paul deposited my backpack into the trunk and gave instructions to the driver. After I had scrambled in, he reached in and kissed me—a devouring, electric kiss that melted my legs and tasted of stale wine. Then he pulled away and slammed the door.

Still reeling from his kiss, I watched through the rear window as another taxi stopped, and Paul got in just as we turned the corner and began rushing along the Seine. Paul's taxi disappeared at the next intersection. In less than twenty minutes, we had arrived at the Gare du Nord, and I was dashing towards the platform, where at the end I saw Madame, pacing outside a blue sleeping car with Mimi prancing alongside her. Only ten more minutes before departure. Most of the passengers had already boarded the train; a few hardcore smokers were puffing on the platform.

Mimi yapped furiously as I ran towards the car. Madame Rosier waved. "Ah, here she is! My American niece!"

The conductor eyed me once and scratched me off his list as I handed him my ticket and passport. After he had helped Madame and Mimi climb on, I swung my backpack up into the train and hopped on just seconds before it lurched forward.

The attendant made up our bunks. Madame Rosier was assigned the lower bunk; I, the upper one. He showed us how to lock the door to the compartment.

"Whatever happens, don't open this door until morning, even if someone knocks and don't go out! There's a lot of thieving goes on in the night," he said.

"Oh, I'm not worried. Mimi is a good watchdog. She will protect us." She cuddled Mimi to her breast, and the creature blinked and lapped up some crumbs from its furry jowls.

"But what if I have to go?" I asked. "I sometimes have to get up in the night."

The attendant pointed to the little sink mounted on a column by the window, where sealed paper cups of safe drinking water had been provided for us to brush our teeth.

"That's not what I mean," I said, "I might have to use the...."

Impatiently, he crouched down and jerked open a drawer at the foot of the sink, where a chamber pot of flesh-colored plastic was neatly tucked on a rack, beneath which you could see the train tracks and the ground below.

"You use, then throw out, you see? But not when the train is standing in the station."

I nodded, wondering how that would work out.

Madame Rosier beamed. "That will do fine for Mimi. You won't have to take the dog out when we stop in the middle of the night."

"If you need anything, *Mesdames,* I will be in the compartment at the head of the carriage."

After we were settled in, I stepped out to the corridor to give Madame some privacy while she got ready for bed. Watching the lights streak by in the blackened window, I felt increasingly excited about the trip. I had never been to the south of France, and I welcomed the chance to mull over my feelings for Paul.

Most of the compartments were empty. This was a first class *wagon lit*, and not the cheap second class couchette I was used to as a student traveler. I didn't mind traveling in style. The door was open to the attendant's compartment, and I could hear him bantering with someone. Then the attendant came out, followed by a tall man with a briefcase, and led him to a compartment three doors down from ours. I pressed myself to the wall and glanced at the stranger as he squeezed past me. Tall with stooped shoulders—long, lanky hair, a patchy beard and thick moustache. Dark glasses shielded his eyes. It was only a glimpse, I couldn't tell much; still I felt uneasy. Why would he be wearing dark glasses at midnight in such a dimly lit train? I heard the lock click shut in his compartment. Could this possibly be the same man I had seen at the hospital or at the Café Metro: a private detective who kept changing his disguise? Or was I just imagining things because Madame had suggested them?

I made a visit to the lavatory located at the rear of the car, and when I returned Madame Rosier lifted the blind and tapped on the window to let me know I could come in again. Stepping inside, I found her dressed in a fuchsia velour track suit, stretched on the lower bunk with Mimi on a gold pillow at her feet, next to a small Vuitton overnight case.

Two glasses and a demi bottle of champagne were nestled in the washbasin.

"Open it! Let's have a nightcap, and drink to the success of our trip."

This was certainly a crazy journey I was embarking on. But nevertheless, here I was. I opened the bottle, somewhat inexpertly, and poured out two flutes of champagne as the train jerked and rumbled beneath us, and foam spattered to the floor where Mimi licked it up.

"To Jeanne and Modi," she offered, and we clinked glasses. We sipped in silence. Then, "Brooding about your boyfriend?" she asked.

How could she know? But I shook my head, "I believe I saw someone I recognized on this train."

"Who?"

"I may have seen him before at the hospital, that first time I visited you. And then maybe again when I met Ravi, and perhaps at the Café Metro. But he always looks different: different hair, different beard. I am not really sure it's the same person at all. I might be imagining things." I drained my glass.

"Oh?"

"It's so dim in the corridor."

"You haven't told anyone anything about what we are doing?"

What *are* we doing, I wondered, but only said, "I told a friend I was going away for the weekend."

She nodded. "I hope you have mentioned nothing about the portrait or the diary or the drawings I showed you?" Her voice held a hook of suspicion.

"No, of course not." Which wasn't exactly true—I had mentioned the portrait to Paul, but I didn't tell her that.

"I don't like the sound of this. The same man. But you aren't sure?"

"No."

"As I said, my niece may have hired a detective to follow us. Or perhaps even to steal Mimi back! Well, you heard what the train man said. Don't go out on any account. Use the pot if you must." She clasped Mimi to her breast and kissed the dog's head. "I'd hate to lose my darling."

I removed my parka, took off my boots, and climbed up to the top bunk where I arranged myself between my backpack and Madame Rosier's large suitcase, an oversized Vuitton, crammed in the overhead rack. I kept my jeans and jeans jacket on and lay face down on the berth, with my neck purse stuck in my bra, so that any thief intending to rob me would have to wake me up and roll me over. I thought I should try to stay awake for a while, but the rhythm of the train soon rocked me to sleep as I dreamed of lying in Paul's arms.

I hadn't realized how gray Paris was until I peeked behind the window shade to greet the sky at dawn—tufts of pink and tangerine brightening to pure white. At eight o'clock, the attendant brought us steaming, freshly brewed coffee and a hot croissant, which was a welcome treat. On my way to the lavatory, I noted that the door to the strange man's compartment was open, and when we got to Nice and queued up along the corridor to disembark around eleven, I saw the compartment was empty. He must have gotten off at an earlier station—which was a relief. It didn't look as though he were following us after all.

We had more coffee and hot croissants at the railway café where I accompanied Mimi out to do her business in a flowerbed in front of the station. When I returned to the café, Madame Rosier paid for our snack, and I hoisted on my backpack, picked up her heavy Vuitton suitcase, and grabbed Mimi's leash. Madame managed her cane and her smaller Vuitton overnight case.

From the station, we took a bus to Cagnes-sur-Mer, and from there, a taxi to Rue Planastel. Narrow cobbled streets ran straight up the hillsides from the sea, flanked by little houses of pinkish stones or pale yellow stucco. Lush little gardens of dark citrus trees laden with lemons and oranges flourished behind stone walls and black iron gates. From the hilltop, one could see shimmering stretches of a turquoise sea wedged in between brown terraces and red rooftops.

Madame Rosier and Mimi descended from the cab, leaving me to handle the luggage and pay the driver. We stood outside an old house four stories high, defying the notion of 90 degree angles, where each story had been added on obliquely, retreating further from the street, all cobbled together by sagging balconies, collapsing arches, and teetering stairs. A prickly purple bougainvillea covered the front of the house, and the large windows on the upper floors sported bright green shutters. It was a *maison ivre* exuding storybook charm.

A young woman exited the house and came down the stairs to greet us.

"*Bonjour, Mademoiselle*", chirped Madame Rosier. "Could you please call someone to help with our bags?"

"I am afraid you have made a mistake. This is a restaurant, not a hotel. The hotel is a little further along this road. I can call you a taxi if you wish."

"No mistake. You must be Mathilde's daughter, Lise. Could you please tell Madame Mathilde that I am here? My name is Annie Rosier. And could you also please bring me a chair? I am rather old as you can see."

A folding lawnchair was produced, and Madame Rosier settled herself into it while the young woman, a bit annoyed, went to relay the message to Madame Mathilde, whom I assumed was the owner or manager of this place, where a sign read *Modigliani & Co.*

"You will like it here. The food is some of the best in France, in the South, anyway. Mathilde is a superb cook, or at least she was." She fanned herself with the bus schedule we had picked up at the station, although the air wasn't that warm. "Poor Mimi needs water. Bring me that bottle of Evian in my traveling case."

Opening the case, I found Madame's water bottle nestled next to the mailing tube containing the drawings, carefully wrapped in plastic. I handed her the bottle. Madame took a swig, then leaned down to Mimi to pour a trickle of water, which the dog lapped up so daintily that its little black lips never touched the bottle.

"That is where Modigliani stayed," she said, taking another sip of water, pointing up to the top floor—to a large window and terrace on the right. "The room next to it in the middle with the slanting roof, that was where Soutine slept. Zborowski and Hanka were on the second floor. Jeanne and her mother were just down the road. I was here too, you see. Hanka had me come for a few weeks to help with domestic chores while Ortiz and his family were away from Paris. I was glad to get away from Big Bertha!"

"I was so surprised to read in the notebooks that Jeanne had come to Nice with her mother."

"Madame Hébuterne probably suspected that her daughter was in a family way, and that is why she decided to accompany her. Probably even before Jeanne realized her situation. She was very naïve."

A middle-aged woman in a white chef's jacket now appeared in the doorway, frowning. She had short, frosted blond hair and was as tanned and muscular as a tennis pro.

"Annie?"

"Mathilde!"

Madame wobbled up from her lawnchair and let herself be embraced by the younger woman, while Mimi scampered about their feet. Lise observed this reunion from the doorway, not at all pleased.

"And this is my assistant, Mademoiselle…."

"Smith," I said and gave Mathilde my hand.

"You should have told me you were coming." She eyed our bags: Madame's matching Vuitton set and my battered backpack. "We are not really equipped to receive guests."

"It will only be for a couple of nights. I thought we would stay up there, in the studios— I in Modigliani's and Mademoiselle Smith in Soutine's. Mademoiselle is an art history scholar, working on Modigliani, Jeanne Hébuterne, and Soutine."

Madame Mathilde nodded, with a semi-frozen smile, trying to size me up.

"And I thought she would appreciate seeing the place where they actually lived during their mythical sojourn in the South."

"I see. But the smaller studio is now my office and the other is my bedroom."

"You can arrange something for us, just for a couple of nights. I know you have several rooms."

"I will see. But you must be tired after your trip. Please come into the house." Madame handed me the smaller Vuitton case as Lise and Mathilde took charge of the remaining bags. We entered a lobby filled with prints of Modigliani nudes and portraits alongside landscapes by Soutine. There were lithos of Modigliani drawings and some ceramic sculptures on sideboards, resembling his Polynesian figures.

"Let me get you a glass of water, or champagne?"

"Champagne, naturally."

"Water, please," I said.

I eagerly studied the prints on the walls, but Madame Rosier peered over my shoulder, whispering, "Very bad copies indeed," then ensconced herself in an armchair.

Mathilde joined Madame Rosier for a glass of champagne while I sipped a Perrier.

"Quite a lovely place you have got here. And a Michelin star as well! Here's to your continued success," Madame effused, and they touched glasses.

"I must thank you and Renzo," Mathilde said uneasily, "without your help this never would have happened."

Madame Rosier only smiled knowingly and sipped her champagne, while magnificent smells wafted forth from the adjacent kitchen, where three young chefs were manipulating copper sauce pans. By now it was after three o'clock, and I was starving.

"I am sure you are hungry. Come into the dining room. We are open only for dinner in this season, but I can arrange you a late lunch."

We freshened up in the ladies room off the lobby and then were shown into the dining room. Mathilde sat across from us while a waiter served cold plates of salmon, goat cheese, ham, olives, and peppers preserved in oil, which we soaked up with crusty bread and washed down with rosé. Mimi was fed little tidbits throughout.

Although the two French women spoke very quickly in a language of their own full of allusions, I could make out most of what they said. Mathilde's daughter stood behind the counter, eavesdropping while pretending to polish some silver.

"Look, Annie, I haven't got it. That big…portrait." She paused and shot me a sidelong glance.

"It's all right. You can speak freely in front of her."

"Renzo took it back to Rome. Over three years ago, or so. I couldn't keep it here safely. We have had a couple of break-ins."

"Why didn't you tell me?" Madame tapped her knife on the table-top in irritation.

"You never asked about it. And I would have assumed Renzo should have been the one to tell you. Anyway, if it was so precious to you, you should have kept it in a vault in Paris." Mathilde poured herself a glass of rosé and downed it in one swallow.

"Renzo couldn't have told me. They put him in jail, you know, and then he died after his release. And I couldn't possibly have kept it in Paris. I was afraid Danielle or her lawyer would get their hands on it. And now I have Renzo's sister to deal with! That bitch, Rosa!"

I had rarely heard her express herself so crudely. I could see she was very upset.

"I was terribly sad to hear Renzo had passed away. Forgive me for not sending my condolences," said Mathilde.

"Thank you. His son by his first wife has taken over the business, so I hear. We will just head on to Rome when we leave here and hope that Renzo has kept his word," said Madame Rosier.

I looked at her, and asked, "Rome?" but both women ignored me.

"How do you mean?" Mathilde asked.

"We had a plan B, as to where to keep it safe in case it should be removed from this place."

"I see. You should know that you aren't the only person who has asked about it," said Mathilde.

"What are you saying?" Madame asked.

"An art historian, or so he said, came here some weeks ago, asking around about private collectors and galleries that might have items of interest. He even wanted to see what was in the priest's cellar. He'd heard the story of Modigliani having an illegitimate son who became a priest. He had got my name from somewhere, but I just showed him the prints downstairs, fed him an especially nice meal, and sent him on his way."

"You didn't tell him about the Soutine? You still have that?"

"That is my daughter's future, and the future of her heirs. It is under lock and key. No one knows it's here. But he had a picture of that painting of yours. An old photograph, perhaps from back before the War."

"He showed it to you then?" Now Madame Rosier seemed alarmed.

"Yes. He wanted to know if I had ever seen this painting or heard it talked about. He called it the *Sacrée Famille au Cirque*.

Her eyes widened. "Hah! And what did you tell him?"

"That I hadn't, of course!"

"From Metz. He must have got the photograph from Metz." She rubbed her chin nervously and plucked at a hair. "Can you describe him, this art historian?"

"I can do better than that. He was interviewed by the local paper. I clipped out the article and saved it. I thought of sending it to you— but here you are! Lise! Bring me that album by the cash register."

"You have always been very resourceful." Madame beamed at Mathilde and patted her hand.

Lise brought a large leather volume with gold trim to the table, and Mathilde leafed through it.

"This is the album we keep of famous guests, postcards, autographs. Et cetera." From photos and newspaper clippings stuck among the pages, I saw that Isabelle Adjani, Gérard Depardieu, and Jean Reno were all frequent patrons of the restaurant. "Here we are," she handed Madame Rosier a folded piece of newsprint.

"My eyes are bad, even with these glasses." Madame squinted at the photo. "I thought it might be the Israeli fellow who came asking about that photograph I have of Jeanne and Modigliani in their studio. But I don't think I recognize the man in this photo."

She perused the article carefully while caressing the crease between her eyebrows. "It is disturbing to know this person, whoever he is, has a photo of that portrait, and may have discovered its secret. And even more disturbing that he has traced it to you and to this place."

"Don't read too much into it. He interviewed almost everyone in town. He probably thought I might have found some souvenirs or even paintings here in the villa when we first bought it and began our renovating."

Madame Rosier chuckled at that. The women exchanged a sly, meaningful glance.

"I dissuaded him from such a silly idea," Mathilde said.

You couldn't tell much from the grainy photo on wrinkled newsprint, but I recognized the person immediately: Professor Jules Renard. But I kept that information to myself.

After our meal, Mathilde took us upstairs to our rooms. I was to sleep in the Soutine room, a sort of alcove with a low ceiling and a terrace. Furnished with a writing desk, filing cabinets, and bookcases crammed with cookbooks, binders, and photographs, it obviously served as an office and archive. The narrow bunk below the window was to be my bed. Madame would sleep in the adjoining room, which had been Modigliani's studio and was now a bedroom in tasteful southern style.

I carried Madame's bags into her room, where she collapsed in an armchair, gathering the dog on her lap.

"Very lovely, *n'est-ce pas?*" Raising her cane, she tapped on the door of the wardrobe across from her. "Show her your little treasure."

Opening the wardrobe, Mathilde shoved aside a row of dark woolen coats and removed a panel in the back, which slid out revealing a niche with a padlock. Slipping a key from round her neck, tucked out of sight beneath her chef jacket, she unlocked the niche and switched on a light inside the wardrobe.

I found myself looking at a painting about twelve inches square, mounted on a black velvet background, like a jewel. I felt as though I were peering at an enchanted world through a keyhole— uncanny, secretive, and unreal.

A yellow road swirled up among tipsy pink houses with peaked red roofs, keeling over left and right, stairs tumbling upwards and palms bending low, as if all were churning in an earthquake and caught in a convex mirror. Among the cluster of tospy-turvy houses was this very one in which I stood. For a moment I was drawn into the picture's hallucinatory vision and I seized the back of a chair to steady myself as the floor buckled into waves.

Madame Rosier grabbed my hand. "You feel it too! The power of his art! Magnificent! Chaim painted this during that crazy holiday they spent here in 1918. Chaim Soutine painted this house at least three times. One of those paintings is in a museum in New York; another is owned by a private collector in Tokyo. No one knows the whereabouts of the third."

The two women smiled at each other. Then Mathilde said, "I could never sell it. I sometimes feel that if I look close enough, I will see my own face in a window there, or my figure moving about the room. And I am very superstitious. It is as though Soutine has captured the soul of this house, and if it were ever to leave my possession, then this house itself would die. Or I would. I know, I am talking like a madwoman."

"There is a power in making images," said Madame Rosier thoughtfully. "That is why the Jewish religion prohibits it… and why some people will do anything, murder their own mothers, to possess an original like this."

We admired it in silence a few moments longer. Then: "Tell her where you got it from."

"It was here," said Mathilde, grinning. "In a trunk in the cellar. No one knew what it was. Or what it was worth. Modigliani and Soutine used to exchange their paintings to pay for their rent or for food and drink. Everyone thought their pictures were worthless. Most of them were destroyed, but this one was saved. Now it's worth tens of thousands, but in twenty years, it will be worth millions!"

"Poor Soutine," sighed Madame Rosier. "He had such a miserable death. They tried to make him wear the yellow star, but he kept it in his pocket. But he was never taken to the camps. Not like Nussbaum. Modigliani would have met a similar fate to Nussbaum. Had he lived…."

Mathilde switched off the light, closed the niche, locked it, replaced the panel, and rearranged the coats to conceal her hiding place.

"I am tired now," said Madame Rosier. "I will have a rest before dinner."

I took a walk around the town, imagining Jeanne and Modigliani walking hand in hand down the cobbled streets. I looked for the pink villa with a turret where they made love hidden in a garden but

couldn't find it. When I returned to the restaurant, the scent of grill-
ing meat wafted out from the terrace, where a chef was ministering to
a flaming barbecue. A table had been prepared for us in a private dining room upstairs, out of sight of the other patrons. Mathilde did not
join us, and Madame ate hardly anything, complaining of indigestion.
She fed tidbits of entrecôte and liver to the pup, and then retired to
bed, while I finished dinner and dessert alone.

Situated beneath an uninsulated roof, the alcove was freezing,
with only a tepid radiator for warmth, so I wore a sweatshirt and thick
socks to bed. Reproductions of works by Soutine and Modigliani surrounded me. Over the mantelpiece, a yellowed photograph showed
Modigliani and Soutine sitting under a bougainvillea in bloom in
front of this very house. Although it had been a very long day, visiting
these rooms, where these artists had lived and painted, had excited my
imagination. I kept musing over Mathilde's superstitious attachment
to Soutine's picture of her house, and when I fell asleep, I dreamed of
being in a painting myself, but the details were very unclear. Still, no
ghosts came to trouble me until the door opened around three a.m.
and someone gently shook me awake.

I blinked. Madame in a pink silk peignoir, curlers tucked beneath
a gold hair net, bent over my bed. Mimi crouched in the doorway
whining faintly.

"Mimi needs to go out," she whispered. "Would you please oblige
me?"

I pulled on my jeans and reached for my boots, but Madame said,
"Wait till you are downstairs to put those on. We don't want to wake
our hosts."

Boots in hand, I tiptoed down to the front door with Mimi scrambling ahead of me at the end of her leash.

I was still half asleep, but the cold air outside roused me. It took
Mimi over twenty minutes to do what we had come for, as she was
much more interested in sniffing shrubs and exploring unfamiliar
smells. Then something agitated her, and she barked loudly, dragging
me towards the shadows.

"*Tais-toi!* You will wake the whole house!"

Twigs crackled in a hedge flanking the villa. Out shot a black-clad
figure and I was shoved aside and sent tumbling. I managed to dodge

away from the sharp edge of a low brick wall but fell into the bougain-villea, while Mimi raced down the road after the intruder. When the dog finally returned, I was still painfully untangling myself from the brambles. My jeans had offered protection, but my face was scratched and bleeding. I blotted it with a tissue from my jeans pocket.

"My poor dear! I hope you aren't hurt!" Turning round I was aston-ished to see Madame Rosier standing in the doorway, fully dressed, clutching her cane and Vuitton overnight case. She had changed back into her pink Chanel suit and was staring down the road, where the prowler had disappeared.

"Bravo Mimi! A true watch dog!" She fished a tidbit out of her pocket and held it to Mimi's eager black lips. "*On ne peut pas rester ici.* We must leave immediately. As you have just seen, it isn't safe here. I will wait here with Mimi while you get ready and bring down our bags. Take off your boots before going upstairs."

"At this hour?" I asked incredulously.

Madame nodded and went into the front bar on the ground floor, where I heard her make a phone call.

Her bag was ready in her room, where the bed had been neatly remade. I carried it down in my stocking feet, then returned upstairs to pack and fetch my things. The creaking of the ancient wooden stairway must have woken Mathilde, for she called out from the second floor where she and her daughter had occupied a guest bedroom for the night. "Annie? What's happening?" Her voice was heavy with sleep.

Madame Rosier answered from the bottom of the stairs. "Mimi needed to go out, that's all—go back to sleep."

It must have been past four in the morning, and as yet no trace of dawn. Outside, not a soul was up at this early hour, except a street sweeper who appeared around the corner with a broom of twigs. He stared at us and our bags. "*Bonjour, Mesdames,*" he mumbled.

I realized I must still have blood of my face and probably looked a fright. I murmured a reply.

Madame Rosier ignored him. "The taxi will be waiting at the end of the street."

"Why are we running off like this?"

"The sooner we get to Rome, the better the chances of finding what we are searching for—before someone else does."

"Won't Mathilde be upset?"

"She will be glad to get rid of us. And as I told you, it's not safe for us to stay here."

We were soon aboard a slow train for Rome.

ROME

We sat, Mimi and I, waiting on the stairs with the bags—the Vuitton overnight case anchored to my arm—as Monday morning travelers tramped through the entrails of the metro and swarthy men with inquisitive eyes sidled up to us, commenting on my hat. After nearly two hours, a pink ghost appeared through the frosted glass of the *Albergo Diurno* under Termini Station, and Madame stepped forth freshly manicured and coiffed—even her hair was lightly glazed with a pink rinse. Once outside the station, where we garnered much attention, we bundled into a taxi and set out for the Pantheon, to have a proper breakfast.

With the backdrop of that somber dome and its colossal pillars, it was pleasant to sit in the cold, sunny *piazza*, drinking cappuccino and eating hot *cornetti* filled with apricot jam. Mimi, on patrol against the invasive pigeons, was rewarded with little bites of the sweet, sticky rolls.

"I lived here in Rome, many years ago, with Renzo, my second husband," said Madame, looking up with delight at the red and yellow façades fronting the Piazza della Rotonda. "I got the flat when we divorced. It's right around the corner from here, a lovely *monolocale*." With a napkin she wiped some jam from Mimi's wispy white beard.

"Is that where you were planning for us to stay?" I spooned up the foam from the bottom of my cup.

"Oh no, no. An old friend, actually my former sister-in-law, has been living there. We will just leave our bags there for the day while I arrange for some more suitable accommodations."

After breakfast, I managed to drag our luggage into a narrow alley leading off the *piazza*, where tall buildings pressed close on either side, leaving only a narrow wedge of blue sky at the top. At the very end stood a pale yellow *palazzo* with stucco flaking off the façade. Its massive front door was open to the street, and inside a nasal voice sang in melancholy quartertones, accompanied by the sloshing of a

285

very wet mop. As we stepped into the entryway, the woman swabbing down the floor stopped singing and stared at us, and, suddenly recognizing Madame, gave a shout. Throwing down her mop, she embraced Madame, kissing her effusively on both cheeks, and the two began babbling away in Italian as Mimi bounced around them, her paws skidding on the wet marble floor. The *portiera* grabbed Madame's big Vuitton suitcase and lugged it up the steps to the second floor, and I followed, as I well as I could manage, with my backpack and Madame's overnight case.

Paris stairs swirl, but these wide, shallow steps of gray flecked stone flowed straight down like a waterfall, fitted with a solid wrought iron banister, to which Madame Rosier tenaciously clung. She seemed quite winded when she reached the top, and I was concerned she might be overdoing it. After all, she had just been in the hospital, and I had no idea of her physical condition or even her real age. The train trip and our early departure from Nice must have been enervating for her as well.

Depositing the bag on the landing, the *portiera* kissed Madame Rosier again twice and scurried back down to her chores. We waited a moment outside a door, listening to the tinny voices of a radio inside. Madame paused to catch her breath, then rang the brass doorbell.

When the door swung open, a plumpish, naked woman peered out at us and screamed, then tried to shut the door in our faces, but Madame Rosier, with very quick reflexes, blocked the door with her cane. The commotion upset Mimi, who starting yapping.

"Annie!" shrieked the woman, through the crack of the door. "You are the last person I expected to see. You should have let me know you were coming." She spoke French with a heavy Italian accent.

Madame, as usual, manifested unruffled aplomb. "How could I if you have disconnected the telephone? May we come in?"

"Just wait there a minute." We could hear her rustling about the room as we waited in the doorway. The radio was turned down but not off. "I was expecting someone you see. I thought he was early. He likes to find me ready," she called from inside. "You may come in." I followed Madame inside, with the bags.

The woman, in her late sixties, perhaps, with dyed black hair, had put on a short, red satin dressing gown with unstitched hem, in sharp contrast to the bare, blue-veined legs beneath. She stood in the middle of the room, arms crossed, under an ornate chandelier dangling overhead from the ten foot ceiling like a giant spider. The sepulchral light of its ten-watt bulbs barely illuminated the room, which resembled more a baroque burial chapel than a boudoir with its green marbled walls and brass ornaments. In a corner, a kitchenette with a bar, worn vinyl sofa, and dressing table with professional make-up mirror all looked incongruously out of place. Brimming ashtrays and empty wine bottles were scattered here and there. Propped on an easel was a painting in process of the lady herself, sprawled naked on the sofa. Mimi sniffed around the room excitedly, growling at a fat Persian cat which had taken refuge on top of a cupboard. The cat followed our movements with huge yellow eyes and seemed to mesmerize Mimi.

"I have been meaning to catch up with the rent, but. . ." the woman said nervously, snatching a pack of cigarettes from the dressing table and lighting up.

"Well, at least you can give me some of it." Madame waved the smoke away from her nose. "Those things will kill you, you know." Addressing me, she said, "Just put the bags down by the door."

The woman flicked her head towards me. "Who's this girl with the cute hat and the suitcases?"

"My assistant. I am not here to chase you out of the flat, Rosa, as long as you give me an advance on what you owe."

"Well, I don't know, things have been so difficult ever since Renzo... You should have warned me," she looked away and contemplated the blank wall. She seemed on the verge of tears. "But all right," she said hotly, stubbing out her cigarette.

Opening a drawer of the dressing table, she took out some cash and handed it to Madame, who in turn gave the bundle of bills to me without counting them, saying simply, "Put it in my case."

Obeying, I opened the overnight case and stuffed in the money, and as I did so, I noticed that a thick package, about fifteen inches square and wrapped in newspaper, had been added to the contents.

"May I sit down?" Without waiting for an answer, Madame settled on the sofa and Mimi scrambled up beside her. The cat now sprang from its perch to the floor and paraded about our bags, poking delicately about with its pink nose while Mimi nearly went mad.

Rosa picked up the cat and put him out the door. Then, greedily studying Madame's Vuitton luggage, said "If those aren't real, they are a damn good imitation."

"Of course they're real."

Rosa snorted in apparent disbelief. "You have got some nerve, you know, showing up now."

Madame petted Mimi with long, meditative strokes. "You can't blame me for what happened to your brother. It was his own fault. He had become reckless, and you know I am right. And I tried to make it up to you, by letting you live here almost for free, all this time."

"Eighteen months in prison destroyed him. He tried to turn over a new leaf, opened a frame shop, but he didn't have the heart for it."

"Yes, I can imagine, such a waste of talent."

Rosa glared at her. "My nephew Maurizio took over the business and has made it a success. He does fancy framing for museums, big shows, but none of that other stuff. Besides, times have changed. Buyers won't touch a painting now without a certificate as long as your arm."

The bells jangled out in the *piazza*. "I am expecting someone. I hope you don't mind. I have to get ready for my next modeling session." She sat down at the dressing table and began to make up her face.

"And the house in Monte Sacro? Is Maurizio living there?"

"Oh, not there at the moment. It's all run down, you see. Some squatters got in while Renzo was away, and they nearly wrecked the place." She rubbed in dark foundation and patted it with pink powder. In the bright light of the mirror, her face appeared hideously purple. "And it's not really settled who's going to get it. Some distant cousin has come forward with a claim. Maurizio's nicely settled elsewhere." Applying scarlet lipstick, she smacked her lips and blotted them with a tissue. The red lips made her teeth look obscenely yellow, like those of a carnival ghoul.

"So it hasn't been sold. Is it empty?" Even I could tell from Madame's studiedly neutral manner that she was keenly interested in this house.

Rosa squinted at Madame Rosier in the mirror. "Why are you asking about the house in Monte Sacro? You want to buy it? I will trade it for this one."

"I doubt if it is yours to trade. No, I was thinking we might stay there while here in Rome. Only for a week or two."

A week! What was she thinking of? I had to get back to Paris. I had another lecture to give in a few days. Rent to pay. Professor Renard to contact, my thesis to work on, and, I hoped, Paul to see. If I was going to be away for much longer, I'd need to make some phone calls and think up some excuse for why I couldn't get back. I couldn't just disappear without risking my grant, which was my only means of support, meager as it was.

Rosa considered Madame's proposal, then drawled, "I suppose you could stay there—if you extinguish my past debt with what I have just given you and lower the rent from now on." She began to tease her hair with a comb, producing a dry, scratching sound, like rat claws in the walls.

I found this woman and her flat very distasteful.

"It could be arranged," Rosa continued. "I go there to feed the cats and do a bit of cleaning, so I am still in possession of the keys—although the lawyer doesn't know that I kept a set—so you'd have to be careful. And discreet." A cloying gust of hairspray filled the room like incense.

"Cats?"

"Wild cats in the garden, but they would be no threat to that neutered bunny of yours."

Madame Rosier yawned. "The utilities are still on? I don't want to be camping out."

Rosa nodded. "Everything works and is perfectly functional."

"Very well, you have paid what was owing up to this month. As of next month, your rent will be lowered to forty-thousand lire."

"Thirty."

"Thirty-five, take it or leave it."

"All right. And you must promise not to attract attention."

"We will be as quiet as mice."

"Just take the 60 bus from Largo Argentina. The route still goes all the way there. Number 632B. You remember the street, Via Cimone. I keep the key to the backdoor under a geranium pot just inside the gate."

Rosa got up now and made a pirouette under the chandelier. "How do I look?"

"My dear, like the cadaver in the picture," Madame nodded towards the easel, and Rosa grimaced.

"We'll leave our bags here and my assistant will come back later for them. In any case, should anyone contact you to find out where I am, you will say you haven't seen me?" Her voice trembled slightly, or so it seemed to me.

"You aren't running from the police again?"

Rosa winked at me.

"Don't be ridiculous. I am trying to avoid a confrontation with my niece. I checked myself out of a hospital and she doesn't approve."

"You ill? Hah! *Erba cattiva non muore mai.*"

"Only because she has been poisoning me. Away from her, I am perfectly fine." Madame rose from the sagging couch with the help of her cane. Out the window, bells struck noon. "We shall leave you to your artist." As she shuffled to the door, she paused to examine the canvas on the easel.

"You know, I think your fellow has talent. If he is looking for well-paid work, tell him to get in touch with me."

And we went out, leaving all our bags but the Vuitton overnight case, which Madame entrusted to me.

"We will go for lunch at Pier Luigi's at the Chiesa Nuova," she suggested once we were out in the street.

By one o'clock, it was quite warm in the square, so we sat outside without our coats. Here, too, she was welcomed like a prodigal daughter, and we were served raw artichoke and parmesan salad, grilled sole followed by strawberries with whipped cream; all washed down by Vermentino. Mimi curled at our feet under the table and received nibbles now and then. At Madame's instruction, I kept her small Vuitton case clamped between my ankles.

"Modigliani was in Rome briefly for his studies—it must have been the winter of 1904. He copied paintings in churches. Caravaggio, Reni. There is a church right near, just around the corner, San Luigi dei Francesi. You must see the Caravaggios there later. From here he went to Venice, and that is where he met Ortiz, who told him stories of Paris, Cézanne, Montmartre, and Montparnasse, which enticed him to move there. It is odd to think that it was also Ortiz to carry him down the stairs and deliver him to the taxi which would take him to the place of his death. So Ortiz was for Modigliani a sort of guide, a herald, like Mercury. Jeanne's brother came to Rome for two years to paint, in 1922, and traveled on to Algeria, Morocco, and Corsica. He made his living in the end painting exotic French landscapes for wealthy foreign collectors. Still Rome, in our time, has not been a city for art. Not like Paris. But in Paris, it was over so quickly. By 1930, all the artists who counted had either died, moved away, or become bourgeois. And then came the war and things were never ever the same again. The bubble burst."

I leaned my cheek on my hand as I listened and had another sip of wine. A fountain gurgled in the background, and the warm sun slanted into my eyes. I never tired of her rambling stories—whether fabrications or not, as Professor Renard had insinuated. She had such a command of characters and details that she made the people and places of the period stir to vivid life. By now Jeanne, Modigliani, Soutine, and André Hébuterne were familiar, bodily presences that I almost expected to find waiting for us around the corner at the next café.

After lunch we boarded the 60 bus to Via Cimone—it crawled down the long Via Nomentana, a magnificent boulevard lined with villas, embassies, and parks, where cypress trees, umbrella pines, and cedars towered behind decrepit yellow walls. Creeping at a snail's pace with Mimi on my lap, we crossed a narrow bridge glutted with traffic, took a looping road, and finally halted at the top of a hill, where we were the only passengers left on the bus. Small villas and gated gardens bordered the street, at the bottom of which we found the entrance to the villa at number 632B. The place was entangled with yellow flowering vines that reached out over the sidewalk, and large, splayed leaves like the fingers of a hand.

A dozen cats rushed at us as we came in, intimidating Mimi, then slunk off hissing when they found we had brought them no food. After we had checked under several potted geraniums, the key was located, and, following Rosa's instructions, we went round to the back.

The once charming garden was an overgrown ruin—persimmon trees with rotten fruit fallen to the ground weeks ago; straggly winter roses dying on a toppled trellis; a fountain choked with algae and dead goldfish; daffodils sprouting along a winding path strewn with crumpled newspapers and spaghetti scraps, probably Rosa's leavings for the cats. The scarred red door of the rear entrance looked as though it had been pried open dozens of times with a crowbar. After some fumbling with the key, I managed to unlock it.

It was freezing inside and smelled of mold, but the lights came on when I groped for the switch. A dusty marble stairway led upward. Right at the top, a set of double doors sealed off a room along a corridor. To the left was the kitchen and bathroom; to the right, a living room and study. From this landing, stairs continued up to another floor.

Madame burst open the double doors to reveal a blue bedroom, with a huge bed and red tile floor. She sighed with pleasure. "It's just as I recall it, from thirty years ago. Just put my case on the bed here. You can sleep on the couch in the little salon." She shivered and touched the dusty radiator beneath the shuttered window, then wiped her hand on a handkerchief. "I imagine that the heat hasn't been on in years. I hope the boiler still works. Go have a look upstairs."

I found the boiler in a storeroom on the next landing. Tentatively, I pressed a button and the contraption rumbled to life.

Across from the storeroom, a door stood ajar. Peeking inside, I discovered an atelier, which once must have served as a framing workshop and painting studio. Frames of all sizes and blank canvases on stretchers were propped against the walls and piled on chairs. There was a worktable scattered with tools, paint-blotted palettes, pots full of brushes, glue, varnish, and against one wall, a cupboard holding sheets of glass. Everything was coated with a layer of gummy dust. No one had set foot in here in ages. Dozens of ugly abstract paintings and prints hung on the walls, while other canvases were rolled up and stuffed in cubbyholes reaching up to the ceiling.

"It's working. The hot water's on. What are you doing up there?" she called from the landing below, and I went back downstairs to check out the room where I would be sleeping. The first thing I noted were the bookshelves lining the walls, a desk with a slim Lettera 22 typewriter zipped into its case, a balcony with stiff blue curtains, and an ancient wisteria twisted round the railing. The books in the case were mostly art books and catalogues. I searched the shelves for the name Manuel Ortiz de Zarate but found nothing, although there were several volumes on Modigliani. Spotting a gray telephone on an end table, I picked up the receiver, but there was no signal.

Stepping into the room with her overnight case in hand, Madame frowned when she saw me holding the telephone. "Do you need to call someone?"

I put the receiver down, feeling inexplicably guilty. "I should call someone in Paris," I said. "Especially if you are planning for us to stay here for long."

"Don't you worry. We will only be three or four days at most. Then you can go back to your boyfriend."

I shrugged. "It's not that. I have to give some lectures for my grant. I have to inform them if I am not going to be there. In any case, the phone doesn't work."

She seemed relieved. "Just as well. We wouldn't want to be disturbed. Besides, there is probably somebody listening." Scanning the book-filled walls, she said, "There used to be a safe hidden behind here somewhere, but I can't remember where it was exactly. We need to find a place for this," she said, indicating the Vuitton case, "where no one would think to look, especially Rosa, or whoever else may have the keys to this place."

"Maybe upstairs," I suggested. "There are lots of cubbyholes in that studio."

"So you have found the atelier. Good idea," she said.

It was only a few steps, which were not very steep, but I could see Madame was overexerting herself when we got to the top, for she was very short of breath.

"Maybe you need to lie down and rest," I said. "It has been a very long day."

"Nonsense," she said, giving me a dirty look. "Don't start acting like my niece."

I demurred.

"Ah, yes," she said, as we stepped into the studio and flicked on a light. "You can't imagine how many great works of art were produced in this room. Renzo had an incredible talent. Many of his works hang in the homes of millionaires and even in museums."

"You mean he produced fakes?" I dared ask. Not that I was all that surprised from what I had seen and heard over the last few days.

Madame laughed, a bit condescendingly, I thought. "There are fakes, my dear, and there are artistic copies. Some people will pay large sums to have an accurate copy of a Gauguin or Renoir, or why not, Modigliani, hanging in their living room—or in a small local museum. You would be surprised how many illustrious museums and galleries hold my ex-husband's work. Never forget: the value of an artwork is in the eye and heart of the beholder as well as in his wallet."

She studied the shelves and cubbyholes built into the wall and chose one on the very bottom behind the table, where it was hard to reach. Pulling out the rolled up canvases tucked in there, she stuck the case towards the very back, then piled some rags and other canvases in front of it. "There now. No one knows it's there, except you and me." She gave me a quirky little wink.

We went back downstairs again. I felt quite tired and thought I should go lie down for a bit in the living room. Taking off my hat and jacket, I stretched out on the couch and gazed up at the walls of books. I don't know why, but I felt so comfortable lying in that room. In just the few moments I had been there, both the house and garden had cast a spell on me. I could imagine living there forever and wished it was all mine: the yellow kitchen; the rundown garden with its ancient wisteria; all those moldy art books and the portable typewriter. The rusted radiator groaned as hot water murmured in its coils. I closed my eyes and must have drifted off for a few minutes, for when I opened them again, Madame was smiling at me from the doorway, and I could hear water running in the bathroom at the end of the hall.

"I am going to have a hot bath now and then I will fix myself a cup of tea. You should fetch our things before it gets too late. Take a taxi on your way back." She handed me some lira and a well- worn map of Rome. "On your way home, you might find us something to eat. There will be some shops still open in the square at the Pantheon. Bring us some nice white wine."

I donned my hat and parka. As I was heading out the door, she called down the stairs, "By the way, there is a telephone and telegraph office by the Pantheon. You can probably make a call from there. If it is absolutely necessary. But please don't tell anyone exactly where we are."

It took me over an hour to get back to the Pantheon by bus. The front door to Rosa's building was still open, but Rosa was out. The *portiera* communicated with fingers that she would probably return in an hour or two. I rambled to the Pantheon to search for the telephone office, where I bought a cupful of tokens for the payphone. I managed to get through to the school secretary before the office closed to explain I had been called away by a family emergency and wouldn't be back in Paris for a week. Then the tokens clinked through and the connection was cut off. I wasn't in time to catch the secretary's reply, but I supposed it would be all right.

I found the church Madame Rosier had mentioned, intending to see the Caravaggios, but a late service was being held, so I didn't go in. I drifted back to the Pantheon, thinking I should have an aperitif or a coffee while waiting at the café where we had had breakfast that morning.

It was the mustard-colored sweater I recognized first as I came around the corner from Sant' Eustachio. A dark painterly ochre. And then the red tennis shoes. Same sweater, same shoes, different man: the young man who sat sipping a drink at the Pantheon café was clean-shaven with lanky blond hair combed straight back from his forehead. I gawked. I gaped. Yes, it was Paul. Another version of Paul—well-groomed and wearing wire-rimmed eyeglasses, reading a newspaper. Not just reading it, but making notes on it with a pen.

I stared at him in disbelief—at this improbable transformation and at his inexplicable presence in Rome, not knowing what to do. He must have followed me from Paris, but why? Should I be pleased or worried? Confront him or conceal myself? I sat down on the steps to the obelisk fountain in the center of the square and pretended to study the map Madame Rosier had given me, shielding my face with it as I spied on him. Surprised, I saw him rise and nod, not to me, but to someone coming from the *piazza* behind me. A man approached Paul's table. Bewildered, I recognized the man from the train, and, as I scrutinized his face in the strong afternoon light, *this time* I had no doubt that he was the same person I had seen outside the hospital when I had visited Madame Rosier and also at the Café Metro. Was it the same man I had seen at the bookstall when I went searching for Monsieur Ravi? Of this, I was not certain. But what was he doing here, talking to Paul? In any case, it was a good thing Paul hadn't seen me and that I had not made my presence known.

They shook hands quite formally, then Paul tossed some change on the newspaper left lying on the little tin table, and the two went off together and climbed into a taxi. After it had driven off, I walked over to the table Paul had just vacated, collected the newspaper lying there, and plunked myself down. The newspaper was the latest evening edition of *The Daily American*, folded to the funnies and a crossword puzzle, half-filled out, which I presumed Paul had been working on. I skimmed the puzzle and was amazed to see that he had filled in the squares with the letters of my name in blue ink. What could that possibly mean, if not that he was thinking of me?

The waiter interrupted my absorption and glancing up, I ordered a prosecco with Campari.

"Wait a minute," he said, shaking a stern finger at me. "I remember you. The girl in the hat. You were here this morning with that old lady and the dog."

"Yes," I said, perplexed. "Is there something wrong?"

"You went off without paying. That's fifteen thousand lire for the breakfast, which I had to pay out of my own pocket."

"I am terribly sorry," I said, embarrassed, fumbling in my neck purse for two ten thousand lire notes. "I had no idea. My granny is sometimes forgetful. Please keep the change."

"All right," he said, pocketing the money. "But you watch out for that sneaky old bird. She'll get you into trouble."

While waiting for my drink, I studied my name in the crossword puzzle. I had no idea what to think or feel, after that unforgettable—at least for me—kiss in the taxi. He had followed me here and was now in cahoots with a private detective, who was trying to trace Madame Rosier and her pup. Or maybe the detective was trailing me! But that didn't make any sense.

I perused the front page, where the news was all about the engagement of Prince Charles and Diana Spencer. When my aperitif arrived, I nibbled some peanuts and took a sip, then nearly choked when I turned the page. A headline blared out: FAMOUS FRENCH CHEF DEAD. The article ran:

Haut de Cagnes- sur-Mer. Mathilde Debonnet, chef and proprietor of the renowned restaurant on the Cote D'Azur, Modigliani & Co., and

daughter were found dead Sunday morning, poisoned in their beds by car-
bon monoxide released by a malfunctioning stove. The incident is being
treated by the police as a potential homicide, or possible suicide, as the
exhaust pipe of the stove was found blocked with a wad of old rags. Police
are searching for two persons who may have been guests at the restaurant:
an elderly woman and a younger woman in a large hat, seen leaving the
area at four a.m. by a city employee. Persons answering to that description
were accompanied by a taxi to the train station in Nice and are believed
to have set out for Italy.

A phone number for Interpol was provided at the end of the article for anyone having information about the crime. Someone, Paul
presumably, had underlined the part about the two women and had
circled the phone number in blue ink.

I felt sick to my stomach, and, with a shiver that shook my whole being,
realized that we, too, might have died, poisoned by the stove, if we hadn't
left early that morning. But Mathilde was still alive when we left. I had
heard her call out to Annie. If we had realized something was amiss, would
we have been able to save them? As I pondered this, a cold knowing swept
through me, and I remembered my surprise at seeing Madame Rosier fully
dressed in the doorway after I had taken Mimi out for her business. Sweat
prickled along my forehead right under the crown of my hat—a very conspicuous hat, so I took it off and tossed it on the seat beside me.

I leafed through the newspaper to see if there was anything else
of interest and found hidden between the last two pages a business
card advertising the *Hotel del Sole*, with a phone number scribbled in
blue ink on the back. I tore out the article and stuffed it into my neck
purse along with the business card. Without finishing my drink, I left
a generous tip and discreetly moved my hat to a chair drawn up to
the next table, hoping it wouldn't be noticed right away. Studying the
shops on the square, I noted a grocery store where I thought I might
pick up some bread, wine, and cheese, and when I was halfway across
the *piazza*, I heard a shout behind me.

"*Signorina! Il suo cappello!*"

The waiter ran over to me, holding out my hat. "You and your
granny are a bit distracted, aren't you?"

"Yes," I said, "Thank you so much."

I managed to buy some groceries for our dinner before making my way through an alley to Rosa's *palazzo*. At the far end of the street, I spotted a dumpster where, after first checking that no one was looking, I threw my hat into the garbage.

I stood for a few moments outside the entrance to Rosa's *palazzo*. Had Mathilde and Rosa known each other? It was possible. Might she already have heard or read about Mathilde's death? That, too, was possible. Although she might not have bought today's paper, she did listen to the radio. Madame Rosier had said nothing to her about our having just been in Nice, at least that I recalled, so there was no reason why she might connect us to what had just happened in Cagnes-sur-Mer.

But if Rosa had heard or read any reports similar to the one printed in *The Daily American*, she might well have recognized us in the description of the two women, or anyway, suspect us. Thank goodness there had been no mention of the dog! In *that* case, it might not be safe for me to retrieve our things from her flat, or even for us to stay in the villa. Still, I had to get my backpack from Rosa's place. Jeanne Hébuterne's diary was in there, along with all my stuff.

I rang her bell, and a young man answered her door. He did not object to me collecting our things and even helped me take them down to the street, where I found a taxi at the stand outside the Pantheon. The driver loaded the bags in the back. So far, so good, but my anxiety was mounting. I would have to confront Madame Rosier about what had happened to Mathilde and maybe tell her about Paul and that man. Maybe.

My stomach was in knots as we were stuck in traffic for quite a while heading out of the city center. The hair rose on the nape of my neck at the screech of every siren. For two hours that morning, upon arriving in Rome, I had sat in full view at Termini station, wearing my hat and waiting for Madame Rosier to have her hair done. The two of us had been noted by hundreds of people. Perhaps the police already knew where we were staying.

There were angles to this story I simply did not understand. What was Paul doing here? And why was he with the detective trailing Madame Rosier, if that is who he was? Was I in danger? If Madame Rosier had killed her friends so nonchalantly, might she not do the same to me? But then again, it might have been the prowler who had stuffed rags in the stovepipe, not Madame Rosier at all. Then I thought, what if Paul or that man had been the prowler?

I was still in time to make an escape—to ditch Madame Rosier's bag by the roadside, buy a ticket with my credit card, and catch the next train back to Paris. But then what? Using my credit card was not wise, and I didn't have enough cash on me for a ticket to Paris, where I was easily traceable. Besides, there was something in Madame Rosier's overnight case that I now considered mine: that drawing by Jeanne Hébuterne. If I left now, I would never see it again.

It was already quite dark by the time I got back to the villa on Via Cimone. The yowling cats seemed even hungrier when I struggled through the gate with our bags, dragging them through the garden to the rear entrance, where the door stood open a crack.

Puzzled, I pushed it open. Inside, I found all the lights ablaze, and a strong smell of burning on the stairs—somewhere Mimi was barking her head off. I dropped the luggage at the bottom of the stairway and ran up to the kitchen, where I found a kettle with all the water boiled away, roasting red hot on the gas stove. Fortunately, it hadn't yet caught fire, but the handle had begun to smoke. Turning off the flame, I dashed the kettle in the sink, turned the water on full blast, producing a small geyser. Mimi, still locked out on the kitchen balcony, scratched at the door, howling. When I let her in, she bolted through the room and down the hall to Madame's bedroom where the white doors were firmly closed. In desperation the dog threw itself against the door, yelping and pawing at the wood.

"Madame Rosier?" I called, knocking at the door. I turned the handle, but the door was inexplicably locked with the key on the outside, I now noted. How could she possibly have locked herself in if the key was outside? "You left the kettle on. Are you all right?"

I turned the key. When the door opened, the dog dashed between my legs, nearly making me trip. Madame Rosier lay on her side in the bed, wrapped in a sheet, with her back towards me. One bare pink leg sticking out from under the sheet seemed to be caught in a seizure.

"Madame Rosier," I shrieked, running to the bedside. When she looked at me, her eyes were wild, and the left side of her mouth seemed frozen. An unintelligible sound welled up from deep in her throat.

I had no idea what to do. We had no telephone—and who would I call? At best I could run to a neighbor, but I couldn't speak Italian. I stared at her, paralyzed, as she bobbed her head and repeated that sound, which I finally made out was *"En haut."* Up. Or perhaps, "upstairs." Jumping up on the bed, Mimi began to lick Madame's face and her inert left arm.

Only then did I become aware of the room around us and what must have happened there. The place was a mess: drawers and cupboards yanked open and emptied of their contents. Everything was heaped on the floor and lamps were overturned. Her little shoulder bag had spilled out on the bed. Thieves had come. Perhaps they had frightened her so badly, her heart had given out and she had had a stroke. Maybe the intruders were still in the house—*"en haut,"* and she was trying to warn me.

I pulled the dog away, thinking Mimi might hurt her. "I will get a doctor, an ambulance," I said.

But this provoked a strong protest—though I don't know if it was the idea I might leave her to fetch help or my attempt to deprive her of Mimi's presence, which upset her so much. A spasm traveled through her whole body—her eyes stared; a tiny explosion flared deep within her pupils; her head dropped to the pillow.

"No," I cried, "Not like this!" I listened for her heart and took her pulse. I tried banging on her chest, but she was gone. I gaped at her in a state of sheer panic. I had never seen anyone die before—the only corpses I had ever seen had been beautified at a funeral parlor. I covered her with the sheet. Mimi curled up despondently at the foot of the bed, whimpering, and I began to cry. I had to leave the house immediately. That was clear. I might be in danger. Even if the thief or thieves had already fled, I couldn't stay here in this house with a dead woman who was suspected of murder. I would have to get the Vuitton case hidden upstairs, unless it had already been removed from the premises.

"Up! Up! Up!" she had repeated insistently—but that might be interpreted many different ways. Downstairs, the back door slammed so hard, the floor tiles trembled. With my heart pounding in my throat, I went to the window, where the shutter was unlatched, and peered out. Someone was running through the tall weeds. I heard the crushing of gravel underfoot, and then a skirted shape trundled through the gate and out to the street. Rosa! I thought. From that rapid glance, she didn't appear to be carrying bags or objects—so maybe Madame's precious case had not been touched. She might come back, I realized. Perhaps with the police or perhaps with her friends, and I didn't want to meet either party.

More boldly now, I headed upstairs where I found the boiler rumbling ominously, with a row of warning lights flashing, so I switched it off. The lights were on in the atelier, but nothing seemed amiss. I reached into the shelf under the table to pull out the overnight case Madame had hidden there earlier that day. Inside, I was relieved to find Rosa's bundle of lira notes, which I badly needed, as I had almost no cash of my own left. The mailing tube was still tucked inside, and beneath Madame's gold brocade scarf was the square package wrapped in newspapers. From the bulk and size, I could guess what it was: Mathilde's Soutine of the tipsy house that Madame Rosier had snitched before—perhaps—murdering her friend and escaping. I snapped the case shut. Hearing a noise downstairs, I panicked again, but it was only Mimi scratching to go out.

On my way out of the atelier, something caught my eye: in plain sight, right on top of the worktable, a large canvas was rolled up and sticking out from under some old newspapers. I hadn't noticed it before—perhaps Madame Rosier had been up there while I was out and had put it there for me to find—or perhaps not. An edge of the canvas was folded back so the painted surface was visible—a distinctive luminous red background with a strip of dark heavenly blue.

I unrolled it and there it was: unmistakable! *La Sacrée Famille au Cirque*. Jeanne with her auburn hair and turquoise eye sockets with no pupils, both turned inward, swathed in a blue—*carta da zucchero*—robe with stars splashed along the hem. A fringed shawl of red and yellow was thrown around her shoulders and bundled in her arms was a sleeping infant, with long spidery lashes and thin angelic lips. On Jeanne's left wrist glinted a circlet of blue-green: the Venetian glass bracelet which now adorned my arm! Modigliani, in a red harlequin costume, stood beside her, with one arm on her shoulder. The loose-limbed body with elbows oddly angled did not quite match his melancholy face. In the background, a gypsy cart stood ready to roll—and strewn about the canvas were small Hebrew letters, numbers, and occult symbols, spelling out a message for the initiated few.

But I couldn't linger there to decipher it. I rolled the canvas back up and tucked it under my arm. Grabbing the overnight case, I flew back down the stairs to find poor Mimi waiting forlornly by the door, wagging her tail. There was one more thing I thought I should take with me: the Lettera 22 typewriter, which might come in handy if I didn't make it back to Paris to pick up my things. I managed to fit it into my backpack, then, wrestling on my load, I scooped up the dog, and went out to get the bus.

Part 5
Afterlife:
Jeanne on Gauguin's Island
A fantasy

I WAKE UP TO THE PUNGENT SMELL of smoke, then hear the crackling of a fire I cannot see. Overhead, a roof of yellow bamboo. In between the cracks, strips of azure so bright they burn my eyes. No walls enclose me, and beyond lies a wide, blurred expanse of brilliant blue, sky or sea, I can't tell. Incredulous, I stare at it and drink in the color, not so much with my eyes, straining at the glare, but with my whole body—I am so thirsty for blue. I stir and manage to move my head, despite the torpor of my limbs. I am lying not in the sand where I was washed ashore exhausted, but in a hammock strung between two lanky palm trees, shaded by jagged fronds.

Soon I am aware of a presence, and soft puffs of warm air on my face. A black figure crouches next to me, waving a fan of palm leaves and muttering words I can't understand. My eyes focus on a dusky-skinned Polynesian woman in a stiff black dress with lace collar. She smiles as I study her, somewhat perplexed, for I believe I have seen her before.

"Where am I? Who are you?" I ask—my mouth so dry I can hardly speak, but she drops the fan and runs away.

Leaves rustle and swish, a shadow moves through a hedge of crimson hibiscus, then a tanned face atop a yellow shirt bends over me to peer into my eyes.

"You are awake at last," he says. "How are you feeling today?"

As I stare in wonder, joy spurts throughout my being. I know I must have reached my destination, and Modi cannot be far away for I recognize the mournful, goat-like face, the pointed chin and drooping mustache. I have seen these same gentle eyes in a dozen self-portraits. "*Bonjour*, Monsieur Gauguin."

"*C'est incroyable. Vous êtes belle, jeune, française, e vous me connais-sez.* To whom do I have the privilege of speaking?"

I am so excited, I can hardly string my words together. "*Je m'appelle Jeanne Hébuterne. Je suis la femme du peintre Amedeo Modigliani et je voudrais savoir, Monsieur, si je suis arrivée à île de l'immortalité* and if my husband is here."

He frowns at me, astonished, then bursts out laughing.

"*Mais non*, Madame, you are on my private island; my personal paradise." He waves his large brown hand towards the blue behind him, then reaching for a stool carved from a stump, plunks it next to me on the sand. "As for your husband, I do not believe I know him and most certainly he is not here."

I taste tears on my lips. "Then I must go," I say, twisting my body round, attempting to climb out of the hammock, but I am far too weak. My legs won't move, and my feet become entangled in the folds of the rough fabric.

"Wait—I found you water-logged like a sponge, and you are not quite recovered yet. You are in no condition to set out upon any further journeys. You must stay here until you are strong again. That will not take long—I assure you. Here the sun, the sea, the air are all revitalizing."

A golden-skinned native girl emerges from the hibiscus hedge. Her hips are wrapped in bright orange cloth, and her nipples poke out through garlands of pale pink orchids. Taking him by the wrist, she pulls him away from me.

"You must rest some more," he calls. "Later, we will talk again." He waves at me—perhaps a sort of benediction. Sun splinters on my eyelashes. I let my eyes close as I smell the salt of the sea and a spicy scent of ginger, perhaps, or vanilla.

When I open my eyes again, fragrant petals of orchids and jasmine float in a basin set on a stool beside me. I stir the water with a finger to make the petals spin. I am lying face down, naked on white sheets, in a pleasant room, or at least an enclosed space. The walls are made of bamboo and the sun shines in between the slats. The sea sounds further away, muted.

The girl in the black dress has returned to bathe me. Dipping her yellow sponge into the water, she draws it down my body in long, clean strokes—humming snatches of a strange song, which makes me want to sleep again. As the cool water drips down my back and hips, I feel as though encrustations of salt and sorrow are being rinsed away. She dries me with a soft cloth, then rubs me all over with coconut oil, even the toughened soles of my tar-spotted feet.

"Sit," she says, in French, and props me up on the pillows so that my hair can be combed. It is full of seaweed, pebbles, and tiny shells, which she picks out and throws on the ground.

As the fishbone comb rakes my scalp, I gaze around the room, still puzzled by the way it looks so familiar. A bright piece of green print-ed fabric hangs on the wall. Next to it, a battered dresser with gilt-framed mirror and a terracotta figurine of a Polynesian idol looped with strings of black pearls. All these things I somehow know. Per-haps I have dreamed then.

When the bathing and combing are done, I am wrapped in a red cloth. Red hibiscus are pinned in my hair and wreaths of gardenias strung around my neck. The silky petals graze my throat like kisses. Still chattering to me in her sleepy language, the black-clad girl holds a hand mirror to my face. I blink in amazement. How is it I can see myself and yet not recognize what I see? My skin has turned almost as dusky as hers. It glistens with oil.

A bare-chested young man in loose white cotton trousers pads into the room. He helps the girl lift me from the bed, and they lead me out-side, where Monsieur Gauguin and the gold-skinned girl are waiting, sitting on rough wooden chairs facing the sea. There is a third chair, for me, evidently. Supported by the girl in black and the boy in white, I walk steadily towards it, my feet shuffling in the warm, velvety sand.

Monsieur Gauguin smiles and nods encouragingly, like a dutiful father. "You are beautiful, Jeanne!" I touch the crisp red cloth, the soft white petals, and smile too. It feels odd to smile, my lips curved in a sweet tension I have almost forgotten.

The young man settles me into the empty chair beside Monsieur Gauguin, and I feast my eyes again on the sea. The golden girl exam-ines me but does not speak or smile. As Gauguin chats with me, she holds his hand, playing with his fingers. Her eyes slide towards me from time to time, studying me cautiously, but she never says a word. I do not know if she understands our language.

"To tell the truth, it makes no sense for you to be here. For it is impossible for anyone to reach these shores unless I invite them. So you are an interloper. *Mais en même temps*, you are most welcome. How did you come here?"

"I swam. I meant to swim all the way to the shores of Immortality, but then a wave overpowered me. And here I am."

"You swam, but from where?"

"I don't know, it was a putrid ocean, underground." I shudder, recalling the presences those waters contained.

"And why were you swimming to the shores of Immortality?"

"That is where my husband is, and all I want in the world is to find him again."

"You say your husband is a painter."

"His name is Amedeo Modigliani. He is Italian by birth, but came to Paris in 1906."

"That is why I don't know of him. I have been in this realm since 1903."

"I think you would like his work: his nudes and his colors and his sculptures. He was very fond of yours. We lived together at number 8 Rue de la Grande Chaumière in the flat above the studio you occupied, and then he died and I died too."

I feel uncomfortable pronouncing that word *die* in this luminous realm of fragrance and color. If I am here, how can death exist? How can Modi be dead if Paul Gauguin is here alive with me?

"*C'est vrai?* So we are neighbors?" He ruminates awhile as the sea licks our toes. "You loved him deeply to come so far."

I nod.

"But I don't see how I can help you," he concludes with a sigh. "As I said, he is not here."

My eyes scan the shoreline that seems to go on forever, while behind us rise green-furred peaks so vivid I almost expect to see them move. Perhaps this is only a small corner of paradise, and further away, or beyond those mountains, Modi is waiting for me.

"How big is this island?"

"As big as I wish. Come—are you strong enough to walk? I will show you."

I rise, and leaning on his arm, I walk along the strand where our feet leave no impress. The golden girl walks beside us. The white sands stretch on, fringed with dense palm groves.

There are banana trees in bloom, hibiscus in every tone of pink and scarlet, and bougainvillea—purple and magenta—surging over trellises. Orchids entwined in tall waxy shrubs brush our faces as we walk. Slim naked boys with sleek, dripping hair dance around a fire, flinging droplets of water into the air. Girls lounge among ferns, petting red dogs, laughing and watching the boys dance. Tall boys with girded loins pick red fruit. On sun-drenched walls, lizards preen, and wise birds nestle in the shadows, where they produce liquid, quivering sounds. A dark stone idol broods in a niche. I stare hard at these scenes—how familiar they seem. Then I realize where I have seen them before: not in a dream at all, but in Gauguin's paintings. Here they have been brought to life.

"*Where do we come from? What are we? Where are we going?*" I murmur.

He laughs and slides his arm around my waist to pull me closer, pleased that I know the name of this masterpiece, but the golden girl pouts and tugs at his other arm. When he ignores her, she breaks away, unties the cloth around her hips, and struts into the sea. Now he stops to admire her as she stands in the foam, facing the horizon with raised arms, then dives into the surf.

"Magnificent, isn't she? I must have painted her a hundred times."

"I know. I have seen your pictures."

"*Bien,*" he muses.

"I would like to see your studio."

Again, he laughs, though this time, it seems, a little sadly, and shakes his head. "No, I have no studio here."

"You no longer wish to paint?" I cannot imagine that. To be surrounded by so much beauty and color, by all these harmonious forms, and not to paint would be a torture.

"What you see springs from my own mind. To create this, I don't need paint or canvas. I only need to think it and feel it, the way you can remember music in your head even when it makes no sound."

He turns to me now, stepping closer, and tilts my face towards his. "That is why it is so extraordinary that you are here. For I must have created you myself, and yet you say you are another man's wife and that you swam here of your own accord. I do not understand how you could have found my island, much less entered my mind. I must have been dreaming of you and desiring you without even knowing it."

He reaches for my hand and brings it to his lips. His fingers are cold, and his moustache scratches my skin. "Why not stay here forever with me and enjoy what I have made?"

The naked girl is watching us from the waves—and I can see she is angry. But she needn't be. I do not want to become Paul Gauguin's mistress or remain frozen forever in one of his ideas for an unpainted picture. She stalks out of the sea and goes to sit with the other girls, scowling at us through the sharp-bladed aloes.

"Monsieur, I am sorry. This is not what I want. I admire you very much, but I cannot love you and I cannot stay here."

"Don't you see, there is nothing else than this? This is who we are and where have come from." He presses my hand to his breast. "In any case, I don't see how you can leave. Even if I wished for you to go, which I do not."

I stare out to sea with a dismal sense of foreboding as he squeezes my hand harder. The colors that gave me such joy upon finding myself here now weigh heavy, unreal and cloying, like colors in a drugged dream. No trace of any other land on the horizon meets my gaze, nothing but blue and turquoise sweeps, crested with white and the undulating silver line of the coral reefs breaking through the water. This heaven would be my hell.

Then a black spot appears before my eyes. I blink, perhaps it is a tiny insect caught in my eyelash, but no, it's moving on the horizon.

"What's that?" I ask. Curious, we observe it zigzagging speedily towards us, dropping, bouncing, slipping behind a wave and lifting again in a peculiar way.

"I don't know," he murmurs. He lets go my hand and wades into the waves, staring at the bobbing dot on the horizon, as the sea soaks his trousers. Turning to shore, he shouts "*A hi'o! Haere mai!*" The young men stop their dancing, and the girls rise from the ferns in alarm. They run to join us at the water's edge, where we stare in consternation at an approaching vessel: a three-master, with a tattered white sail and all but one mast broken, atop which perches a crow with folded wings.

Gauguin turns to me, "I don't understand it. No one but you has ever come, and now we have more visitors."

"Pirates?" I ask, squinting at the crow.

"Impossible. Don't be afraid. There can be no violence in my paradise." He clasps my hand, and with his other hand draws the golden girl near to protect her.

The ship comes as close as it dares, dropping anchor just beyond the reef. Aboard the ship stand two men: one at the helm, dark as an African, waving, grinning like a bronze skull—a pistol in his waistband and a bloody rag tied around one knee. The other, wrapped in a black robe flapping in the wind, clings for dear life to a broken mast. The sun glints on his eyeglasses and I recognize him—it is Jacob Rabinowitz.

Now within earshot above the sea, the tanned, withered man declaims a poem I know by heart.

... je me suis baigné dans le Poème
De la Mer, infusé d'astres, et lactescent,
Dévorant les azurs verts; où, flottaison blême
Et ravie, un noyé pensif parfois descend ;

I weep at those words Modi used to recite, whispering into my ear on insomniac nights. *I bathed in the Poem of the Sea....*

"*Mon dieu!* I should have known!" chortles Gauguin. "Arthur! Arthur Rimbaud, welcome!"

A canoe full of young men shoots out to greet the newcomers and help them disembark. Rimbaud tosses a rope ladder over the side of the ship and scuttles down as swift as a cockroach, while poor Rabinowitz, clutching a briefcase, gets his robe entangled in the rope and has to be rescued by the laughing young men. Once on shore, Rimbaud and Gauguin embrace. The inquisitive girls swarm around them.

Rabinowitz looks quite ill, and Gauguin has a boy bring a stump for him to sit on. Wiping his salt-spotted eyeglasses with the edge of his sleeve, he pulls out a damp piece of parchment from his briefcase, which he then hands to me.

"*Bonjour*, Jeanne. I have good news. Your petition to join the Immortals has been accepted."

It is an official decree. At the top of the page I read: *Mairie des Morts de Paris.*

"The reunion shall take place in Venice, in March 2021," Rabinowitz continued. "I have the honor of accompanying you there."

And so, we left Gauguin and his island. To his great dismay, his favorite golden girl and some of the young men sailed away with Arthur Rimbaud.

I don't know how long we navigated, or how many ships or worlds we passed, how many wars and hurricanes we sailed through. But there were bodies in the sea and ghostly hulks that paid us no attention as we cruised through mist and smoke. Finally, one splendid morning at winter's end, we reached the Grand Canal. Throughout our journey, the crow clung to the mast, but when the tower of San Marco came into view, he flew away.

Domes, towers, and arches floated in the water as we skimmed across a mirror and docked along a quay where leviathans were berthed. Hordes of people were surging off the ships, pulling suitcases on trolleys, making an infernal sound.

Rimbaud threw out the gangplank to the dock. "This is where I leave you, Jeanne."

I looked at Rabinowitz for confirmation.

"Someone will be here to fetch you," he said. "You just have to be patient a little while longer."

"Who will come? Modi?" But Rabinowitz smiled without reply.

I crossed the plank to the quay and was soon lost among strangers while Rimbaud's ship departed. I walked from one end of the dock to the other, as the crowds swarmed on and off the white ships chugging in and maneuvering out again with a booming of their horns. For an endless time, I sat on a bollard, staring out to sea. Then a thin tenor voice I recognized crept across the waters. There he stood in a gondola, wearing a yellow straw hat with a black feather tucked in the band, rowing towards me, singing a song I used to know, about a withered rose whose perfume never fades. *Un seul désir, un seul espoir, te revoir…* And then I was in his arms.

As we embraced on the rocking waves, my being dissolved into liquid gold and I understood everything I had ever wanted to know. Modi and I had never been apart and we could never die. And all those we loved were still part of us.

"I think we should go look for Giovanna, André, and Soutine," I suggested as the run rose above us. "They must be here somewhere."

"We'll have all the time in the world for that," he said, "but first I have to take you to an exhibition."

Part 6
The Holy Family of the Circus
Venice, 2021

AFTER CLEARING OFF MY DESK at the museum of all the remaining paperwork—shooting off some press releases, answering last minute, miscellaneous correspondence, and filing away the invoices and insurance forms—I still needed to make the rounds of the exhibition rooms for one last check before going home that evening. This was the most important show I had curated as yet, and my first for the Raphael Foundation of Venice. Everything had to be perfect. I wanted there to be no unpleasant surprises when the great bronze doors of the Palazzo swung open to receive a host of dignitaries: the mayor of Venice, the Italian minister of culture, the director of the Biennale, and the international press, for their short private viewing. Their tour would be followed by the admission of the general public and a *vernissage* to be held in the courtyard at half past one, weather permitting. Yet the purplish gray clouds billowing on the horizon boded no good, and were likely to bring cold rain, thick fog, *acqua alta*, and doubtless, cancellations.

As I had learned in my several-month stay in this unreal city, the Foundation, located on its own island, could occasionally be cut off from the rest of Venice, when the waters got too rough and the vaporettos declined to make this only-on-request stop. That would be a very disappointing way to begin. The Foundation director, Enrico Bellucci, would not be pleased if the opening were deserted and all the catering delicacies—pickled octopus and fried squares of *baccalà*—should go to waste. Fortunately, I had had nothing to do with the catering. That had been handled by his secretary, Signora Simoncini, so in no way could I be blamed if anything went wrong in that department. For the rest, I had done it all with a staff of three: me, myself, and I. I selected the artworks, contacted owners and convinced them to loan them. I wrote and edited the catalogue, the labels, the notes. I made an educational video with my iPad and arranged everything from insurance and security to PR, and even did some of the framing.

With my checklist in hand, I went downstairs and asked Guido, head security guard and general fix-it man, to unlock the bookshop, where I was relieved to see the catalogues, postcards, and posters attractively displayed according to my instructions, taking precedence over the rotating gondola LED lamps, gaudy glass bead key chains, cat calendars, and other junk the Foundation was obliged to sell in order to make a little cash. There had been a bit of a mishap after lunch when the catalogues finally arrived by speedboat from the printers. While being unloaded onto the Foundation landing, a carton of fifty catalogues had almost fallen into the canal, but thanks to Guido's quick reflexes, this had been avoided.

As I had too much on my hands to do and the girl who staffed the bookshop had left before lunch, I had entreated Signora Simoncini to deal with the unpacking and display of the catalogues, although she was very annoyed at being assigned such a menial task. She could barely tolerate me, anyway. I believe she felt these events were rather a nuisance, interrupting the calm, languid days when she had nothing to do but prepare decaf for the director and see to his personal correspondence.

After inspecting the bookshop, we passed on to the AV room, where my video about artists in Montparnasse was to be shown at intervals, with the melancholy notes of a Satie *Gymnopédie* playing in the background. The speakers and Wi-Fi projectors were working fine; I had made sure the faulty lightbulb had been replaced. With the music still playing, we unlocked the main gallery, where I asked Guido to leave me alone for a few moments, so I could enjoy in solitude the show I had so painstakingly built over the last twelve months. *An Embrace Eternal – Amedeo Modigliani and Jeanne Hébuterne: Friends and Lovers in Montparnasse*, featuring two lesser known portraits of Jeanne by Modigliani, twenty-five sketches, and three oil portraits by Jeanne herself.

In many ways, this show was a coming home for Jeanne Hébuterne, whose first exhibition ever had taken place in this city twenty-one years earlier in 2000, when her heirs finally released her artwork for public viewing eighty years after her death. In the time that had elapsed since then, pieces had been sold to collectors around the world and a single sketch, once considered memorabilia at the time of her first show, now brought 60,000 euros at Christie's.

I went through the gallery slowly, examining each piece, scrutinizing the labels to check for typos, wrong dates, or translation errors, making sure the angle of the lighting was to the best advantage of each piece, that the security chains were firmly in place so that no one could get too close to the more valuable paintings: the two Modigliani portraits of Jeanne. One dated from the early days of their relationship and showed her thin, turquoise-eyed and dreamy; the other, from the late period, showed her plumpish and brooding with a double-chin and unflattering expression, standing in front of a dark blue door. It was generally thought that this portrait signaled a cooling off of Modigliani's love for Jeanne, who appears dowdy and worn, while the door has often been interpreted as a symbol of their impending exit.

I stood in the doorway for one last look, trying to get a sense of the whole. It was not going to be a knock-your-socks-off show, but rather a sentimental overview of Jeanne Hébuterne and Modigliani's life in Montparnasse, with a few sketches and portraits done by their friends Soutine, Marevna, Kisling, and even a watercolor by Jeanne's brother, André. There were no eye-popping revelations or newly discovered works to excite journalists. Still, Modigliani's signature on two of those portraits, along with Jeanne's own work, were bound to draw crowds.

The Hébuterne heirs had contributed only three sketches. Other works had been obtained on loan from museums and collectors. Among those was a nude self-portrait sketch by Jeanne and an oil portrait with unfinished face against the background of a Spanish shawl in gaudy colors, on loan from a museum in Geneva. We also had a handful of rarely published photographs and memorabilia provided by the Modigliani Foundation of Leghorn. I had hoped for a more substantial show, but this was the best I could do. I had even tried to track down a missing piece sometimes attributed to Jeanne and sometimes to Modigliani: a collaborative portrait of Jeanne, Modigliani, and their baby near a gypsy cart. But after long research, I had concluded it was apocryphal, for only one critic had ever mentioned it in the literature, a certain Jules Renard of the Sorbonne, who died a decade ago. Or so I found out when I tried to look him up after reading an article on Academia Edu. Or perhaps it was just lost to history, as sometimes happens.

The worn red carpet at my feet looked a bit tawdry, pockmarked here and there with chewing gum. The cleaners would be in at eight the next morning with their industrial vacuum cleaner to freshen it a bit. Satisfied that everything was in order, I told Guido, who was manning the front desk, to lock up, and I went upstairs to my office to get my raincoat. I would be just in time to catch the *vaporetto* back to Cannaregio, where I was staying in an apartment belonging to the Foundation.

Wind whistled through the chinks in the leaden window seams as I slipped on my raincoat. The dusk gleamed cobalt in the tinted glass, where a crescent moon sliced through dark clouds. Carnival had just concluded—perhaps not the best timing for our exhibition, as tourists were leaving Venice, but the director had insisted on those dates, hoping that the opportunity to view a Modigliani show in such an illustrious setting would convince the Carnival crowds to remain. The real purpose of this particular show was to gain new patrons for the Foundation. Its finances were a mess, or so I had recently learned, and the building was rotting and desperately in need, like all of Venice, of urgent, costly repairs. The long quarantine for the coronavirus the year before had been a great economic strain for the entire city.

Stepping out to the corridor, I heard animated voices upstairs in the director's office. He worked late into the evenings, and I believe sometimes even slept there, having some problem at home with his wife, or so the gossip about him and Signora Simoncini went. Although an attractive man, he was a bit saturnine and taciturn, rarely mixing with the museum staff.

I descended to the entrance hall, now in darkness, where Guido had deserted his post at the main desk. Perhaps he was in the bathroom or had gone up to see the director, I mused. His absence made me inexplicably anxious, given the valuable artworks in our custody at the moment. Had he remembered to lock up after I had exited the gallery? The gallery doors were shut, just as I had left them, and, jiggling the brass handle, I was relieved to see that they were indeed locked, as was the little anteroom which served as the bookshop. Reassured that all was safe, I buzzed myself out the door.

Stepping out on those corroded marble steps, I was met with a cold gust of brine tainted with rotting seaweed and sewage: the classic Venice late winter stench that stings in your nostrils for hours. Turning up the collar of my raincoat, I walked to the *vaporetto* stop. The attendant in the glass booth had gone home as well. I stuck my pass into the jaws of the ticket machine, undid the chain, and crossed the plank onto the floating platform. I switched on a light, which would signal to the *vaporetto* that there were passengers to be picked up on request. Otherwise, it would have gone straight past us. I could see it now, chugging towards the island through the rolling mist.

As the platform bobbed on the oily black water, I surveyed the ghostly shapes of the houses across the way with their dim, flickering lights. The air was bitter cold and damp and yet exhilarating, and I knew I would always look back on these days in Venice as a unique privilege. Despite the difficulties of daily life here, I would miss it immensely when my stay ended. The show would run for four months, after which I would have two weeks to disassemble it and say my goodbyes to the Foundation. Then I would be back to applying for grants, scrounging up an adjunct post perhaps in some American study abroad program, and, if nothing else turned up, moving back in with my great aunt Elisabetta in Florence. Nearly thirty-five with no real job in sight and no stable relationship, either, I had hoped, if this show were a success, that the Foundation might take me on for a year or two. But when I discovered how poor their finances were, I realized there was little chance of that. Still, having organized this show was an achievement. Something to put in bold caps on my résumé for the next round of job applications.

The platform dipped and lurched as the *vaporetto* approached, bumping so hard against the landing that I almost lost my balance. The ferry was nearly empty, and a passenger stood right at the exit, blocking my way. "Excuse me," I said, when he didn't step aside to let me board, and was amazed when the attendant curtly ordered me to wait until the passenger had disembarked. Who could be getting off here so late in the evening? Our glances met in the faint glow of the lantern above the platform. Tall, sixtyish, with peculiar gray eyes, and a scar on a stubbled cheek, this stranger in a rumpled overcoat exuded a slight smell of *grappa*, as do many men in the Veneto at this time of year. He could only be on his way to see the director. Aside from the Foundation, there was nothing and nobody else on the island. "*Buona sera*," I said. Mumbling an unintelligible reply, he rudely brushed past me.

It took over an hour to get home to my flat in Cannaregio. Cramped, cold, with smelly drains, opulent furnishings, and a magnificent view of laundry flapping over the canal, it was quintessentially Venetian. I had just come in, looking forward to a hot dish of *risi and bisi,* rice with peas, followed by a boiling bath in the four-footed tub, then early to bed, when my mobile buzzed. I was in the kitchenette, chopping up an onion, so I didn't answer on the first ring as my hands were sticky with onion juice. I was expecting my great aunt to call. I knew she wouldn't be coming to the show opening tomorrow, so she was probably calling now to give me her good wishes—her *auguri.* Wiping my hands on a dishtowel and reaching for the phone, I saw, from the number flashing on the display, it was the Foundation calling: the director's line. I hardly had any direct contact with him usually. It was the secretary who was always our go-between. Then I thought, perhaps something has happened. And the stranger on the platform came to mind. God help me, I said to myself and answered the phone.

"*Si?*"

"*Dottoressa?*"

"*Si?*"

"*Sono* Guido."

"Yes, Guido, what is it?"

"I'm calling for the Director. He says you have to come back immediately."

I was so anxious I could barely speak. Something had gone wrong. A robbery! Damage to one of the artworks. God knows what. I tried to modulate my voice. "Oh dear. Has something happened?"

"It could be about that big package that came for you this afternoon."

I was mystified. "What package?"

"I told the delivery boy to take it up to your office."

"I don't know what you are talking about. I didn't receive any package."

"Miss Simoncini said she would make sure you got it."

"Oh," I said. That explained it. Whatever it was in the package, she had probably thrown it into the canal.

"Well, you better get over here as soon as you can. He says he is sending you a water taxi. Just go down to the Cannaregio stop and wait."

A water taxi! I could hardly afford that, so I hoped the director would pay.

I went out. It had started to drizzle again, and I made my way through the dark alleys. Venice seemed exhausted after Carnival. Trampled confetti lay engrained in between paving stones. A discarded mask and a deflated Japanese lantern had blown into the canal. I stopped at a corner bar and bought some fried octopus and polenta cubes wrapped in brown paper to nibble on my way over. The water taxi had already arrived when I got to the stop. I climbed down the slimy steps into the boat and settled myself on the plastic cushions in the back. The black water had become choppy. I was very ill at ease. Why was I being called back? Was I about to get the sack just hours before the exhibition opened? What was this about a package? I couldn't understand it. Then I thought: it might have something to do with the collectors who had loaned their works. Some had been particularly picky about every single detail, fussing over a misplaced accent in the catalogue, or a contested dating. Had I committed some faux pas with the Hébuterne or Soutine estates? Was that why the stranger had come to the museum?

In twenty minutes, we had arrived. I climbed the slick steps under pelting rain, hurried up to the Foundation entrance, and rang the bell. Sheltering myself as well as I could against the wall beneath the pouring rain, as I had forgotten my umbrella, I had to wait a few minutes before Guido unlocked the doors.

Upstairs in his office, the director sat at his desk in the company of the man I had glimpsed on the *vaporetto* landing. As I entered, the stranger gave me a piercing look and a curt nod of recognition. He was older than I had thought at first. Seventy at least. The secretary, Signora Simoncini, was not present and that made me feel relieved. A bottle of *grappa* and two shot glasses were placed on the otherwise empty desk, next to the telephone. Beside the desk stood an easel, where a large canvas on stretchers was propped up, covered with a white cloth, immediately arousing my curiosity.

"Good evening, *Dottoressa*. Thank you for coming. I hope I haven't called you back from a dinner engagement," the director said.

"Not exactly," I said, unsure as to how to interpret his tone. His voice sounded tired but not hostile. Was I about to be fired or not? I stood at attention before his desk, like a schoolgirl. I was a bit out of breath from running up the stairs. "It is rather late, and tomorrow is a big day."

"Quite. Sit down please."

I obeyed, still in my wet raincoat, nestling my briefcase on my lap. Bracing his elbows on the desk, he propped his chin on his clasped hands and studied me gravely, as if he had never really noticed me before and was surprised to see I was not what he had expected.

Nervously, I tucked a strand of damp hair behind my ear and waited. The conversation continued in English, as it seemed the stranger did not understand Italian.

"Let me introduce you to Josef Perez. Josef, this is our curator, *Dottoressa* Cuomo."

"Good evening," I said. "I believe our paths crossed at the *vaporetto* stop."

"Pleased to meet you," he said drily. I couldn't place his accent: not American or British, European but from where I couldn't say. I didn't offer him my hand, as it stilled smelled faintly of onion and octopus, and he did not move forward to offer his.

"Mr. Perez is involved in the recovery of artworks plundered from Jewish owners during the war," the director continued.

I stared at Perez while I racked my brains. Was it possible that some piece we had on loan for the exhibition might fall into this category? Which one? If ownership were contended, could we still exhibit the work, if the other party did not grant permission? If we were not allowed to display the work, a huge hole would be gouged out in the show I had built with such loving care. And what would the legal consequences be? My mind ran on imagining disastrous scenarios.

"A package was delivered to you today. With no return address." The director ploughed into my thoughts.

"Guido said—but I never received it." I was getting a bit annoyed with this story of the package, as I assumed the secretary was to blame for its going astray.

Josef Perez arched an eyebrow.

"Were you expecting something to be delivered?" the director asked.

"No, not that I recall." Oh God, what had I done? What had I forgotten?

"As you know, given recent disagreeable episodes of terrorism against sensitive cultural targets, the unusually large dimensions of the package, and due to the pending visit of leading political figures here on our premises, I felt obliged to engage the assistance of the police to investigate its contents."

I gawked at him as the meaning of the director's convoluted speech sank in. "You had the police open a package addressed to me, without informing me first?" Adding, after a pause, "The bomb squad?" My voice squeaked unpleasantly.

He nodded. "You realize that I believed the safety of the Foundation and the staff was at stake. Including yourself."

"Of course." I could feel Perez's colorless eyes moving across my face. He must be with the police, I thought. Maybe he thinks I am involved with terrorists, and that's why I have been summoned. It was a horrifying thought.

"I also assumed that anything addressed to you here would not be personal, but would be concerned with your work here, for which I am ultimately responsible," the director said.

I bristled at that. But what could I say? The idea that a bomb might have been addressed to me was as terrifying as it was absurd.

"Fortunately, it wasn't a bomb—at least not literally speaking."

"Thank God for that." As the knot in my chest relaxed, I realized that I had been sitting on the edge of my chair and that a nail from the worn upholstery was cutting into my flesh, and had probably ruined my rain-spattered stocking.

"Would you like to see what was in the package?"

"Yes," I said meekly. I had no idea what to prepare myself for.

When he turned to the easel and lifted the cloth to reveal the painting it concealed, I was dumbfounded—it portrayed Jeanne Hébuterne holding a baby, standing next to Modigliani dressed as a harlequin in a fanciful circus setting. It could only be *La Sacra Famiglia del Circo!* The Holy Family of the Circus, the legendary painting by Jeanne and Modigliani that few people had seen and that I had first read about in an article by Jules Renard.

"What can you tell me about this?" the director asked.

I was speechless.

"Nothing. It looks like a Modigliani. Or at least part of it does." I fought to get the words out. "I thought this was only a legend!"

"So you have heard of this painting?" Perez asked suspiciously.

"Yes, I have read about it, but I didn't think it really existed. To my knowledge, it is not in any official catalogue."

"Can you explain how this came to be in a package sent to you?" the director asked.

I shook my head in bewilderment. "Is it authentic?" I asked dubiously and peered closer at the signature in the upper right hand corner, but certainly didn't have the expertise to tell the real from the fake.

"Too soon to determine. But after a cursory inspection," he nodded towards Perez, "it seems likely. Naturally a more thorough investigation will be required with infrared spectrometry."

I nodded, though I still didn't understand what this all had to do with me.

Perez now leaned forward, his eyes boring into mine. "My people have been looking for this painting since 1949." He drew a faded black and white photograph from his breast pocket and showed it to me: it pictured what appeared to be this very painting, a bit out of focus, but definitely recognizable.

"It belonged to the great collector and critic Armand Metz, who died at Auschwitz, and whose galleries and personal collection were plundered by the Nazis during the Paris occupation."

"Oh dear."

"This painting may be connected to a crime—to a murder, in fact, to the disappearance of an American citizen, and to several episodes of fraud perpetrated by a ring of art forgers operating in Italy and France between 1965 and 1990," Perez continued.

I understood that I was being accused of something, though I wasn't sure what. "I have no knowledge of any of that," I said slowly, "and I am willing to make a statement to the authorities to that effect, as soon as I have consulted my lawyer." I didn't know any lawyers I could call on at a short notice, but I hoped Aunt Elisabetta would surely be able to recommend someone. One thing puzzled me. If the painting had just been discovered that afternoon in a package sent to me, how was it that Perez had found out so soon? Adddressing him, I asked, "How did you know it was here?"

"Serendipity," Perez replied.

"Signor Perez is an old colleague of mine," the director explained. "I was aware of his search for this portrait being carried out with the help of a mutual friend, the renowned Modigliani critic, the late Jules Renard. I knew Josef was in Berlin this month for work. I felt obliged to notify him, and he flew out immediately."

"I got the last seat on the plane," Perez added.

"There was something else in the package," the director said. He fished a large yellow envelope out of his desk drawer and dropped it in front of me. I undid the clasp and out slid three worn-looking, fragile cahiers with many loose pages bound together by a frayed gold ribbon.

"This document is a diary, supposedly written by Jeanne Hébuterne, in three notebooks."

For a moment, I stopped breathing. I had read apocryphal stories by journalists about a diary of Jeanne's, which had supposedly disappeared. I examined the brittle, yellowed paper of the notebooks. They certainly looked old.

"May I?"

"The package *was* addressed to you."

I opened the first notebook and studied the crabby handwriting in sepia ink, the scrawled dates, loose photographs, and postcards with postmarks dating back one hundred years or more. As I turned the pages, my perplexity gave way to total absorption, and out slid a cold circlet of blue-green glass into my lap. It was a bracelet, a bangle.

And then I understood who must have sent the package: that woman at the Rapolano Spa Hotel, where I had stayed with my great aunt last September.

I had noticed her eating alone at a table in the very back, never removing either her sunglasses or the gold brocade scarf wrapped round her gray hair, untidy tufts of which stuck out here and there. She seemed to be on a similar schedule as my aunt Elisabetta, for meals, mud baths, and sinus treatments, and the two would nod to each other across the desert of spotless white linen tablecloths and sparkling silver that spanned the dining hall. I had accompanied my aunt to the sulfur spa because the friend who usually came along on her jaunts had cancelled at the last minute, and Aunt Elisabetta claimed she was too old to go alone. I had also just been through a rather disappointing affair with a married man, and she thought that a visit to the spa would cheer me up. At the time, I was editing the catalogue notes, which I thought I could do just as well at a hotel in the Sienese countryside as in a library in Venice.

"You'll enjoy it. There are more younger people now," she had said on the phone, hoping to entice me—younger people for her, being in their fifties. "And some attractive young doctors." She had always hoped I would marry a man of some noble profession: doctor, lawyer, notary, or university professor, but I had disappointed her by remaining unattached.

The Tuscan spa had also been recently discovered by a few foreign celebrities in Italy—rock stars, models, and their entourages, which might make for amusing people-watching, so I had agreed to meet her there. I had filled up a bag with books and swim gear, and something to wear to dinner, had taken the train to Siena, and then a cab.

The hotel had been nearly empty, except for my aunt, myself, an elderly German couple, and the solitary woman who seemed to be incognito, but given her age and shabby appearance, she didn't look much like a rock star in disguise.

After two or three days of observing her there alone at her table, I found her more peculiar than mysterious, and I asked my aunt about her.

"She has been coming here for years. I believe she is British, or is it American? She was once married to that famous French art critic. The one who went to jail but was really innocent and was found dead in his cell. There was a big fuss in the newspapers. What was his name?"

"Do you mean Paul Marteau?" I said, biting into our chicken liver crostini. I was immediately intrigued, as Paul Marteau had been involved in a scandal regarding forgeries of Soutine and Modigliani. He had been tried and convicted, but in the appeal had been acquitted—posthumously, however, as the day before the sentence was announced, he died in mysterious circumstances while still in custody, supposedly of natural causes.

"That's the one," she beamed. "For a while we'd see her every other year with a different wig after her husband died."

"Different wig? How funny."

Aunt Elisabetta clicked her tongue. "No, my dear. You don't understand. Chemo."

We observed the solitary woman eating her dish of crostini and sipping her red wine. She looked sad and lonely, and I felt a stab of pity for her, knowing she was a cancer survivor and a widow.

"Poor woman."

"Poor is not an adequate adjective in this particular case. She is actually very wealthy," my aunt said, crossing the heavy silver knife and fork on her plate.

"She certainly doesn't look it."

"The truly wealthy never do, my dear."

The waiter brought our next course: for my aunt just salad, and for me a small plate of grilled porcini, and we focused our attention on the food.

The next day, I was out walking among the arid hills in the afternoon, where I had discovered a gazebo above a vineyard, a perfect place to curl up with a book. So I settled on the wooden bench, and took out the new biography of Modigliani I was reading. It was a hardback, with a flashy picture on the cover showing the artist wild-eyed and raven-haired, and the title in big red letters: *Maudit Modi*.

A half hour later, inky clouds gathered overhead, and suddenly we were in a downpour. The rain pattering on the broad grape leaves and half ripe grape clusters released a pungent scent of tangy fruit and red clay. Just then a figure in a purple hoodie, huge sunglasses, and black sweatpants came running down a path among the vines, darting into the gazebo just as the rain intensified.

"Pardon the interruption," she said, plunking down out of breath on the bench across from me. It was the solitary woman. She pulled out a water bottle and took a long drink. As she did, I noted a glass bangle on her bony wrist.

"There is plenty of room here," I said, smiling.

She nodded and glanced up at the rain for a few moments. Then, studying me through her sunglasses, she must have noticed the book in my hand. "Tell me," she said, gesturing with her water bottle towards the book. "What do they have to say about his wife, Jeanne?"

This was unexpected. Jeanne Hébuterne isn't by any means a household name. But then I knew this woman had once been married to an art critic.

"Only that she was taciturn and moody, and a very bad mother. And that he stopped loving her at the end."

"They would say that. Poor girl. She deserved better." She took another drink, and then from the smell, I could tell what she was drinking wasn't water but gin.

"She did," I agreed. "Did you know," I ventured, "she was also an artist, although her work isn't well known? And as it happens, I am curating a show of a few of her works that is going to be held in Venice. At the Raphael Foundation," I added, hoping to impress her.

"Are you really?" Her lips curled in surprise, but I couldn't gauge her expression because of the Dior sunglasses concealing half her face. She took another sip from her bottle and mumbled in a barely audible voice, "I knew someone who knew her."

"Did you?" That was rather remarkable, as Jeanne had died in 1920.

"You must think I am mad. At the time I was very young, and she was very old, and when she knew Jeanne, she must have been about seventeen."

"I see."

"She had modeled, not for Modigliani, but for Ortiz de Zarate, who lived downstairs."

I stared at her, astonished. Here was a detail that only art scholars were likely to know: that Modigliani and Ortiz de Zarate were neighbors. What else might she be able to tell me about Jeanne Hébuterne? It occurred to me that a long chat might be very worth the while.

"Well, you will have to come to the show. Let me give you my card. If you send me an email, I will have the Foundation send you an invitation." I fished a visiting card with my contact info out of my bag. She took it reluctantly and put it in her pocket without looking at it.

"Thank you, but I don't travel much anymore."

Her voice trailed off, and we listened to the rain for a few moments.

Then pushing up her sleeve, she showed me the bangle on her wrist, saying, "This belonged to Jeanne, and Modigliani painted her wearing it." From the compressed emotion in her voice, I felt as though she were confessing a long kept secret.

"Did he really?" I scrutinized the bangle, but couldn't remember having seen a portrait with Jeanne wearing a bracelet. It occurred to me that this woman might be a pathological liar or that it was the gin talking. "How did it come into your possession?"

She gave me a wan smile. "It's a long story."

"I'd love to hear it."

She tucked her bottle back into the pocket of her hoodie and stood up. The rain had stopped. I realized I had made her uncomfortable.

"Perhaps some other time," she said. "I have an appointment for my massage." She ran out of the gazebo and jogged down a side path now turned to mud.

I planned to speak to her again that evening, but she didn't come down for dinner, nor did we see her the next day at lunch. When I enquired at the desk, the clerk informed me that she had been called away unexpectedly and had left the hotel. All that he could tell me was that her name was "Madame Smith" and he apologized for being unable to disclose anything further.

I hadn't really thought of her again—until that bangle fell out of the notebook.

I related this episode to the two men, leaving out a few details, for example about the bracelet belonging to Jeanne or the woman having been married to the infamous Paul Marteau. Perez stared at me bug-eyed with disbelief, while the director listened with his hand over his mouth. He had perked up at the mention of the Rapolano Spa Hotel, and I gathered he was another habitué, himself. I could sense his mind ticking away. When I dropped my hands to my lap and slid the bangle on my wrist, neither of the men noticed.

"Do you think it was your elusive American?" the director asked Perez.

He shrugged. "Quite possibly. If so, she's not going to get away from me again." Now he fixed those colorless eyes on me. "She said her name was Smith?"

"The hotel clerk said her name was Smith. We were never properly introduced. Believe me, I wouldn't even be able to recognize her if I saw her again. But you could contact the hotel."

"Indeed, we shall. This painting, as I said, is connected to a long chain of crimes."

"Well," the director said, folding his hands on his chest in a gesture that usually preceded an official utterance, "I have fulfilled my obligation by informing you that a picture matching your description has been located, and I believe you now have some elements to trace its recent history, thanks to the *Dottoressa* here, who seems to be extraneous to its discovery. Although in any investigation, I am sure she will be called as a witness." He gave me a slight nod, of gratitude or dismissal, I couldn't say. "But if you are hoping to pack this up and take it away tonight, I am afraid you will be disappointed. I don't intend to turn it over to you until it has been ascertained that this is indeed the portrait you have been looking for, that it has been proven authentic, and a court order has been issued recognizing your client as its rightful owner. If the results are positive on all three counts, I am sure there will also be a reward."

Perez jumped to his feet. "That wasn't our agreement." He paced around the room, fuming.

The director was imperturbable. "I don't believe you can ask me to do any more than that at the present time. By informing you at all, I have given proof of my good will in this matter, which should satisfy your client. I could have kept it to myself." He flashed me a patronizing smile. "Thank you again for giving us your time. Your contribution has been most helpful, but I won't trouble you any longer. I will arrange for you to return home with a water taxi." He reached for the notebooks I had placed on the desk. "As for these, I am sure both the Modigliani and Hébuterne heirs will lay claim to them, so it is best if they are kept locked in my safe, until they can be evaluated by experts."

I didn't intend to be shoved aside like this, especially if a reward was due.

"Excuse me," I said clamping my hand down on the bundle of papers and snatching it from his grasp. "But you seem to have forgotten that these items were donated to me anonymously. And I consider myself their legal owner until a qualified authority informs me otherwise. So I am not giving them up." I was talking off the top of my head, and most astonishingly, the men seemed to listen attentively. No way was I going to let this treasure slip out of my hands. I put the diary back into the envelope and stuffed it into my briefcase. My mind was racing ahead, trying to decide what the next move should be, and then I had a flash of inspiration. "However, given the circumstances, that I am unable to keep this in my custody as I have no safe place to put it, I entrust the portrait to the care of the Foundation—on one condition." The director gaped at me, not quite believing his ears. "I request it be included in the show tomorrow," I added in Italian, looking straight into his eyes.

I thought this might have been his intention all along: to keep the portrait at least until the closing of the show. Even if it should turn out to be a fake in the end, as not a few Modigliani portraits have done, this would still be advantageous for the Foundation. A boost in visits, catalogues, sales, postcards, interviews, articles, donations.

His face lit up—he was delighted by my suggestion.

"I am sorry, Josef, but after hearing the *Dottoressa's* opinion, I can only agree with her that she at present must be recognized as the owner of this artwork, so for the time being, this painting stays here."

"We'll see about that," Perez grumbled, grabbing his overcoat from a rack. As he lifted his arm, I saw the bulge of the gun he carried strapped under his jacket.

"You will regret this," he sneered, struggling into the sleeves of his coat.

"I will have Guido call for a water taxi to take you to your hotel."

"I assure you, my client will be on the next plane from New York with a court order."

"And I assure you, he will be most welcome at the Raphael Foundation."

Now Perez sputtered at me, "Until it returns to its rightful owner, that picture will cause nothing but pain, and you may have abetted a crime."

He stalked out the door. We could hear his heavy footsteps echo on the marble stairway.

"There is no time to lose," I said. "We have got work to do if we are going to include it in the exhibition."

The director picked up his phone and punched a button. "Guido—call the gentleman a water taxi, then come up at once."

The three of us worked feverishly all through the night. While our handyman hunted for a suitable frame downstairs in the cellar, I took several photographs of the portrait, and, using templates, quickly created a poster and a postcard, which I shot off in an urgent message to the print-shop. Although it was nearly midnight, the director managed to get the printer, who was a friend of his brother-in-law, on his private cellphone to arrange for a last minute run of 5000 postcards and 1000 posters to be delivered before eleven—promising to pay quadruple the standard price. Meanwhile I wrote up a press release about the miraculous recovery of this legendary portrait, thanks to an anonymous donor, and emailed it as URGENT to our contact list of 3,000 journalists.

When the portrait was framed, we rearranged the order of the artworks and hung it in the central position, dominating the show so that the red carpet, worn as it was, made a beeline for it from the main entrance. Frumpy-looking Jeanne was moved to the side. I typed up a label reading *La Sacra Famiglia del Circo, 1920* and pinned it up next to the painting. Guido moved a small bench for three in front of it, where I sat smiling in bliss, gazing at the portrait. It was then I noticed, peeping out from an edge of the shawl in which the baby was wrapped, barely visible on Jeanne's wrist, a glinting strip of blue-green—the very bracelet I was wearing.

"Cara *Dottoressa*," said the director, offering me a cup of tasteless black liquid from the vending machine, "You need to rest. Come up to my office and lie down on the couch."

Weary and excited, I complied.

A bright ray pierced the milky blue. I stirred awake, feeling chilly, confused by the sticky surface to which my cheek adhered, rather than a smooth cotton sheet, then realized I was stretched out on the worn leather couch in the director's office, with his jacket thrown over my shoulders. The director was slumped shoeless, asleep in an adjacent armchair, one hand reaching out to touch my tussled hair. His long legs stuck out to the center of the room, toes pointing at the door, which now opened to reveal Signora Simoncini, holding a bag of hot *cornetti* from the bakery.

"Good morning, Marta. Thank goodness, you're early," he said, promptly withdrawing his hand and sitting up to recompose himself.

"As you can probably imagine, we have had quite a night here. Do make us some real coffee."

Signora Simoncini was too surprised to speak and managed only to blurt out, "Not decaf?"

"Espresso. Arabica," he ordered curtly, and her eyes popped in astonishment, perhaps at his change of habit and the new, decisive tone of voice.

I sat up bleary-eyed to say good morning and hastily began buttoning my blouse back up, which had somehow come undone. Laying his jacket aside on the couch, I put on my shoes, retrieved my purse, and got up. "I'll just go freshen up," I said, tucking in my blouse and leaving him to do any explaining. As I headed back to my office, I could hear a vacuum cleaner whirring through the gallery downstairs.

Thank goodness I have always kept a survival kit in the bottom drawer of my desk, at Aunt Elisabetta's suggestion. I pulled out a bag containing a fresh blouse, stockings, perfume, comb, and make-up pouch. Fifteen minutes later, I was back in Enrico's office, perfectly presentable and sipping coffee with him, although Signora Simoncini clearly did not relish my presence. Through the window, I could see it was going to be a beautiful day, crisp and sunny, not at all the apocalyptic gloom the weatherman had predicted. There was even a regatta of some kind out in the Grand Canal—sailboats, gondolas, row boats. A young man in a yellow hat with a black feather stuck in the band was rowing his girlfriend in a gondola towards our island. Straggling carnival revelers still in costume, I thought, although the poor girl must have been freezing in that skimpy red sarong she was wearing.

The director—Enrico—was yakking on his mobile, boasting of the miraculous loan they had received from a mysterious patron. Some of the press releases I had sent off by email late the night before must have already been opened and read: once the phones started ringing that morning at nine when the office officially opened, they never stopped. Signora Simoncini and Guido had to fend them off the best they could. The postcards and posters arrived from the printers at ten, and I went down to meet the delivery men and helped the bookshop girl arrange everything all over again. We papered the walls of the bookshop with the magnificent new posters of *La Sacra Fami-*

glia del Circo. Meanwhile, the caterers had arrived and started setting up their folding tables, fridges, and chafing dishes in the courtyard. I peeked in while Enrico was speaking with the woman organizing the buffet.

"You know," he said, smiling up at the square of luminous blue enclosed within our courtyard as he popped a sesame-coated shrimp into his mouth, "I think you have brought us luck today, *carissima*." And he drew me to him and pressed my hand warmly. Signora Simoncini, who had been following him around, taking notes on her phone, turned bright crimson at the sight.

The gallery was unlocked, and the two guards, Guido and an assistant, took their places, positioned so their eyes would be trained on the more valuable works. Through the open doors, the new portrait with its strong primary colors stuck out so conspicuously, radiating whimsy, gaiety, youth, and promise: all those things that we love so much in a work of art, those values that make art worth living for, and, perhaps, even dying for. The gypsy cart suggested freedom and imminent escape. And yet I knew how cruel and sad the end had been for all three: Jeanne, Modi, and their daughter. I thought of Perez's dismal warning and found it impossible to believe that this vibrant work of love and tenderness could be connected to crimes, fraud, or war.

The dignitaries arrived now for their special viewing an hour before the public was to be admitted. In trooped the mayor with a slew of politicians in charcoal gray suits and accompanying paparazzi, as Enrico led them around the show and offered the explanations I had prepared for him on notecards. Everyone wanted a selfie with the *Sacra Famiglia*, and Enrico himself posed for a photo, which would run twenty-four hours later in every newspaper from New York to Tokyo.

When they had finished viewing, Enrico introduced me to the mayor, the minister, and the director of the biennale, and all complimented me on what a fine show I had built—if only they knew! The three men could not stay for the buffet, as they were off to a meeting in Milan. The minister and his retinue had to leave by the rear entrance because of the multitude waiting to get in. Word had got out about the show's recovered lost portrait. Nearly seven hundred people had congregated on the steps and in the little square fronting the building, a line was reported to stretch down to the *vaporetto* landing, where more crowds were spilling off the ferries.

I had gone upstairs to the ladies' room to freshen my face, and as I turned the cold water off, the knob came away in my hand and black slime gurgled up from the drain. Well, I thought, at least we will probably make enough money to call in a plumber. On the way out, from the top of the landing, I saw Guido at the front desk on the phone, trying to get through to the transportation authorities in hopes of arranging some extra *vaporetto* runs, as there would be problems getting all these people off our tiny island by nightfall. I observed him arguing for a few minutes, and then it struck me: he isn't in the right place. He should be in the gallery. Perhaps, I thought, Enrico was still in there, but I ought to go and make sure, as the public would be storming in any minute.

As I was halfway down the stairs, the main door opened, and a whoosh of bracing air blew in, sending banners flapping and whirling the postcards and brochures all around the entrance hall, like bats escaping from an attic. But I wasn't in time to pick up any of the clutter, for the crowd surged forward towards the ticket booth and on to the gallery.

Yet, the moment, the first viewers crossed the threshold into the gallery, absolute silence cast its net. Every viewer stood in awe of the portrait and the longings it transmitted. All were caught in a moment of suspension, as the bells of the San Marco tower pealed across the waters. In ways I could not understand, I had somehow contributed to this magic. Then, a whisper broke the spell, and someone coughed; stirred. The line edged forward, and more people poured through the doors, voices amplified to a buzzing ocean. I stared at the heads bobbing forward towards the gallery and spotted Perez's grizzled gray hair and seedy, brown overcoat. Then a thin woman, with a gold brocade headscarf and sunglasses—my mysterious donor had shown up, after all. The youngish gondolier in a yellow hat with a black feather stuck in the band had made it to our island, but the long-haired girl clinging to his arm was only a blur of red as they slipped through the mob. Later peeking in, I saw them standing hand in hand before the portrait, riveted by its beauty, oblivious to the crowd seething around them. When I looked for them again later, they had vanished.

The day wore on. More people kept coming. The buffet was an immense success; everything was cleaned out in half an hour. By three p.m., the catalogues, postcards, and posters had all sold out, and more were ordered. Calls had come in from TV networks, news agencies, and documentary producers, all wanting interviews, photographs; information. A troop arrived from the BBC World Service with cameras and sound equipment. Would I kindly, Enrico asked, provide what they needed? I would be paid extra for this.

At seven o'clock, dusk deepened to night, the last stragglers were coaxed out, the gallery inspected and locked up, and the front door closed. Nearly 4,000 viewers had visited the gallery on that first day. We could all have a rest before it started all over again, perhaps even more hectic than before. Signora Simonicini was the first staff member to leave at her usual schedule, refusing to work late that evening. Enrico begged me to stay until nine, at which time we'd go by water taxi to have dinner at a little place he knew on the Giudecca. I had hoped to go home for a shower and a change of clothes, but that would have to wait. He had several projects he wished to talk to me about, including a renewal of my contract for two years.

As we were coming down the stairs, I said, prompted by some instinct, "Let's have a last look at the *Holy Family of the Circus.*"

"I locked up with Guido; everything is fine. We want to get to Giudecca before they close up the kitchen."

"Only for a moment, *caro.* I'd just like to make sure," I said, laying my hand on his arm as we stood before the double doors.

"Of course, my dear." Fishing the key out of his pocket, he fitted it into the lock and pulled the door to the gallery open. His head lifted as he gazed towards the painting, and the benign expression on his face crumpled into incredulity and fear. I thought he was having a heart attack.

"It's gone," he stuttered, but I had already seen it, too. The gilt frame still hung on the wall, but the canvas inside had been cut away. All that remained was a blank, eyeless rectangle like the window Jeanne fell backwards through a century ago.

The End

AUTHOR'S NOTE

This project, like many important things in my life, began entirely by chance, when, stumbling out of my car on a rainy October evening in 2000, I caught the name "Beatrice Hastings" printed on a poster plastered on a wall just around the corner from my apartment in Rome. It attracted me at once because at that time, I was immersed in researching the rivalry and friendship between Beatrice Hastings and Katherine Mansfield, who was the subject of a new novel I was writing, *Katherine's Wish*. Hastings had been the mistress of Mansfield's mentor, Richard Orage, and a contributor to Orage's literary journal, the *New Age*. After leaving Orage, Hastings had moved to Paris and become Amedeo Modigliani's lover and model.

Stopping to peruse the poster, I noted Hastings' name listed among Modigliani's most intimate friends, who formed the focus of an exhibition which had just opened in Venice, entitled *Modigliani e i Suoi*. The Italian term "i suoi" for third person; "i miei" for first person, generally refers to family – here it was being used to denote the Italian painter's closest associates.

Hoping to learn something more about Hastings, at the end of October, I set off for Venice. The show, held at the Fondazione Giorgio Cini, curated by the well-known Modigliani critic, Christian Parisot, was an eye-opener and for some, a heart-stopper, featuring works by artists in Modigliani's circle. The surprise star of the show was not Modigliani at all, but his common-law wife, Jeanne Hébuterne, whose sketches and paintings were on exhibition for the first time ever, eighty years after her death. Mostly sketches from a single cahier loaned to Parisot by the Hébuterne heirs for the occasion, the works on display revealed a startling, provocative talent, along with a very determined, unique personality quite in contrast with the picture of Jeanne as bland, brooding and clinging, usually given in period memoirs.

Instantly captivated by Jeanne's story, I bought the catalog, and my research began, leading to an essay. "Missing Person in Montparnasse:

The Case of Jeanne Hébuterne," published in *The Literary Review* and nominated for a Pushcart prize. I eventually also contacted Parisot, and had the pleasure of interviewing him once at his home in Paris, and several times by email, before he became embroiled in the legal intricacies which have dampened his career. After my essay was published online, I received numerous emails from passionate fans of Jeanne Hébuterne around the world, all wanting to know more about Jeanne's art. I heard from writers, scholars, television directors, and even from someone who claimed to be Modigliani's great-grandchild, through one of his undocumented children.

Since the Venice show, the value of Jeanne's work has skyrocketed in twenty years' time. Each sketch now brings about 60,000 euros at Christie's and one of her paintings sold for $450,000 in 2019. Not bad for an art student whose work was out of circulation for eight decades! Prior to 2000, her remaining sketches and paintings had been stored in her brother's studio in Paris and were released for public viewing only after his death, for the Venice show.

If Jeanne Hébuterne has captured the imagination of countless admirers, many of whom are young women, it is thanks primarily to the efforts of three people. Firstly, her brother, the painter, André Hébuterne, who, after Jeanne committed suicide, locked her artwork away in his studio and refused to speak about his sister when researchers tried to interview him, as his pain was too great. How unfair, you might think, to hide her artwork away from the world. Yet by doing so, he preserved it. Having died without establishing a reputation, except for that of being Modigliani's wife and favorite model, Jeanne Hébuterne could not have hoped to be remembered for her art, at least not back then, in 1920. The works of minor women painters of the period have not been as well-preserved as those of men, as we know from the case of Victorine Meurent, Manet's model, who was also an accomplished painter. Only one of Meurent's paintings has survived, recovered in 2004. Others disappeared from record after 1930. So if we know anything of Jeanne Hébuterne's work at all, it is thanks to the time capsule deposited in 1920 by her brother in Rue de Seine.

Secondly, we must thank Jeanne Modigliani aka Giovanna Modigliani, the daughter of Modigliani and Jeanne Hébuterne, who, dissatisfied with the myth of Modigliani *maudit*, genial drunk of Montparnasse, as portrayed in many memoirs, tried to unearth the truth about her parents and reclaim her maternal heritage. Her two books about Modigliani shine a light in the muddy depths of Modigliani's complex personality. Having discovered the existence of a treasure trove of documents, photos, and sketchbooks pertaining to her mother, all kept in custody by her uncle, André, Jeanne Modigliani tried to negotiate with the Hébuternes for their release. She died in 1984, before this could happen.

In her contacts with the Hébuternes, she was assisted by a young art researcher, Christian Parisot, who carried on her efforts after her death, and for a time, exercised authority over the Modigliani Archives. By 2000, Parisot evidently felt the time was ripe and began to promote Jeanne Hébuterne's works and her story through various shows and writings. However, the Hébuterne heirs withdrew their support and refused to let their carnet of drawings circulate any further after the Venice show. Parisot then came into possession of a second series of drawings purportedly by Jeanne Hébuterne, which the Hébuterne heirs contested as forgeries.

Upon examination of the drawings by experts appointed by a Spanish court, it was found that the contested drawings were in part pastiches and in part photocopies of originals. Parisot was convicted of fraud and given a two-year suspended sentence, the mere beginning of a scandal that shook the artworld. The Hébuterne heirs turned to another younger art critic, Marc Restellini, a rival of Parisot's, who curated future shows devoted to Jeanne Hébuterne and prepared the first and only catalogue raisonné of her work. And yet, the third person we must thank for bringing Jeanne Hébuterne to vivid life and keeping her story before the public eye, is Christian Parisot. Without his promotion of Jeanne as a forgotten artist, we would know little about her today.

Jeanne Hébuterne, whose time on earth was fairly brief but very intense, has also had an adventurous afterlife.

In creating my portrait of Jeanne Hébuterne as a ghost, an adolescent, and artist, I consulted many texts, images, and films. First, Jeanne Modigliani's *Modigliani Senza Leggenda* (1968), and *Modigliani Mio Padre* (2005). Secondly, I must mention Patrice Chaplin's haunting narrative of her own search for Jeanne Hébuterne, *Into the*

Darkness Laughing (1990), which when I started researching Jeanne in 2000 was one of the few texts available. Chaplin dug up a stash of letters from Jeanne to her friend Germaine, from which she assembles a fascinating mosaic. She also mentions a diary which may have gone missing from the studio where Modigliani and Jeanne lived. Other resources I used include André Salmon's *Modigliani, a Memoir* (1961), Charles Douglas' *Artist Quarter* (1941), Pierre Sichel's *Modigliani* (1967), Dan Franck's *Bohemian Paris :Picasso, Modigliani, Matisse* (1998), and Marevna's *Life with the Painters of La Ruche*. To get a sense of Paris atmospheres, I dipped into the writings of Francis Carco, Jean Rhys, Anais Nin, Nina Hamnett, among many others.

Jeffrey Meyers' study of Modigliani from 2006 is an interesting read, but he tends to dismiss Jeanne Hébuterne, while Meryl Secrest offers the most sympathetic and detailed view of Jeanne and Modigliani's relationship in *Modigliani A Life* (2011), though by the time it was published, I had already consolidated my own portrait of Jeanne. For those seeking more information about Jeanne Hébuterne as an artist, the catalogs of exhibitions curated by Christian Parisot and Marc Restellini offer a wealth of information. Among those are Parisot's *Modigliani e i Suoi* and Restellini's *Le Silence Eternelle*, which includes the catalogue raisonné of Hébuterne's artworks.

ACKNOWLEDGMENTS

I would like to thank all those who assisted me in this long project and shared their enthusiasm and advice at various twistings and turnings: Thomas E. Kennedy, Walter Cummins, Thomas Wilhelmus, and the late David Applefield, who have given me great moral support throughout my writing career. I would also like to thank Pamela and Jim Leavy for their Parisian hospitality along with Rebecca DeFraites and Meredith Mullins; Miriam Polli for her reminders and insightful feedback; Amalia Melis and the writers at the Aegean Arts Circle workshop in Andros who heard the first bits read aloud; Lauren Grosskopf for her chic cover design; Meghan Ducey for help with French; and Natalie Cannon for her editing. And of course, thanks to my husband Sergio without whose help on so many levels none of this would ever have been possible.

Linda Lappin is the prize-winning author of four novels: *The Etruscan* (Wynkin deWorde, 2004), *Katherine's Wish* (Wordcraft, 2008), *Signatures in Stone: A Bomarzo Mystery* (Pleasureboat Studio, 2013), and *Loving Modigliani: The Afterlife of Jeanne Hébuterne* (Serving House Books, 2020). *Signatures in Stone* was the overall winner of the Daphne DuMaurier prize for best mystery novel of 2013. She is also the author of *The Soul of Place: Ideas and Exercises for Conjuring the Genius Loci* (Travelers Tales, 2015), which won a Nautilus Award in the category of creativity in 2015. A former Fulbright scholar to Italy, she has lived mainly in Rome for over thirty years. Her website is www.lindalappin.net.